Acclaim for John Gregory Dunne's

NOTHING LOST

"Pitch-perfect." —*The New York Times Book Review*

"Astonishingly wicked and deliriously well-paced. . . . Genuinely well-plotted, full of surprises, without skimping on emotional and metaphorical resonance." —*The Baltimore Sun*

"Reads like a John Grisham story as rewritten by Carl Hiaasen. . . . Dunne brings his characters alive, even the outrageous ones. And he'll leave you with a bittersweet feeling that may haunt you for a day or two. It's *that* good a book." —*St. Louis Post-Dispatch*

"[This] novel is fertilized with blood. And with stinging cynicism, political hypocrisy, betrayal, and, if you can imagine, worse. . . . Nothing lost by spending a few days with this splendidly dark entertainment." —*Chicago Tribune*

"[A] deliciously cynical page-turner." —*W* magazine

"Sardonic, bemused and, beneath thickets of thorns, wistful. . . . Imagine F. Scott Fitzgerald and John O'Hara sitting elbow to elbow in the same bar arguing over the latest tabloid scandal and you have some idea of how *Nothing Lost* flows through your inner ear." —*Newsday*

"Dunne effectively skewers shibboleths of both left and right while vividly delineating the hidden links between America's elite and its forgotten underclass." —*Entertainment Weekly*

John Gregory Dunne

Nothing Lost

John Gregory Dunne wrote five other novels—*Vegas*; *True Confessions*; *Dutch Shea, Jr.*; *The Red White and Blue*; and *Playland*—and seven works of nonfiction, among which are the memoirlike *Harp* and two books that look at Hollywood, *The Studio* and *Monster*. Born in West Hartford, Connecticut, in 1932, he graduated from Princeton in 1954. He collaborated with his wife, the writer Joan Didion, on many screenplays, including *Panic in Needle Park* and *True Confessions*. John Gregory Dunne died in December 2003.

NOTHING LOST

NOTHING LOST

A NOVEL

JOHN GREGORY DUNNE

VINTAGE CONTEMPORARIES
VINTAGE BOOKS
A DIVISION OF RANDOM HOUSE, INC.
NEW YORK

FIRST VINTAGE CONTEMPORARIES EDITION, MAY 2005

The Library of Congress has cataloged the Knopf edition as follows:
Dunne, John Gregory, [date]
Nothing lost / by John Gregory Dunne.—1st ed.
p. cm.
1. African American men—Crimes against—Fiction. I. Title.
PS3554.U493N68 2004
813'.54—dc22
2004000552

Vintage ISBN: 1-4000-3501-5

Book design by Robert C. Olsson

www.vintagebooks.com

Printed in the United States of America
10 9 8 7 6 5 4 3 2 1

This book is for

Sharon DeLano
Barbara Jackson
Susan Muska
Greta Olafsdottir

O love is the crooked thing,
There is nobody wise enough
To find out all that is in it.

—William Butler Yeats, "Brown Penny"

For nothing is lost, nothing is ever lost. There is always the clue,
the canceled check, the smear of lipstick, the footprint in the canna
bed, the condom in the park path, the twitch in the old wound,
the baby shoes dipped in bronze, the taint in the blood stream.

—Jack Burden in Robert Penn Warren's *All the King's Men*

BOOK ONE

SUSPECTS

PART ONE

ANGKOR WAT

She appeared as if an apparition on the surveillance tape. The tape was black and white, the definition jumpy, unstable. She was there, not there, shielded from view. It could have been. Might have been. Was. Probably. Maybe. A glimpse of a white blouse, a dark blazer slung over a shoulder, held by the forefinger of her right hand, dark pleated trousers, sunglasses anchored in her hair, a cigarette in her hand.

So she was smoking again.

If she had ever really given it up.

Room for doubt.

Remember the Tic Tacs.

Her substitute for nicotine addiction. Only one and a half calories each. She said.

She had reason to start smoking again.

God knows.

Her stride was steady, unhurried. The digital clock counting at the bottom of the tape said 20:47:42. At 20:47:49 the woman was blocked by what seemed an extended family exiting the elevator. An elderly man in a motorized wheelchair carrying a cane in his lap, a woman approximately the same age wearing a straw cowboy hat hovering close to the wheelchair's arm rail, two grown women and their two overweight male companions in floral Hawaiian shirts, the top two buttons open to show an abundance of chest hair. The elderly man in the motorized wheelchair reached up with his stick and brushed the cowboy hat off the older woman's head. 20:47:53. The woman in the white blouse again. She did not look back as one of the younger women picked up the straw cowboy hat and returned it to the older woman. The elderly man knocked it from her hands, his cane flailing, catching her hard on the wrists. The two overweight men in the Hawaiian shirts began waving their arms, one at the older woman, the other at the elderly man in the wheelchair, then began pushing each other. One security guard materialized, then a second. The surveillance camera zoomed in on the scuffle for a moment, then resumed its sweep.

20:48:06. Another glimpse of the woman in the white blouse. She was no longer smoking. And was now wearing her blazer. Her sunglasses were shielding her eyes. It would have been easy to miss her.

Chapter One

That is the end of the story.

Or almost the end.

I'm not sure I'm the one who should be telling it, but if I don't, nobody will, so what the hell.

We live in a litigious time, and as I do not wish to be the focus of any litigation, I've located the major events of what follows in a state I call South Midland. By its name you can intuit a couple of things. Midland suggests the middle of the country, that part grandiosely identified as the Great Plains. South Midland suggests that there is a North Midland, as indeed there is. North Midlanders proudly claim to have the largest Paul Bunyan statue in the world, and perhaps they do, since to the best of my knowledge there are no other claimants. With that highly developed sense of humor we all recognize as indigenous to the Great Plains, South Midlanders say that the best thing in North Midland is Interstate 90 leading to South Midland. People in North Midland often group the two states together as Midlandia, but people in South Midland never do.

The biggest city in South Midland is Kiowa, which of course is Indian or, as we now say, Native American. When traveling out of state, Kiowans often refer to Kiowa as the Chicago of the north-central states. I have never heard a Chicagoan refer to his home as the Kiowa of the Midwest. Our state capital is called, with the imagination we also know as indigenous to the Great Plains, Capital City, usually shortened to Cap City. The University of South Midland, whose main campus is located in Cap City, has never had a Nobel laureate, but its football team has been the national champion three times in the last eight years, and its coach, Dr. John Strong, has been on the cover of *Time, Newsweek, U.S. News,* and *Sports Illustrated* (three times, twice as he was doused with Gatorade by his team and assistant coaches after a victory); the editorial page of *The Wall Street Journal* has even floated his name as a future Republican vice-presidential candidate because of his devotion both to winning and to American ideals. All the university sports teams are named the Rhinos, although there is no palaeontological evidence that herds of rhinoceroses ever roamed the empty vistas of the Great Plains.

I teach a night school course in criminal law at Osceola County Community College in Cap City, and at the first class meeting each semester I tell my students that when I open the Kiowa *Times-Ledger* and the Capital City *Herald* every morning, I turn first to the obituary page. In an obit, I say, the spaces between the lines tell all. What is omitted is often more interesting than what is said. Example, from yesterday's *Herald,* the deceased, a forty-nine-year-old professor of agronomy at the university, unknown to me, killed by a hit-and-run driver in a Kmart parking lot; said driver, just turned fifteen and without a license, apprehended two blocks from the accident site after blindsiding a brand-new Volvo SUV on a pre-purchase trial spin: "He is survived by his second wife, from whom he was recently divorced, and by a stepson from his first marriage." Think of the moral and sexual misdemeanors woven into that simple sentence, the mosaic of small, mean betrayals. The mind has difficulty entertaining all the agronomist's sins and discontents, mortal and venial, the permutations and possibilities of discarded and discarding spouses. And that is before we consider the teenage jerkoff who thought the Kmart parking lot was the Talledega Superspeedway.

Then, to reinforce my point, I drop in Henry James. Although in the academic slum where Osceola Community is resident, *The Golden Bowl* is not exactly required reading. (Due diligence requires me to admit that I never actually finished it—I was bored by the Ververs—but I did see the movie and thought the actor who played Prince Amerigo not unattractive.) Anyway, James once wrote in an essay I saw quoted on the Net that the power to guess the unseen from the seen, to trace the implication of things, to judge the whole piece by the pattern—that constitutes experience.

Henry James, I tell them, would have made a great criminal attorney. That would no doubt send him spinning in his grave, and it makes those of my students who know who he was (four, perhaps five, no more) laugh nervously.

I know most of the principals in the story I am about to tell, and a number of the walk-ons as well. I am even, as you will find out soon enough, a minor character. Some of the carnage that ensued I witnessed. Some of it was told to me. On the record, off the record, who cares now? Some of the principals did not realize they were telling me. Sealed audiotapes. Film, as in "Film at 11." I went to the printed record, voluminous if you know where to look. Court transcripts. Discussions in chambers with a court reporter present. Proceedings of the South Midland Bar Association. Testimony before the Judiciary Committee of the State Legislature. Interviews in the legal journals.

I broke an Internet password. Read the spaces between the lines. Traced the implication of things. Guessed the unseen from the seen. Judged the whole piece by the pattern. Surmised. Triangulated. Extrapolated.

Anything that passed through my filter carries my shadows, my imprimatur. As fact, it might be suspect, but as truth it is as close as I can get. If you were the filter, your facts, or your memory of them, might be equally suspect, but the truth, presupposing your honesty, or as close as you could get to it.

But you weren't there, and I was, so fuck off.

I think I got it right.

Mostly.

And if I didn't, it's the available version.

Of course it began with Edgar Parlance.

His death, and the obscene brutality of it, immediately captured the headlines and the newsbreaks of the gluttonous 24/7 news cycle, searching as always for the correct and visually gratifying metaphor to validate the American experience, or, better yet, to provide a dark parable about that same experience. It is my own feeling that life began going downhill with "You give us twenty-two minutes, we'll give you the world." I think

I would have preferred to live in the age of the pony express, allowing as it did, I would like to think, a time for contemplation before action was deemed necessary. 24/7, plus the transitory involvement of a president looking for a way to act presidential as the second term of his forgettable administration was winding down to its unlamented conclusion, gave Edgar Parlance's murder the push it needed to become a major media event, bringing with it the usual suspects, talking heads prattling about race hatred and the phenomenon of what they insisted on calling "Terror in the Heartland." It was a heartland that existed only in their fevered imaginations, neighborly values and small-town ways, stoked not by reality but by Oscar Hammerstein, we know we belong to the land, and the land we belong to is grand. Crap, of course. This land was fertilized with blood. Jesse and Frank James, Bonnie Parker and Clyde Barrow, killers all, sanitized into public darlings by Tyrone Power and Henry Fonda, Warren Beatty and Faye Dunaway.

Dixon McCall didn't mention Jesse or Frank, Bonnie or Clyde.

PRESIDENT TO ATTEND PARLANCE FUNERAL

Washington, D.C. (CNN 12:42 P.M. EDT)—President Dixon McCall will interrupt his Midwestern fundraising trip to attend the funeral of Edgar Parlance, White House deputy press secretary Anita Bowne announced today. Parlance, a 39-year-old African American, was the victim of a brutal race-related torture slaying earlier this week outside the small town of Regent, South Midland.

The President, who has often feuded with civil rights leaders and the Congressional Black Caucus in the past, has asked the Reverend Jesse Jackson to accompany him from Capital City to Regent in the presidential helicopter.

In a statement Bowne released to reporters, the President said, "Let the healing begin."

Dixon McCall's special rhetorical skills always seemed to begin with the construction "Let." As in, "Let us look forward, not back," "Let us walk together," "Let the sun shine through," "Let the forces of light persevere," "Let us put our differences behind us." (All from *Dix: Finding the Words That Defined the McCall Presidency*, from a speechwriter unhappily influenced by the "thousand points of light" template.)

The autopsy and forensic photos indicated that Parlance had been skinned alive, the meat on his upper thighs sliced with a razor, box cutter, or sharp knife and then pulled away slice by slice with a pair of pliers. The same pliers that had pulled the tongue from his mouth so that he was not able to scream. Edgar Parlance was thirty-nine, a big man, six feet tall, 180 pounds, leading the investigators from the Loomis County Sheriff's Office and the South Midland Bureau of Investigation to speculate that because of his size it must have taken two or more people to kill him. Then the autopsy report concluded that it wasn't even the skinning that finished him off. It was a hollow-point from a .38-caliber DS-II Detective Special that blew the back of his head off. One of his knees had been shattered, probably with a tire iron, and what remained of the left side of his face was crushed, apparently by the boots of his assailants. Indicating that Edgar had put up an uncommon struggle before he succumbed. And what turned out to be the most interesting fact of the crime was that his shirt had been torn open and the letter *P* carved into his chest with what was later identified as a thirteen-inch double-edged knife its manufacturer picturesquely called, in the gunshow catalogues, a Tennessee Toothpick. The assumption of the SMBI detectives and the Loomis County Sheriff's Department was that the *P* stood for Parlance, meaning that the killers, whoever they were, were probably familiar with their victim.

As it happened, the first part of the assumption was wrong.

I wonder how long the story would have played had it not been a slow news period. It was a nonelection fall, the economy was stumbling along as it had throughout the McCall administration, the rising indicators balancing out the falling, Wall Street was bullish one week, bearish the next, the war clouds of August were blown away by the Berne proposals of September. No scandals had captured the public imagination (a House counsel in a men's room, an undersecretary's wife with her minister—sorry stuff), Halloween loomed, Thanksgiving, that most tedious and unnecessary of national holidays, threatened, promising only Christmas, and with it the obligation to think about, and pretend we believe in, the concept of family and giving, the holly and the ivy. The murder of Edgar Parlance was unspeakably barbaric, but blacks have been strung up, roasted, crucified, mutilated, castrated, and decapitated as a form of public entertainment throughout our history. What is a Tennessee Toothpick, after all, but a lethal artifact of the entertainment culture? Dead, Edgar Parlance had a legitimacy that he never had alive. Dead, he had become an icon. Because dead, people did not have to associate with him. He was a victim, a convenient symbol of man's inhumanity to man, the kind of black man white people can most easily grasp unto themselves. To prove to themselves that the aberrant behavior of the lowest of their kind against the racially less fortunate will not be tolerated. Like limpets, sentiment and innocence attach themselves to a victim. *The New York Times,* the newspaper of record, is exhibit number one:

EASYGOING MAN, EASYGOING TOWN

By FELIPE DELL and CAMERON KEOGH

Regent, SM, November 1—Everyone who knew him called him "Gar," the diminutive of his given name, Edgar. And no one had a bad word for Gar Parlance in this sleepy cattle and farming community in the southeastern corner of South Midland tangent to Kansas and Missouri. He mowed their lawns, he hauled their trash, and when the weather was warm and jobs were available, and if he felt like it, he did manual labor for the Department of Highways or the Burlington Northern Railroad.

And if he did not feel like it, which was more often than not, he would spend the afternoons napping and fishing out by Loomis Falls, a nineteenth-century man-made waterfall that diverted the path of the Albion River so that it irrigated the rich farm flatlands of northern Loomis County.

"I'm like tumbleweed," Parlance once told local barber Joe Salmon, whose lawn he mowed every Saturday afternoon until the snows came. "Wherever I go, I always tumble right on back to Regent."

His affection for his hometown is the main reason residents cannot fathom how Parlance became the victim in one of the most grotesque racial murders in recent American history, his flesh torn from his body with pliers, the letter *P* carved into his chest like an engraving, and his tongue severed from his mouth. For two days, his body went undiscovered until a dog belonging to farmer Eugene Hicks found his remains in a field outside town, and barked until his master came to see what was the matter.

"I guess we just thought Gar was tumbling again," Mr. Salmon said.

"Regent—A Place Fit for Kings" read the road signs leading into town. "Pop. 3,679." Claude Applewhite, pastor of the Bethany Methodist Church, looked sadly at the sign this week and remarked, "I guess we're down to 3,678 now that Gar's gone."

Regent takes its name from the English-owned Regent Cattle Company, which settled the town immediately after the Civil War, when younger sons of landed British nobility came to the New World to make their fortune. It was a rough-and-tumble time. The English aristocrats built the Loomis Waterfall, and the diversion of the Albion River nearly precipitated a range war with the ranchers of neighboring Albion County.

The Regent Cattle Company went bankrupt around the turn of the century, when beef prices tumbled. A check of county tax and property records reveals that none of its English supervisors—people with names like Lovat and Angell and Simsbury and Stuart—chose to remain when times were no longer flush and the longhorns disappeared from the rolling plains. What they gave to Regent were the names of the four cobblestone streets bordering the Loomis County Courthouse, on the lawn outside of which stands a scaled-down man-sized Statue of Liberty.

Yellow ribbons adorn the clothes of most people in Regent this week. Those who did not personally know Parlance remember his daily wanderings through town. "He was always smiling," town librarian and resident local historian Marjorie Hudnut said. "He'd come into the library and say, 'Miss Marjorie, give me something new to read.' He liked to read naval stories. *Horatio Hornblower,* that sort of thing. I can't say he ever really finished any of them. I think the library was just a place for him to take a nap."

It seems particularly ironic that here in the middle of the American heartland, Parlance would dream of the four winds and the seven seas.

No one seems to know exactly when Parlance sank his roots in Regent. "He was here, then he wasn't, then just as you began to miss him, he was back again," Miss Hudnut said. "He'd be gone for a year, sometimes two, you'd say, 'Gosh, I haven't seen Gar in a bit,' then he wasn't gone anymore. It was like he never left."

"Gar was like that Forrest Gump fella," Marcus Garvey Case, the local African-American undertaker, recalled. "He said there wasn't a state in the union he hadn't walked through."

"Forrest Gump was a runner, Marcus," Pastor Applewhite said.

"Gar was no runner," Mr. Salmon said. "He was a walker. He had two speeds."

"Slow and slower," Miss Hudnut said.

Parlance had no known survivors. "He said his daddy run off when he was a little one," Mr. Salmon said. "After his momma died," Miss Hudnut said.

"That's when he first hit the road," Loomis County Sheriff Brutus Mayes said. "Keep moving, that was Gar's motto."

Mayes was a former All-Pro linebacker for the Detroit Lions until his knee blew out. When injuries forced him into retirement, he entered law enforcement in the town where he was raised. Last year, he was reelected to a second term, winning 72 percent of the vote.

Parlance lived in a tiny, immaculately clean one-room apartment above Claude Applewhite's garage. Its only decorations were a number of melted wax votive candles twisted into bizarre shapes.

Parlance never managed to put together enough money to buy even a used car. "Gar would say, 'A car don't matter in a town this size,' " Mr. Case recalled. " 'I got the best two wheels in the world—my own two feet.' "

Perhaps the reason Parlance never drove is that when he was 19 he was sentenced to a four-year prison term at the Colorado State Penitentiary for stealing an automobile in Alamosa. "All I was trying to do was get back to Regent in a big damn hurry," he told undertaker Case. " 'If I'd walked,' " Mr. Case reported him saying this week, " 'I'd have got back here a lot quicker than that four I spent in Colorado.' "

Sheriff Mayes said he occasionally had to lock Parlance up for public drunkenness, but he was always out by the next morning. No charges were ever filed, nor was any record of arrest registered. "It was just a place for him to sleep it off on a cold night," Sheriff Mayes said. "It's a funny thing to say, but he was a pleasure to have in my jail. He'd talk my ear off about places he'd been. New Hampshire. Places like that. 'They got no taxes in New Hampshire, Brutus,' he'd say. 'You got to go there.' "

Today in Regent, Sheriff Mayes, Miss Hudnut, Mr. Case, Mr. Salmon and Pastor Applewhite tied a yellow ribbon on the miniature Statue of Liberty outside the Loomis County Courthouse.

It will remain there until the killer or killers of Edgar Parlance are arrested and brought before the bar of justice.

Remember those votive candles.

Everyone wanted a piece of the Parlance saga. Johnnie L. Cochran announced that he would represent the Parlance family interest in any civil litigation and negotiate any subsidiary motion picture or literary rights. Even the Klan, after a fashion, signed on. In Waco, the grand dragon denied that the Klan had anything to do with the murder of "this so-called African American," but he added that there were "many good white Americans" who felt as if they had been "bypassed by government toadying to the Negro rabble-rousing element, and may have decided that some sort of compensatory action was necessary." When pressed about the definition of "compensatory action," he did allow that "maybe the lesson went a bit too far." Brutus Mayes became a chat-show regular, with more airtime than he had since he was in the NFL. "We don't have no Aryan Nation or KKK deal here in Regent," he told CNN, Fox 5, and MSNBC. "Our friends in the white community are as appalled at this Parlance deal as black folks are." At a prayer vigil in Los Angeles, Jamaal Jefferson of the Los Angeles Clippers announced that he would pay for Parlance's funeral, and said he had lobbied NBA president Steven Silver to set up an annual Parlance Trophy, to be given each year to that NBA player who best promotes the idea of racial tolerance and understanding. The first contributor to the Parlance Fund was Cyrus Ichabod, CEO of I-Bod, the sneaker and sportswear conglomerate that paid Jamaal Jefferson $11 million annually to promote its sporting goods.

Hollywood of course got on the bandwagon. A director named Sydney Allen said that he and his producing partner, Martin Magnin, were negotiating to secure the rights to the Parlance story. "This will be a major motion picture about race," Magnin told CNN, "but we want to concentrate on the man." Cyrus Ichabod said he planned to invest in the picture, his first venture in the film industry. "Jamaal Jefferson would be perfect for the part," Martin Magnin told all available outlets. "It would open a whole new career for him. We see him as a kind of young Morgan Freeman." That Jamaal Jefferson was fifteen years younger than Edgar Parlance did not pose a problem, or at least none that could not be remedied. "Maybe Morgan Freeman could play Gar, and Jamaal would be his young friend."

What the late Edgar Parlance had become was a lottery ticket on the money tree.

If I may mix a metaphor.

I watched Edgar Parlance's funeral on TV. Bethany Methodist in Regent was the place to be in South Midland that day. An SRO crowd inside the church and closed-circuit monitors for the throng of public and press gathered outside. Speaking from the pulpit, Dixon McCall was in his let mode: "Let us inoculate the land against the fevers of hate." Jesse was there, and Johnnie Cochran in an iridescent heliotrope Buck and the Preacher suit, and Jamaal Jefferson and Cyrus Ichabod and Martin Magnin, who let it slip to MSNBC as he entered the church that he would be "scouting locations" in and around Regent after paying his "last respects." None of South Midland's political hierarchy could afford to miss the event. You'd never have known that Guy Kennedy, the Democratic governor in a generally Republican state, was the political equivalent of a dead man walking the way he bounced up the aisle shaking every hand as if he were entering the Hall of Delegates to address the state legislature. The Secret Service tried to direct the governor into a pew three rows behind the president, but Kennedy slipped past them and sat across the aisle from Dixon McCall with Jesse, Jamaal Jefferson, and Cyrus Ichabod. The Worm was also there. The Worm is Jerrold ("Gerry") Wormwold, South Midland's attorney general. The Worm was gearing up to run against Kennedy, and even though he had not announced, the polls gave him a double-digit lead. The Worm was a born-again Christian, and he sat in the front pew next to Dixon McCall, practically hugging him. If you intuit that I am less than enthusiastic about the Worm, your instinct would be correct. More later.

Poppy was also there, sitting on the other side of Dixon McCall. Congresswoman Sonora ("Poppy") McClure, La Pasionara of the Republican right wing, and the Worm's worst nightmare. Poppy had floated the notion that she might run for governor herself, and because of her combative high-octane style, she was the best-known politician in the state, one who, unlike the Worm, could guarantee maximum national media coverage. What the Worm was best known for was his unfortunate nickname, a name that gave Poppy an opening to make all kinds of allusions, veiled and otherwise, to squishy invertebrates absent backbones. I am not all that sure that Poppy could have beaten the Worm in a primary. I think she was counting on scaring him into folding by promising a scorched-earth primary that she was well aware could ultimately end up delivering the state to Guy Kennedy in the general election.

Outside Bethany Methodist at the end of the service, Jamaal Jefferson led the crowd in a hip-hop version of "Amazing Grace." Poppy linked arms with Jesse and Johnnie Cochran and hip-hopped right along with them as if she had spent her life down and dirty.

The Worm thought Jesse and Jamaal and Johnnie were agents of Satan.

He did not think much more highly of Poppy McClure.

Coincidentally, two days after Edgar Parlance's funeral, South Midland was scheduled to conduct its first execution since 1959. Small potatoes when compared to Texas or Florida. The condemned man was a pedophile sex murderer named Percy Darrow, who had been convicted of sexually assaulting and murdering nine-year-old twin brothers named Patrick and Lyman James. The James twins were found buried and largely decomposed in a shallow trench in Phil Sheridan County by a brace of retrievers on the first day of duck season. I was the head of the Homicide Bureau in the state attorney general's office in those days, and I assigned myself to prosecute Percy Darrow. The legislature had just reinstituted the death penalty, I favor capital punishment, the case was open and shut, and at some future date, when all Darrow's appeals were exhausted, he would be strapped into the electric chair at the state penitentiary on Durango Avenue in Cap City. Durango Avenue is the oldest of the three maximum-security prisons maintained by the South Midland Department of Corrections (there was one in Halloween County and a recently opened supermax in Sunflower County), and the facility where all executions as far back as hanging days had historically been held. The Worm, however, had other ideas. Shortly after he was elected attorney general, he had me removed from the case. It's a long story that I'll get into presently, accounting as it does for one of the reasons I find myself narrating these events. I was replaced by my number two in the Homicide Bureau, James Joseph McClure. J.J. was also Poppy McClure's husband. The Worm no doubt thought he was not only getting rid of me, but doing Poppy a favor.

Proving that no good deed goes unpunished.

It was J.J. who would get to attend Percy Darrow's execution.

J.J., by the way, did not accompany Poppy to Edgar Parlance's funeral.

There was another story below the fold on the front pages of the Kiowa *Times-Ledger* and the Capital City *Herald* that week. The Rhinos from South Midland University were set to play Florida State in the Orange Bowl New Year's night for the national college football championship. In South Midland, football was the secular religion, more important than God, certainly more important than Edgar Parlance or Percy Darrow. What kept the football fever in check and the Orange Bowl coverage muted was whether the Rhinos' All-American nose tackle, Ralph ("Jocko") Cannon, Jr., would be allowed to dress for the game. Jocko was not medicating a football injury. Rather, a coed named Brittany Barnes had accused him of dragging her down three flights of stairs in Rhino Land, the dormitory and student-center complex that accommodated all of USM's athletic teams, male and female, segregating them from the rest of the undergraduate population as the Romans did with their gladiators. Brittany Barnes's skull was fractured, her cheekbone shattered, and her two front teeth knocked so far into her palate that she needed oral surgery to dig them out.

Jocko Cannon was unavailable for comment. A university spokesman said he was in seclusion with the Cannon family minister and spiritual advisor, the Reverend Hardy Luther of the United Church of Almighty God. Rhino football coach Dr. John Strong promised to lead a campus candlelight vigil asking Jesus to watch over both Brittany Barnes and Jocko Cannon in what Strong called "their common hour of need."

The Worm wanted no part of the Jocko Cannon case. USM *v.* FSU with Jocko Cannon unavailable to suit up for the Rhinos because of a possible criminal investigation conducted by his office was the Worm's idea of a political nightmare. Jocko Cannon's father, Ralph Cannon, Sr., was the finance chairman of the Republican Party in South Midland. Without the benediction of Ralph Cannon, Sr., the Worm as Republican candidate for governor was dead in the water.

So he did what he thought was the smart thing. He bumped the case to J.J. McClure. Let Poppy's husband handle it. Indirectly letting Poppy take the heat. Maybe Poppy was right: the Worm would fold if the pressure got too heavy.

There was one more newsbreak that week:

XXXXX DRUDGE REPORT XXXXX NOVEMBER 4,
17:26:02 XXXXX

Two white men in custody for Parlance slaying

Duane Lajoie, 21, and Bryant Gover, 23, were arrested today in South Midland after trying to crash through a roadblock set up at the county line separating Loomis and Albion counties, the *Drudge Report* has learned. There was immediate speculation that the two men, both unemployed and both said to be ex-convicts, would be charged with the murder of Edgar Parlance.

MORE MORE MORE

CHAPTER TWO

Cline: originally Kleinbaum in the Galician railhead of Lemberg; then Klein in Graz, the family destination in the former Austro-Hungarian Empire after Marshal Pilsudski tried to cut a deal with the Russian Whites; then Cline in Galveston, where the former Kleinbaum/Kleins finally disembarked in the New World, after a stopover at Ellis Island. It is better for you Cline, the immigration officer at Ellis Island said as he stamped the papers and changed the spelling. His name was Helms, formerly Hersh. At least that was the story told by my great-grandfather, who spent every Shabbat wailing about the loss of the family name, as if it had been Connaught or Carnegie. Every Shabbat actually only meant the six weeks he spent in Galveston before he was run over by a Reo when he tried to cross a street waving his cane to stop the traffic, which did not stop. Imagine a Reo, my grandfather would say, as if the Reo's pedigree made the death of my great-grandfather, his father, somehow more honorable than a mundane street accident. The Clines moved north to Kansas, then to Nebraska, and finally to South Midland. My grandfather said the climate reminded him of Galicia, where actually he had never lived, having been born in Salina, Kansas. Nothing in this family history quite checks out, but telling stories was what the Clines were good at.

My name is Max Cline. I'm queer. I'm a Jew. And I'm a lawyer. In South Midland, that trifecta is not exactly a winning ticket in the social sweepstakes. My significant other is named Stanley. Stanley Poindexter, M.D. Stanley is a psychiatrist. Another long shot in the local social sweeps. Stanley used to be a married psychiatrist in Kansas City, with children, but he switched leagues several significant others before me. I made the mistake early on of asking his ex-wife's name, and he told me it was none of my fucking business. Fair enough. So I called an investigator I knew in the Kansas City D.A.'s office and got the information. Wife Audrey, children Kara and Karl. Audrey has a boyfriend. First name Dutton, last name Fearing. Dutton Fearing. I wonder what it would be like to have a last-name first name. Grunwald Cline. After my mother's maiden name.

Grun Cline.

It doesn't make it.

Stanley is also an Episcopalian. I've often thought that an Episcopalian psychiatrist is an oxymoron, but there you are. We've been together four years. I've been monogamous, except occasionally in my heart, for the odd closeted movie star. Stanley attends five or six professional meetings a year, even one in London last summer. I try not to wonder how he behaves when he's out of town.

For sixteen years I was a prosecutor in the state attorney general's office. A lifer. I have no problem with the penal system. I don't want to reform it. Incarceration benefits society. Some people belong behind the walls. My opinion is: the rougher, the better. Coils of razor-sharp concertina wire, electric fences, the hole, cattle prods, the works. I once argued successfully that a fourteen-year-old should do his time at the Durango Avenue adult facility rather than at the juvenile correction center in Kiowa County. He'd crushed the skull of a Chinese takeout deliveryman with a brick for no other reason than that he had ordered General Tso chicken and in a mix-up of orders got Kung Pao shrimp instead. Because of his age, he only got nine-to-life. Of course he was buggered at Durango Avenue, and finally, at fifteen and a half, he was drowned by a fellow psychopath who held him facedown in a toilet full of excrement.

At the trial I made a meal about the deliveryman's pregnant wife and three children under four.

I didn't mention that the deliveryman was also running smack along with the MSG.

That I was queer was never an apparent problem when I was with the A.G.'s office. I assumed people knew, I was discreet, I didn't dress up, I had the highest conviction rate in the office, I played rugby for the Department of Corrections in a league composed of teams from the legislature and the state agencies (I lost four front teeth in a scrum during a match against the Department of Public Safety, a very butch thing to do), and I taught a course in criminal law at the university.

Then Gerry Wormwold was elected attorney general. The Worm never missed an opportunity to punch the Christian ticket on his way to higher office. Poppy McClure liked to say that he thought the initials "A.G." stood for "aspiring governor." A divorce from his first wife seemed to be a speed bump on the Worm's career highway, but the first Mrs. Wormwold agreed to sign an affidavit acknowledging that her infidelity was the predicate cause of the breakup. The first Mrs. Wormwold said it was the Christian thing to do, that she had renounced adultery and rededicated her life to Jesus, and that she had received no favors in return for the affidavit.

Objection overruled.

The second and current Mrs. Wormwold, the former Aphrodite Anderson, had her name legally changed to Nancy Reagan Anderson, in honor of the woman she most admired in the world, and when the A.G. announced their engagement, Nancy Reagan Anderson produced a doctor's certificate that she was a virgin, hymen intact, who would save herself for her wedding night with her fiancé, the presumptive candidate for attorney general.

During his campaign, the Worm had also pledged not to violate his Christian principles by appointing a gay person to a senior management position in the A.G.'s office. It was a pledge that really only applied to me. He could not legally fire me, which would have made him subject to a discrimination suit that I in fact never would have filed, but he could take me off the Darrow case. The grounds, never stated in so many words, were that as I was what he would call sexually ambiguous, I might have a conflict of interest. J.J. got the case, and I was reassigned from head of the Homicide Bureau to arraignment hearings and the misdemeanor courts. I quit the A.G., which of course was what the Worm was hoping I would do, and naturally he appointed J.J. my replacement, a move I suspect he has since come to regret.

I also lost my lectureship at the university law school. Again courtesy of the Worm. A word here, a word there, proposed budget cuts, a restructuring of course schedules, a cutback in electives, and I was gone. Not that it really mattered. I signed on as a night school professor at Osceola Community College's unaccredited law school. And I prospered, more or less, as a member of the defense bar, defending those I used to put behind bars, often, I regret to say, successfully.

That was a more efficient way to get under the Worm's skin.

About J.J.

He was someone who got where he was by playing the angles. When he worked for me in the Homicide Bureau, he had a reputation as an operator, a fixer, someone whose eye was always on the desired result. Where it remained when he took over from me. And as much as I dislike admitting it, he was also a very skillful attorney.

It was a skill inherited from his father. Walter McClure had been crippled by polio when he was in grade school in the town of Hamlet, in Parker County, and spent the rest of his life in a wheelchair. Hamlet was not named after the Dane, but took its name from its size, and as it grew larger saw no reason to change. This was a part of South Midland where few words were wasted. Towns and counties bore names like Adverse and Badland, and the place-names established without unnecessary explanation local attitudes toward outsiders who entered the city limits or crossed the county line. Walter McClure had gone to South Midland University, then to the university law school, where he was on the law review, and after his graduation, had turned down corporate practice with the larger firms in Kiowa and Capital City to be a country lawyer in Hamlet. Where, at the age of thirty, he was elected Parker County attorney.

County attorney was a job Walter McClure said he loved, though it paid him only seventy-five hundred dollars a year (stretched out with some money from his wife, Emily, who was always referred to as a St.

Louis girl, as if her Missouri genes explained the source of her dowry). The cases weren't much of a challenge—repos, unpaid taxes, DWIs, domestic abuse, drunk and disorderly, hunting or fishing out of season, bigamy, incest, crimes against nature (farmers and sheep), indecent exposure, embezzlement, fraud, grand theft larceny, a litany from the low end of the civil and penal codes—but Walter treated every one as if it would ultimately end up being reviewed by the Supreme Court. He was always cheerful, never complained about his useless legs, and for seven consecutive two-year terms he was elected president of the state bar association. It was an unpaid job nobody really wanted, and by electing someone who was handicapped, the state bar bureaucrats could congratulate themselves on doing a noble deed for good old crippled Walter McClure, what a damn shame, he could've been one of the best. What they didn't say was that having Walter on the case spared electing a Jew from Cap City or Kiowa. And I was never entirely sure that Walter disagreed with that assessment. He was, after all, from Parker County, which wasn't all that crazy about Catholics either.

To be honest, I could not stand Walter McClure. An unsentimental verdict about someone whose legs were wrapped in metal braces, and got a lot of unearned mileage out of it. I always had the sense that Walter was trying out for one of those "Most Unforgettable Characters I Ever Met" who used to turn up in the *Reader's Digest* but hadn't made the cut. He used to say he wanted to write a book about the life of a county attorney. And what was the most important thing he had learned as a county attorney?

That there were three stages in a man's life—birth, puberty, and adultery.

You see what I mean.

Walter and Emily had J.J., and then four years later, Emmett.

Emmett drowned when he was three, in the pond beyond the McClures' farmhouse in Parker County.

Five months before J.J. and Poppy were married, Walter McClure steered his wheelchair into the barn and shot himself with a single-action Colt .45 he had inherited from his father, who had inherited it from his father, and he from his father.

A story of the Old West.

I guess Walter was more complicated than I gave him credit for.

Y̲ou can't discuss J.J. without discussing Poppy.

Born Sonora Ford, the Sonora from the state in northern Mexico where her mother's family owned 212,000 acres richly veined with minerals. Margarita Ochoa Reyes had married Jim Ford, a fly-by-night prospector, and done him the favor of dying the day after their only child was born. A postpartum hemorrhage that made Jim Ford a rich man and a single parent on the same day. He was a doting father for over three decades until he was hit by a bolt of lightning on a golf course he was developing for a resort hotel he had underwritten outside Tangier. Except for charitable contributions and cash bequests to loyal retainers, Poppy was the primary beneficiary of Jim Ford's largely unleveraged estate, which she used to finance her first congressional campaign and a substantial portion of her three subsequent races.

Poppy never discouraged the notion that her nickname was affectionately given her by her father, but in fact it was bestowed on her when she was a student at Foxcroft. Her four years at Foxcroft are never mentioned in her campaign biographies, only that she went from "high school in Virginia" (never identified) to Wellesley, where she was exposed to what she now called "the pernicious virus of liberalism." It was at Wellesley, she claimed, that she learned to hate tree huggers. "The most beautiful thing about a tree," she says in her campaign literature, "is what you do with it after you cut it down."

The literature did not say that the line was lifted from Rush Limbaugh.

From the moment she took her seat in the House, Poppy was in demand. She was beautiful, she was rich, she would say whatever was on her mind, and she would say it outrageously. It was treason to imply that the world's ecosystem was fragile. Liberals only win elections by pretending they're not liberals. Feminism is a twelve-step program for homely women. Prison construction is the only necessary public housing program. She was preaching to the converted, but the converted ate it up, and faltering Republican candidates begged her to show up at their fundraising events. Poppy on the dais meant headlines for her and big bucks for the party coffers. Publicity was her crack, a microphone her crack house. The Sunday-show bookers all had her on speed dial, knowing that Poppy McClure on air guaranteed a quotable sound bite. I sometimes think that the network and cable anchors, and the talk-show hosts, knew Poppy better than J.J. did.

It occurs to me, as I am sure it had occurred to J.J., that death had twice been a fortuitous silent partner in the Ford family accomplishments. Poppy's considerable treasure allowed J.J. to forsake the uncertainties of the private sector and remain a prominent presence in the A.G.'s office, however uncomfortable that presence made the Worm. J.J. was also too smart not to know that his role as a high-profile prosecutor boosted his political asset as husband, another complication in his and Poppy's already complicated relationship.

J.J. in effect was a weekend husband. He saw Poppy only when she flew back to her district on those Thursday nights when she was not booked on a talk show the following Sunday. It was common gossip among the local political reporters who covered her that, on her daily schedule, Poppy and J.J.'s occasional coupling was euphemized as "Private Time," as in "Sunday 12:30 to 1 p.m.—Private Time." Unless there was a fundraiser. Raising money always took precedence over copulation. It is not surprising that J.J.'s eye occasionally wandered between Poppy's takeoff for Washington Sunday evening in the private jet she had inherited from her father and her return home to Cap City the following Thursday night. One can assume Poppy knew. There was little she didn't know. As long as discretion was maintained, it was a trade-off she could handle.

Poppy was a piece of work.

Occasionally I would see J.J. in the courthouse. He had stopped saying we should get together sometime for lunch. I think I had him nervous. I hope so. He didn't like to be read, and he thought I could read him.

I thought I could, too.

Begin with his appearance.

You can pick up things there.

He was a forty-two regular, high-end off-the-rack, nothing Italian, of course, I doubt there was a single Armani in Cap City, maybe Blass or Hilfiger with the designer label removed, he would be scrupulous about that, he wouldn't want people whispering at the office Christmas party that he bought the basics on Poppy's ticket, and although he wasn't tall, five-ten or so, but definitely under six, he did a very good languid. He seemed born to put his feet up on a desk or a conference table, kicking first one shoe off and then the other, loafers usually, never lace-ups, they were for the five-hundred-an-hour corporate boys, he would say, sometimes black Mephistos for the common touch, and he made his feet on the table seem an act of grace. He didn't work out that I knew of, no jogging, no aerobics, no StairMasters, exercycles or treadmills, no gym membership, but he didn't carry weight either, and his hair always looked as if it was the day before a cut, not long, not short, no discernible after-forty loss, no scalp desert and definitely no comb-over; he had a private way of pointing out to a jury when opposing counsel was wearing a hairpiece, he'd keep running his hands through his hair at a lawyers' sidebar with the judge, he thought wigs were funny, wigs were untrustworthy, a bad piece might tip a juror toward a guilty verdict, and a defendant might be remanded to Durango Avenue in part because of his court-appointed attorney's unfortunate head ornament.

Women thought he was attractive. Which is why he tried to stack juries with them.

J.J. knew I had known his father, probably even that I wasn't sold on Walter's relentless bonhomie, but his name never came up. It was as if he had no family. After Walter's suicide, I wrote J.J. the usual platitudes, and on the bottom of the printed card I received in return—THE FAMILY OF WALTER MCCLURE APPRECIATES YOUR EXPRESSION OF CONDOLENCE—he had scratched three words, *Max—Thanks—J.J.*

I suppose what I am trying to say is that J.J. did not encourage intimacy, but then who among us does. Christ, I wouldn't want anyone poking around my memory closet.

Take his brother, Emmett. A very complicated story, that. As it turned out. But first the day that Percy Darrow was executed.

I think I can put together a plausible narrative.

Chapter Three

J.J.

J.J. closed the door of the conference room, checked his digital Casio, then took his seat at the head of the empty conference table. The sandwich Allie had bought sat on a paper plate in front of his chair. Along with a plastic knife and fork and split of bottled water. Lunch. He took a bite and a swallow. The water was room temperature, the sandwich ice cold. He picked up the remote and clicked on *News at One*.

Poor Percy Darrow. Probably the last day of his life, the first man to die in the state's electric chair in over forty years, and the poor son of a bitch didn't even lead the news. "Holding on to life is like holding on to a handful of sand," Percy Darrow had said in his *NewsFront* interview the night before, hands and feet shackled, wearing an orange prison jumpsuit. Not bad as last-day quotes go. Manufactured by one of his New York and Los Angeles pro bono death-penalty lawyers. Probably Elsie Brand. She had a gift for the telling phrase, befitting an entertainment lawyer from Century City. And a former federal prosecutor with the U.S. Attorney in San Francisco, she had taken pains to tell him. While posting signals that she might be available for a prairie interlude.

A mistake he did not make.

Parlance was still the big story. How often does a Republican president come to an unemployed black man's funeral in a state he won with 61 percent of the vote, and hug Jesse Jackson in the bargain? On the screen there was film on Duane Lajoie and Bryant Gover. Both in shack-

28

les, both in prison orange, both slight, feral, shifty-eyed. They could have been twins. One had a receding chin, the other reddish-blond hair, a few strands of which he had twirled into what looked like a shoulder-length rat's tail. A bugger grip, the hacks at Durango Avenue called that effect. As the prisoner would find out soon enough. J.J. shook his head. He knew what their rap sheets and probation reports would say. Violence is the way stupid people try to level the playing field. To make up for mobile homes, public housing, foster parents, grungy rentals, domestic abuse, deficient IQs, sexual molestation, juvenile detention, substance abuse, paternity tests, unpaid child support, petty crime, felony convictions, and penitentiary hard time, probably with a little buttfucking thrown in. The bumper sticker on Lajoie's pickup said FUCK THE TELEPHONE COMPANY. It might just as well have said ARREST ME. A witness remembered seeing the bumper sticker the night of the murder, on an '89 Ford 4x4 with a four-pin trailer-tow harness, driving at a high rate of speed on County Road 21 a mile east of the field where Parlance's body was discovered two days later. In the ranching counties, people knew pickups and trailer tows better than they knew their own children. "Helped me change a tire once," a woman of indeterminate age and hair that looked as if it had been combed with a rake told a TV reporter about Duane Lajoie. Or was it the other one? They had once been residents of the same trailer park. "Pretty much of a loner, though. A drifter, like."

The loner and the drifter. Twin carbuncles on the body politic. J.J. wondered which one would dime the other out first. It was going to happen. Bet the house, break the bank. The Worm won't give me this one, thank God. Too much ink for Poppy's husband. And ink for Poppy's husband meant ink for Poppy. The last thing the Worm wanted.

Poppy's husband. As he would always be identified. There were worse fates.

Maybe.

Percy Darrow finally got airtime after the Frito-Lay commercial, his rapidly diminishing future hanging on the decision expected any moment of an en banc meeting of the Twelfth Circuit in Chicago. DECISION DAY was the slug line over a still photo of Percy Darrow, a Bible clutched to his chest, a WWJD tattoo displayed on his left hand, one letter on each knuckle. WHAT WOULD JESUS DO? Not for the first time it occurred to him that Jesus found a lot of converts among the constituents detained by the Department of Corrections. At least the parents of the murdered James twins would not be in attendance at Durango Avenue for the festivities. The seven-year wait for decision day had taken its toll. Mother dead of breast cancer three years earlier, father lost in a twister in Phil Sheridan County the following spring. The only other living relative was the mother's sister, a Carmelite nun in Oregon who had taken a vow of silence. So there would be no bullshit about closure. That terrible feel-good word. There is no end to grief. It's there, a constant, layer upon layer over the years. Like barnacles on a sunken ship.

Is it grief I feel about Emmett? Or guilt?

It was thirty-five years since it happened, but now he was dreaming about it again. It. Never a more specific designation. The dream was not exactly a nightmare. Just something that woke him up. Not every night. But more nights than he wished. Often enough so that he came to anticipate it. And to feel relief the nights it didn't wake him. The dream was like instant replay, viewed from every angle, slo-mo and super-slo-mo.

Back to the present. The past was too dangerous.

A live update of the crowds already beginning to picket outside Durango Avenue. There was a thin blanket of snow on the ground, with more promised, and the cameras picked up the frozen breath of the picketers. And the tinted plastic masks of the Capital City riot police who were already in place. He hoped for a blizzard. A blizzard wouldn't cancel the execution, but snow and below-zero wind chill meant thinner crowds. Thinner crowds might mean no Ted Koppel. And no Ted Koppel meant no Poppy. Poppy, who was going to Durango Avenue to represent the James family.

The weather was not cooperating. Clear skies, temperatures not expected to drop below freezing.

Poppy would not be there yet. Poppy was prime time only. Poppy would have a few words to say about what Jesus should do to Percy Darrow. In her role as the representative of the James family. Bringing closure.

God, Poppy could be a pain in the ass!

A thought that was constantly percolating beneath the impenetrable imperturbability that J.J. chose to present to the world.

Another commercial. Then a still of Jocko Cannon in studious black glasses holding three Cap City kindergarteners on his lap at the annual Reach Out Festival the university sports information department conducted at the end of spring practice every year. Followed by a clip of the Reverend Hardy Luther in wire-rimmed aviator glasses leading the Rhino football team in a pre-game locker-room prayer. A second clip of Jocko Cannon in full pads and Rhino black and silver doing a sack dance over the crumbled form of K-State quarterback Kareem Cox. A cut to Dr. John Strong holding a candle at the campus vigil he had organized, protected by a phalanx of Rhino linemen, all holding candles. A head shot of Brittany Barnes circled in a photo of the women's swimming team, then stock footage of her last-place finish in the backstroke at the conference championships.

It was as if finishing last justified what happened to her.

Allegedly happened to her.

The presumption of innocence must be maintained.

As Gerry Wormwold had stressed within the hour.

That investigator of yours is off the reservation, the A.G. had said.

Miss Vasquez is not my investigator, General. She represents the department. Over which you preside.

Are you blaming me? She works directly for you.

I'll talk to her.

Call me when you do.

A weather update, another commercial, then Nathalie Hubbard, as always looking as if her clothes were two sizes too small. Nothing but violations of the penal code on *News at One* today. J.J. raised the volume slightly. "We're outside the Criminal Courts Building, Des, where local nightclub owner Bobby Toledo"—film of Bobby Toledo entering the courthouse, head hidden under a raincoat—"accused of the murder of convicted drug dealer Tone Vaccaro . . ." A traveling shot of Murray Lubin scurrying down the courthouse steps. Known as Not-to-Worry Murray, Murray was Bobby Toledo's lawyer. "You know what I like about murder cases?" Murray Lubin liked to say. "One less witness to worry about." Murray Lubin said he had no comment, he would try the case in a court of law, not the court of public opinion. "No comment" meant Not-to-Worry Murray was worried. And maybe ready to deal. Tone Vaccaro was no loss. Back to Nathalie Hubbard: "This morning in Department Thirty-three, lead prosecutor J.J. McClure, with his usual flair for courtroom pyrotechnics, ridiculed the defense contention that Mr. Toledo was trying to protect his ex-girlfriend Carmen Capote."

Then J.J. trying to push his way past the cameras. Nathalie Hubbard blocked his way. She knew he would stop for her. The legacy of a long-ago post-midnight entanglement in the back of her Volvo station wagon after a department Christmas party. He had bumped his head on a child's safety seat, and there were Fruit Loops stuck to the soles of his shoes. "J.J., would you characterize this as a good morning or a bad morning for the prosecution, up or down, who was today's top scorer." Stop. To the camera. "This is a murder trial, Ms. Hubbard, we don't keep a running score . . . now if you'll excuse me." Over his shoulder: ". . . a drug deal gone bad, no more no less."

"J.J., will you be involved with the Parlance case?"

"I have no comment on pending cases."

"J.J., a question about Percy Darrow, will you be at Durango Avenue tonight . . ."

Unfortunately, yes. But not an answer he was willing to share with the viewers of *News at One.*

He had never seen anyone die. Scratch that. He had seen Emmett drown.

The door to the conference room opened suddenly. J.J. quickly clicked off the remote. Not quick enough.

"Don't you ever knock?" J.J. said.

MAX

Allie enters the story here. Allie Vasquez. An investigator in the A.G.'s office. I had hired her when I was still there, and J.J. kept her on, even though the Worm had wanted him to get rid of all my people. Allie was also a student of mine. At Osceola Community Law School. The night division. Allie was bright. If she hung in, she would pass the bar. It might take a couple of tries, but she wouldn't back off, she'd keep taking the bar exam until she got it right. She was thirty-three, and a single mother. I hate that phrase. She got drunk, she got laid, she got knocked up, she had a kid, she couldn't tell you who the father was, and so she was a single mother. Or maybe she wasn't drunk, she forgot to wear her diaphragm or take the pill or the guy didn't want to wear a rubber. Or maybe the father was a shit or a one-night stand and she didn't want him around. Her daughter's name was Rhea. Rhea was six.

I liked Allie. She could be a bit of a cunt, but she would keep me up on things at the A.G.'s. The gossip. What was going down. Nothing that would compromise a case. Just a touch here, a shading there, a peek at the computer records, if I asked, or a phone call. Sometimes she would say no. Fair enough. She had a kid to support, she needed the A.G. job. Getting fired was not on her agenda. She didn't expect a break on her grade, and I didn't give her one.

She was also a special friend of J.J.'s. Or had been. Anyway, that's what people said. There were not many secrets in a place as incestuous as the courthouse.

Some of them were even true.

"Don't you ever knock?" J.J. said to Allie.

"Why? You might find something interesting. You can always say excuse me, you walk in on something you shouldn't have walked in on." He doubted she had ever said excuse me about anything. "Watching yourself on the tube?"

"No," J.J. said. He straightened his tie and slipped on his shoes. "Of course not."

"The remote's by your hand."

"So?" Of course Allie would have noticed the remote. And of course she would have called him on the pointless prevarication. Little escaped her. It was what made her a good investigator. Her in-your-face style had antagonized both her superiors and her male partners when she was a detective in the Cap City P.D. It was why the commissioner was so willing to unload her when the A.G.'s office requested another investigator. And no doubt why Max had hired her. Now the Worm was on her case.

J.J. stared at her for a moment, then pointed to the sandwich. "What in the name of Christ do you call that?"

"A tuna on rye, hold the mayo, hold the lettuce."

"It tastes like tuna-fish sherbet."

"J.J., I'm an investigator, I'm not your fucking waitress; you want somebody to nuke your tuna on rye, get yourself a sandwich babe. Patsy maybe." Patsy Feiffer was the most junior of his attorneys, just a month or two out of arraignments. "She's so good with the precedents and the case law and all that shit, she shouldn't have any trouble keeping your order straight."

"You don't like Patsy, do you?"

"What's there to like? She's a babycake." Babycake was the name the nonlawyers in the office called the junior assistant state's attorneys. Always out of earshot. Except for Allie. She wore her class resentment like a wound stripe. "I forgot. Babycakes don't do sandwich orders."

"What I like about you, Allie, is your gift for holding your tongue."

"What you like about me is—"

J.J. cut her off. Change the subject. Work up to the Worm. "How's Rhea?"

"A pain in the ass."

"She's six years old."

Allie reached over and scraped away a dab of tuna he had not realized had adhered to his chin. "The only thing you know about kids is you don't have any. So if I say Rhea's a pain in the ass, buy into it." She licked the tuna from her finger. A simple gesture she could make seem salacious. Conversation with Allie was like hand-to-hand combat. Blade to blade. The trick was not to engage. Rhetorical argument led nowhere. "Look, I'm due back in court in an hour, then I've got to head out to Durango Avenue." Be matter-of-fact. Cool. An afterthought. "Bring me up to speed on Jocko Cannon."

"He's a fat fuck."

A predictable response. "That's not an indictable offense."

"All right. He's a three-hundred-pound All-American nose-tackle, fat fuck." Allie scratched her cheek. "What's a nose tackle anyway?"

She knew what a nose tackle was as well as he did. In South Midland, schoolchildren practically learned to call defensive signals for the Rhinos as part of their curriculum.

"Think of a walking Coke machine that falls on people," he said.

"And hurts them."

"If that happens, nobody gets too twisted out of shape."

"That explains it then. He was doing what comes naturally. And nobody got too twisted out of shape about it."

J.J. did not respond.

"So," she said finally when he kept staring wordlessly at her, "this walking Coke machine dragged . . ."

"Allegedly dragged . . ."

Allie didn't pause. "Brittany Barnes . . . sophomore, nineteen, no, twenty last Thursday, athletic scholarship, swimming team . . ." She consulted her notebook. ". . . down three flights of stairs in Rhino Hall . . . leaving her with . . ."

"The injuries are established. Whether Jocko Cannon is the perp is not. Or whether there even was a perp. Eyewitnesses?"

"Jesus, J.J., of course there's no eyewitnesses. A national championship's on the line. New Year's Night. Moon over Miami." She syncopated a cheer. " 'We're Num-ber One.' BFD." Big fucking deal. Allie Vasquez's mantra. "The people I talked to in Rhino Land all have the same fucking story. She got loaded and jumped from the fourth-floor stairwell. Bombed on Ecstasy, with a Diet Coke chaser."

"Any evidence backing up her story?"

"Clumps of her hair were found on all three landings."

"Blood test?"

"Negative on both alcohol and controlled substances." Allie closed her notebook. "Then there's fallback position two."

J.J. massaged his temples. He knew what was coming next. The Worm had floated the possibility when they met. "Which is?"

"She was working her way through the football team. Having already serviced the basketball team. And the track team is in the starting blocks."

The A.G. had missed the track team. "And she still wants to go ahead with this?"

"Wouldn't you?"

"Just give me a yes or no, Allie," he said irritably.

"She's not going to withdraw the charges."

"Jocko's lawyered up, you know."

"He was lawyered up before anyone dialed 911. Which means no DNA or hair samples without a court order. No way. Every judge in the

state has season tickets at Rhino Stadium. Comped. Prime location."
Allie leaned close. "Look, J.J., you don't have to spell it out. The Worm
wants a way out of this; he doesn't want to take Jocko to the grand jury."
J.J. discouraged his subordinates from calling the A.G. by his nickname.
A restriction Allie did not think applied to her. "He wants to be governor. Without the support of Jocko's old man, he's dead. Q.E.D. You've
got me spinning my wheels so it looks like we're doing something."

The point was not arguable. The Worm could not afford to incur the
wrath of Ralph Cannon, Sr. Which is why he wanted Allie Vasquez fired.
For overstepping her authority, he had said. It's your responsibility,
you're her immediate superior, take care of it. Thus getting Ralph Cannon, Sr., off the A.G.'s case. And Jocko in the Orange Bowl. "Tell me
about your meeting with Strong."

"I make an appointment, I go see him. Surprise. He's got a university
lawyer there."

"Leo Cassady." A regent and full-time university enabler to the state
legislature. "Enabler" was a kind word for "fixer."

"Leo. That's the one. And some dude from the sports information
department. I sit down, I say, 'Mr. Strong, I have a couple of questions,'
and the flack interrupts and tells me I have to call him 'Coach.' Or 'Doctor.' And that he prefers 'Doctor.' Doctor of what, for Christ's sake?"

"Sports psychology."

"I thought you had to take a pulse to be called 'Doctor.' "

Another unarguable point. "What happened then?"

"The flack puts a tape recorder on the table. 'To verify the accuracy
of the interview,' he says. 'Policy of the sports information department.'
'Fine,' I say, 'I've got no problem with that,' and I take a Sony M-405 out
of my bag, slip in a microcassette, and click it on. 'It's better if we both
have a record,' I say. The flack says that won't be necessary, they'll provide me with a copy of their tape, and it looks like it's all over before we
get started; there's no fucking way I'm going to use their tape. Then
Strong shakes his head at the flack, and he says, 'No, Larry'—that must
be the flack—'this young lady represents the legal establishment of this
great state, and we assume its veracity, as we have learned not to assume
any such thing with your brethren in the press.' Then the million-watt
smile. 'So anytime you're ready, young lady.' He's jerking me around."

As if she were a wide receiver he was recruiting. "Get on with it, Allie. Without the editorials."

"I was just . . ."

"Allie . . ."

"You want to hear my tape?"

"Your own words."

"Okay." She paused for effect. "I said I had a couple of questions about Ralph Cannon, Jr., aka Jocko Cannon, and the lawyer . . ."

"Leo Cassady . . ."

"Leo, right. Leo says no charges have been filed against Mr. Cannon, and the flack says he's a leading contender for the Outland Trophy, whatever the fuck that is . . ."

"Collegiate interior lineman of the year."

"I should've known you'd know that, J.J. It's a guy thing, right."

J.J. picked at a soggy crust of rye bread. Allie's version of the story was not going to improve.

"Anyway." Allie consulted her notebook. She was enjoying this. "The lawyer, what's-his-face, Mr. Fixit . . ."

"Leo Cassady . . ."

"So you said. Sorry. Right." She paused. "So Mr. Fixit, he says that Ralph Cannon, Sr., is a prominent alumnus, a figure of some importance and influence in this state, so on and so forth, and I say that Ralph Cannon, Sr., did indeed honor this great state, it was a privilege being allowed to walk on the same ground he did . . ."

"Allie, for Christ's sake . . ."

". . . but that this important and influential man was not the reason I was there, what I wanted to know was why Dr. Strong—I called him 'Doctor,' J.J., it's on the tape—twice felt he had to suspend Ralph Cannon, Jr., the aforementioned Jocko, from the team, and the flack said that was covered in the press at the time, and I said, right, I read the clips, but on both occasions Dr. Strong said he would not entertain any questions from the media, so I'd just like to hear him talk now in his own words about these incidents—you know, in a kind of shoot-the-shit way, 'That Jocko, he's some kind of dude,' don't give me that look, J.J., of course I didn't say that—and the flack says they weren't 'incidents,' and I said, Okay, we'll call them 'suspensions,' like the press releases did, and the flack says Dr. Strong doesn't air team matters in the press, and Leo says, 'Let me give you a little background, which I think will allow you to put this situation in some perspective . . .' "

Leo Cassady thought everyone had his hand out. It was only the amount that had to be decided. He hadn't met anyone like Allie in years. If he ever had. "And you said . . ."

Of course he knew what she had said. Broad strokes via the Worm.

"I say, What you call a situation, Section 242 of the Penal Code calls battery, to wit, 'Any willful and unlawful use of force or violence upon the person of another.' And he says, this Leo character, 'I'm an attorney, Ms. Vasquez, and I don't need a night school law student to explain the penal code to me.' " Allie permitted a smile. "I give him that one, he did some checking on me; how does he know I go to law school at night? I bet the Worm had something to do with it."

Her instincts were like gold.

"I wonder what else he knows."

He pretended not to hear.

"I mean, he's not as dumb as I thought."

"Allie . . ."

Another smile. Point made. "So I say to Mr. Fixit, Okay, I'd like to get your heads-up on this 'situation,' this 'perspective,' you mention. And he points to Strong—he's sitting there like he's the fucking pope, and just as infallible—and he says, 'What I see in Dr. Strong is thirty-five years of good judgment in the service of his God, his country, this state, and this university.' The band was there, it would've broken into the Rhino fight song. Then he gets all confidential, Leo, and he says, 'I have greater access to information than either you or the general public regarding Mr. Cannon, and I am in complete agreement with Dr. Strong and the action he took. This action,' he's practically whispering, like he's talking to a jury when he knows his client is hip-deep in shit, 'this action doesn't say what happened was right, this action says that if it happened to John Q. Student, John Q. Student would not be banned from extracurricular activities for as long as he was a student.'

"I give him a lot of heavy nodding, like I'm buying in to this, and then I say, like I'm really trying to work my way through it, 'But this didn't happen to John Q. Student; John Q. Student, in the person of Ralph

Cannon, Jr., is alleged . . .'—I did say 'alleged,' J.J., check the tape—'to have caused it to happen to Ms. Brittany Barnes, who is the aggrieved party here, not Mr. Cannon, Jr., and in the meantime I did not forget the question I was supposed to forget I asked . . .'—I should've said 'when you were blowing smoke up my ass,' but I didn't—'and the question was, why Dr. Strong thought it was necessary to suspend Ralph Cannon, Jr., from the team on those previous occasions.' And Leo says, 'Dr. Strong, you don't have to answer that,' but he raises his hand, and he says, 'I'm comfortable answering that, Leo, it's been covered extensively, however unfairly, in the media.' "

Any criticism of John Strong was unfair. Ipso facto. He was unassailable. He had always believed it. Rhino boosters thought it was the secret of his coaching success.

Allie waited for J.J. to respond, and when he didn't, she continued. "He says, 'Yes, Miss— Vasquez, is it? Such a lovely Spanish name, Rafael Huerta, our strong safety, is of Hispanic heritage, and yes, on two occasions I did suspend Mr. Cannon from our program, in fairness to my other kids, on the first occasion for one game, as you know, on the second for two.' And he smiles, like he's some straight-from-the-shoulder guy." Allie leaned forward. "J.J., what is this shit about the football program?"

"What shit about the football program?"

"The word. 'Program.' When I was at Cap City Community, we never called the criminology department the 'criminology program.' "

"Right."

"And the professors called us students. Not 'my kids.' He a fag?"

The thought had flickered across his mind. Not that John Strong was gay. Just the idea of coaches and their "kids." Avoid that. "Allie, get on with it."

"Okay, J.J. Calm down. So . . ." She paused for effect. "I said, 'Let's talk about those two suspensions. I want to hear Dr. Strong,' and Strong looks at Leo, and Leo says, 'Mr. Cannon had anger issues.' I remind him that on one of those occasions, Jocko had hit a student water boy in the face with his helmet, breaking his nose in the process. And the flack, Larry, he says, 'Because he didn't have any Gatorade.' I'm working my way around the no-Gatorade defense when Strong realizes how it must sound. 'I'm a firm believer in counseling and anger management therapy. Mr. Cannon is not a dangerous person, he's not an O.J. Simpson, he has a problem with anger, and he has occasional outbursts.' I let 'occasional outbursts' pass, and he says, 'So I admitted him back to the program because I felt he would benefit by the kind of structured setting that I and my coaching staff and other kids in the program could provide for him. I firmly believe in the inherent worth of young people, and giving everyone the opportunity to correct mistakes.' Then he says, 'I could've done the popular thing and dismissed Mr. Cannon from the program. But I wanted to do the right thing. I'm willing to take the heat for my kids, and I'm prepared to live with my decision.' And I say I'm relieved to hear that. And he says, 'You know, young lady, this alleged incident is going to do harm to a good young man.' Now he sounds like Father Flanagan, he's running Boys Town out there, there's no such thing as a bad boy. Or a bad nose tackle. At least until his eligibility expires . . ."

"Allie . . ."

"Okay." She ran her fingers through her hair. "So I ask him in what way Jocko could be harmed. And the flack says, 'It could affect how high he's taken in the NFL draft. And if he's not a top-ten pick, that could cost him a lot of money.' So now we've got Jocko as the real victim, and Strong says, really confidential, 'I think there are special interests involved with an agenda of their own.' I ask what special interests he has in mind, I assume he means women, but he just stands up, and he says, 'I don't want to get into that, I want to take the high road.' Then real confidential. 'I hope this has been helpful, young lady,' he says, and I say it certainly has been educational, but that Brittany Barnes was not going to withdraw her charges. And Leo says, 'Well, we'll see how well she adapts to a courtroom environment.' "

It was the sort of stupid thing Leo Cassady would say. He'd grown sloppy renting the legislature. "Then what?" J.J. said. As if he didn't already know.

"I sling my bag over my shoulder, I say thank you very much, I head for the door, and when I get there, I turn around and I say, like Columbo, 'I just have one more question, Dr. Strong.' 'Fire away,' he says. Cool. Like he's on the sideline. Time running out. Watch the clock. Make every play count. Go for the two-point conversion. But like Leo the lawyer, I've done a little homework myself. And I say, 'Your daughter.

Riley.' 'The apple of my eye,' he says. 'Nineteen,' I say. 'Lacrosse player.' You know where this is going, don't you?"

All too well.

"And I say, 'If it'd been Riley dragged down three flights of stairs, sneezing out her teeth like they were enameled snot, would you re-admit Jocko to the program, treat his anger issues?' That did it. Strong gets in my face, waving his finger under my nose, and he says, 'Just one minute, young lady,' and I say, 'Forget "young lady," I'm a state investigator. I carry a badge, I carry a gun, and I have the power to arrest.' Leo says this interview's over and the flack says this could cost Jocko the Outland Trophy."

"That explains it then," J.J. said.

"Explains what?"

"Cassady's got the A.G. on the horn before you hit your car, and the Worm brings me in for a heart-to-heart, he says, actual words, you're off the reservation."

"My name is Vasquez, not Geronimo."

"Very good, Allie. Very, very good."

"He wants to fire me."

"No. He wants me to fire you."

"So I guess I'm not your sandwich babe anymore."

J.J. made her wait for a moment. "I told him I wanted to hear your version," he said finally. "And I've got to say it's a good deal more colorful than I was led to believe."

"That means you don't believe it."

"No. It means the truth is in the details. The Gatorade and the Outland Trophy. And Leo Cassady threatening Ms. Barnes with a courtroom environment. You can't make that up." He paused, taking her in. "This is all on tape?"

Allie nodded.

"You make a duplicate?"

She nodded again. Of course. Allie would have made sure she was covered in case the Worm made a move against her. She always covered her back. And her flanks. Minority thinking. "Give it to me, and I'll give it to the A.G."

"That should make his day." She looked at J.J. "Is Poppy really going to run against him?"

He tried to maintain a professional posture. As ridiculous as he knew he sounded. "This office is not influenced by the career ambitions of the state's elected representatives."

"You go right on believing that, J.J."

There was a knock at the conference room door, and Harvey Niland, his number two chair, entered, followed by Patsy Feiffer dragging a wheeled evidence trunk behind her. Harvey was nearing retirement. How I do not want to end up, J.J. thought. Harvey Niland at sixty. Looking tired, thinking tired. For ten years, Harvey had waited to be appointed to the bench, but every year the Committee on Judicial Appointments had passed him by, always listing him as "Qualified," its lowest recommendation. The only qualification needed for "Qualified" was still to be breathing.

"You were so good on *News at One,*" Patsy Feiffer said, hefting the evidence trunk onto the conference table. She was blond and limber, and whatever the season wore mix-and-match pastels, even on the most frigid winter days when the wind cut to the bone and the snow stung the face. She never missed an opportunity to compliment him. "That's so right about not keeping score at a murder trial. I mean, it's not a game, is it, J.J.?"

J.J. looked over at Allie. His face was a mask. "Allie and I were talking about you, Patsy." He wore his bad cold smile. His take-no-prisoners smile, Allie called it. Patsy glanced quickly at Allie, acknowledging her presence for the first time with the briefest of nods, then expectantly back at J.J., waiting to hear why she had been under discussion. "Allie doesn't like you," he said pleasantly. "She thinks you're a babycake." Patsy appeared stricken. Allie was impassive. Harvey Niland seemed not present, as if counting the days to his retirement. J.J. bored ahead. "Pampered. Entitled." Nothing I had actually said, Allie recalled later. But in the ballpark. "Lady Bountiful." The kind of frontal attack that was his courtroom trademark. "Always high-hatting her."

Patsy tried to gather a response. "I don't really see why you and . . ." She pointed at Allie as if she could not bear to say her name.

"Try 'Allie,' " J.J. interrupted. "Short for Altagracia. Allie. Vasquez." Then cutting each word off as if with a knife, he said, "And I really don't see why you don't have a response ready." His voice lowered dangerously.

"In a courtroom, you have to be prepared for every surprise. It never goes the way you want it to go. If you don't answer, if you look as if you're going to cry, as you do right now, then you're lost, throw in the towel. 'Your Honor, the prosecution asks for a directed verdict of not guilty by reason of prosecutorial incompetence.' " J.J. tented his fingers. "I assume you want to try cases . . ."

Patsy nodded blankly.

"Then give me an answer." He raised his voice. "Now."

"I don't see any justification for this . . ." Patsy began.

"Justification?" His voice was contemptuous. "You think a lion needs justification to take down a zebra? His justification is he's hungry. His justification is he can." He was in her face. "You say, 'BFD.' You ever hear Allie say that? 'Big fucking deal.' You probably didn't know what it meant. Or you say, 'Of course she doesn't, I'm a lawyer, she's not, she takes night courses at an unaccredited law school from a homo who was fired from this office.' You say, 'Of course she doesn't, she's an envious bitch.' You say, 'Of course she doesn't, she knows you want to get in my pants.' "

Patsy seemed near tears. J.J. leaned close to her. "It doesn't matter what you say," he said quietly. "Just say something. The more outrageous the better. And if you're in trial and the judge says you're out of order, skirting contempt, BFD, you got the jury's attention back. You're the lion. The lioness. Belching after you eat the zebra." He reached down and patted her hand. "You just learned more about criminal court behavior than you picked up in three years of law school. Don't forget that." He sat back in his chair. "And Allie thinks you're just swell. Right, Allie?"

"Just swell," Allie said.

"Good." A big smile. "Harvey, you awake?"

Harvey Niland removed a file from the Toledo evidence trunk. "Tadeusz Lynch."

"He arrived from Durango Avenue yet?"

"He's in the holding tank."

"You got him dressed? I don't want him showing up in his orange jumpsuit."

"He's shaky, J.J."

"Of course he's shaky. He's going to rat out Toledo."

43

"Patsy thinks we should ask for a continuance." Typical Harvey. His idea, but he laid it off on Patsy in case it got shot down.

J.J. turned to Patsy. She seemed to have regained some of her composure. "Why?"

"I think he needs a little prepping."

"His resolve needs stiffening, you mean? He wants to be clear on what he gets for turning rat? How big a chunk of cheese he's looking at?"

Patsy nodded.

"Let me tell you a story," J.J. said after a moment. "Three years ago. Ellen Tracy's court downstairs. I'm examining my witness. One Wendell Z. I have successfully established that Z stands for just that. Z. He is Mr. Z. So I ask Mr. Z—Wendell—what exactly the accused, one Luscious Odelle, said to him immediately prior to committing the three counts of homicide that had brought us to Judge Tracy's court. Wendell answers, and I quote, within reasonable parameters of accuracy, and believing that my memory still has most of its pixels: Wendell says, 'Luscious say Nadine messing around with Antoyne. Luscious say he mean to take care of Nadine. Then he mean to take care of Antoyne.' So I ask Wendell if Luscious mentioned how he meant to take care of Nadine. 'With his blade,' Wendell said. I asked Wendell what Luscious meant to do with the blade in question, which had already been entered as a prosecution exhibit, and Wendell says, 'Luscious say he going to hit Nadine upside the head, and then he going to take that blade . . .'" J.J. paused to see if he had everyone's attention. "'. . . he going to take that blade and cut out her pussy.' That did it. Four bells. Defcon 2. Ellen Tracy leans so far over the bench her size-six triple-A's clear the floor . . ."

"J.J.," Patsy Feiffer said, "is this relevant to the Toledo trial?"

J.J. ignored her. "'Whoa, whoa, whoa,' Tracy says. "'In this courtroom, we refer to the sexual organs by their clinical terms. In this case, the vagina. Understood?'"

"J.J.," Patsy insisted.

"In due time, Patsy. 'Wendell,' I say, 'you heard Her Honor's admonition.' And he just stares at me, 'admonition' not being a word common to the purviews where the Z family operates. So I spell out what Tracy had said, and I say, 'You understand, right?' Wendell nods, and I resume my line of questioning. 'Wendell,' I say, 'under the strictures laid down by the court, please continue your account of what happened the afternoon in question. 'Well, Luscious be mad,' Wendell said, 'because Nadine messing around with Antoyne . . .' "

"J.J., we have a motion to frame," Patsy Feiffer said.

"For the last time, Patsy," J.J. said, "shut up and let me finish. Understood?"

Patsy nodded unhappily.

" 'Luscious go looking for Nadine,' Wendell says. 'And when Luscious found Nadine?' I say. 'He hit her upside the head,' Wendell says. I now have his full attention. Wendell is on the program. 'What happened then?' I say. And Wendell says, 'Luscious grabs Nadine . . .' Then he breaks off. He's looking for help. 'Judge,' he says finally, 'what's that word you say I got to use instead of "pussy"?' "

Allie laughed.

"I don't find that amusing," Patsy Feiffer said, without looking at Allie.

"You think it's suggestive and could be construed as sexual harassment?" J.J. said.

Patsy did not reply.

"You think it's an inappropriate story to tell in the middle of a murder trial?"

"Yes."

"You would prefer full focus on *The People* v. *Toledo*."

"Yes."

"Full attention on his motion for a continuance?"

"Yes."

"So we can stiffen Tadeusz Lynch's backbone?"

"Yes."

"And make sure his story rhymes?"

"Yes."

"You don't think Murray Lubin would welcome that motion? You don't think he'd love a continuance so he could gin up his own line on Mr. Lynch?" J.J. let the question sink in. "Give Murray two more days and he would rip Lynch's heart out." Patsy started to speak, then stopped. "We don't give him that chance. We put Lynch on first thing. He places the murder weapon in Bobby Toledo's hand. Murray maybe gives him a bloody nose, but that's all, nothing we can't handle, Tadeusz is back in leg irons and on the bus home to Durango Avenue before the afternoon break." J.J. looked from Patsy to Harvey. "Any objections?" Neither spoke. "Didn't think so. See you in court."

Patsy closed the evidence trunk and wrestled it to the floor. When she opened the door, J.J. said, "Patsy, could you get me a bottle of water and put it under my chair." Patsy hesitated, her back stiffening. She did not turn around. "And make sure it's cold."

Patsy maneuvered the wheels of the trunk over the door saddle and let the door slam behind her.

After a moment, Allie said, "What did that story about Wendell X . . ."

"Z . . ."

". . . have to do with the Toledo case?"

"Nothing. I just thought the tension level needed to be lowered a bit."

"Good thinking. It really did the trick for Patsy."

"Sarcasm's not your long suit."

"I thought you were giving yourself time to figure out why a continu- ance motion was a crappy idea. Say something. Isn't that what you told Patsy?"

J.J. rose and slipped his jacket on. "On the money." He stared at her for a moment. "Max Cline might turn you into a pretty good lawyer."

"When Max told that story, Wendell's name was *X. Mustafa X.*"

J.J. smiled. "It's a courthouse classic. I was betting Patsy had never heard it. And Harvey's brain-dead."

"You're a real shit."

"Agreed."

MAX

Allie gave me chapter and verse later, after a class in cross-examination in my role as mentor-savant to the less than privileged, the not quite Cau- casian, and the first-language-anything-but-English minorities who were my students at Osceola Community.

"Why was he so beastly to what's-her-name?"

"Patsy."

"Softening her up?"

Allie shrugged.

"So that she's *soooo* surprised when she winds up in the kip with him?"

Another shrug.

"That his MO with you?"

"MOs don't work with me, Max. Just a good stiff dick."

Chapter Four

The warden's office at the state penitentiary on Durango Avenue over-looked the visitors' parking lot. On the wall opposite the warden's desk, there were monitors showing each cellblock, and in the death-row hold-ing cell a ceiling camera recorded what promised to be the last hours of Percy Darrow's life.

"Who do you think designed the electric chair?" Charley Buckles said.

"A matter of some dispute, Charley," J.J. McClure said. "Thomas Alva Edison was in the running. A direct-current man. George Westing-house favored alternating. AC and DC. Each trying to corner the elec-tricity market. Capitalism at work. Edison juiced a horse to make the case for DC. A prison electrician wired up the actual piece of furniture. He used AC. A fellow named Kemmler was the first to sit in it. His girl-friend had run into the business end of his axe. He needed a couple of jolts, but it worked. The newspapers said he'd been Westinghoused."

"You been reading up, J.J.," Charley Buckles said disapprovingly. Charley Buckles was the Osceola County medical examiner. And had been for as long as anyone could remember.

"Observing the courtesies of the occasion, Charley."

"Edison thought it would only take four seconds. He got that one wrong. Took four minutes." Edison's fallibility seemed to please Charley Buckles. "Two thousand volts for the first four seconds in this state, a thousand volts for the next seven, then two hundred and eight volts for

48

two minutes. Depending on body weight. Eight amps should take care of Percy."

"After which you take out your stethoscope and do the honors."

"They were never quite sure the hot squat would take care of business," Charley Buckles said. His interest in the way people died was inexhaustible. "That's why they mandated immediate autopsies. To finish the job, so to speak." He laughed heavily and leaned toward J.J. Even when he whispered, his voice was like gravel. "I did the post on that Parlance fellow. The pathologist down there in Regent thought it was a little beyond his capabilities. He does mostly highway and hunting accidents. Farmers who get sliced and diced falling into combines they can't afford that their widows end up handing over to the bank, the odd suicide swinging in the barn, that sort of thing, nothing of the homicide variety." He paused. "Your dad ever have a homicide out there in Parker County?"

J.J. shook his head. Charley, why bring up suicides in a barn? J.J. thought of his father and the old single-action Colt he had put in his mouth and triggered with his thumb in the tack room. It was as if his face had never existed. He wondered if swinging from a beam in the barn would have been easier to take. Would he have cut him down or waited for the sheriff?

No, he would have left him up. Maintained the integrity of the crime scene.

"Good man, Walter," Charley Buckles said, nodding his head slowly, as if processing what he seemed to have momentarily forgotten, the way Walter McClure had died. He plunged on. "One thing I did not want to do was drive all the goddamn way down to Regent. I can hardly fit behind the wheel of my automobile anymore. I get the wheel pushing in my stomach and it makes me sleepy." His eyes closed for a moment, and then he snapped awake. "Well, I thought I'd seen just about everything in the homicide line. I'd have to say those two young gentlemen did not like Parlance much. The skinning you know about. He was alive when they did it. Cut out his tongue so he couldn't scream. Shot off his fingers, stomped his chest with their cowboy boots. He must've been some tough bird. It was the hollow-point that took him out for good." He appraised J.J. "You ain't going to do this one, are you?"

Plead ignorance. "It's up to the A.G."

"Fat chance," Charley Buckles grunted. "He's looking at a primary against your wife, she decides to run. The last thing he wants is you on a case that brings Jamaal Jefferson and the president of the You-nited States to Regent."

J.J. wondered how Charley Buckles, who spent all his working life with the recently dead, had such perfect pitch for the politics of his home state.

"You know why I went into the pathology line after I finished medical school?"

A Charley Buckles perennial. It was easier to pretend it was the first time he had heard it. And it moved him away from the Parlance trial. "Why, Charley?"

"Because your mistakes can't kill people," Charley Buckles said, swallowing a tobacco laugh. "They're already dead."

"Funny, Charley."

"J.J.," Charley Buckles said. "One thing I always wondered. Why the initials? What's the matter with James?"

"My family called me Jamie," J.J. said after a moment. There was something about Charley Buckles that invited unintended confidences. It might have been his ridiculous name. Or his medicine-ball shape.

"I think I see the problem," Charley Buckles said, clearing his throat, a sound like the rumble of thunder. His face was beet red, and his breathing came in quick spurts heavy with phlegm and nicotine. "People named Jamie don't generally ask for the death penalty."

J.J. nodded. As if to himself, he said, "It's a frivolous name." A sudden sharp memory. Emmett called him Jamie even as he was drowning. Death was much on his mind this evening.

"And riding the lightning is a most unfrivolous penalty," Charley Buckles said, his words lost inside a wheezy laugh. Another change of direction. "Listen. I saw Poppy outside when I got here. Signing autographs, enjoying the hell out of herself."

"She says she's representing the mother and father."

"They're lucky they died, you ask me."

An unexpected take. "Lucky, Charley?"

"Hell, J.J., they would've been in the victim business." He hawked some phlegm and left it in the blue bandanna he used as a handkerchief. "Selling T-shirts. NO MERCY FOR PERCY or some such. It's a funny goddamn kind of famous, waiting for somebody like Percy Darrow to die.

If they was still alive, they'd wake up tomorrow, wishing he was still around, wondering what the hell they're going to do with the rest of their lives. Nobody on the TV wanting to talk to them. No cameras. No notebooks. They'd end up missing that son of a bitch."

Charley Buckles still had the capacity to surprise.

"That Poppy." Charley Buckles had switched gears again. "I see her on that fat one's show. Rosie something. And that blonde, what's-her-name, married to the bald guy with no eyebrows, her show. She's going to be on *Nightline* tonight, I hear." Another snort. "That fellow Poppel will have his hands full with her."

"Koppel," Harold Pugh said. "Not Poppel." Harold Pugh had slipped back into his office, as always unnoticed, after yet another trip to ensure that the wiring attached to the electric chair would not short out when the governor's office ordered the execution to proceed. Practice makes perfect, the warden had said. You can't over prepare. Harold is a compendium of the obvious, J.J. thought. In the A.G.'s office, the warden, as elusive and recessive as a piece of ectoplasm, was known as The Shadow. That night's scheduled execution was the biggest event in Harold Pugh's twenty-five years of silent and uncomplaining service in the Department of Corrections. It was an effort for him not to show his resentment that Poppy McClure would be talking to Ted Koppel in the parking lot while he was attending to the needs of Percy Darrow's last meal and waiting for the governor's message that all appeals had been exhausted. "And the reason he's here is because it's the first execution in this state since 1959, not because . . ."

Harold Pugh caught J.J.'s eye and left the sentence dangling. He had made his point. No reason to mention Poppy. It was he who would ask Percy Darrow if he had any last words, he who would order the switch pulled, he who would announce to the media that the sentence had been carried out and the will of the people observed. But it would be Poppy McClure on *Nightline,* not he. He would not have occasion to tell Mr. Koppel about the two Big Macs, the six-pack of Pepsi, and the bag of jelly beans Percy Darrow had ordered for his last meal, or about his demeanor as he sat in the electric chair, a leather hood covering his head and face.

"I bet Big Macs are the last meal of choice," Charley Buckles said, his breathing still labored. "I mean, around the country."

"I didn't think it would be sweetbreads," J.J. said. Every time he was with Charley Buckles he felt like a straight man.

"It could be a hell of an ad campaign," Charley Buckles said. "You get Ronald McDonald. And he says, 'To all my friends on death row, think McDonald's.' "

"I don't think that's appropriate," Harold Pugh said.

"Shit, what is?" Charley Buckles said. "Gordy Sunday had cheese steak." Gordon Sunday was the last man executed in the state's electric chair. "I was there. Representing the Osceola County coroner's office. They called us coroners those days. A good word. Now it's medical examiner. And even that's too much for some people." He wheezed a cough. "They say M.E." He elongated the two letters: EMMMM EEEEE. "J.J., I want you to promise that when I die, my obituary says that I was the coroner in this county for forty-two years, not some damn M.E."

"I'll take care of it, Charley." His beeper rang. It was Gerry Wormwold's callback number. The A.G. had wanted to attend Darrow's execution himself, but his advisors had counseled that a potential gubernatorial candidate should keep himself aloof from the proceedings and use his office instead as a pulpit to accuse the anti-death-penalty protestors who had gathered outside of "cynically manipulating the system." It was an attempt at even-handedness that his handlers thought might assist him in getting past his nickname. And so around the state at 4-H Club meetings and Rhino booster lunches, the A.G. did not miss an opportunity to toss in the phrase "cynically manipulating the system."

J.J. dialed Wormwold's number.

"J.J., what's the delay?"

"No delay, General. The governor hasn't called yet."

"You think that Democrat son of a bitch Kennedy is stalling?"

"I think he's waiting for the Twelfth Circuit to finish writing its decision."

"They'll turn it down, right?"

"Unless hell freezes over. Then the governor's office has to make sure copies get in the hands of all the involved parties."

"I know what has to be done," Wormwold said irritably. He paused for a second. "I just got off the phone with Niland. Murray Lubin wants to deal."

I called that one right, J.J. thought. It was in the wind. "I'll put together a package."

"Toledo does time."

"No problem."

"Heavy duty."

"A touch."

Wormwold hesitated. "Write it up and run it past me in the morning." J.J. was sure the A.G. had little interest in the Toledo case. He had something else on his mind, and he was having trouble getting to it. "Your wife's outside over there." There it was. Poppy was getting airtime and he wasn't. He and Harold Pugh should compare notes. "Talking to all those TV boys." Wormwold paused as if wondering if he should continue. He plunged on. "I know she's your wife, but . . ." His voice trailed off. He was not ready to come right out and say that Poppy was cynically manipulating the system. As of course she was. Better to leave it hanging.

"I'm giving the Parlance case to Maurice Dodd," the A.G. said disagreeably after waiting an unseemly number of seconds for a response. "You've got a full plate."

Surprise, surprise. "Maurice could use the exposure."

"What's that supposed to mean?"

"Nothing at all, General."

"It's a slam dunk."

"As long as he doesn't bounce it off the rim," J.J. said. Wormwold started to speak, then hung up without another word. Blowing a layup was always a possibility with Maurice Dodd. Maurice the Uncontaminated. Maurice the Incorruptible. Maurice the Inflexible. Harvey Niland with attitude. A more effective gauleiter than trial lawyer, J.J. had said more than once about Maurice Dodd. Among other things.

Maurice Dodd was equally charitable about J.J.

Poppy McClure's husband, he would say.

On the holding-cell monitor, J.J. watched Percy Darrow sitting on a bunk, wearing only Jockey shorts and a T-shirt. His head had been shaved, his legs, even his eyebrows and his pubic hair. It would give the wrong impression to the witnesses if his eyebrows or the hair around his testicles caught fire when the electricity jolted him. He had his hand inside his shorts, and seemed to be masturbating. Not something Jesus would do, but why not. One last spasm. Like the two loads he left on the James twins. J.J. had read the execution procedures Harold Pugh had written. Percy Darrow's Big Macs would be laced with Dulcolax to ensure that he would evacuate his bowels before he was led the fifteen steps from the holding cell to the execution chamber. He would be given a clean white shirt and freshly laundered jeans, with both pant legs split up the side to make it easier to roll them up and attach the restraining straps. He would wear a rubber diaper because the first jolt of electricity would loosen his sphincter. Clockwork was what Harold Pugh was after, and to that end he and his guard commander had drilled the seven-man tie-down team as if they were Riverdancers. Thirty-five seconds from entry into the chamber until ready-to-go was Harold Pugh's timetable. There was a right-leg man to do the right-leg strap, a left-leg man to do the left-leg strap, a right-arm man and a left-arm man to do the same with the upper limbs, a guard to stick a gag into Percy Darrow's mouth, a guard to stick the leather hood over his head, and a guard to screw the head electrode with its circular sponge down on top of his skull. Three guards pushed outlet buttons, but only one of the buttons was connected to the electrical source, so as to keep the identity of the real executioner unknown.

His cell phone rang. Poppy from the parking lot. Looking for electric-chair chat that would surely end up on *Nightline.* No way. He had asked her not to come to Durango Avenue, but asking her to avoid press coverage was like asking the sun not to rise.

"Gas Station Gordy," Charley Buckles suddenly said. He seemed to have been sleeping. Gordon Sunday was on his mind. Even more than Percy Darrow. The past was an infinitely more interesting place for Charley Buckles than the present. "That's what they called him. First four people he shot ran convenience stores out on the Interstate. I swear, all by himself he shut down every gas station in the state. From the Big Muddy to the Wyoming line. Must've passed through Parker County. Walter ever mention it to you?" J.J. shook his head. "Probably before your time. Might've shot Walter, he stopped off there. Then I guess you wouldn't be here, if he had." A spittled laugh. "Funny the way things work out." He wiped his mouth with the back of his hand. "Nobody dared get in their car. Your grandma died, they kept her on ice until it was safe to plant her. Gordy and that little bit of fluff he drove with. Sue something." He searched his memory. "Sue Carol Hayes. Convenience-store Bonnie and Clydes was what they were. I mean, they shot eleven people in nine days. The only reason they got caught was because there was nobody on the highway, and they just run out of gas."

Another rumble of phlegm, some of which Charley Buckles caught in the palm of his right hand. He wiped it off on a trouser leg. "Sixteen months from the day he got caught to the day he got the juice. They knew how to do things those days. Of course Sue Carol said she was Gordy's prisoner, she hardly knew him. No way he'd been porking her. She was a good girl. Shit. Cowboy Collins ever got into her, he wouldn't have touched the sides." Cowboy Collins was another South Midland luminary, the star of a thousand porno films, now retired to anonymity and cattle ranching somewhere in the state, the immense weapon that had serviced two generations of adult cinema actresses now only unholstered, it was claimed, for his male companion. "So anyway, I was there. July 14, 1959. They wanted to do the job right, so they set the generator so high Gordy sizzled like bacon in a pan. The room stank, a greasy smell like fatty pork when it catches fire in the oven, and those were the days when there were no air fresheners. My stethoscope sunk into him like he was a goddamn swamp."

Charley Buckles pulled the blue bandanna from his pocket and mopped the sweat from his face. "That smell of pork still upsets my stomach. You take care of that, Harold?"

Harold Pugh ignored the question.

Charley Buckles motioned J.J. to come closer. "I hear the Cowboy contributes to Poppy's campaign," he said confidentially.

"I wouldn't think so."

It would have been political nitro for Poppy to accept a contribution from Cowboy Collins. But then, Charley was plugged in all over the state; he could've heard something.

"You might have her check out if she got something from the Loomis Cattle Company." Charley Buckles's whisper was like a shout. "That's the Cowboy. She might think about returning it if she did."

His face contorted into another explosive cough.

"You okay, Charley?"

"Just let me catch my breath." He gulped air. It was a moment before his breathing evened out. "You going to indict Jocko Cannon?"

"Privileged information, Charley."

"It'll knock the shit out of that dance down in the Orange Bowl, you do. That big son of a bitch is a number one draft choice, he plays and the Rhinos win the national championship." He pronounced it "champeen-ship." "Three hundred pounds of mean. Those Rhino boosters will be all over the Worm's ass he indicts Jocko. He must be squirming on that one. Those boosters can raise a lot of money."

For Poppy as well as Wormwold.

"How big was that little girl anyway?"

"What little girl?"

"The little girl Jocko dragged down three flights of stairs by her hair."

" 'Allegedly' dragged."

"If that's the way you want it, J.J." Another coughing fit. This time some of the spray landed on Harold Pugh's desk. Harold Pugh jumped back, nearly falling from his chair, then examined his shirt with distaste, looking for residue.

"The one with the fractured skull and all her teeth rearranged is the one I mean," Charley Buckles said without looking at Harold Pugh. "They sure got some strange idea about consensual sex these days over there in Rhino Land. That's his defense, right? Me Tarzan, you Tiffany."

"Brittany." J.J. knew he would have to recuse himself if Ralph Cannon could not buy off Brittany Barnes. An unlikely scenario if, as he did not doubt, Allie had read the situation correctly. Poppy was simply too tight with Ralph Cannon. He was not only the finance chairman of the state Republican Party, he had also developed shopping centers with her father.

From the parking lot, the lights on the TV satellite trucks reflected off the windows of the warden's office. Harold Pugh fiddled with the remote, then as if in a fit of pique clicked on the TV. I knew he couldn't resist, J.J. thought. The appeal of Poppy power. On-screen the cameras panned over the crude handmade signs in the prison parking lot. A line drawing of Christ on the cross over the words MAYBE THE DEATH PENALTY SHOULD HAVE BEEN ELIMINATED A LONG TIME AGO. Then the balance:

MURDERERS SHALL SURELY BE PUT TO DEATH. NUMBERS 35:16–21. Anti: THEY'RE DYING TO GET US ELECTED. Pro: GOD SAYS, "YOU SHALL NOT PITY HIM." DEUTERONOMY 19:11–13. And another: ELECTRICITY—A SHOCK TO THE SYSTEM. It's like a minstrel show out there, J.J. thought. It's as if the signs and the demonstrators are shipped from death row to death row, another opening, another show. Then from his studio in Washington, Ted Koppel. It struck J.J. how much he looked like Alfred E. Neuman. He turned to share the observation with Charley Buckles, but Charley was dozing in his chair, his chin resting on his chest. Perhaps dreaming about Gordy Sunday sizzling like bacon. Anyway, he doubted that Charley would know who Alfred E. Neuman was. Or had even heard of *Mad* magazine.

"Next," Ted Koppel said, "we go to the state penitentiary in Capital City, South Midland, where . . ."

Cut to Poppy in the prison parking lot. A vision in a black leather Jil Sander shearling-lined duffel, her high cheekbones and the mane of raven hair from the Ochoa Reyes gene pool flecked with snow. She was hemmed in by demonstrators, many of whom, like Poppy herself, were wearing large white campaign buttons with orangey letters declaring POPPY POWER.

"Now Congresswoman McClure . . ."

"Ted, let me interrupt." J.J. wondered if the thick wet snow and condensed breath clouded her view of the monitor on which Koppel was appearing. No. Nothing would get in the way of Poppy and live air. "You can call me Poppy or Congressman, but not Congresswoman, I hate gender specificity, it's part of the social dry rot that is undermining . . ."

"Congresswoman, let's cut past the rhetoric, we're here tonight to talk about the death penalty . . ."

"Excuse me again, Ted, but I'm here to wish good riddance to Percy Darrow, a pedophile child murderer." She waved documents at the camera. "I have right here in my hand the autopsy reports on little Patrick and little Lyman . . ."

J.J. swore silently. Poppy must have taken the reports from the duplicate files he kept in his office at home. There was no point in losing his temper here. Not for the benefit of Harold Pugh. He would have this out with Poppy later.

" 'Their nude bodies were found buried in the woods,' " Poppy was reading. " 'Soil at a temperature of fifty degrees preserves that which is buried in it.' " Poppy stared at the camera. "Which is why their little bodies were not in an advanced state of decomposition, Ted."

Charley Buckles's eyes were still closed, his heavy breathing punctuated by irregular quiet snorts. Thank God, J.J. thought. Charley had done the autopsy reports on the James twins. It would offend his sense of professional propriety that so many years later they were being used to make points on a television interview show.

"Congresswoman, you seem to be using the bodies of those two children to troll for votes," Koppel said. "I noticed you passing out campaign buttons. You even tried to pin them on our crew."

Poppy was not dismayed. "You know what I say, Ted."

"I have no doubt that you'll tell me, Congresswoman."

"I'd sweep the system clean." The James twins had served their use. Now back on message. "No more getting off on technicalities. Didn't read Miranda, didn't have a warrant, didn't this, didn't that. I say no more plea bargaining, no more Miranda, give the accused one day in court, one day only, then a no-return ticket to the penitentiary, and to death row . . ."

"Everybody?"

"We don't need less death penalty offenses, Ted, we need more. That's the best way to stabilize the inmate population."

"Congresswoman, will that be your campaign theme if you compete against Attorney General Wormwold for the Republican gubernatorial nomination? 'Poppy will execute more than Gerry.' Are you going to put a moving sidewalk from death row to the electric chair? Open up a death-row gift shop?"

Score one for Koppel.

J.J. wondered exactly what Poppy would do next. Something off the wall, he was sure. It was like a programmed gene when someone was trying to pin her against the ropes. Fingers through her thick black hair, framed now by a tiara of snow. A dazzling smile. The power of her sexiness setting up the unexpected curve ball.

"Do you read George Bernard Shaw, Ted? *Pygmalion*? *St. Joan*?"

"Congresswoman McClure, I'm not sure what George Bernard Shaw has to do with the first execution in . . ."

"Ted, are you telling me you are not aware of Shaw's attitudes on the death penalty? Even as soft on Communist Russia as he and the Webbs were?" Koppel hesitated. "Beatrice and Sydney Webb," Poppy added, as if Koppel might not have known. The killer Poppy smile. J.J. knew that Willie Erskine had been surfing the Internet again. Willie Erskine was Poppy's chief of staff. The Internet was made for a poisonous idiot like Willie Erskine. And for a magpie intelligence like Poppy's. Not just Shaw, but the Webbs, too. Poppy's parlay. "Let me quote GBS for you, Ted. From a letter to *The Times* of London in 1947, when socialist England was debating whether or not to quit hanging murderers. 'The public right and power of civilized states to kill the unprofitable or incorrigibly mischievous in self-defense is a right that can never be abrogated.' "

Willie Erskine's browser would have been working overtime as soon as Poppy got the call from *Nightline,* and she would have committed the quote to memory, ready to pop it at the opportune moment. Her captivating capriciousness and her unfailing memory were what made her in such demand as a guest talking head.

Ted Koppel changed the subject. Shaw had not been on his agenda. "Congresswoman McClure, Mr. Darrow is going to die in your state's electric chair, perhaps before the end of the program. Many states have instituted more humane . . ."

"Killers don't deserve humanity, Ted. Which is why I am absolutely opposed to lethal injections as a means of ending their lives. Sodium pentathol to put them to sleep. Why let them snooze? Go right to the potassium chloride, I say. Down in Texas, at Huntsville, a killer began to snore on the gurney from the sodium pentathol. That's an outrage. What you call humane is just a way of insulating our way into a liberal feel-good cocoon. Garrote them, as the Spanish used to do. The guillotine, like the French did before they got all squishy. Faceup, eyes taped open, so their last look is the blade coming down. Death for the likes of Percy Darrow should be as horrible as the death he inflicted on his victims . . ."

"You are aware that in Florida a few years ago the electric chair malfunctioned, and the condemned man's head burst into flames—"

"You know what I say to that, Ted?"

"I can't wait, Congresswoman."

"If people don't want to burn up when they're electrocuted, then they should commit their capital offenses in some other state . . ."

The telephone on Harold Pugh's desk began to ring.

"Hold that thought, Congresswoman," Ted Koppel said on the TV screen. "I'll get back to you and our other guests, but first we have to go to a commercial break."

Harold Pugh straightened his shoulders, clicked off the remote, picked up the phone, and announced officially, "Warden Pugh."

J.J. looked over at Charley Buckles. The wheezing had stopped. He still appeared to be napping. J.J. tapped him on the shoulder. "Charley." Again. Louder. "Charley?"

Harold Pugh hung up. "It's time. The governor's faxing over the order. We can bring in the witnesses and proceed with . . ." His voice trailed off. "I'll get Darrow; you and Dr. Buckles—"

"I think Charley's dead," J.J. McClure said.

Chapter Five

Poppy blew J.J. a kiss from her perch on the bed when he opened the bedroom door. She was resting against a wall of pillows, as always in black—black lace slip, black stockings, and black Manolo Blahnik slingbacks—and as always a cell phone was plugged in to her ear. "Willie, can we fit in the Rural Caucus brunch Thursday at nine."

Willie Erskine, sitting cross-legged next to her on the bed, punched up Poppy's calendar on her laptop. "No. The issues-and-answers coffee is at nine. And there's also the Republican mayors' pancake breakfast."

"Shoes off the bed, Willie," J.J. said.

Willie Erskine looked at Poppy. She glanced quickly at J.J., then motioned Willie off the bed.

"I'll make all three," Poppy said into her phone as Willie Erskine slid into the chair next to the bed. "Meet and greet, the basic 'Hello, how are you, Bud. Randy. Phyllis.' No pancakes, no brunch, no bagels, just tea with lemon, forget the sugar, then out of there, 'Good to see you all, I'll nail all those Washington do-gooders, count on it, count on Poppy,' and on to the next stop."

She dropped the cell phone into her lap. "So what happened?"

J.J. contemplated himself in the mirror. Poppy's mastery of political choreography still impressed him. It confounded him in equal measure. Most things about Poppy did. He ran his nails over his stubble. He needed to shave, shower, and change his clothes. No time for a catnap. He had promised Wormwold he would have the Toledo package in time for the Worm's noon press conference. Involuntary manslaughter, three-to-six, out in eighteen months with good time. The Worm would hate it. Murray Lubin would think he had died and gone to heaven. Think of the upside, he would tell the Worm. A guilty plea and Tone Vaccaro is in the ground. What he would not say is that it might deflect questions about the Darrow fuckup. In the mirror he saw Poppy waiting for an answer. "He died."

"What of?"

"Being seventy-three years old. A hundred pounds overweight. Heart disease. Five packs of cigarettes a day. Emphysema. Maybe he hated George Bernard Shaw, too." Willie Erskine looked up quickly, as if his handiwork had been challenged. "Charley didn't much like anyone from out of state. And maybe he just didn't want to see another execution. He was at the last one. I didn't know that. It's funny what you learn about someone a half hour before they die."

"What did you learn about Percy Darrow?"

"Electricity kills. It takes a long time. In this case two and a half minutes."

"That doesn't seem long," Willie Erskine said.

"Maybe you had to be there," J.J. said. "Put your finger in a light socket, Willie. See how long you can keep it there."

No one spoke.

Poppy's cell phone broke the silence. "Congressman McClure." She listened for a moment. "You tell him if he's still interested in keeping his seat, he'd better get his ass home from Maui and start dialing for dollars. While's he's learning the hula, his numbers are heading for single digits." She rang off Poppy style, without a goodbye. "Willie's got something to ask you."

"As long as you're here, J.J., can I say you're running with Poppy tomorrow?"

J.J. looked at him.

"Hispanic Circle's Winter 5-K Fun Run. You and Poppy. It's a natural. She's a Reyes, and you, you're a . . ."

Willie Erskine's voice trailed off.

"The poster boy for the electric chair? The prosecutor who put the juice back into the system?"

Willie Erskine concentrated on his shoes. He rubbed first one, then the other, on the back of his trouser legs.

"I think I'll take a pass on the Fun Run, Willie." J.J. was suddenly very tired. He knew he should not say what he was going to say, but he did not care. "I also want you to get the fuck out of our bedroom." Willie Erskine turned toward Poppy. "Don't look at Poppy." His tone was deliberate. "Just get out of here."

Willie closed Poppy's laptop carefully, placed it on the bed, and slipped silently past J.J. Poppy watched him without comment. As he opened the door, she said, "Willie, ink me in for the Fun Run tomorrow." Willie nodded without looking back. "And Willie, it's Ochoa Reyes. Not just Reyes. Things like that matter to the Hispanic Circle." When the door closed, Poppy regarded J.J. for a moment. "That make you feel better?"

"Absolutely." J.J. stretched out on the bed. "That autopsy report you read on *Nightline* last night . . ."

"It was on your desk."

"And what's mine is yours?"

"And vice versa."

An allusion to her substantial fortune. Always a sensitive subject, never out in the open. He switched tracks. "You stick around after the cameras left?"

Poppy was back on relatively unmined ground. "What took so long?"

"It took three hours to certify that Charley was dead. The paramedics tried to revive him, and then they had to load him on a gurney and cart him out of there. He weighed two hundred seventy-five pounds, for Christ's sake. On five feet five inches. It was like he was glued to that goddamn chair. Then his next of kin had to be notified. I thought his wife had died. She had. The first one, that is. Four or five years ago. Turns out he got married again last summer."

"To whom?" Of course she would have met Charley Buckles. Pressed flesh with him at some event or other. He was—or had been—a constituent, and she wanted to know and file every piece of information about a constituent. Even a dead one. You never knew when it might be useful.

"The hostess at the Safety Blitz. The sports bar. Downtown."

"Across from Rhino Stadium?"

J.J. nodded. "Where every bookie in town lays off his action. That's where Charley did his drinking and placed his bets."

"And the widow Buckles?"

"Forty years younger than Charley is. Was. With two little kids. And, I gather, a taste for older men. She dropped a couple of husbands along the way. Gentlemen of some considerable years. One in South Carolina, one in Kansas. Her name's Darlene."

"A waitress name."

It struck him that you can take the girl out of Foxcroft, but you can't take the Foxcroft out of the girl. "I like your common touch, Poppy."

Poppy paid no attention. "You can see it on those little plastic name tags they wear pushing trays in coffee shops. Crystal. LaVerne. Darlene."

All of whom would vote for her, J.J. thought. Thinking she was one of them. "I guess Charley was embarrassed. He never told anyone. Except his two grown children, and they stopped speaking to him. They told me about her, but flat out they refused to call her. Wouldn't even give me her telephone number." He had got it from Allie. No reason to mention that to Poppy. He woke Allie up, and she called back with the number in five minutes. Even at 2 a.m.

"How'd you break it to her?" The logistics of personal tragedy had always absorbed Poppy.

" 'Hi, I'm Deputy State Attorney James J. McClure, sorry to call you at this hour, but I thought you'd like to know your new hubby Charley beat Percy Darrow to the end zone.' Sports talk. The kind you hear at the Blitz. 'Did you have the over or the under?' Betting lingo. Cut the pain. And you know what 'Hi, I'm Darlene, I'll be your hostess tonight' said right out of the box, she was so cut up by the call?"

"She said, 'Did Charley leave a will?' "

J.J. propped himself up on a pillow. "How'd you know that?"

"It's what Darlenes would do. And LuAnnes. Elisabeths tend to be straight."

Sometimes Poppy was good value. More often than he liked to admit. "Well, I don't think Charley left her in hog heaven, but maybe she won't have to cadge tips at the Blitz anymore. Or put up with all those Rhino boosters trying to cop a cheap feel." He noticed a faraway look in Poppy's eyes. Her interest in Charley Buckles's family situation was beginning to fade. He was, after all, dead, and Darlene would move on. "The bright side is he didn't have to watch Percy Darrow die."

Poppy was on safer ground. "You're not getting all bleeding heart on me, are you? Percy Darrow was a bad guy."

"I know he was a bad guy, Poppy. I convicted him, I knew all the sad stories about what a tough life he had." He held up his hand as a caution not to interrupt. "I suppose there's a lot of guys out there who watched their sisters suck off their old man, and these guys didn't end up killing two twelve-year-olds and then jerking off in their faces, like Percy did. They might even have turned into solid citizens, these guys. Internet tycoons. Venture capitalists. IPO specialists. Contributors to Poppy McClure's campaign fund. Foursquare with Poppy for the garrote, the gallows, and the guillotine. Auto-da-fé. Decollation. Defenestration. Drawn and quartered. Disemboweled. Noyade. Bastinado. Lapidation. Impalement. Firing squad. Buried alive. Burned at the stake. Or maybe that's auto-da-fé, I'm not all that up-to-date on the Inquisition."

Poppy let him ramble. He felt as if he were talking in his sleep, free-associating, trying to find the thread. Then he had it again.

"It's now three o'clock in the morning, and no pathologist wants to get out of his warm bed and come down to Durango Avenue to preside at the execution of some pansy psycho in an electric chair they don't know if it's going to work or not. When chances are the stiff is going to smell like overcooked fatty pork. That's a little piece of information Charley passed on to me before he cooled. And there's going to be a little puddle of piss around his feet. That's something else I discovered. The governor's having a shit fit, the warden's afraid he's going to lose his job, as if he's responsible for Charley's death, plus the Worm's pissed off at me, which means he's really pissed off at you, because of that lesson on Shaw you got to give on *Nightline*—that was really smooth, Poppy, Willie earned his pay on that one."

J.J. took a deep breath.

"And then there's Percy Darrow. He was ready to go at eleven. Made his peace with his maker, he'd pay the penalty, he even offered his organs. Eyes. Liver. Kidneys. I thought the chair would microwave them. Guess not. Then he has to wait for eight hours. That's a long time to wait for the man with the hood." Poppy waited for him to continue. "He did not go gentle into that good night." J.J. smiled wearily. "Another Celtic playwright heard from. After this one, Poppy, I think I might I exit public service."

"I'm not sure you have a private-sector personality."

He supposed she meant a gift for solvency. Count on Poppy to shoot from the lip. He was an expense on her tax return. A depreciable item.

Poppy's cell phone rang again. "Congressman McClure." She listened. The caller seemed to irritate her. Or more probably I had, J.J. thought. Poppy carefully enunciated every word, as if in disbelief. "The Rhino boosters want an advance copy of my remarks. Since when." The impertinence of the request turned her voice edgy. "It's the red-meat speech. 'You elect Poppy McClure, you elect a flat-out, unashamed, unabashed sworn foe of the federal government. You send a message to the welfare bureaucrats. To the fascist in-your-face environmentalists. To all the do-gooder something-for-nothing boys who don't know an honest dollar when they pick it from your pocket' . . . blah, blah, blah. And no, you don't get a copy."

Poppy tossed the phone away in disgust.

"You know what I like best about the red-meat speech?" J.J. said after a moment.

Poppy eyed him carefully. "What?"

"The blah, blah, blah."

She reached for the mirror she kept on the bedside table, the mirror he often said would fall and break in the middle of the night and bring her seven years of bad luck, but she did not pick it up. "Do you vote for me?"

"We get our picture taken at the polling booth on Election Day. Then I pull the curtain shut behind me and exercise the franchise."

"And?"

"I have never voted against you."

Poppy chose not to pursue the point. "You don't like politics."

J.J. stretched and put his hands behind his head. "Every time I think I might weaken, I run into Willie Erskine. He pulls me back to reality."

She did not come to Willie's defense. He worked for her. Performed the necessary unpleasant services with relish and always with her benediction. When the zeal for the unseemly diminished and he had outlived his usefulness, as it would most certainly would, he would be dismissed without a thought. "I do like it. In fact I love it. It's like I grew up and got to join the circus." Poppy stood up and smoothed her slip. It clung to her angular figure. Small breasts, small waist, small hips, prominent hipbones. My Dolores Del Rio look, she called it. "I'm good at it. It's the only thing in my life I did get really good at. All by myself."

"All by yourself?" He let the statement sink in. He knew it was diffi-cult to get under her skin, but he saw no reason to stop trying. It was like cross-examination. It sharpened his skills. This was payback time. The appreciation of the depreciable item. "That's one way to put it."

Poppy wet a forefinger and checked a possible flaw in her panty hose. Good legs. Trim ankles. "How would you put it?"

"I might say that the last will and testament of Jim Ford might have helped get the ball rolling."

Her answer was equable. "You're a real pain in the ass this morning."

"It's not every morning I've seen two people die the night before. One I didn't get all that choked up about. The other was a bit of a surprise."

"And you're feeling sorry for yourself?"

J.J. closed his eyes. "Just tired." After a moment, he heard water splashing in the bathroom sink. "By the way, Poppy. You ever hear of the Loomis Cattle Company?"

A piece of information that the bizarre events of the evening had not jarred from his memory drum. Precipitating a second call to Allie from Warden Pugh's office as the sun rose over Durango Avenue. Check the property taxes of all the major landholders in Loomis County, he had told her. Why? she had said. Just do it, he had said.

Poppy came to the bathroom door, a face towel in her hand. "It's a contributor."

"Believes in what you stand for?"

She disappeared back into the bathroom. "Get some sleep, J.J." Then she was in the doorway again. She had an acutely sensitive early warn-ing system. J.J. normally evinced no interest in her public life. Which meant he had something on his mind. Something that would affect her. Of that she was sure. "What's your sudden interest in the Loomis Cattle Company?"

"One Lewis Colin. Formerly Colinsky. Born in the San Fernando Valley. That's in California someplace."

"Los Angeles."

He knew where the San Fernando Valley was. He just wanted to keep

Poppy's attention. When she was off balance, not in total command, she was desirable. Private time was her way of staying in charge. Controlling, not cuntable.

He detected the slightest quiver of urgency. "Get to the point, J.J."

"Lewis Colin. Owns the Loomis Cattle Company."

"So."

"In the world of adult cinema, Lewis Colin is known as . . ." He made her wait. "Cowboy Collins."

"Shit."

"The Trail Rider himself. The Cowboy and his trusty Chinese side-kick, Hard Ahn."

"Jesus." The morning was turning into a minefield for Poppy. "Where did you pick that up?"

He did not offer an answer. Poppy would know he would not pass on that kind of information just to make mischief. Nor would he volunteer how he got it. She would not believe a lead from Charley Buckles. Even with Allie nailing it down. Listen to Charley when he was alive and you could get an unauthorized history of South Midland. Dead men tell tales, Charley liked to say. Don't believe that other stuff. "Have Willie check it out. You wouldn't want the Worm to get hold of that. Too bad Koppel didn't have it. Been a lot more interesting than George Bernard Shaw."

She was already punching in a number on her cell phone.

"Protector of family values like yourself, and your campaign's being backed by the films of Cowboy Collins. You have a favorite? *Bucking Brenda*?"

She ignored him. Insistently into the phone: "Pick up, Willie, pick up." Finally.

"Willie. What took you so long? The Loomis Cattle Company . . ."

". . . *Riding Regina*? *Cowboy and Indians* . . ."

Poppy wheeled toward him. "Will you shut up?"

J.J. picked up the harmonic tremor of unhappiness. He rolled over contentedly, tucking a pillow under his head.

He dozed. In the fading background he could hear Poppy ordering Willie Erskine to find out all he could about a contribution from the Loomis Cattle Company, and to figure out a way to return it quickly and quietly. In the haze of half-sleep, he wondered if Poppy had ever slept with Willie Erskine. No. Willie was double-locked and dead-bolted in the closet. And Poppy would never sleep with anyone on the payroll. Too risky. Too much economic incentive. A vineyard of extortion or exposure. No man is a hero to his valet, or whatever the female equivalent is. Even with the confidentiality clause in the employment contract she made all her staff sign. Easy to sneak around that one. No, no, no, no. If Poppy did it, she would insist on someone who regarded avoidance of risk as not just a virtue but a necessity. Probably married. Definitely someone important. Or better yet, self-important. Maybe a woman. No. Don't think so. But. But what? There were whispers. A hint. No. Let that rest. I'm liberated. To a point.

He turned over, fighting sleep. Why? Why these bad thoughts, like dark scudding clouds in a twister? He knew why. So he didn't have to think about Emmett. He could scarcely remember what his brother looked like. The only photograph he still had was sealed in an unmarked envelope in a locked desk drawer at his office. Forgetting what happened was not an option. As hard as he tried. Would still try. Emmett grasping for air, going under, his spindly three-year-old arms flailing in the water, then floating, facedown under the boat dock. And up on the hill, Walter, chained to his wheelchair. Trying to get to the dock. Falling forward, the braces on his polio-withered legs locked so that he could not move. Crawling. Pulling himself forward, his fingers digging into the grass and into the soft turf. It's not your fault, Jamie, he had said. It's not your fault. He knew. J.J. knew that he knew. Think of something else. God, Charley Buckles was fat. And there was Percy Darrow with duct tape over his mouth to stop his screaming, handcuffed, carried feet first from the holding cell into the chamber with his legs in plastic restraints. The restraint team was wearing hard hats, tinted face shields, and body armor. "A cell extraction," the tie-down manual called it. Extraction. What dentists did to a diseased tooth. Percy Darrow was a diseased tooth. Q.E.D.

Poppy was shaking him. Poppy was dressed. Poppy in severe designer black.

"J.J."

He snapped awake.

"I've got Willie on that."

J.J. did not think he had ever seen a Dolores Del Rio movie. "You want to fuck?"

"I have a coffee." She picked up her bag. "Then a women's forum. But tomorrow. After the 5-K Run. I'll make some private time."

"Private time lacks a certain spontaneity."

Poppy checked her appearance in the mirror until her eyes caught his. "Is that what you have with Allie? Spontaneity?"

Of course she would have known about Allie Vasquez. Willie would have heard. Willie would have dropped hints.

"Spontaneity, yes." He wondered why she brought it up now. All right. Her way. "And enthusiasm."

Accused Parlance Killers: "Not Guilty"

WEB POSTED 13:29

Regent, SM (ABCNEWS.COM)—In a brief arraignment at the Loomis County Courthouse today, court-appointed lawyers for Bryant Gover and Duane Lajoie, accused of the brutal slaying of Edgar Parlance last month, pleaded their clients not guilty before Judge Ellen Tracy, who will preside over the trial.

The state was represented by Maurice Dodd, a senior prosecutor in the Attorney General's office. Dodd said that he would press vigorously for the death penalty for both defendants.

Gover is represented by Francis Howar of Regent and Lajoie by Earle Lincoln from nearby Questa. Refusing to answer questions after the arraignment, Howar told reporters that he would argue his client's case in court and not in the press. Lincoln, who only passed the bar in June, also declined comment.

Because of the sensitivity of the case, which is expected to draw full media coverage, Judge Tracy, a veteran jurist, was selected by lottery from a pool of senior judges.

Present at the arraignment was Los Angeles Clippers superstar Jamaal Jefferson, who flew in to Regent by chartered helicopter after his private jet brought him to Capital City from Indianapolis, where the Pacers beat the Clippers last night 107–92.

Jefferson had paid for the Parlance funeral last week.

On behalf of the NBA and Cyrus Ichabod, CEO of I-Bod, the sneaker and sportswear conglomerate, Jefferson presented a

$10,000 check to Clyde Ray, 59, who identified Lajoie's pickup as it sped from the location where Parlance was killed on the night of the murder. This identification led to the arrest of the two former ex-felons.

Ray was able to remember the 1989 Ford pickup by an obscene sticker on its rear bumper.

PART TWO

CHAPTER ONE

This is a story Teresa Kean told me.

If I were a writer, not a lawyer, or as good a writer as I am a lawyer, I would have introduced her earlier. Since you could say this narrative is about her. Because without Teresa, there is no narrative. If you were giving billing, she is above the title.

Prima inter pares.

J.J.'s above the title, too. And I suppose Carlyle.

Although you haven't met her yet either.

In due course.

Anyway.

My elaboration on Teresa's story.

During Poppy's first two terms in Congress, J.J. would occasionally visit her when the House was sitting. "What do you do, Mr. McClure?" a party functionary once asked him at a Heritage Foundation cocktail party. "Other than being Poppy's husband, that is."

"I put people in prison," J.J. said. "Other than being Poppy's husband, that is."

You can see why he hated it there.

He spent an awful lot of time in green rooms waiting for Poppy to finish whatever chat show she was on. The last time he went to Washington, Poppy was interviewed on C-Span by Brian Lamb. J.J. was alone in the green room with all the morning papers and a table covered with Snapple iced tea and bottled water and bagels and cream cheese. Poppy was live on one of the two monitors, and on the other there was a rerun of a three-hour interview about books with Joyce Carol Oates. About halfway through Poppy's show, a P.A. came in and asked if he needed anything. She was tall, blond, coltish, about twenty-seven, wearing a black T-shirt, black linen culottes, and a black cotton sweater knotted around her waist. Her hair was pulled together with a tortoiseshell barrette. She said she was a great fan of Joyce Carol Oates's, that an old boyfriend would give her copies of Oates's books as birthday and Christmas presents. She said she no longer had the boyfriend, but still had the books. Then she asked again if there was anything she could do for him.

Yes, J.J. said.

He never did get her name.

They began going at it while Poppy was on live, taking listener calls, doing her rap. On the other monitor, Joyce Carol Oates hid behind her tinted glasses. The P.A. said someone might walk in and see them, they had to stop or go in the bathroom, lock the door, and do it in there. J.J. brought the cream cheese with him. He pulled up her T-shirt, spread cream cheese on her breasts, and started to lick it away. She pushed him onto the toilet seat and began sucking him off. J.J. lifted her off her knees, turned her around, bent her over the sink, and fucked her. When he was done, he pulled up his trousers and started to wipe the remains of the cream cheese from her breasts with a damp paper towel. She took the towel from him, said she would do it herself, and sent him back to the green room while she finished getting dressed.

On the monitors, Poppy was finishing up her interview, while Joyce Carol Oates was deep into an explanation of how the literary ecology between the senator who was not Ted Kennedy and the young woman who was not Mary Jo Kopechne led her to write *Black Water*. Brian Lamb signed off, and a moment or so later Poppy walked into the green room. J.J. was sitting on the couch. Good job, he said, as in the bathroom the toilet flushed and the P.A. exited, carrying the dish of cream cheese, a dab of which had stuck to her black T-shirt.

Poppy looked from J.J. to the P.A. and then back at J.J. There was a small smear of cheese on his upper lip.

You didn't, she said equably. It was as if the P.A. were not present.

Poppy, you are embarrassing this young woman, J.J. said. Then he guided Poppy out of the green room, out of the C-Span building, and into her waiting car.

J.J. never returned to Washington after that visit.

I may have added some details, but the cream cheese came from Teresa.

Chapter Two

From an unpublished manuscript written by Teresa Kean and stored on her laptop in a locked folder called RECIPES. *Also in the folder was a haphazard collection of notes, observations, and miscellaneous journal entries.*

My father was a gangster. He was, in fact, a murderer. I don't know how many people he actually killed, but there were two cut-and-paste biographies about him and about his role in the opening up of Las Vegas, and he is listed in *The Encyclopedia of American Crime* as a top hit man, the murderer of twenty or so people, perhaps even more. He did not of course advertise the number and names of his alleged victims, or the means by which he allegedly dispatched them, but then neither did he deny the claims, his silence only further gilding the myth he seemed, according the tattered clippings about his life, to so enjoy. Firearms, piano wire, explosive devices, claw hammers, screwdrivers, suffocation, battery, drowning—his chroniclers claimed there was no form of mayhem in which he did not exhibit a master's skill.

My father never knew he was my father. He was shotgunned to death before he knew my mother was pregnant. He was building a hotel in Las Vegas called King's Playland (his name was Jacob King), and there were shortfalls and overruns, and he was hit. The shooter was a childhood friend. ("Hit" and "shooter" were in the rhetorical style of both books written about Jacob King, books which, when I finally read them, I found essentially worthless, a compendium of clips and rumors and self-aggrandizement, but then of course I had an emotional investment in believing in their paltriness and inconsequence.) It was only after my father was murdered that my mother discovered that she was pregnant. They were of course not married. My mother was a movie star. A child movie star who was trying to cross over and become a grown-up movie star. Her name was Blue Tyler, and if she is remembered now largely as a crossword puzzle entry or a question on *Jeopardy!*, there was a time in her prepubescent and adolescent years in which her name on a marquee was a guarantee of gold. The crossover did not happen. Jacob King's occupation and his dramatic and bloody demise, both of which fell under the moral-turpitude clause in a motion-picture contract, were two good reasons, my mother's putative talent for fellatio and her equally putative appreciation of a prominent phallus were two more, two that to a certain degree are my only inheritance from her.

I never knew my mother. She worked for a while in Europe, and then she disappeared for nearly forty years until Jack—dear, dear Jack—found her quite by accident in Detroit, and although he patiently dug into her past, and pieced together my identity and that of my adoptive parents, he refused to engage in any public or private discussion about these discoveries or about my mother's subsequent gruesomely unpleasant death (she was crushed under the wheels of an eighteen-wheel refrigerator rig), which may have been suicide or, equally possible, the result of a final descent into madness. Daddy—my adoptive father, Brendan Kean—knew my real father even before Jacob King met my real mother. Brendan Kean was a former homicide prosecutor in Queens turned criminal defense attorney in private practice, and in 1947, in Department 50, the Manhattan Criminal Courthouse on Centre Street, he defended Jacob King on a charge of first-degree murder, a murder he almost certainly committed, and won him an acquittal. The not-guilty verdict was a significant reason why Jacob King left New York for California, where he took up with my mother, so it might be argued that Brendan Kean played a crucial, if unintentional, role in charting the destiny of my parents, and I suppose mine too.

Daddy always insisted that he did not know the identity of my birth parents (I hate that phrase; it is so clinical and professional, so absent the tears and feelings that scald relationships), but he was no less dogged than Jack. Given Daddy's background as both prosecutor and defense counsel in the city's five boroughs, and the concomitant network of allegiances he had built up in the criminal and civil bar, it is not a leap to suppose that he made discreet inquiries, probate searches in the records of the Manhattan Surrogate Court, and educated guesses that supplied enough circumstantial evidence for him to intuit who my natural parents were, at the very least to an indisputable level of probability. The measure of Brendan Kean, and of his ability to keep his own counsel, is that he never imparted any of this information, or speculation, to me.

He and my mother, Moira Twomey Kean, were childless, but I suspect it was Daddy's successful representation of Jacob King, coupled with his professional ability to sidestep unnecessary and perhaps troubling legal and moral questions, that ultimately led Blue Tyler's advisors and the ex-officio executors of Jacob King's affairs (some, perhaps even most, it is safe to surmise, on the shady side of the law), acting in concert, to offer Brendan and Moira Kean the opportunity to adopt the six-pound-thirteen-ounce daughter they named Teresa. Daddy, in his seventies, was still vigorously practicing when he died in a small plane crash on the way to his summer house on that stretch of the Jersey shore called the Irish Riviera; at Manhattan Federal Court, on the Wednesday morning he was killed, he had an insider trading case dismissed for official misconduct, and decided to fly down to Mantoloking and spend the rest of the week celebrating with my mother. She now lives in a retirement community in northern Virginia, drifting in and out of Alzheimer's. I regularly send her gifts—fruit baskets, expensive chocolates, Pratesi robes, even electronic gadgets I know she cannot possibly master, like an eight-band shortwave radio or a five-inch color television that she can perch on her lap—to paper over my guilt for not going to see her more regularly, since more often than not she does not recognize me. Yet occasionally she flashes like a lightbulb before its filament burns out, and I receive a note in her spidery arthritic hand. *Dear Teresa Kean* is always the salutation on these communiqués, as if she corresponded with more than one Teresa.

Here is an example:

> Dear Teresa Kean,
>
> God bless you for sending the toy television set. It is so cute. I watched a show yesterday about a lawyer, and I thought about your dear father and my dear husband Brendan. I don't know if you knew he was a lawyer, but he was, Brendan Kean, Attorney-at-Law. Mrs. Eisenhower in the next room is 85 years of age, and since she came here five years ago, she has always had a TV, a color model. I do not know why she calls herself Eisenhower, because I know for a fact that she was not married to the general. She has such airs, like she was. In all those five years, she never invited me once into her room to look at her color TV. Yesterday her color TV fell to the floor and broke. It made a terrible noise, and it made her very sad. She knocked on my door and she asked if she could come into my room and look at the toy TV you sent me, and I said, Fuck you.
>
> Your loving mother,
> Moira Twomey Kean

My father was Queens born and bred, having worked his way up the social ladder from the top floor of an underheated three-family house in Ozone Park, with grottoes to the Immaculate Heart on every balcony, to a community in Forest Hills Gardens with lawns and a twenty-four-hour private security patrol in unmarked cars, and every summer the house in Mantoloking. His father, my grandfather, was a bus driver for the Transit Authority and on election days stuffed ballot boxes for the Queens Democratic Party, purely as a precaution, according to Daddy, and not because they needed to be stuffed. He died when my father was ten. Daddy called Manhattan "the city" and the subway "the train," and every morning he took the E-train from Continental Avenue to his law office and the courthouses downtown, returning from the Chambers Street station on the E-train back to Forest Hills every evening. Playing hockey in the seventh grade at St. Cyril's in Ozone Park, he had his features rearranged by a hockey puck that flattened his nose and gave him the look of a man who in a fight would come after you with a beer bottle in his hand. Belligerence came naturally to him and revealed itself in the most unexpected way. He hated the pageantry of police funerals, to which he had often been summoned when he was a prosecutor, hated even more the skirl of bagpipes that attended the deceased and had the same effect on him as fingernails scraping down a blackboard. It's just a photo op so the mayor and the commissioner can throw their arms around the grieving widow and get their pictures in the *News*, he would tell me. Christ, just once I'd like some cop widow to say, Blow it out your ass, Mr. Mayor, I don't want you or your bagpipes here when I plant Sean, he got on top of me six times in eleven years, that's the five girls and Sean, Jr., who's slow.

Daddy went to mass every Sunday at St. Pius V in Forest Hills, and smoked outside, winter and summer, one unfiltered Camel after another, never entering the church, waiting there until the service was over and my mother appeared clutching the Sunday announcements. He was thirty years into his marriage before he learned that Moira Kean believed in God no more than he. "You never asked," my mother said when he wondered why she had never told him. And he never had. It was the kind of mistake he never would make in the courtroom, and perhaps indicated the state of their marriage. And yet as far as I know, he was faithful to her, I would guess out of some residual parochial-school training. (That she might have been unfaithful to him was beyond my powers of invention.) I knew there were women within the legal system who were attracted to him, but outside of a smile and an Irish joke, he would never return the signals he must have received.

I was divorced twice before I was twenty-six. My first wedding took place the week before I graduated from Smith, three months pregnant; the marriage lasted until I miscarried. The name of the impregnator was Chipper, which says more than needs to be said about that liaison. My second husband was Furlong Budd Doheny, called Budd—the Furlongs, the Budds, and the Dohenys on his side of the marriage bed all vying for which was the richest entity. Budd Doheny's only real skills were sailing, skiing, and screwing, and with his access to the multiple family fortunes, he was never out of season and rarely out of bed. Sex with him was, more often than I care to remember, a group production, with many of its moments captured on film, both still and video, all of which he carefully catalogued. Budd's powers of invention seldom waned— he was the only person I was ever aware of who used vanilla extract as a sex aid—I will leave it to your imagination where he applied it on his person—but in time the appeal of esoteric erotica paled (to this day I detest the taste of vanilla and the smell of vanilla beans), and we went our separate ways more or less amicably, in large part because in the divorce I made no claim on the vast resources of the Furlongs, the Budds, or the Dohenys. A few years and several wives later, Budd Doheny drowned in a one-man-one-boat ocean race, the victim of rogue waves and 60-knot winds somewhere in the rolling Tasman deep between Auckland and Hobart (his bodily remains were lashed to his splintered mainmast when the wreckage of his capsized boat was finally discovered after the freakish winds calmed). My mourning for him was perfunctory, but I confess to wondering occasionally, as middle age and the decorum attendant to it make their inroads, about the disposition of his catalogue of film and photographic erotica, or at least that part of it in which I might appear.

After my second divorce, I applied to Yale Law School, and when I graduated, I passed the bar and went to work with my father (although I chose to live on Manhattan's Upper East Side and not in Queens). Criminal law suited me, as it suited him. I was good at it, and in and out of court he was both mentor and unruffled presence at my side. The first thing he taught me was never try to convince myself that a client was innocent, it only messes you up and makes you a bad lawyer. If a client turns out to be innocent, that's a bonus: just don't count on it, he probably did something worse: a courtroom's not a cathedral and you're not the coadjutor bishop. He was comfortable with the criminal attorney's code. When the facts are against you, he said, argue the law; when the law is against you, argue the facts; when both are against you, attack the other side. Murder and the more egregious violations of the penal code did not usually attract high-powered attorneys. The reason is simple: There is not that much money in it. Outside of mystery novels, criminal defendants are rarely propertied; they tend to live on the frayed margins of society, and often do not speak the language of the courts where their cases are heard. However often they invoke the right of every defendant to have an attorney, good lawyers, as opposed to the incompetents and the shysters, tend to avoid this redlined legal zip code unless, like my father, they enjoy the game. The odds are against them. In the interest of what they call "justice," D.A.'s really do think that defense lawyers should calibrate the vigor of their argument to the larger societal need of putting perps behind bars. Whatever their public position, prosecutors seem to regard the presumption of innocence as a kind of devil worship, and reasonable doubt as justice not served. I never asked, but I would have bet that even my father worked that side of the street when he was in the Queens D.A.'s office. The law is situational, he liked to say.

The second thing Daddy taught me was that defense attorneys do not win cases so much as prosecutors lose them. What a good defense attorney does is exploit error, because running beneath prosecutorial error is a filigree of reasonable doubt. Innocence need not be proven; guilt does. For eight years we prospered, but when he died, Kean & Kean and the prospect of continuing as a solo practitioner lost its attractiveness. At the first opportunity, I dissolved the firm and moved to Washington as an advocate for an organization lobbying on behalf of victims' rights. It was called, with a noticeable absence of imagination, Justice for All, and in time I became its president and public spokesperson on chat shows and at seminars, luncheons, conferences, and every kind of public forum. Jack said my involvement was not without irony, considering Jacob King's propensity for making victims. He said that during the twelve hours I knew him.

CHAPTER THREE

MAX

It seemed a kind of exorcism, a way to distance herself from her DNA. Her sense of privacy was so acute that I can't imagine that she ever planned for anyone to see it. Certainly not me, who professed to be her friend. I showed this bit to Stanley (remember Stanley Poindexter, M.D., my psychiatrist companion, partner, or what have you, each term worse than the next), and Stanley said it was a kind of computer therapy, a way to own up to one's life without having to face a therapist's questions. Like all shrinks, Stanley thinks he has an answer for every eventuality, which is horseshit, of course. Was there any more, he wanted to know, and I said no, although I don't think he believed me, rightly enough. What was there was not mine to share, and so I told him there was just the usual sediment one finds in every computer: a telephone directory, an appointment calendar, e-mails, search engines, news sites, *The New York Times,* Navigator, penal and civil codes in all fifty states, the judiciary and elected officials in those same fifty states, a militia website (interesting!), websites for the FBI, the CIA, the Securities and Exchange Commission, and other agencies, the U.S. Constitution, the Bible and the complete works of Shakespeare (I would guess for a handy quote), a dozen daily newspapers, too many magazines, the Internet Movie Database, MovieLink—Search by Theater, music sites, shopping (the e-mail addresses and 800 numbers of the usual stores—Saks, Armani: You name it, she had it, including her personal shoppers), et cetera and so forth.

Her word processing files were not much more interesting. Speeches (a commencement address at Smith, a luncheon talk to the American Bar Association, essentially one canned talk configured to fit the audience at hand), case files, trial transcripts, a file (actually dossiers) on people she would guest with on talk shows, seminars, and panel discussions—their quirks, C.V.'s, legislation they had sponsored or supported, personal and political antipathies (her folder on Poppy McClure had the cream cheese story; she was Brian Lamb's guest the next night, it turned out, and the show staff whispered the details to her, or as much as they thought they knew or could make up, including the firing of the leggy P.A.), guest lists for parties and official events, travel plans, household repairs and renovations (including letters threatening contractors with legal action, scary and very well done, quoting the appropriate district statutes and clauses in the construction contracts), and recipes.

Recipes.

Nothing wrong with that. Except. The entrance to her RECIPES folder was blocked by a password. Nothing else on the computer was, not the e-mails, the case files, or her mini-dossiers. Why? She did not wish to share her recipes for navarin or albóndigas or chartreuse of pheasant?

I don't think so.

That was the old prosecutor in me. What could be blander than RECIPES? A folder one would normally slide right by.

Breaking the password was not especially difficult. It never is. I went to her entry in *Who's Who.* Lawyer. Advocate. Born Forest Hills, Queens, N.Y. (no DOB, I noticed); d. Brendan and Moira Kean (Twomey); B.A. Smith College, 1980; m. Roger Chipworth, May 25, 1980 (div.), m. Furlong B. Doheny, April 17, 1982 (dec.).

NORTHAMPTON did it.

Of course I already knew, by the time I got into Teresa's computer, most of the personal information buried in RECIPES. It had been massaged and distorted through the great American publicity machine, turning Teresa into what I knew was her worst nightmare, a fifteen-minute celebrity.

I think I knew her better than anyone (except perhaps Marty Buick), and I suppose I always loved her, not enough to make me go straight, but in the way a queer can love a woman, by understanding and appreciating without all the collateral damage of sex. What I didn't know, until I cracked the password into RECIPES, was how she felt about the step-by-step chain of events that led her inexorably into my life. So forgive me if I take the liberty of casting the links of that chain of events in Teresa's voice.

It begins at the White House.

CHAPTER FOUR

In Teresa's voice: I remember every moment of my time with Jack.

We met at the president's annual black-tie dinner for the justices of the Supreme Court. I was sitting at the attorney general's table. I can't say that Margaret Dudley and I were friends, but she was an imposing woman with whom, in my capacity as president of Justice for All, I had often appeared on the Sunday shows, and at her urging I had testified before both the House and the Senate judiciary committees on behalf of a victims' rights bill the administration was sponsoring, a bill that was constitutionally suspect but which, in an election year, of course passed with overwhelming bipartisan support and was signed into law. White House dinners were usually a trial, with bad food geographically allocated and elaborately explained on individual menus written in a calligrapher's script—Chesapeake Bay Crab Mousse, Bow Tie Louisiana Gruyère Twists, Medallion of Veal in Napa Valley Champagne, Gnocchi à la Chicago, Turban of California Carrots with Oregon Yellow Squash, Pennsylvania Nasturtium Flower Salad, Ohio Brie Cheese with Mississippi Almonds, Vermont Caramel, Petits Fours Sec, a Washington State Merlot, a New York State Zinfandel, and an Arizona Grappa. The guest list was the usual assortment of campaign contributors and congressional pirates seeking favors and who, in turn, when said favors (a dam or a submarine base) were granted, would, as a quid pro quo, provide favors by way of votes or campaign contributions, or so the president hoped. At my table, besides the attorney general, there was the governor of Massachusetts, a pontificating CEO, an airhead from the Senate Judiciary Committee, assorted spouses and consorts, and John Broderick. He was seated across the table from me, and I overheard him tell the wife of a black appellate judge from Missouri that it was the first time he had been at the White House since his brother worked there as an advisor to former President Frederick Finn. I of course knew who he was. His late father was a famously blunt and famously randy billionaire with the manners, it was said, of a tire iron; his brother, the presidential advisor, a Benedictine priest who was assassinated by a crazed schizophrenic in San Francisco along with John Broderick's first wife, Leah, a noted radical criminal attorney. His second wife was an immensely rich collector of husbands, his third wife was killed in an automobile accident, he had written a number of movies and two books, and in spite of considerable pressure he had never revealed what he had learned about Blue Tyler and Jacob King. He had a disconcerting stare that I found focused on me whenever I looked up during dinner.

The evening wore on. The president toasted the honorable justices, the chief justice toasted President McCall, a soprano from the Metropolitan Opera sang a Massenet aria from *Cendrillon* followed by "He's Got the Whole World in His Hand," and then the dancing began. Margaret Dudley rose and danced with John Broderick, and then brought him back to my seat.

"Thank you for letting me take you to my considerable bosom," Margaret Dudley said to John Broderick.

"I wouldn't use the word 'considerable,' General . . ."

"Jack, we've known each other much too long for you to call me 'General.' Now. You know Teresa Kean?"

"Only by reputation."

"Then go out on the dance floor and get to know each other better."

The orchestra was attempting Gershwin's "Summertime." He was not a good dancer and did not seem to care that he wasn't. He must have been in his early sixties, maybe sixty-five, trim, but too old for dancing to be an important part of his life, if it ever had been. Again I found myself the target of that disconcerting stare. He made no effort to speak. To make conversation, I said, "You really haven't been here since Fritz Finn was president?"

He nodded.

"You must have been asked."

Another nod.

"Then why come tonight?"

"Duncan Dudley asked if I would be available." Margaret Dudley's husband. "We knew each other at Princeton."

"So that's the reason."

"No."

His rudeness was like a baffle, useful in deflecting inquiry. I had the sense that he wanted to see if I would persist. Okay. His way then. "Do you ever give anything beside name, rank, and serial number?"

"Usually, not even that." He looked at me directly for the first time and half smiled. "Actually I don't like Duncan. Never did. He's a burr of public life. Always attaching himself to someone who might do him some good. Dix McCall now, Margaret at the get-go. When she was young and fat. But he was smart enough to know she was very, very, very smart. Which is three verys smarter than he is. He'd fuck a pencil sharpener. And has. I never understood what Margaret saw in him. She's all right."

It was not the sort of measured conversation one usually hears at a White House dinner. I knew it was his way of not answering my question, but I was too good a lawyer not to continue my cross-examination, whatever his rudeness. "Why then?"

He pretended to listen to the music. "I hate Gershwin."

He was dodging. I bored in. "Why?"

"Lush and sentimental. 'Old Man River' crap. 'Tote dat barge, lift dat bale.' "

"Forget Gershwin. Why did you come tonight?"

" 'I got plenty of nothin', and nothin' is plenty for me.' "

Again. "Why?"

A pause. "You don't give up, do you?" Another pause. "Duncan mentioned that you'd be here."

I felt a chill. I knew what was coming.

"I knew your mother."

"Why did she do it?"

We were in the bedroom in the carriage house just off Capitol Hill where I lived, the dinner for the Supreme Court justices already forgotten. He had told me in exact detail about my mother's thirty-five-year odyssey as an itinerant bag lady, one with a small anonymous annuity from those who had been charged to protect her when she was young, famous, and solvent, one whose truest love in those halcyon years was a killer unimpressed by her fame and wealth and whose daughter she had borne and given up for adoption after he was murdered, one who as a woman in her increasingly unstable later years had married and discarded nine, ten, or eleven husbands. "I mean, why did she choose to live the way she did?"

"I don't do why."

I was startled. "What?"

"Motivation is a very poor explanation of character." His tone was brusque, peremptory. "People behave the way they do because that's the way they are. Change their circumstances and their behavior won't change for the better or the worse. Put Jesse James on Molokai, he's not going to turn into Father Damien." He paused, as if considering whether he should continue. "Like your mother." He propped himself up on his elbow. "Did you ever suspect?"

"A little," I said after a moment. "When the story first began to come out. I really didn't follow it that closely, but people wouldn't let it go, and you wouldn't talk. I was impressed by that. It was like something my father would do. Daddy—I'm a woman who has not led a sheltered life, but I still call him Daddy. I knew he was well regarded in the legal community—Pat Moynihan came to his rosary, and the mayor and Jack Javits to the funeral. Oh, God, I hate people who drop names. Forgive me for doing that."

He shrugged.

"He would never talk once he made up his mind not to. I never gave who I was much thought, but I knew he knew. He'd defended Jacob King right after the war—it was mentioned in all his obituaries—and so I found the trial transcript and I found the billing receipts and as the executor of his estate I had access to all his financial records and saw that there was a blind trust set up about the time I was adopted, one where I was the ultimate beneficiary. It was something I just didn't want to investigate, and when I finally got interested, my mother couldn't tell me anything—she has trouble remembering my name. Because of you, or not you, really, because you never said a word, but what others made of what you weren't saying, I knew more or less when Blue Tyler's daughter was born, I knew when I was adopted, I knew when the trust went into effect. As a lawyer you make inductive leaps, you're taught to use the facts to present a credible story to the jury. That we were the same person was a story that seemed . . ." I looked for the proper word. "Tenable." Then I added, "Possible."

"You never tried to contact me."

"You wouldn't have told me."

"Right."

I traced the vertical foot-long white scar on his sternum that indicated open-heart surgery, then ran my hand over the hairs on his lower stomach. "Why now?"

"I'm sixty-two," he said, tapping the scar on his chest. "I have a prosthetic aortic valve, a plastic St. Jude model—the only reason I tell you that is because I suspect you have a lawyer's passion for specificity. Anyway. I had the copyright to your mother's life, and I wanted to pass it on to the one person to whom it could possibly matter." His dinner jacket and pleated shirt were thrown over a chair, and his studs and cuff links littered the floor. A small smile. "Before . . ."

I knew where "before" led, and I did not want to go there.

He waited for a moment, then rolled over and ran his finger over the aureole of my right breast. "Well . . ."

"Yes."

He swung his legs over the side of the bed and walked to the chair over which his tuxedo jacket was hung. From an inside pocket he removed what seemed to be a small sewing kit, and then sat on the edge of the bed. "I suppose I should have told you this before," he said after a moment. There was a thin hypodermic needle, a small medical bottle, and some alcohol wipes inside the kit. "At a certain age, one becomes close in the most unseemly way with one's urologist. He becomes like"— he hesitated—"a penile priest."

Sex was suddenly on hold.

"Mine is a Bengali Sikh. Dr. Singh. Dinakar Singh." It was if he was in a confessional, explaining some form of aberrant behavior to a priest. As I had done too often when I still believed, after a fashion, in God and Holy Mother the Church. "Actually I'm not sure I could have talked about this to someone not from the third world. Jerry Caplan at Beverly Hills Medical, say. Leonard Lewis at UCLA. Bucky Kantor at Cedars. Phyllis Haney at St. John's." He was talking too fast. "A Haitian would have been fine. A Samoan. An Eskimo. The best goddamn man in Sri Lanka. But not someone I might see at Spago. Dr. Singh wanted me to have a penile implant."

"I'm not sure I want to hear this."

"Then you don't have a passion for specificity?"

Was there any way to end this conversation in a lighthearted manner? No. Just go with it. As far as it goes.

"My . . ." He pointed to his flaccid equipment. "What word are you comfortable with? Penis? Dick? Prick? Cock? Johnson?"

"Johnson," I said too quickly. I had a very extensive lexicon on this subject, largely but not wholly learned while engaged in bedroom acrobatics with Budd Doheny, but this was one I'd never used before.

"Then johnson it is. And you might have noticed, Mr. Johnson here is shaped like a T square."

I had noticed that.

"A condition called Peyronie's disease." He saw my blank look. "Do you floss regularly? Morning and evening and after meals?"

Where was this going? How do you answer? "When I think of it."

"Why?"

"Because the hygienist says I should."

"To get rid of what?"

A Budd Doheny photo session with umbrellas and reflectors was never as strange as this. "Plaque."

"Right. Plaque. That's what Peyronie's disease is. Plaque. But instead of in your teeth or your gums, it's in your johnson. And you don't go to a periodontist for it, you go to a urologist. When I was a kid, I was told hair would grow on my hands if I masturbated too much. Forget the hair on your hands. It's plaque in your johnson. From overuse, I hope. And the plaque makes it difficult to . . ." A deep breath. ". . . get it up."

I confess he had my attention. In a criminal courtroom, a lawyer sops up information. About calibers and the particularity of exit wounds and DNA. This was my learning curve on Peyronie's plaque.

"So Dr. Singh's solution was a penile implant. A reservoir under your abdominal muscles, a pump in your scrotum, and two cylinders surgically implanted in Mr. Johnson. 'Squeeze that pump,' Dr. Singh said, 'and you will be hard as a rock.' " He mimicked a subcontinent accent. " 'Hard as a rock, Mr. Broderick.' No, thank you, I said, I already have one prosthetic device . . ." He pointed to the foot-long scar on his chest. ". . . my St. Jude valve, and two would be pressing my luck. And anyway, the only person I ever heard of who had a tube in his johnson was Paul Castellano, and he ended up getting shot in front of Spark's Steak House by John Gotti's guys. He was seventy-five years old, and he had the tube so he could screw his Puerto Rican maid; she looked like a sumo wrestler from her pictures. He deserved what happened outside Spark's for that alone. So what's your backup? I asked Dr. Singh." He removed the needle from its kit and inserted it through the rubber stopper on the medical vial. "Penile injections."

I was furious. I sat bolt upright, and tried to cover my nakedness with a pillow. "You brought that with you tonight? You thought you were going to score? At the White House? With me?"

He smiled reasonably. "When you go out at night, you don't slip a package of condoms in your purse. Or your diaphragm? Or an RU-486 pill?"

How did he know? Because he had spent a lifetime in the trenches of the sexual battlefield, of course. Not unlike me. "It's not the same."

He brushed away my answer. "I could do it in the bathroom, I could do it here, or I could leave. Your call."

I waited for a moment. "I'm not sure I could watch." Which meant that leaving was not the call.

"Because it's anti-romantic?"

I nodded.

"At a certain age, romance becomes problematic," he said. "Transient and overrated." He took the needle in one hand, and rested his semi-tumescent cock on his thigh with the other. "This, however, is interesting." He smiled, holding the hypodermic for a moment. "A 30-gauge ultrafine needle." Another smile. "It takes some getting used to. Closing your eyes is not the best way to proceed." He was like a dentist explaining a root canal. A driblet of liquid appeared at the top of the needle. "Two raindrops of a high-potency corticosteroid, by name prostaglandin E-1, into the spongy tissue here . . ." He showed me. ". . . where there's no nerve ends, and where you can take the needle . . . and poke it in . . ."

He thrust, humming the mournful dirge of the bull ring. ". . . like a bullfighter finishing off a bull."

I shuddered and turned away. When I looked back, he was smiling. "It takes a moment, but it works."

It did.

We watched *Nightline* afterwards. Live from an execution at a prison somewhere in the Midwest. There was Poppy McClure wearing a black designer duffel in the prison parking lot. Lecturing Ted Koppel in his Washington studio about George Bernard Shaw's views on the death penalty. "Ted." She was fiddling with her earpiece. "Are you telling me you are not aware of Shaw's attitudes on the death penalty? Even as soft on Communist Russia as he and the Webbs were?"

"Do you know her?" Jack said.

"Only from the various green rooms we've been in together."

"She's a horror."

"Actually, she's rather funny. Once you get past her politics."

"Is there anything else?"

I suppose he had a point. I still liked her. "I was on C-Span a few years go. She'd been on a day or so before. The story I heard was her husband was screwing an intern in the green room while she was on the air."

"Serves her right."

"For what?"

He looked at me for what he seemed to assume would be a lecture. On-screen there was a shot of the ambulance that would remove the body of the deceased from the prison premises and then a tight shot of a window on the second floor that was identified as the room where the electric chair was located. Most of the victims whose rights I lobbied for were in favor of the death penalty. I wasn't, but it was an opinion I chose never to make public, and always cut off any discussion of what my view actually was.

I changed the subject. "I read you were going to write a movie about that black man who was skinned alive out there. Parlance. Edgar Parlance. And the two who killed him."

He shook his head. "No one to root for."

"Parlance."

"You don't root for a dead man. What's his backstory? Will anyone give a shit three years from now when a picture, if it's made, which I doubt, comes out?" He yawned and stretched. Mr. Johnson still stood tall. It suddenly reminded me of the field hockey stick I used as a teenager at St. Pius V Intermediate School. Sister Boniface was the coach. What she told my parents about me was that I was a delicate stick handler. A skill perfected, after field hockey, in more one-night stands than I preferred to count. "That's the upside of the needle," Jack said when he saw me staring.

Again I traced the scar on his chest and then moved my finger slowly south of his navel. Dr. Singh's proposed implant with its pump, reservoir, and dual cylinders could not possibly have been any more efficient than the needle carrying the two raindrops of prostaglandin E-1. Maybe Jack was right about romance. There was something to be said for efficiency. And for stick handling. "Some upside."

The wakeup radio switched on to NPR as it did automatically every morning at five. Weekends I did not do the StairMaster or the rowing machine in the exercise room I had fitted out in the large pantry off the kitchen. There was no *BBC World Update* on Saturdays, just concert music. Mozart's Concerto number 3 in G major, with Itzhak Perlman on the violin and James Levine conducting. I listened for a moment, stretching and wiping the sleep from my eyes. When I finally put my feet on the floor, I stepped on one of his cuff links. I looked back at him. He still had a hard-on. His right leg hung out of the bed, but his cock stood up like a rocket on a launching pad. I was full of cock metaphors. Lacrosse stick last night, rocket this morning. The needle and the vial of prostaglandin E-1 were on the bedside table along with their tiny carrying case. I wondered if he had given himself an extra boost. As a way of wishing me good morning. I massaged the hard-on for a moment, getting in the mood, but he did not move. His eyes were closed, his face peaceful but drained of color. Even before I said "Jack," I knew he was dead. I felt for a pulse in his neck, but there was none. On his wrist he wore a MedicAlert bracelet. I read the instructions: "Aortic valve prosthesis—takes anticoagulants—allergic to penicillin." Already there was evidence of postmortem lividity pooling at his thighs. I could not think of what to do, so I gathered his studs and cuff links from the floor and put them on the table next to his penile injection kit. Then I took his credit cards, California driver's license, and money clip from his tuxedo trousers and placed them next to the studs and cuff links. Next I folded his pleated dinner shirt and hung it and his bow tie and his dinner jacket in the closet. Then I sat in the chair and tried to follow Itzhak Perlman. Mozart soothed my nerves as I tried to guess what had happened, and what I had to do next. In my criminal practice I had read countless death certificates. I knew the words appropriate to the failure of an aortic prosthesis. Myocardial infarction. Pulmonary embolism. Rheumatic valvulitis with stenosis and/or insufficiency. Bacterial endo-carditis. Stroke. Suddenly I got up, went over to the bed, and tried to pull his paisley boxer shorts over his buttocks. Over his fucking cock. His body fell heavily onto the floor. Oh, Jesus. Oh, God. So much for getting him dressed. For a moment I felt like crying, then went into the bathroom and looked at myself in the mirror. I was still naked. His come stained the sheet and was crusted on my stomach. Shower. I could always think in the shower. I let the water flow over me and for some demented reason decided to wash my hair. I felt like Mary Martin in *South Pacific.* I'm gonna wash that man right out of my hair, wash that man right out of my hair, and send him on his way. Except he was dead. Not that easy. Was this worth learning about my mother? And my father? I always tend to forget him. What did Jack say? About my being a victim's rights lawyer and my father being a steady provider of victims. Goddamn Jack. What would it cost to disappear him? Who could do it? No. Pull yourself together. Do not do anything illegal. Better to be embarrassed than disbarred. I dried myself off, pulled on a pair of jeans and a cashmere sweater. My nipples looked like chestnuts under the cashmere. Not something I wanted the boys from EMS to see. Under the circumstances. With a stiff and his still-stiff johnson alongside my bed. I pulled off the sweater, found a bra, wadded toilet paper in the cups, put it on, and then the sweater over it.

No more chestnuts.

It was still not five-thirty. Take stock. I lived on a cul-de-sac. The Bonaventures next door were on a frequent-flier trip to Albuquerque visiting the daughter they didn't like and the granddaughter they did. The O'Learys across the street were in Japan for the economic summit.

The Ackerman house on the other side had been empty since Marvin Ackerman's posting as DCM in Warsaw. The Nigerian economic attaché who had rented it would not move in until March. The Sheridans were in the middle of a messy divorce and the bank had taken over their house. That pretty much took care of the neighborhood. Saturday. Slow news day. A blessing. His death might not hit the papers until Monday. Look around. See if there is anything to get rid of. The needle and the prostaglandin E-1. Definitely. It was not as if this were a crime scene. No. Not thinking. If there was an autopsy, the toxicology results would indicate the presence of—what did he call it—a corticosteroid in his system. As if his stiff dick was not a dead giveaway. Dead. Why did I think *dead* giveaway? Jesus. Where to put the paraphernalia of erection? In the change pocket of his dinner jacket. Where it might be overlooked. The glasses and the half-empty bottle of red wine. Out of the bedroom and downstairs into the kitchen. Rinse the glasses. A swig of wine, then a cork in the bottle and into the fridge. For cooking. Back to the bedroom. Put his socks in his patent-leather shoes. Try pulling on the paisley shorts once again. Over that fucking thing. Which was what it was. A fucking thing. Why didn't it go down? It was like penile rigor mortis.

Success.

At least a little dignity.

Then the large protuberance made its way out of the fly in his shorts.

What the hell. I couldn't do any more.

R.I.P., John Broderick.

Now, be prepared: 911 brings EMS.

D.C. police will pick up the 911 and dispatch a squad car.

Daddy had taught me how to talk to cops. Look them in the eye. Don't bullshit, but don't tell them anything they do not need to know. Do not lose your nerve.

I dialed 911.

CHAPTER FIVE

EMS was discreet and professional. The paramedics noted the Medic-Alert bracelet with its reference to an aortic valve prosthesis and the necessity of anticoagulants. They asked the name of the deceased individual—"individual" was their word—and how long he had been on the premises and if I had been aware of any signs of cardiac unrest prior to his becoming deceased and when had I noticed that he had in fact expired. I thought credit cards and driver's licenses expire, not people, people die, but "die" was not a word that seemed to figure in the paramedics' professional vocabulary. They made no mention of the residue of sexual activity on the rumpled bed or the still-erect penis sticking out of the shorts on the deceased individual. I was in a penis mode now, not dick, prick, cock, or johnson. I had considered changing the sheets, but another piece of advice from my father was never do anything that might invite suspicion. Humiliation is not an indictable offense. They asked how the deceased happened to be on the floor, and I told them, I hope in a flat uninflected voice, that I had been trying to put on his shorts. By this time, the squad car had arrived, and the paramedics told the senior uniformed officer that the cause of death appeared to be MI, that MI was consistent with the type of heart surgery indicated both by the deceased's MedicAlert bracelet and by the scar on his sternum, that there was no evidence of foul play, that the name of the deceased was John Broderick, his ID was on the bedside table, and perhaps it would be best if they interviewed me in another room as they thought it might be unsettling for me to watch as they bagged the body. As I left the bedroom with the two policemen, I heard one paramedic whisper to the other that they would need a van with a sunroof if the deceased did not lose his wood. Humor on the EMS beat.

Downstairs in the kitchen the officers declined the coffee I had made while waiting for the paramedics. The officer who did the talking looked familiar. His plastic name tag identified him as WILKES, and my inability to immediately recognize him seemed to irritate him, one more proof he did not need that white people thought all black men looked alike. "Two years ago," he said finally. "Alex."

Of course. He was the officer who came to my house that night. Another weekend, another sexual misadventure. Two days on Nantucket with someone else's husband. Name of Kris. As in Kringle, he would say to people he just met. That should have been clue enough. Kris as in Kringle told me he could not leave his wife and marry me because she had not signed a pre-nup, and a divorce would leave her with assets he was not willing to surrender. Getting off Nantucket in mean March weather meant chartering a fishing boat to Hyannis, and more seasickness than I care to remember. Then a rented car for the endless drive to Washington. Fury kept me awake. I should have known by then that someone else's husband was always a bad idea. It was nearly 3 a.m. when I got home. I wanted nothing but a bath and some red wine, the more expensive the better, which in moments of duress I find soothes the fragile psyche no one seems to think I have. I was opening a bottle of Prieuré-Lichine when I saw the red light blinking on my answering machine.

Four messages. First a hang-up. The second from Marty in New York. Martha Buick had been my roommate at Smith. When it was a straight school, she liked to say. Before it became Sappho State. Marty was maid of honor at my first wedding, matron of honor at my second. *Hi,* her message said. *How many times?* Marty had an avid interest in my sex life, enjoying it vicariously, I suspect, more than I did actively. She was married to Jimmy Sebastien, the marriage seemed to work, or at least they did not get in each other's way, they had three kids, Jimmy put seed money into start-up companies and was very rich. While Marty ran a modeling agency she called VVV, the three *V*s standing for *Veni, vidi, vici*—"I came, I saw, I conquered." She was good at it. VVV, or Three V, as it was called in the fashion world, was the agency all the hot young models wanted to join. Marty's home and office was a former warehouse in the West Village. Everything was white, gray, stone, minimal, the floors polished concrete, the spaces lit with photographer's lights, photo blowups of her clients from shoots around the world covering the walls. On the top floor, under a huge skylight, there was a lap pool. Marty traveled to the spring and fall collections in Paris and Milan in Jimmy's G-4, and she was guardian angel and foster mother to some of the weirder specimens of the female gender, many of whom were burned out, in rehab, or DOA by nineteen. She knew all about Budd Doheny's quirks and collection of erotica and of course she would want to know every nuance of my thirty-six hours on Nantucket. She was also the only person to whom I had ever confided my speculation about the identities of my real parents, the speculation that Jack had confirmed in what he did not realize would be his final bequest.

Then an automated message from a bank promising high interest and free travelers' checks if I would open an account, and a chance to enter the draw for a Lexus sedan, with CD player, wraparound sound, alarm system, and a computerized navigator screen. The last message began with a desperate guttural voice. "This is Alex. Listen, I can't meet the schedule, I need more time, you have to give it to me, you owe me that, you fuck . . ." Suddenly he began to cough, that smoker's cough I still remember from the days when my father chain-smoked, two packs a day, maybe three, his face almost purple from the exertion, veins about to burst. Alex seemed to gasp for air, and I could hear a strangled exclamation, "Oh, shit," and then a noise that sounded like the last water in the tub going down the drain.

"Alex," I said. "Alex," as if I were talking to a real person, not a machine, and then there was a banging that cut the message short, the caller had hung up or fallen on his telephone; at any rate the connection was severed. "Sunday, ten forty-eight p.m.," the neutral voice on my answering machine said, logging the time the call came in, and then, "End of final message."

I didn't know any Alex.

Like a good Samaritan I called 911. It took a while to convince the operator that I would like someone to listen to the message from Alex. Officer Wilkes had responded to that call, too. He asked some questions. I recognized the tone. It was the one he would use on possible perps, somewhere between threatening and hostile. Was it my voice on the machine? No. It was computer-generated. Saying? Leave your name, number, and a brief message after the beep. It give your number? No. Let me hear it, he said. My truthfulness was not to be taken for granted. So we were acquaintances, after a fashion. "Did you ever find out . . ."

Wilkes nodded. "Alex Dimanche. Dimanche is French for Sunday, they tell me, although I bet you know that already, I bet you speak it, French." He made it sound like an accusation. "Small-time gambler. Into his shy for twenty-seven K. Couldn't make the vig. Afraid his ankles were going to get broke. Which is what almost happened. The muscle came to rough him up, but he was dead by his telephone. They steal everything they can carry, then being good citizens they call 911, tell 'em where there's a body going rank. Reason he called you was he transposed your number with his shy's."

"I would have appreciated knowing."

"Why?"

More advice from my father: Never argue with a hostile cop unless he's on the stand under oath. Then eat him alive.

"Your friend Broderick, first name John, he live here?" Wilkes asked. I said no. "In D.C.?" I shook my head. "Where's he staying then?" I think the Madison, I said. "You might let them know they have a room free," Wilkes said. "You wouldn't have a Q-tip, would you?"

I found a box in a drawer on the serving island and handed it to him. He cleaned his ears vigorously as I watched, closely examining the wax he had dislodged, then arched the Q-tip toward a wastebasket. It missed. He made no effort to pick it up, just stared silently at me. Resentment seemed to leak from him, like sweat. Finally I retrieved the Q-tip from the kitchen floor and deposited it in the garbage pail under the sink.

The paramedics were bringing the body bag downstairs. They strapped it on a gurney and pushed the gurney into the van.

Officer Wilkes brushed by me without a word, followed by his partner, who had not spoken the entire time he was in the house. Wilkes opened the passenger door on the squad car, and then surveyed me over its roof. "You call the Madison," he said after a moment, pointing a finger at me. He made it seem like a warning. "Hear?"

I closed the door before the EMS van pulled out of the driveway.

It was not yet six-thirty.

I did not call the Madison.

Nor did I call Marty Buick.

I was not up to any more explanations.

The obituary actually did not appear until Tuesday, and then in *The New York Times,* not *The Washington Post.* The cause of death was a heart attack, and the *Times* said he had died at my house. A reporter in the *Times*'s Washington bureau had called to ask how long I had known Mr. Broderick, and I said he was a friend of my mother's, which seemed to satisfy him, and was true, after a fashion; it just wasn't the mother with Alzheimer's across the Potomac in Virginia. The obit was extensive, with an automatic "He was a good friend and a graceful, witty man" quote from former President Finn, but Jack seemed to merit the space allowance only as a lesser member of his own family. He was identified as Hugh Broderick's son, Augustine Broderick's brother, and the ex-husband of his first wife, the murdered radical attorney Leah Kaye. His two books, many screenplays, and discovery of the long-lost Blue Tyler were not mentioned until the penultimate paragraph, after the paragraph saying he was a much sought-after extra man in New York, Los Angeles, and various venues around the world favored by the gilded classes.

The *Times* said funeral arrangements were pending.

The phone began ringing early that morning.

Condolences first from Margaret and Duncan Dudley.

Followed immediately by Marty Buick. Marty assumed the worst, or considering her natural train of thought, the best. She said it reminded her of John Garfield and Spencer Tracy. Both of whom, she felt impelled to explain, died in the saddle. I replied quite sharply that "in the saddle" was an unpleasant figure of speech, and in any case it was inaccurate.

Marty never gave up a position easily. Well, they were both someplace they should not have been. In beds not their own. And why hadn't I called in the first place? I thought I was your best friend.

I did not argue. Nor did I mention the prostaglandin E-1.

His death did not make the *Post* until Wednesday. Washington is a company town, and the *Post* less a newspaper than the government's trade paper, and in its scheme of things a G-12 assistant undersecretary in the Department of Agriculture gets billing over a Hollywood screenwriter. For the self-absorbed of Georgetown and Cleveland Park, Hollywood seems to exist only to give them someplace they think they can look down on, since it would never occur to them that the people who live in what they insist on calling "out there" are richer, smarter, meaner, and tougher than they are. It was only when a *Post* editor remembered Jack's name on the guest list at the president's annual dinner for the Supreme Court that his death was deemed worthy of the Style section. I was screening my calls by this point, and left the Style writer's message on my answering machine. The *Post* is across the street from the Madison, where out-of-town guests at White House events regularly stay, but no reporter bothered to check the concierge to see if the hotel had any information about the late Mr. Broderick. Grudgingly, the *Post* writer picked the bones of the *Times* obit, sneering at several movie stinkers Jack had written and digging up unsubstantiated stories ("Rumors persist . . . sources maintain . . .") about sex and money in the Broderick family.

That evening I moderated a PBS panel in Baltimore on whether civil redress after acquittal in a criminal court constituted double jeopardy. I was so detached from the proceedings that I scarcely noticed when two of the panelists nearly came to blows, and a third suggested that the fourth was an "asshole," an invigorating if unintentional departure from the deadening civility so characteristic of PBS. Afterwards the producer complained that I had so lost control of the panel that he would have to edit the tape rigorously before it was fit for broadcast. I just nodded and headed for my car. When I got home, there was a message on my machine saying simply, "This is Wilkes," and then ten or fifteen seconds of silence before he hung up. And a second message from the writer who did the *Post*'s "Reliable Sources" gossip column, demanding and self-important, he was on deadline and needed me to confirm new information about the circumstances of John Broderick's death.

Circumstances unspecified.

I called Marty and asked if I could come up and lay low with her for a few days until the story blew over.

It was at Marty's that I met Carlyle.

CHAPTER SIX

Carlyle. No last name. Like Madonna. Named after the hotel.

"Not the one in Miami Beach. Deco is for scuzzes. The one in New York. I tell people it's where I popped my cherry is how I picked it." This was in her *Rolling Stone* interview. "It wasn't. Shit, I lost it on the hood of Kile Purdy's Crown Vic when I was like thirteen. Not with Kile. He was puking in the back seat. With Waylon Madden. Who was wearing a dirty T-shirt that said NEVER TAKE A SIX-PACK TO A JOB INTERVIEW. Funnee. The only thing Waylon knew about a job was that he never had one. The hood burned my buns, it was so hot. My buns were the only thing that got hot, you want the truth. Waylon's was about the size of a toothpick. I thought they all looked like that. How was I to know? Him and Kile cracked up that Crown Vic two months later. Skidded into a Burlington Northern grain train at the Albion crossing. Toast. He was always racing trains, Kile. He thought he was Dale Fucking Earnhardt, and look at what happened to that fucker at the Daytona Five. There were twenty-two empty cans of Midlandia Lager in what was left of the Crown Vic. Eleven each. Except that asshole Kile was such a hog I bet he had a couple more than Waylon. I was so pissed. I was supposed to go with them, but I got my period, and Waylon said he didn't want someone riding the cotton pony tagging along. Fuck him, he's dead, I'm not. I just thought Carlyle sounded cool. I mean, I wasn't going to call myself fucking Marriott, was I? Days Inn?"

Her real name was Alice Faith Todt.

She had been on the cover of *Newsweek* when she was fifteen. The slash line was LOST YOUTH: TOO OLD TOO SOON. Carlyle hadn't seen it that way. "What's so great about being a kid anyway?" she had told *Newsweek*. "Chemistry tests? Being a pom-pom girl? Going to the prom? Getting knocked up? Getting totaled in Kile Purdy's Crown Vic?" She was the official face of the Jacquot cosmetic empire, with her own product line. Marty had negotiated a Jacquot deal paying her six million dollars a year, escalating by the end of the contract to nine, plus a hundred thousand dollars a day for public appearances. Her contracts stipulated that she would only travel by private jet. She had been on seventy-seven magazine covers around the world, forty-one of them shot by her favorite photographer, Alex Quintero, who also directed her Jacquot commercials, which he had parlayed into a Hollywood film contract, two one-man photography shows at the Gagosian Gallery, and induction into the Fashion Hall of Fame. On the runway in Paris and Milan, she earned fifty-eight thousand dollars a show, and she was booked three years in advance. Her website—Yo! Carlyle—was the Internet site most visited by men and women under twenty-five. The site had a shop selling Carlyle postcards, Carlyle beauty products, and Carlyle exercise tapes, a bookshelf selling Carlyle's fashion tips, a message board, a fan focus where each month one of Marty's staffers answered five letters in her name: "Yo! Carlyle: Please tell me what I'm supposed to do with my cellulite. I'm 19 years old and maybe just a little overweight. Thank you—Tarawa." And the answer: "Yo, Tarawa: Carlyle's Action Cream is just the ticket for those fat thighs. Use it, love it, get a life—Carlyle."

She was seventeen years old.

She had made nineteen million dollars that year.

She was crouched over a computer in Marty's office, absorbed in a website called Famous Flesh. She was smoking and chewing gum, oblivious to Marty, equally oblivious to me. Famous Flesh (as well as Celebrity Skin, Notable Nookie, Boobs & Pubes, and other soft-core sites) published bootleg photos of models and celebrities taken at fashion shoots where models casually walk around naked backstage between wardrobe changes, plus nude photos taken at isolated and expensive island resorts with long-range lenses, even photos and occasional videos of celebrity copulation. She was of course looking for the latest photographs of herself, not so much in the interest of pursuing litigation as in comparing herself to her contemporaries in the beauty business, with a running and derogatory commentary of their every physical flaw, real and imagined. "Look at that roll on Kate, Kate, you look like a baby elephant . . . Clea, they droop, your tits weigh more than I do . . . Alex says Carrie's got a clit ring . . . what if some sicko dude pulled it . . . hair pie and clit ring . . . Xan, don't you know pubes are gross, get them waxed, a Mohawk's so much cooler."

She was five-eight, according to the computerized fact sheet Marty's staff updated weekly (as they did for all Three V models)—119 pounds; bust, weight, and hips 34-23-34. A rubber band caught her hair, off blond that morning, in a ponytail, and there was a space between her front teeth that softened her otherwise sulky erotic looks. She was wearing jeans and a gray hooded sweatshirt. Printed on the back of the sweatshirt were the words RIKER'S ISLAND. It was a souvenir of a fashion shoot Alex Quintero had done on Riker's, with Carlyle modeling the spring Prada line surrounded by inmates and hacks. The official at the Department of Corrections who sanctioned the shoot was fired, and editorials in the *Post* and the *Times* and *The Wall Street Journal* decried "Prison Chic." The phrase became a battle cry. It also made Carlyle and Alex Quintero famous. Or infamous. Which was essentially the same thing. She had five tattoos (this too from the fact sheet): a shark's tooth bracelet on each wrist, a rose on her navel, and a dragon climbing out of the crack in her ass and up her back. The fifth was an ankh over the scar on her left arm where she had accidentally shot herself when the licensed Manurhin 7.65mm she was carrying in her Kate Spade bag discharged at a Donna Karan AIDS benefit in Miami Beach. One last look at the competition on Famous Flesh: "Lynch, you're so old even your finger won't fuck you."

She twirled around, planted her elbows on Marty's marble-top desk, and looked me up and down, blowing bubbles, not speaking.

"This is Teresa Kean," Marty said finally.

I thought I hadn't registered on her radar screen.

I was wrong.

"Those your own boobs?" was the first thing Carlyle said to me.

The second was "You had a hysterectomy yet?"

And the third: "What are you anyway? Sixty?"

And the fourth: "That guy in Washington, you fucked him to death, right?"

Okay. Smart mouth was the language of criminal courtrooms, committee hearings, and chat-show mud wrestling, nothing I hadn't heard before, and I was better at it than a dim teenager whose every whim was satisfied, and to whom no one ever said no.

Voice soft, eyes steady. Ready, aim, fire. "To question number one, yes. To questions two, three, and four, no." And then a finger pointed at the sweatshirt: "I bet you think that hoody is cute. Let me tell you something." Lean close, almost a whisper now. "You ever spent a night on Riker's, some bitch would razor your nipples off before you hit your cell and then ram a turkey baster so far up your sweetness you'd be sneezing metal filings." A brief pause for effect. A bubble splattered over Carlyle's surprised, sullen face. One final shot. "When you're twenty, you think anyone's going to remember you?"

I apparently made an impression.

Three months later, I got a call from Marty. She got right to the point. Carlyle wanted me to defend her half brother.

What's the charge? I asked.

Murder, Marty said.

PART THREE

CHAPTER ONE

In the three months before Martha Buick called Teresa, not all that much happened.

Poppy McClure spoke on behalf of Republican candidates in eleven states from Maine to New Mexico. The Hasty Pudding Club at Harvard named her its Woman of the Year, and when she accepted the award in Cambridge, she came in full costume as her favorite female politician— Queen Elizabeth I.

Carlyle fired Martha Buick and Three V the day after Thanksgiving, went to Elite, fired Elite, went to Casablanca, fired Casablanca, and returned to Three V in time for the holidays.

Martha Buick bought her a black 290-horsepower Jaguar XK8 convertible as a welcome-home present, and at 5 a.m. New Year's morning, while changing a CD, Carlyle ran the Jaguar into an undercover police van on a stakeout in Union Square.

Carlyle was arrested for driving a vehicle without a seat belt and a valid registration, for being an unlicensed driver, and for reckless endangerment of an ongoing police operation. A Breathalyzer test was negative. The object of the stakeout disappeared in the resulting confusion. The black 290-horsepower Jaguar XK8 convertible was totaled. Carlyle was fined five hundred dollars in Manhattan traffic court and forbidden to operate a motor vehicle in New York for three years. Carlyle told the two New York tabloids and reporters for all the local TV channels that the restriction was no big deal because she always had a driver anyway.

Teresa Kean returned to Washington, and resigned from Justice for All. She said it was time to prepare for a new phase in her career, and that several publishers had asked to see a manuscript about the law she had been polishing for several years.

Martha Buick offered Teresa Kean the house in Sagaponack where she and her husband and children spent their summers. Martha Buick said that Sagaponack in winter was a place where Teresa Kean could work on her book without distraction.

Margaret Dudley gave Teresa Kean a going-away party in Georgetown attended by crime professionals, a deputy White House press secretary, members of the legal community, lobbyists, two cabinet secretaries, Sunday talk-show bookers, a cable-TV host, several print and television reporters, a visiting actress making a film in Washington, one pundit, a weekend anchorwoman, a widower Supreme Court justice with whom the actress was said to be having an affair, three ambassadors, two senators, and four congressmen.

Poppy McClure attended the event briefly. Poppy and the actress had their picture taken together. The photograph of Poppy and the actress appeared on the front page of both the Capital City *Herald* and the Kiowa *Times-Ledger*.

President Dixon McCall sent a note praising Teresa Kean for a job well done.

Maurice Dodd prepared his case against Bryant Gover and Duane Lajoie. He resisted the discovery motions filed by the attorneys for Gover and Lajoie until ordered to comply by Judge Tracy.

There was nothing unexpected in the reports filed by the South Midland Bureau of Investigation that were turned over, under the laws of discovery, to Francis Howar and Earle Lincoln, counsels for the defense. Bryant Gover had a history of violence and had been in constant trouble with the law since his first arrest as a juvenile offender. His arrest and incarceration records were filed as separate attachments to his file. Duane Lajoie had a history of violence and had been in constant trouble with the law since his first arrest as a juvenile offender. His arrest and incarceration records were also filed as separate attachments.

The SMBI had run an extensive background check on Edgar Parlance and found no other entanglements with law enforcement beyond his incarceration at the Colorado State Penitentiary in Canon City for grand theft (auto) twenty years prior to his murder. Documents on file at the Colorado Department of Corrections indicated that Edgar Parlance had been born in Wunder, Arkansas, and that he was nineteen years old at the time of his incarceration. An SMBI check of birth records in Fletcher County, Arkansas, failed to confirm Edgar Parlance's date and place of birth in Wunder, Arkansas. SMBI investigators checked school records and the records of child welfare and foster-care agencies in Kansas, Missouri, Arkansas, South Midland, North Midland, Nebraska, Texas, and Georgia—all states where Edgar Parlance claimed to have lived as a child— and failed to find any mention of an Edgar Parlance whose probable dates corresponded with those of the victim.

Anecdotal evidence, i.e., information supplied by the deceased, indicated that Edgar Parlance was thirty-nine years of age at the time of his death. There was no record that Edgar Parlance had ever been issued a driver's license. He did have a Social Security card, but it appeared to have been bought on the street. The SMBI report said that while Edgar Parlance had a checkered employment history, he enjoyed the support and friendship of all those he came into contact with, including former employers. He was especially active in community activities in Regent and Loomis County during holiday celebrations.

SMBI investigators said that after an exhaustive check they had been unable to discover any prior contact between Edgar Parlance and either Bryant Gover or Duane Lajoie. Their conclusion was that Edgar Parlance was the victim of a random act of violence.

J.J. McClure told the attorney general he was ready to backstop Maurice Dodd any way he could.

The A.G. said he did not think Maurice Dodd needed a backstop.

CHAPTER TWO

Willie Erskine was on the horn from Washington. Stacking up Poppy's outgoing calls like an air traffic controller. She would speak to him in five minutes. The midweek check-in. Would he be available? No. J.J. saw no point in making Willie's life easier. Willie tried to explain. Poppy was talking to the Speaker. He would be her next call. She and the Speaker were going over the agenda for the meeting of the majority caucus. Willie whispered, as if the information were classified. It struck J.J. that people in Washington did not seem to have names. Titles had more significance. The Speaker. The Secretary. The Director. The DCI. Venues also carried weight. HEW. State. Labor. And the ultimate: the White House. J.J. expected Poppy would want to know what he had thought of her letter in that morning's Kiowa *Times-Ledger*. Signed by Poppy, written by Willie. She had sprung to the defense of some preposterously rich cash cow accused of raiding the reserves funding the 401(k)s of his employees. The preposterously rich cash cow, code name CC in the inner sanctums, was a major party contributor from whom the White House, or WH, as Willie called it in a sepulchral whisper, was trying to put some distance. Poppy was on the attack in the *Times-Ledger*, her targets those middle-of-the-road Republicans ready to abandon the preposterously rich cash cow. The MOR Republicans were termites in the temple of conservatism, she said. No better than liberal Democrats. Politically correct. PC was the new McCarthyism. What, she asked, was wrong with the old? The preposterously rich cash cow—why not a cash bull? J.J. wondered—was a self-made man of wealth and position, Poppy/Willie expostulated, free of the commonality that infects the so-called polity. Blunt the inevitable bleats of bigotry that will naturally emanate from the cesspool on the sinister side of the room, the letter continued. Sinister proceeds from the Latin root *sinistra,* and in Latin *sinistra* means left. Left = sinister. Indeed. The letter made no more sense than any of Poppy's other jeremiads, but as always the richness of the invective made him smile. He wondered idly, as he occasionally did, how much Poppy actually believed of what she said. Probably more than I think, he supposed. Not everything, of course. The rhetorical overkill was just a tool. It got her on *Nightline.* A thought he would not share with her.

Willie Erskine was back on the line. Poppy had to take a call from the WH. Himself is in a dither. The president. Leader of the free world. Not likely. Willie still thought J.J. had not mastered the WH's food chain, or how far down it Poppy's caller might be.

I liked sinister, Willie.

That was Poppy.

And those termites.

That was Poppy, too.

Sure it was, Willie.

I just cleaned it up a little, Willie Erskine said. He could not resist. The urge to suggest that he had made some small contribution to Poppy's public pronouncements was too strong. Just a polish. Grammar and punctuation. Then the thought that he might have implied too extensive a contribution, and that J.J. would tattle to Poppy, took over and Willie returned to his officious tone. WH is going to be on for a while.

J.J. wondered what had happened to the P.A. from the C-Span green-room. He thought of her whenever he had a bagel and cream cheese. What is it about you and bagels all of a sudden? Allie said. She had antennae for any sudden or transient irregularity in someone's routine. If there was a change, there was a reason, and beyond the reason usually some dereliction, however slight. A passing fancy, J.J. had said. An answer that was not exactly untrue. Allie did not need cream cheese to get motivated. I can think you off, she had once told him. He did not doubt it. Occasionally in court she would stare at him, her face a mask, not blinking, and he would feel the beginnings of a hard-on. He would busy himself with a transcript or an exhibit or whisper to Harvey Niland or Patsy Feiffer or whatever assistant was at the prosecutor's table until the moment passed. Watching him, she said, she could think herself off, too. He did not see Allie all that much anymore. She lived in a small apartment unit halfway between Capital City and Kiowa, and it did not have the privacy she insisted on. She did not want visitors with Rhea there, or neighbors talking. She'll learn about that stuff soon enough, J.J., I'm not going to push it. Mommy, what's an orgasm is a question I'm not prepared to answer from a kid four years removed from her first period. If I'm lucky. Latin girls grow up faster, that's one thing we all learned, I got my first tampon at eight, Rhea's only half Latin, if who I think is the one *is* the one, and I'm reasonably sure he is, so maybe she's on Anglo slowdown, I hope so.

It was the first time she had ever mentioned Rhea's father. Or a possible father. He wanted no more information. It was not useful. His physical encounters with Allie were quick, unplanned, intense, ingenious, and usually occurred in the courthouse now, because there was something so depressing, so furtive, about the motels available for a late-afternoon before-dinner tumble. Adultery Manors, Allie called them. There was also the possibility of running into someone he or Allie knew. An acquaintance of either sex practicing something more adventurous than the missionary position that was the feature of the marriage bed. Strangely enough, the courthouse was the safest place late at night, he could lock his door and they would climb on the conference table, the cheap Naugahyde couch did not have enough purchase, she said, it made her ass slide around, or her knees when they were in that configuration. Once they even performed on the floor in the A.G.'s office. The Worm and Mrs. Worm—Nancy Reagan Wormwold, that perfect name—were visiting Grand Coulee Dam. Mrs. Worm's father was a hydraulic engineer, she had this thing about dams, and J.J. was acting A.G., with access to the A.G.'s office. It was uncomfortable on the rug but it was worth it, Allie said, imagining what the Worm would have thought had he known. Another time, Allie's idea, standing up in a utility closet by the service elevator shaft, surrounded by pails and mops and brooms and rags and detergents and Dustbusters and industrial vacuums, her legs wrapped around his waist, her arms around his neck. In the pitch-black closet, her bare bottom had bounced against the electrical fixture, suddenly switching on the light, it was so surprising that he dropped her, but she did not stop or cry out, she just grabbed hold of him, sitting on a bucket, and pumped it until he came.

Imagine Patsy in here, Allie said, turning the light off and plunging the closet back into disorienting darkness. It had already occurred to J.J. He tried not to hit a pail with his foot, causing some unnecessary noise that might bring a janitor from the night cleaning crew or a deputy from the sheriff's detachment that guarded all the country buildings in Capital City. Something I should have thought of sooner, he thought. He found a handkerchief in his pocket and vigorously rubbed the stickiness away. A sudden memory. When his father shopped at Parker County Dry Goods in Hamlet, he always bought suits with two pairs of pants ordered from the Sears catalogue. A reminder to J.J. of how much a country boy he actually was. And preferred to forget. A second pair of pants would have been perfect after an occasion such as this. Throw away the soiled pair and he still had the suit. Get rid of the handkerchief, too. He did not want Carmencita picking it out of the dirty laundry basket. Simple though she was, virgin that she probably was, Carmencita would have her suspicions about why the handkerchief seemed glued together. Carmencita was the latest of the women of no known age who arrived periodically at his and Poppy's house from the village in Sonora where Poppy's mother had come from. Poppy's so-very-rich mother. The mother she had never known. Carmencita was preceded by Elena, Elena by Rosario, Rosario by Alcibiades. Guadalupe, Crucita, Arxenta, Natividad, Inocencia, Orquídea. He had lost track of how many had come and gone, what they looked like, what their names were. The women cooked, they cleaned, they wore white uniforms, they spoke Spanish to Poppy when she was in residence, but never to him, although his Spanish was Anglo perfect. They would never meet his eye, and then for no apparent reason other than the frigid South Midland winters they would disappear back to deepest Sonora and immediately be replaced by still another docile inhabitant from the same village. It's not a village, Poppy would say irritably, it's a hacienda. He loved it when Poppy was snooty.

Big deal, Harvard Law School, Allie said. J.J. had never mentioned Alcibiades or Guadalupe or any of the others to Allie. And certainly not the hacienda. She was still musing on Patsy Feiffer. For a moment she placed his hand between her legs, squeezing it with her thighs, then rapidly adjusted her clothes.

UVA, J.J. said.

What's UVA?

For people whose first choice was Harvard Law and didn't get in.

Like SMU Law and Osceola Community?

Something like that, J.J. said.

And this is a starter job for her. She thought she'd come out to the sticks, the people out here aren't so smart as she thinks she is, she'd move up fast, and then she's gone. Chicago. L.A. New York.

Even during sex Allie had the ability to make connections. She's from Connecticut, Allie said.

Farmington.

Where's that?

The fancy part of Hartford. J.J. had of course checked out Patsy's résumé when he conducted the job interview, and hired her. Her father was CFO of a secondary insurance company. Steadman Feiffer. The third. Her mother had been a vice-president of the Hartford Junior League. Her twin brother was autistic and had been in an institution since he was two. Steadman IV. No other siblings. Economics degree, without honors, from Bowdoin. Bowdoin was almost certainly a second choice, or third, as UVA Law School was. No one not from Maine goes to college in Maine as a first choice. Vice-chairman of Campus Republicans. Summer intern for the Republican minority in the Connecticut legislature. Hobbies: golf and tennis. Golf handicap: 7. She actually put that down. She must have known the résumé was thin and needed filling out.

You know a lot about her, Allie said.

And you're asking a lot of questions about her.

You want to fuck her.

No, I don't. She's a harassment suit waiting to happen.

I didn't say she wasn't a harassment suit. I said you wanted to fuck her. You just won't.

It was a discussion J.J. was not prepared to continue. How's Max? Still queer?

If he wasn't, J.J., you'd still be working for him.

I should know better than to have a postcoital discussion in a broom closet, J.J. thought.

Señor J.J., Allie said. She gave it the Spanish pronunciation—Señor Hay-Hay.

"How did it play?" It was Poppy calling direct from one of the hideaways on the House side of the Capitol. She knew J.J. would never remain in Willie Erskine's holding pattern. But she always had Willie try. WH must have rung off. She had waited until a recess during her subcommittee hearing to make the call. The subcommittee had something to do with the economy. She was the chair. Democrats think you can tax this great nation into prosperity, was what she said every time she gaveled a session to order. A Poppy-ism grown a little wilted. Always objected to by the minority. And never sustained by the chair.

"Led the letters page."

"I meant the protest."

Of course. Poppy would be interested in the march of university co-eds and women faculty members who had descended on the A.G.'s office yesterday protesting his decision three days earlier not to prosecute Jocko Cannon for allegedly attacking Brittany Barnes, the SMU sophomore swimmer who had refused to withdraw the battery charges she had filed against him. For allegedly dragging her down three flights of stairs in Rhino Hall. And allegedly fracturing her skull and cheekbone. And allegedly knocking out her two front teeth. "Allegedly" was a word that adhered to Jocko Cannon like a tick. It was whispered in the courthouse that his father, Ralph Cannon, Sr., retained an attorney whose sole function was to monitor the movements of his son, and to be available at odd hours for the spreading of paternal largesse and the removal of potential embarrassments. He's just a company lawyer, Poppy said, no one special, it's what company lawyers do, it bloats their hourly. In other words she did not deny that Ralph Cannon, Sr., kept babysitters watching Jocko around the clock. The A.G.'s decision not to proceed against Jocko would allow him to play against Florida State for the national championship New Year's night in the Orange Bowl. J.J. knew that Poppy's sympathy for Brittany Barnes was nil. Nor did she doubt that her multiple fractures were the work of Jocko Cannon. A bad kid, she had said more than once, someday his father is not going to be able to buy his way out of a scrape. What she cared about was how the A.G.'s decision might inconvenience Gerry Wormwold if she should decide to challenge him in a gubernatorial primary.

"Page four, below the fold, in both the *Herald* and the *Times-Ledger*," J.J. said. "The story was dead when the A.G. said he wasn't going to move forward. Jocko can play. Rhinos versus the Seminoles. That's all that counts. You could hardly call it a protest. A bunch of women marching is just a bunch of women marching."

That had been Allie's verdict.

Allie had been out on the steps in the event the march turned ugly and she had filled him in. The Kiowa and Cap City papers had both estimated a hundred and fifty marchers. A figure that came from the Rhino athletic department. Bigger than that, Allie said. The jock flacks would like to pretend it didn't happen. Closer to three hundred. Plus the football goons. Brittany Barnes had walked with the women. Many of her supporters carried placards showing her in a neck brace, her smile showing the gap in her mouth where her front teeth had been. The football goons also carried photo blowups, theirs of ten or fifteen Rhino players whose teeth had been knocked out in games or scrimmages. One of the toothless Rhinos was Jocko Cannon. HEY, BRIT, GET A DENTIST, the crude lettering on Jocko's poster said. JOCKO DID.

That lawyer paid for the football posters, Allie said.

Leo Cassady, J.J. said.

He also had one made up that said THE TRUTH WILL SET YOU FREE, Allie said. He's a cunt.

The epithet Allie reserved for her special favorites.

Wormwold declined to meet with the marchers. Nor would he answer questions forwarded to him by reporters about pressure from Rhino alumni not to compromise SMU's title hopes by prosecuting Jocko Cannon. A statement was given to the press: "My office is dedicated to the highest principles of the law. We do not bend under pressure. The facts and only the facts decide which cases go forward."

His interpretation of the facts has bumped the Rhinos back up to a twelve-and-a-half-point favorite, Allie said.

Bet your wallet, not your heart, Allie.

Always take twelve and a half points, J.J.

The Athletic Department had also issued a statement over the signature of Dr. John Strong, the Rhino coach. "Miss Barnes," Coach Strong said, "is an honorable young woman who unfortunately is being led astray by special interests with an agenda of their own. I do not think these special interests have the best interests of the university's football program at heart. Nevertheless, it is my intention to invite Miss Barnes and her family to Miami to cheer the Rhinos on against the Seminoles. A vacation in Miami will help the healing process."

Brittany Barnes did not join the healing process at the Orange Bowl.

Poppy did not make it to Miami either.

She had bronchitis. Or was it an inner-ear infection? The A.G. wondered why she was not down in the Orange Bowl with other state officials rooting the Rhinos on from the SMU cheering section. J.J. knew that Poppy did not really care for football, a secret she would not reveal even if lashed to the stake and the Worm had a match in his hand to ignite the kindling. At the hacienda in Bacadéhuachi, the children played soccer, as had Poppy when she was at Foxcroft until someone had called her a fast little Mexican. She always wore a diamond rhino pin designed by Harry Winston, but in fact her only real interest in football was whether John Strong would someday run for public office, and become a possible rival. A far more significant presence than the Worm. She never missed an opportunity to praise him. Gridiron John Strong, she would say. The Rhino football program without John Strong, she would say, is unthinkable.

You should have said you had genital herpes, J.J. said. It's the only excuse that has wheels. Nobody's going to doubt that. Even the Worm.

She kicked him under the covers.

They had spent most of New Year's afternoon in bed at their house in Proctor Park, the wooded section of Cap City where the fortune that Poppy had inherited from Jim Ford allowed them to live. Outside it was snowing, a blizzard in the making, the streets empty. In the kitchen, Esmerelda, the latest import from Bacadéhuachi, was making quesadillas, and occasionally they would hear snatches of a mournful ballad about love in the sun on the Sonoran plateau. It occurred to J.J. that he had never spent so much private time with Poppy since she had first gone to Washington. The congressman and the prosecutor enjoying the New Year.

He wondered if Esmé was the diminutive for Esmerelda.

Even here my attention is wandering, he thought.

They watched the Orange Bowl on the flat thirty-six-inch screen in the bedroom, nibbling Esmerelda's quesadillas and rooting the Rhinos on as everyone else in South Midland was meant to be doing, as if it were a penal violation not to. Nine seconds left, one last desperate play by Florida State, down 30 to 28, a fourth-down Hail Mary pass from mid-field that fell short and was nearly intercepted in the end zone. One second left on the game clock, Rhinos national champions. Except not yet. Penalty flag. Unsportsmanlike conduct on South Midland number 94, Jocko Cannon, for spearing the Florida State quarterback in the head with his helmet as he lay on the ground after the play was completed. The quarterback's name was Vinny Vincent. He was crumpled on the field, not moving, the announcers wondering if he were play-acting, not really hurt. Fifteen-yard penalty, rewind the clock, replay the down, Florida State was in field-goal range. Jocko Cannon became enraged at the referee, Tyler Cohen, and pushed him to the ground. Tyler Cohen immediately ejected Jocko from the game. Jocko went berserk, and began swinging his helmet at the Florida State players. Both benches emptied, meeting in a midfield melee that John Strong and the Seminole coach, Bubba Guillaume, were unable to contain. A real rumble, Guillaume said after the game, an ice pack against his eye. It took Metro-Dade police officers seventeen minutes to restore order on the field. Vinny Vincent was removed in a crash cart, and was later diagnosed at Jackson Memorial Hospital as having a concussion and a subdural hematoma. Fifteen Rhinos and fourteen Seminoles were ejected from the game. With so many ejections, both teams were represented by makeshift lineups when Florida State attempted a winning field goal. The kick from fifty-one yards was good, final score 31–30, once-beaten Florida State took the national championship from the previously unbeaten Rhinos.

J.J. wondered if Allie had gotten a flutter down.

"The referee, Mr. Tyler Cohen, made a questionable call," John Strong said at the postgame press conference. "Jocko was trying to hold up, from my perspective, and I'm sure the film will back my coaching staff and not Mr. Tyler Cohen. Of course, Jocko lost it, and he should not have, but there would have been no reason to if the referee, Mr. Tyler Cohen, had made the proper decision and not succumbed to the moment for whatever reason. We all, and I am including Mr. Tyler Cohen, will have to look in our hearts and see where we went wrong, and how we can improve."

"Especially Mr. Tyler Cohen," J.J. said.

"He's cute, that one," Poppy said about John Strong later that evening. By that time she saw the unpleasantness at the Orange Bowl only as an event that she would try to reconfigure to her advantage at some future date. The here and the now were never long in Poppy's sight line. She was always working three or four moves down the road. In the night, she had settled somewhere else. "This Maurice Dodd. Is he as good as you?"

"No. He is not as good as I am."

"Can you get rid of him?"

"No. I can't get rid of him."

Or perhaps J.J. only imagined Poppy had asked these questions. Because he knew she was thinking them. What was it about Edgar Parlance that rang her bell? Her natural political habitat was not one occupied by Edgar Parlance, African-American handyman who in death had exposed racial intolerance in the heartland and brought a nation closer together. Then it came to J.J. Never underestimate Poppy's reach. You'd think I'd know that by now. She's thinking vice-president two national elections hence. Perhaps not actively yet, but he was sure the seed was germinating. Edgar Parlance was a way to broaden her appeal. Poppy McClure, surrogate healer, was how she would present herself. A long shot, but nevertheless. If the Worm had chosen him and not Maurice Dodd, Poppy would have been at the Loomis County Courthouse every day. Available to the national press that would descend on Regent when the trial began. The big print and broadcast organizations had already booked most of the available hotel and motel space in Regent and surrounding areas. Poppy would see the trial as the J.J. and Poppy McClure Show. Actually as the Poppy McClure Show, co-starring J.J. McClure. Sound bites throughout the broadcast day.

"Prosecutor politics," Alicia Barbara, the anchor for the cable-TV show *Courthouse Square* had called the assignment of Maurice Dodd. "A journeyman career prosecutor who would get the job done," she said. "In his usual unbending way," she said. Absent the "flamboyant style" of J.J. McClure. "A political no-brainer" for Gerry Wormwold.

A cogent analysis, J.J. thought.

In fact, Maurice Dodd was much on his mind.

It was hard to avoid mention of him. Or the enjoyment Maurice Dodd took in the attention he had never before received.

A little envious, are you? Allie had said to J.J.

Maurice Dodd's profile in *The New York Times* was more generous about his abilities than Alicia Barbara had been.

He had joined the A.G.'s office immediately after his graduation from South Midland University Law School twenty-four years earlier. He was from Higgins, a crossroads community in Tribune County near the Wyoming border, population 112. Country, like me, J.J. thought. No. Country perhaps, but not like me. His father, Cletis, was a general storekeeper, his mother, Rebekah, a homemaker who raised Maurice, his four sisters and three brothers. His younger sister, Bethel, had been his secretary during his entire tenure with the A.G. She called him Mr. Dodd, he called her Miss Dodd. A form of address that was continued outside the office. J.J. wondered if anyone had ever made a move on Bethel Dodd. No. She had the sex appeal of a fire hydrant.

Maurice had lost his right arm as an infantry lieutenant in Vietnam. It wasn't a problem, he liked to say, I'm left-handed. An ostentatious way of drawing attention to his disability that infuriated Max Cline when he was running the Homicide Bureau. He was fragged, Max told J.J. one day at lunch. No, really, Max said. I know someone who served with someone who served under Maurice in the Mekong Delta. The gay network, J.J. remembered thinking. Always in touch. The someone who Max's someone knew was a scout assigned to Kilo Company, 199th LIB. That's the outfit whose unit brass Maurice always wears as a lapel pin, Max said. The scout's squad leader was a nineteen-year-old Mexican corporal from East Los Angeles whose mother would regularly send him packages of chile delicacies from the bodegas in Boyle Heights. Like everyone else in Kilo Company, except Maurice Dodd, the corporal wanted out of 'Nam, and one day it hit him that his mother's care packages offered an opportunity to rotate out a little quicker than the army had planned. He knew that a rat bite could send him to the military hospital in Cam Ranh Bay, and if the toxins in the infection were militant enough, it could put him on a plane back to Travis AFB in California. The downside was it might cost him a foot. It was a risk he was willing to take, so he opened a can of *pipián ranchero* and spread the contents between his toes and on the soles of his feet. The *pipián* made the rats in his hooch even more aggressive than usual, Max's source had said. They were about the size of squirrels anyway, he said, and they loved that *chilosa* paste so much they were ready to move to East L.A. Maurice heard about the scheme, however, and had the corporal court-martialed. Cowardice in the face of the enemy, ninety days in Long Binh stockade. Didn't matter. Rat bites became an epidemic in Kilo 199, *pipián ranchero* a rival for Panama Red. Then Maurice brought Article 15 charges against nine men in his platoon who had serenaded him on Christmas Eve with a carol that went:

> *Jingle bells, mortar shells,*
> *VC in the grass.*
> *Take your Merry Christmas cheer*
> *And shove it up your ass.*

Max's informant said that the grenade had landed in Lieutenant Dodd's hooch on New Year's Day.

Jingle bells and *pipián ranchero,* J.J. thought. When connected to Maurice Dodd, each fragment had the sharp idiosyncratic particularity of the believable.

Maurice Dodd told the *Times* he had been wounded in a firefight. No specifics given. The silence of heroism. He said he was proud to have served his country and saw no further reason ever to leave the continental limits, or even the state of South Midland. He said he had never had any interest in becoming a defense attorney. Nor did he chum around with members of the defense bar. He seemed to regard them as more pernicious than the Viet Cong. "I believe in the presumption of innocence," he said. "It is guaranteed. That does not mean that I have to associate with people who defend those who I am certain are guilty of the crimes with which they are charged." He was equally categorical about attorneys who had left the A.G.'s office for private practice. "They have a right to support their families in the best way they see fit," he volunteered to the *Times* reporter. "I have an equal right to cut them out of my life."

As if the arm he lost put him two rungs higher on the ladder of virtue than anyone else, J.J. reflected. He had never mentioned to anyone what Max had told him about the fragging.

Allie knew. Of course.

I would've fragged him, she had said one day. Definitely. I would've finished the fucking job, though. Put him in a shroud, not some pinned-up sleeve he can wave around at juries like it's some kind of fancy vestment priests wear when they say mass.

Max seemed to tell her everything.

If he wasn't queer, J.J., you'd still be working for him.

If Allie was a ballplayer, I'd trade her, J.J. thought. Except she's so well known as a pain in the ass no other law enforcement agency in the city, county, or state would take her. Forget the DMV or Corrections. The municipal school board wouldn't even let her check for grass in the toilets.

Besides which she's the best investigator I have. Even if she is doubling for Max. She doesn't even bother to deny it anymore.

Back to Maurice Dodd. And Bryant Gover. And Duane Lajoie.

"I will bear witness as those two animals are strapped into our electric chair," Maurice told the *Times* reporter, "and I won't lose a wink of sleep over it." To the *Times,* this made him a "typical flinty Midwesterner." J.J. wondered if he knew any typical Midwesterners. Let alone flinty ones. "Rigid" was the word he would use to describe Maurice Dodd. Obdurate. Infrangible. Unadaptable. Adamantine. That had a good sound to it. Adamantine. Not a *Times* word. Too many syllables. Maurice's soft side, according to the *Times,* was that he cultivated roses in his solar-heated backyard greenhouse, where even his wife, Ana, was forbidden entry. In the solitude of his greenhouse, he prepared opening statements, summations, and rebuttals, and tested them "before a jury of tea roses, white Pascalis, and buff-colored Chanelles."

It was the kind of cute factoid the media loved.

J.J. did not believe it for a second.

Maurice the Adamantine. Maurice the Unadaptable. They were like the names of medieval popes. Except Maurice Dodd did not like Catholics all that much. Only slightly more than he liked Jews. No wonder he was such a favorite of the Worm's. Patsy Feiffer now trailed Maurice around the courthouse, looking like a mix-and-match pastel cocker spaniel. Maurice had selected Patsy to be his second chair. Time for that girl to move up, he had told J.J. She's too smart to keep on doing scutwork. Imagine being patronized by Maurice Dodd, J.J. thought. He did not tell Maurice that Patsy was doing scutwork because that was all she was good at. Such airs, Allie said. She acts like she's Sandra Day O'Connor all of a sudden. Waiting for the White House to call. You think Maurice is banging her, J.J.? Slapping that stump across her tiny tits? Maybe in that utility closet, you remember the one. On the fifth floor.

Someday, Allie, you are going to go too far.

Don't count on it, J.J.

In his new grandeur, Maurice Dodd had vehemently objected to Ellen Tracy's decision to let *Courthouse Square* cover the trial live. Cameras in the courtroom will turn the proceedings into "a circus sideshow, O.J. in Loomis County," he told the Cap City *Herald*. J.J. was sure that what really bothered him was not the cameras but the kick in the slats he had received from Alicia Barbara when she wondered why a journeyman prosecutor was in charge of the case. He should have jollied her up, J.J. thought. She was a lesbian, however, and sexual deviation was another category on Maurice Dodd's Does Not Fly list. A pervert, he had called her. That was also how he had referred to Max Cline when Max was his boss. As good a reason as any for Max to tell him the fragging story. A couple of things to remember about Alicia Barbara, other than that she was gay. The accent on her last name was on the second syllable, Bar-*bare*-a, and she took pains to correct your ass if you pronounced it Barbara, as in Santa Barbara. She also wanted in the worst way to get off cable and onto network, and she figured the only way she could do it, considering the not-too-well-kept secret of her sexual orientation, was to be the hard-charging bitch of the airwaves. She worked non-stop, was mean as a snake, tapped off-the-wall and sometimes surprisingly reliable sources, and was probably less inaccurate than anyone else J.J. ever met on the beat, which he guessed fell into the category of left-handed compliment. Maurice Dodd's objection over allowing *Courthouse Square* into the courtroom made an implicit point that J.J. thought did not need to be made: He was as dumb as a post, as well as adamantine, and the proof of it was that he had antagonized Tracy from the get-go, not something you want to do with a trial judge, however open-and-shut the case may appear to be. "My name is Tracy, not Ito, Mr. Dodd," Ellen told him in open court, as reported in both the Cap City *Herald* and the Kiowa *Times-Ledger,* "and it would be your advantage to remember that."

"I beg the court's pardon" is what Maurice should have said, but he didn't, because he was too thick to realize that a judge might not wish, even inferentially, to be compared with Lance Ito. The antagonism of the judge would more than counteract the sympathy he received from his empty sleeve. "No bargains, no deals," he told *The New York Times.* Another dumb thing. "We'll do what we have to do" is what he should have said. But then Maurice isn't asking your advice, is he? J.J. said to himself. The fact was, he didn't think the case against Gover and Lajoie was all that hot. There were no witnesses, the gun that had blown a hole in the back of Edgar Parlance's head hadn't been found, nor the pliers that ripped out his tongue and peeled the skin from his thighs. J.J. ran over all the arguments in his mind. Never publicly. He would never do anything that would seem to undercut Maurice Dodd. Who was looking for any reason to complain to the Worm. No word. No gesture. It's going well, he told Poppy when she called. Maurice is doing a bang-up job. "Bang-up" was not a word he normally used. He's putting his ducks in a row. Putting his ducks in a row, Allie had said in elaborate disbelief.

There're too many pieces missing, Allie said. He needs to cut a deal. Zip it, J.J. said. Have one of them roll over on the other, Allie continued as if he had not spoken. Take the dime. I said zip it, J.J. repeated. Still, he thought, it's a case I'd rather prosecute than defend. A jury would be looking to convict, especially with all the press coverage, and with the jurors' chance for their fifteen minutes of celebrity, all those long thoughts and softball questions on the steps of the Loomis County Courthouse. But Allie was right. It would have been easier to prosecute if one of the accused flipped and testified against his partner. LWOPP for the flipper, the death penalty for the other. The likeliest to rat was Gover, since it was Lajoie's pickup with its FUCK THE TELEPHONE COMPANY bumper sticker that the witness had seen making tracks down

County Road 21 outside of Regent the night of the murder. Gover was a sweetheart, a hyperactive slow learner who would use whatever weapon he could get his hands on—hammer, pencil, knife—to beat up and injure other children in school. He had done one-to-three for road rage after he got drunk, beat up his girlfriend, threw her and her daughter (not by him) out of the car, and drove off. Then he had decided to pound on her again, backed up full speed, and ran over the little girl. She was fifteen months old.

A tragic accident was the defense his court-appointed lawyer put forward.

Involuntary manslaughter the jury ruled.

Three years.

IN THE DISTRICT COURT OF LOOMIS COUNTY, SOUTH MIDLAND

A G R E E M E N T

(1) The State of South Midland agrees not to pursue the death penalty at the sentencing of Bryant William Gover. The State will not present any evidence of any aggravating circumstances in connection with Mr. Gover's sentencing.

(2) All other pending charges against Mr. Gover will be dismissed without prejudice and will not be refiled except in the event of noncompliance with this agreement.

(3) Mr. Gover will agree to testify against Duane NMI Lajoie when requested to do so by the State. He will give complete and truthful testimony and answer all prosecution inquiries to the best of his ability.

(4) Bryant William Gover will be sentenced for the killing after the sentencing of Duane NMI Lajoie.

(5) For the safety of the Defendant and as soon as is practicable, the State of South Midland will assist and make all reasonable efforts to have Mr. Gover transferred to an institution in another state.

Maurice Dodd was defensive about the plea deal he gave Bryant Gover. LWOPP was "no bargain," he told the Kiowa *Times-Ledger*. "Life without possibility of parole is a life without sunlight, a life without hope," he told the Cap City *Herald*. "If that's your idea of a deal, it's not mine," he told Alicia Barbara. "Are we a little testy?" she had retorted live on *Courthouse Square*. "Mr. Gover's testimony is going to strap Duane Lajoie into the electric chair, and I will be there to applaud," Maurice told Channel 3, Channel 8, CNN, MSNBC, Fox News, and *The New York Times*.

Except he would not be there to applaud.

Dodd Death Raises Stakes in Lajoie Trial

By ALICIA BARBARA

WEB POSTED 16:42 CDT

Capital City, SM (Courthouse Square)—South Midland Attorney General Jerrold ("Gerry") Wormwold will be the principal speaker Friday at the funeral of Maurice Dodd, the career prosecutor in the Attorney General's office who died suddenly yesterday of anaphylactic shock after being stung by a bee.

Dodd, 57, was scheduled to present the state's case against Duane Lajoie, the ex-convict accused of murdering Edgar Parlance in a grisly dismemberment killing that riveted the nation last Thanksgiving weekend.

Dodd was an avid gardener, in spite of having lost an arm in the Vietnam War, and cultivated roses in a backyard greenhouse at his home here.

His wife, Ana, said he had never been allergic to bee stings prior to this incident.

Anaphylactic shock closes the air passages and can cause cardiovascular collapse if not treated immediately with antitoxins. When Dodd did not appear for dinner, his wife went to the greenhouse, where she found her husband lying unconscious.

Paramedics said Dodd was dead on arrival at University Hospital.

The chief witness against Lajoie is expected to be Bryant Gover, who was with him the night of the Parlance murder. In a plea deal negotiated by Dodd, Gover will escape the death penalty in return for his testimony. Sources close to the case say that Gover will claim that Lajoie was solely responsible for the murder and threatened to kill him if he did not participate.

Gover's provisional sentence of life without the possibility of parole—or LWOPP, as it is known in legal circles—is contingent on his not recanting the story he told Dodd and co-prosecutor Patsy Feiffer. If he recants, the state can ask the judge to reopen the penalty phase of his case.

Final sentencing will be delayed until the conclusion of the Lajoie trial to ensure that Gover satisfies the terms of his sentencing agreement.

Wormwold has not indicated whom he will appoint to replace Dodd as lead prosecutor. The most likely candidate is Deputy Attorney General J.J. McClure. McClure's wife, Congresswoman Sonora ("Poppy") McClure, is expected to challenge Wormwold for the Republican gubernatorial nomination this summer.

The rivalry between the two prospective political candidates complicates Wormwold's choice, since he passed over prosecutor McClure when the case was first filed.

Wormwold denied that political considerations influenced his choice of Dodd.

"We'll do what we have to do," J.J. McClure told Alicia Barbara on the *Courthouse Square Nightly Wrap-up,* when she asked what facts not currently known he might present in the state's case against Duane Lajoie.

PART FOUR

Chapter One

There is always a moment when, even if doubt is not entirely laid away, you go with your instinct.

A moment usually inconsequential, except that it remains glued to your memory.

This was that moment with Teresa.

That day early in February when we first met.

Remember earlier when I said I had lost four front teeth playing rugby back in my days in the A.G.'s office. Establishing my butch credentials. I had a bridge made, and after it was installed I discovered I could use the bridge to some effect with strangers, or when I was examining or cross-examining witnesses. I would snap it out with my tongue, balance it on my lower lip, and after a moment or so push it back into place. I wanted to see how people reacted to the gap in my mouth, whether they looked away or went off message on whatever story they were trying to spin.

Of course I did it to Teresa.

She did not take her eyes off me.

I waited.

"Bad dentistry?" she said finally. "Or a stagnant genetic pool?"

"I think he should fry," I said.

"You don't equivocate."

"He skinned somebody alive. That takes work. You really have to mean it. It's not like you lose your temper and clip somebody. It's not like you stick up a 7-Eleven or jack a car and get scared and start blasting. It's not like you knock up someone, you've already got a wife, maybe two, you never got divorced, what's the big deal about bigamy, you think whacking the new girl will solve the problem. It's not even you want to see what it feels like, or if it gives you wood." I was trying too hard, and she knew it, but she played along, taking in every word, as if committing them to memory. Slow down. "Skinning someone alive is hard work. These two weren't vascular surgeons, they didn't go to fucking medical school." I was over the top again. "You slice the skin around the thighs with a box cutter or whatever they used, then you pull it away with pliers, you work up a pretty good sweat. Edgar Parlance *en brochette,* is that what they had in mind? The world will be a better place without Duane Lajoie."

"Then you don't want to get involved?"

"I didn't say that."

"You just want to make your feelings known."

"Look. I was a prosecutor for sixteen years. The last case I did was an eighty-six-year-old woman who wrapped her twin sister's head in a plastic garbage bag. The sister was incontinent. She peed in the bed they shared. Nobody wanted to do it. 'The old lady's going to cool, cut her some slack, nobody likes to have someone piss on their leg.' The slack I cut her was twenty-five-to-life. Meaning she would've been one hundred and eleven if she served the full ticket. She died in the ambulance taking her from the courthouse to the prison ward at Osceola County Hospital."

She was not interested. "Why'd you get fired?"

"I didn't get fired."

"Excuse me, you quit." She waited. "Why?"

"I was looking for new opportunities. New situations. A chance to meet new people."

"You don't have an attitude deficit, do you?"

"Never been accused of it, no."

"That's what I heard."

"Then I came highly recommended?"

"Recommended."

"By whom?"

She ignored the question. "In my job, my last job . . ."

"The one *you* quit."

"Resigned."

" 'After eight fulfilling years.' That was in your statement."

The noncommittal stare.

"I found it on the Net. After you called." My way of telling Teresa Kean that I had a few cards of my own. "You're a big ticket on the Net. A lot of hits. The hundred best this, the fifty best that. Women of the bar. Best person to sit next to at another boring Washington dinner party. That's a recommendation to put in your personnel folder. Margaret Dudley's best pal. I guess you never sat home alone with a BLT and a Bud Lite."

"You guess wrong."

"So you had those eight fulfilling years, and you wanted to explore new opportunities too, right?"

She did not bite. All business. "When I had that job, I naturally had occasion to talk to lawyers all over the country."

"And my name came up."

"You had a problem with the attorney general."

"I didn't have a problem with the Worm. The Worm had a problem with me."

"Because you're gay."

"Queer. Gay's a comfortable word straight people use. It makes them feel a little less uncomfortable about something they would never admit makes them uncomfortable."

"You have any other opinions you want to share?"

"*The Godfather.*"

"Whose godfather?"

"Marlon Brando. Vito Corleone. Al Pacino. Michael Corleone. That *Godfather.* Sentimental crap. A Mafia *Gone with the Wind.*"

She waited to see where this would lead.

"Vito and Michael," I said. "Tragic gumbahs. An oxymoron."

A beat. "That's original."

"Fredo and Sonny, on the other hand, they're the genuine articles. One's a fink, the other's a psychopath."

Teresa Kean's gaze was guarded, wary. You could almost hear the tumblers in her brain clicking, searching for the combination. She was dressed with the kind of simplicity that only a great deal of money could buy. The same with her makeup. No jewelry. Her hair was pulled back, tinted auburny, except for a hint of gray at both temples. Vain, but not too. Pretty, but not threateningly so. "And that, I guess," she said finally, "brings us back to Bryant Gover and Duane Lajoie."

She had insisted on seeing me in my office in the Law Building across the street from the Capital City Courthouse. The Law Building is not an edifice that immediately summons the phrase "the majesty of the law." Eight stories of dirty white brick, some of which have popped out and shattered on the setback balconies; one effect is to make the balcony look like a stale wedding cake under attack by rodents. There is a 24-hour Kinko's in the lobby, the three rickety elevators are prone to getting stuck between the floors, sometimes for five minutes, sometimes for five hours, and the building directory lists a doubtful assemblage of bail bondsmen, PIs, steno services, bucket shops, knockdown tax consultants, ambulance chasers, has-beens and never-will-bes. Murray Lubin and I were the best lawyers in the building, in the sense that we got the more difficult court-assigned cases. This was because the judges in Superior Court, most of them politically connected apparatchiks, at the least recognized a degree of professional competence, and, in the interest of what they liked to call justice, nominated us to defend the indefensible. The real lawyers in Capital City, in other words those not sentenced to the ghetto of the criminal courts, resided in the semi-skyscrapers on Rhino Plaza, four blocks farther downtown, in the AgriCorp Building and the Continental Corn Tower, offices with thirty partners and paneled conference rooms and a law library with the leather-bound decisions of the South Midland Supreme Court, as if those decisions were worth collecting, offices with paralegals and notary publics and crosscut shredders and clients absent tattoos and needle tracks on their arms, clients who only wanted to circumvent the tax statutes and the realty laws. My office in the Law Building was the nondescript workstation of a single practitioner, with access to the public men's room and a secretary I shared with three other attorneys on the same corridor. For the common touch, I kept two dog-eared John Grisham paperbacks, neither of which I had actually read, prominently displayed in the metal book-shelves, each flecked with Post-its that seemed to vouch for my legal bona fides; this was a venue where Grisham carried more legal weight than Benjamin Cardozo, my fellow Jew. The only thing of value, besides myself, was a partner's desk, circa 1850, that I had found at a rummage sale, listed at forty dollars. Its provenance, no less suspect than anything else in this part of the world, was that it had come across the plains in a Conestoga wagon, and then been badly burned in an Indian raid. For a few hundred dollars I had it refinished and releathered, and I had developed a genuine affection for it. A law school acquaintance now specializing in wills and inter vivos trusts in the Continental Corn Tower had offered to "take it off my hands for six thou," his too-casual words betraying the hustler's intent, but I had already had it appraised for twice that. I think he had convinced himself that I would jump at the deal because he thought I could use the money in my downscaled post-A.G. phase and in the environment where I now practiced. I did not actually tell him to fuck off, but that was the subtext, and it was clearly understood.

I knew why Teresa wanted to meet me there. She wanted to be in charge, and if our meeting did not go well, the site allowed a quick getaway, don't call me, I'll call you, a pleasure to meet you, and she would be gone, the faint lingering smell of Fracas the only indication that she had been there, diluting the smell of stale urine that seemed to permeate the rest of the building. It was Murray Lubin who told me that she had been making inquiries. She needs someone who knows his way around the courts here, Murray had said, knows the names and numbers of all the players, and where the bodies are buried; I told her you were the only one, especially about where the bodies are buried, the best man in the state. Murray did not expect me to believe that, and I didn't. Murray would have first tried to promote himself into the job; it was a trope with him. He would have licked the soles of Teresa Kean's shoes to get involved with the Lajoie case, would have done it for free just to get the ear of the big-time national crime reporters, not to mention daily face time with Alicia Barbara, who had rented four rooms at the Lovat Hotel in Regent for herself and her crew.

I, on the other hand, claimed not to be particularly interested. Or so I tried to convince myself in the event that I was left only with that lingering scent of Fracas. I was not willing to admit how much I wanted to get back into the game, even on what I knew was the wrong side. There was a premonition of something else, something I was able to sort out only in retrospect. It was the way the rich seam of chance winds its inevitable labyrinthine way under the rough terrain of the everyday. Think of it—a bee sting and a myocardial infarction. If one or the other had not occurred—if Maurice Dodd had not been communing with his hybrid musks in a backyard Capital City greenhouse or if John Broderick's clogged left anterior descending artery had not at a particular moment malfunctioned in a specific Washington bedroom—none of what happened would have happened. Proof again that our lives are funded by the coinage of coincidence.

Chapter Two

Let's do the math on the blood relationship between Alice Todt, aka Carlyle, and Duane Lajoie.

Her half brother. The half brother Alice Todt, aka Carlyle, said she didn't know she had. Until that day her mother said she had to help her half brother Duane out. Her mother said her half brother Duane was being defended by a Zulu. Or whatever they call themselves now. The Zulu she was talking about was Earle Lincoln.

I had taught Earle Lincoln at Osceola Community College of Law. Tutored him when he finally passed the bar. At age thirty-nine. On his fifth try. BARTENDER PASSES BAR was the way the weekly newspaper in Questa headlined the event. Earle Lincoln still tended bar at night in Questa. To pay the rent. And child support. And alimony to two former wives. I failed to tell him during our teacher-student relationship that he had more future tapping kegs than he had as a lawyer. Duane Lajoie was his fourth client. The other three had been DUIs. All found guilty.

On the subject of Alice Todt's mother. Also the mother of Duane Lajoie.

There's a lot to assimilate here. Josefa Carmody Todt Barr Sledge Das. Three husbands followed by a religious rebirth. She was now a disciple of Roshi Gurjanwaia. With a new name. Shehnaz Das. And a new enthusiasm. The Gurjanwaia Method of Meditation.

Shehnaz Das ran seminars on the Gurjanwaia Method of Meditation (always referred to by its full name) at Amritsar University of Mental

Purification in Divide County, North Dakota. As Josefa Sledge (her third husband was Conway Sledge, a part-time pimp and bookmaker), she had taken a voyage of personal exploration to the Indian subcontinent where at Varanasi she bathed in the Ganges and nearly died of dysentery. Upon her return to South Midland, she left Conway Sledge, changed her name to Shehnaz Das, and dedicated her life to Roshi Gurjanwaia. Shehnaz Das claimed that the dysentery she had picked up in the Ganges had purged her body and mind of all their evils.

The evils possessing Josefa Carmody Todt Barr Sledge, before she became Shehnaz Das, had not been in short supply.

Allie Vasquez had checked her out. For J.J., of course. I had asked her to bring me up to speed after Murray Lubin told me about Teresa's inquiries. Allie showed me the discovery, and I spent half the night copying it at the Kinko's downstairs. Allie was waiting for me outside Kinko's at five-thirty. She took the file and got into her car without a word. I had little doubt that J.J. knew I was on her private distribution list. At some point it might become useful to him. Give him the edge he was always looking for.

Shehnaz Das was still only thirty-five, Allie said.

Josefa Carmody Todt Barr Sledge Das had led a full life.

She had exploded into puberty as part of a floating hegemony of rootless children, the flotsam of feckless parents and random liaisons, blowing through the underside of Kiowa and Cap City, in and out of crash pads of friends and boyfriends, a week here, three days there. Human repos in an environment where dreams were the currency of hope.

Josefa Carmody found herself pregnant and alone at thirteen. On her fourteenth birthday, she gave birth to a premature three-pound-eleven-ounce son at St. Fintan of Cloneagh Foundling Hospital in Halloween County, just across the Midlandia Wash from Kiowa. The baby's umbilical cord was wrapped around its neck, so that the oxygen supply to its brain was cut off until the emergency room staff could disentangle it. Josefa Carmody told the admitting Sister of Mercy at St. Fintan's that the father of her son could be one of three possibilities, none of whom she could identify with any degree of certainty. The admitting nun told Josefa Carmody that a good home would be found for her son, and that she could, if she wished, give the boy a Christian name, as it was possible that some time might pass before proper foster parents could be located, since special children needed special parents. Josefa Carmody said she would like him called Duane, and when the nun asked if any of the possible fathers might be named Duane, Josefa Carmody said no, Duane Box was the lead singer of an Amarillo rock group called Duane & The Dudes that she had heard on WROK, "The Voice of Rock in Rhino Land." Josefa Carmody thought Duane had a cool sound.

The nun's name was Sister Alice Faith. Last name Maguire. Sister Alice Faith did not tell Josefa Carmody that the oxygen deprivation endured by her son at birth had perhaps left him brain-damaged, which was why he fell into the category of special child.

Sister Alice Faith said that Saint Faith was the patron saint of prisoners.

Josefa Carmody said that if she ever had a daughter she would name her Alice Faith. Because Sister Alice Faith had been so much nicer to her than her own bitch mother had ever been. Alice Faith Todt was born three years later. Her putative father was Karil Todt, aka Bruiser Todt.

Bruiser Todt was a long-haul driver who long-hauled himself out of Josefa Todt's life shortly after the child who carried his surname was born, and after laying a bruising on his wife, who was ten weeks pregnant when they got married.

Bruiser Todt had only known Josefa Carmody five days when they exchanged their wedding vows at Feathers, the keno bar on the Chippewa reservation in Chippewa County where she worked as a waitress and a keno runner, sticking whatever tips she received down between her pushed-up tits, and where she was available when she was off the clock, freelance, hire your own lawyer if Chippewa County vice moved in, which they only did if someone pulled a blade.

Bruiser Todt said an eight-pound-nine-ounce baby did not compute as premature.

Seventeen years later, terminally ill with pancreatic cancer, Sister Alice Faith wrote to Josefa Carmody, now Shehnaz Das. An attendant with dreadlocks in the hospice in Duluth where Sister Alice Faith was waiting to die had searched and found Josefa Carmody's latest name and last known address on the Internet as a way of perfecting his computer skills, in the hope that said skills would offer the opportunity of a better job than cleaning up the drool, vomit, and excretions of old people. With death so near, Sister Alice Faith no longer felt constrained by the strictures of silence she had sworn to observe. In her letter, she said she had never forgotten the frightened little girl who on her fourteenth birthday gave birth to a baby boy she named Duane. When Duane was four, Sister Alice Faith wrote, he had been placed in the care of a French-Canadian family named Lajoie in Albion County, and the Lajoies had subsequently adopted him. She had hoped, Sister Alice Faith wrote, that Duane, special child that he was, would lead an exemplary Christian life.

But apparently he had not.

His adoptive parents weren't much of a help, Allie Vasquez reported.

They were killed in a hunting accident when Duane was eight. Pascal Lajoie, called Pete, shot his wife Mercury in the back of the head with a .22-caliber CZ 452 Deluxe while hunting white-tailed deer out of season. Pete said it was an accident, one of the deer had spooked Mercury, she had stood up just as he was trying to take the deer down, but the Albion County sheriffs said that until somebody proved different they were calling this one a homicide. Mercury, it seems, was a regular at the Albion County Emergency Room, broken ribs, broken cheekbone, household accidents, she said, she was always falling down the stairs to the root cellar. Little Duane, or Dummy Duane, as his father called him, was another frequent visitor to County Emergency, his list of injuries including a broken wrist, a broken pelvis, each injury credited to that root cellar again, although the root cellar did not seem to explain the cigarette burns on his back and arms. Pete said he'd plead to hunting deer out of season, that was clear enough, but he was no damn murderer, and he grabbed the CZ 452 Deluxe from a deputy, and put it in his mouth.

Oh, hell, call it a hunting accident, Lew Lodge, the Albion County sheriff, said. Pete shot himself out of grief, anyone would. Too much paperwork the other way. Duane went to a foster home. He lived in twelve foster homes in all. He ran away from every one. When he was eleven, a juvenile court declared him uncontrollable, and he became a ward of the state.

Sister Alice Faith Maguire died before her letter to Josefa Carmody was delivered.

Duane Lajoie had the same birthday as Josefa Carmody Todt Barr Sledge Das.

Shehnaz Das telephoned her daughter.

He looks like you, she told her daughter Carlyle. He has a space between his front teeth. Just like you. Just like me. My little boy Duane wouldn't do anything like that. You got to help your brother Duane. What do you mean, you never knew you had a brother Duane? I was trying to give you a chance in life. You were my number one priority. That doesn't mean I forgot little Duane. Who got you that job modeling at Teen Town? All that time you spent ditching school and going to Rhino Mall, you finally made it pay off because I knew Denise what's-her-face at Teen Town. You remember the way you were when Waylon and Kile got killed? You were hysterical. Waylon was the love of your life, you think I didn't know you and him were doing it? I washed your panties, I washed your jeans, I know what that stuff is, he must've done a bucketful. The night before he died, you don't think I knew what you and him were doing back there? I never yet been in a trailer that was sound-proofed, and I have lived in more trailers than boys you've done it with. Who dragged you down to the Three V traveling show, you said you were so sad you wouldn't go, you missed Waylon, you missed Kile, and I said they were dead and you had a life to lead, well, we know what happened, and look where you are today, and where Waylon and Kile are, you tell me who is better off, and it is because of me and Denise what's-her-name, and now you won't help your brother Duane, he's got some Zulu lawyer from Questa, not even Regent or Cap City, look at the picture I sent you and tell me if that's not your brother.

Chapter Three

Carlyle called Martha Buick.

Marty Buick called Teresa Kean in Sagaponack.

I haven't been in a courtroom in five years, Teresa Kean said. I haven't done a murder trial in nearly eight.

She wants you. No one else. You.

Marty, I've been doing victims' rights. I can't just up and defend a murderer. And not just any murderer.

Oh. How about a rapist?

Give it a rest.

Tell me what you're going to do.

I've got options.

Which are?

The civil side. Taxes.

Depreciation. Book-value depletion. 8-Ks. Offshore partnerships. Asset redeployment. Monetization.

Okay, so you know all the terms.

I run my own company.

The only reason you're calling me is because she fired you.

And she hired me back.

And this is the sort of thing you'd do to keep her?

Yes.

So you don't get fired again.

I'm her agent.

You're my friend.

It'll bring you back into the world, Teresa.

I haven't left the world. I like it out here.

Last week you told me you were thinking of screwing the guy who plowed the driveway. The same guy who mows our lawn in the summer and bags the leaves in the fall.

Well, I didn't. He can keep on mowing your lawn.

The week before it was the bag boy at the market. He was thirteen.

He was six feet five. How was I to know he was only thirteen?

His voice hasn't changed.

All right. I should've noticed. Anyway. I'm working on the book. It's going well.

How far along are you?

Outlining. Making notes. I'll probably start writing next week.

What're you going to call it? *Not Just Another Lawyer's Memoir?*

Teresa hung up. A moment later she dialed Martha Buick's private number. Marty, she said, why does she want me?

Because you told her that when she was twenty no one was going to remember her.

Tell her I'll talk to her.

The picture was a mug shot, Teresa Kean told Max Cline. Full face, right and left profiles.

What an awful picture, Carlyle had said. I mean, maybe you could Sytex it.

Alex said the guy who shot it shouldn't be allowed to hold a camera, Carlyle had said.

"Duane" is so my mother, Carlyle said. Why couldn't she call him Matthew? Or Jason? Or Bret?

At least she didn't call him Mohandas, Carlyle said. Like that Gandhi guy who wore the dress. You know. The one that Donna Karan copied.

It might be cool, Carlyle said after some consideration.

I suppose then I'd have to meet this guy, Carlyle said then. Duane.

Alex said maybe we would work in a shoot, Carlyle said.

A coffee-table book, Carlyle said. Me at my brother's trial. Black and white, no color. Black and white gives it a mood. Full-page bleed into the gutter, sprockets for reality. Grease-pencil cropping instructions. I mean, like you are fucking *there.*

Maybe I could have a sty in my eye, Carlyle said. Like to show the strain at the trial, my life's not all that shallow glamour shit.

Alex said don't give up the motion-picture rights, Carlyle said.

Shehnaz Das is such a lame name, Carlyle said.

"Alex is the photographer?"

"Quintero."

"Is she really that awful?"

"She's interesting in a way."

Nothing more volunteered. I realize now that why Carlyle was interesting to Teresa at that point was still only an instinct, a shimmer, perhaps even a sense of foreboding. It took me a long time to pick up what it was, and even now I am not sure I ever did. An educated guess is the closest I can come. With, God help me, some input from Stanley.

"Carlyle says Duane has a girlfriend," Teresa said.

"Then she's checking in with the folks back home?"

"Almost daily."

Of course she would. There was nothing more satisfying than the return of the native. I hoped her interest level would be as transitory as that of any other self-absorbed teen. If not I suspected we would have a hard time keeping her on a leash. A suspicion that unfortunately proved all too prescient.

"Carlyle says she's seventeen, she's fat, and she has zits. She also has a son she claims is Duane's. Carlyle says it's not."

"The girlfriend's name is Merle Orvis." I took an envelope from my desk and slid it across to her. Inside was a set of color Xeroxes, copies of Polaroid snapshots Merle Orvis had tried to send to Duane Lajoie at the Capital City Correctional Center, where he was undergoing psychiatric observation. The hacks at the CCCC had confiscated the pictures and sent them to the A.G.'s office. Allie had passed me copies. "She's actually eighteen, she is fat, she does have zits, and the kid is almost three. He's called Boy. He's also half black. Which lets Duane off the hook."

Teresa examined the pictures. Merle Orvis naked on a sheet doing herself with her finger. With a dildo. With a banana. There was a small boy lying naked on the corner of the sheet, which seemed to have some shit on it. Teresa replaced the snapshots in the envelope and handed them back. "How did you come by these?"

"A friend."

"A useful friend to have." She didn't press it further. When the time came, I would tell her about Allie, but at that point in the preliminaries we both understood it was not yet a done deal, we were still feeling each other out, it might still go south. She also refrained from asking who took the pictures. Considering what I now know about Teresa, it would be surprising if the unexpected exposure to this primitive home pornography had not bared some residual uneasiness about the disposition of the film and video library maintained by her late second ex-husband.

That was later. And not the course I was on that morning. That morning I was in my former prosecutor mode. "Are you doing this for the money?"

It was as if I asked her what time it was. "No."

"I've heard five hundred K."

"Less the ten I gave to Earle Lincoln."

"That's more than Earle's seen in a lifetime. Or will ever see."

"Less expenses. That leaves about four hundred."

"What were you planning to offer me?"

"What do you want? Half? More?"

It was as if money was of no interest to her. There was something deep down that I did not yet understand, something I am now quite sure that Teresa did not understand either. Something it took me a long time to dig out. I stalled. "If it wasn't for the death penalty, this wouldn't be such a big deal."

"Right."

I tried again. "You think Alice Todt would hire you if her brother Duane was only up for rape or armed robbery or vehicular homicide?"

"No."

I felt as if I were talking to myself. And could not stop. "Not a chance. No coffee-table book in that. Who needs a case like this? It takes so much time it destroys your private practice . . ." Her eyes seemed fixed on the two copies of John Grisham in my aluminum bookcases. So much for the exigency and profitability of my private practice. I plunged on. ". . . he's going to be found guilty anyway, we both know that, so then there's a penalty phase, death or LWOPP, that's another chunk of time, you have to explain away his sheet, you have checked his sheet, haven't you?"

She would not be insulted. "Yes, Mr. Cline, I have checked his sheet."

"Arson, assault . . ." There was something about her. I was blustering.

She picked up the litany. "Dealing. Pimping. Burglary . . ."

I persisted, though she had obviously studied Duane Lajoie's copious rap sheet as assiduously as I had. "Auto theft in Oklahoma. Hijacked an eighteen-wheeler, that takes doing."

"He rolled it over on Interstate 35, that didn't."

"And landed it on top of a VW van."

"Full of German tourists." Her voice was mild. "I wonder what they were doing in Oklahoma." She caught the look of surprise on my face. "The German tour group. They were from Düsseldorf."

The seemingly nonresponsive comment from a totally different direction was something I would come to expect from Teresa. I don't think it was entirely conscious—notice the qualification of "entirely"—but it served the useful purpose of deflecting hostility and lowering the temperature. J.J. had the same ability. It might have been one of the things that put them on the same wavelength. Not that there weren't others. That said, it was disconcerting in her at first until I got used to it. And even later, after I learned how to translate. I thought I knew her, but I was never truly fluent in her many internal languages.

I considered the Düsseldorfers. "I don't think they were figuring on spending the next three or four months mending their bones in the Okmulgee County Hospital in Henryetta."

She was of course by now off the Germans. "Why do you steal an eighteen-wheeler?"

This at least was familiar ground. "Because it was something to steal."

"A whim."

"He did thirteen months in McAlester. That's a tough joint for a whim."

She shrugged. "Most prisons are."

We stared at each other across the desk, a couple of chess players plotting the next move.

"Look," I said finally. "A successful defense on this one means LWOPP, you don't get it, then there's an automatic appeal, you get fired, the new appellate attorney, some pro bono guy from a civil firm downtown who wears hundred-dollar suspenders says you gave your client incompetent representation, and that and that alone is why Duane Lajoie got the death penalty."

That cool look. As if I was telling her something she didn't already know. "Right."

"For that little fuck. He's been in deep shit since seventh, eighth grade. At Johnny Page Junior High School in Kiowa. You know who Johnny Page is?"

She looked as if she did not care who Johnny Page was, but was too polite to yawn.

"A Rhino wide receiver and punt returner. All-American. Heisman finalist. That's who they name high schools after in this state."

That almost-smile of hers I would come to know so well. She was letting me ramble. "Eighth grade your boy shows up two days. That's it. Two days. Not even two whole days. The first day he hits an English teacher, a woman, she wants him to take a reading test, so he belts her and gets suspended for the rest of the term. Then the first day of the winter term, back to school, Welcome back, Kotter. Except there's this gang bang in a stairwell. Duane, four buddies, and a retard ninth-grader. Black. Tits like watermelons. They stuck a broomstick up her vagina. They're juveniles, so the court record is sealed, but I've still got friends over there, and I got a copy of the transcript. Granted my knowledge of what women want is not encyclopedic, but I'd bet most women would hesitate to put a broomstick at the top of the charts when it comes to foreign objects they would like introduced into their person. It was consensual, they all say. The juvie judge, he says there are inconsistencies in the retard's story, he finds for the defendants. My own feeling is a broomstick might lead to inconsistencies, but what do I know. Duane gets thrown out of school again, big deal, that's all he wanted anyway. Never went to school again."

She did not take her eyes off me, even as she eased the skin on her face back toward her ears. It was that thing I had often seen women of a certain age do, a subliminal sense that a wrinkle might be taking shape, push it away until lotions and potions and balms could be applied and the telltale signs of encroaching years momentarily arrested.

"You know," I said slowly, "I never did a gang bang when I was a prosecutor. There was one question I always wanted to ask the fourth guy or the fifth or sixth or seventh guy who popped his wad in her. I wanted to get right in his face, nose to nose, and I wanted to say What was it like being last in line? A little gooey? A little slippery?"

Teresa reached over the side of her chair and picked up her bag. It was black and braided, probably a thousand dollars' worth of leather.

"Am I boring you?"

"No. Just looking for some moisturizer."

"Meaning?"

"Meaning I'm going to stay awhile. I like watching the way your mind works. You know all the reasons you don't want to do this, and I want to hear them all, but I know—even if you make the most convincing case for not doing it, and so far your reasons are on the money—" She concentrated on unscrewing the cap on the small plastic jar of Visible Difference, then looked up. "But end of day, you're going to do it."

She was a quick study. She didn't back off. And of course she was right. I knew it was bad business ever to let the personal intervene in such a situation, but I knew it was a relationship that would work. I chose my words carefully. "I may have . . ."

My voice trailed off. She completed the sentence. "A foot in the door." When I hesitated, she said, "The foot that wants to kick the A.G."

I gave in. The nod said yes.

"And the foot outside the door?"

"I want to know why . . ." I hesitated as I never would have if I had been prosecuting. "I want to know why . . . *you* . . . are involved in this."

It was a logical thing to wonder. She had already been semi-anointed by the fame accruing even to those residing at the county line of the national political landscape, and been granted a visa into the green rooms of people in the loop. She was the voice of victims' rights, a not-inconsiderable portfolio for chatterers in the know. Then she agreed to defend Edgar Parlance's accused murderer. Her green room visa was canceled. She had sold out, her thirty pieces of silver a cashier's check for $500,000. Drawn on the ready reserves of a teenager. A teenager who had done a fashion shoot on Riker's Island. Yo, Carlyle.

It took a long time for me to find the answer to my question. There was never anything definitive. Her life was like a jigsaw puzzle with pieces spread all over the table. Occasionally she would say things, and I would add the new pieces to those already on the table, joining them together if they fit. I knew she had come to detest Washington, its self-regard and the indifference that people in the loop had for perceptions other than their own, but there were other more amiable places for her to go than Cap City. This was deliberate, she wanted to find out something, and it took a long time before I could intuit what it was.

Teresa never really did respond. She was not ready to admit why she chose to defend Duane Lajoie. If she even knew at that point. It was a simple reason, really. Once all the pieces were on the table.

They weren't yet.

"You're not going to answer?" I said finally.

She dropped the jar of moisturizer into her bag.

"Shit is coming down."

"I have an umbrella." As quietly as if she were talking about a spring shower. She stood up. She was too well bred to stretch after such a long sit, but years of exercise, I was sure with a trainer, had taught her to unkink her muscles in a ladylike way. "By the way. Carlyle's rented a big old place outside Regent. A ranch, she said. Owned by some cattle company up there."

"Down there."

"Down there then. She and Alex will stay there when they're in town. Plus her assistants. And his assistants. Gofers. Camera loaders. Technicians. Location scouts. Household help. Cook. The place must be huge. She suggested that . . ." It was as if it were a thought she wished not to suggest. ". . . that her legal team might like to stay there, too."

"Over my dead body."

She smiled. "I guess that means you're in."

PART FIVE

CHAPTER ONE

Fast-forward—J.J.'s dream:

Thinking of Emmett, dreaming of him. Emmett, Emmett, Emmett. Push me, Jamie, pushmepushmepushme. It never changes. I always do what he wants, my hand on his head, counting the seconds, going the limit, stretching the limit. At the last minute, I lift my hand. Always. And he shoots to the surface, gasping for air, laughing, this hysterical kid laughter. Do it again, Jamie, doitagaindoitagaindoitagain, running the words together. Then Walter looks up. Sitting in his wheelchair on the rise that sloped down to the dock and the pond, the brakes set, that floppy white Panama hat protecting his bald head from the sun, I used to wonder if I'd get bald, and that book in his lap.

It was always the same tattered paperback. About a barrister at the Old Bailey. Not Rumpole, just some old Brit like that. Black robe and periwig, M'Lord this, M'Lord that, can you imagine that? The most important case Walter ever handled was a farmer who sodomized a neighbor's ewe. That's what he called it. A ewe. To differentiate it from a ram, I suppose. He was always such a goddamn didact. It's funny what you remember. I mean, I still remember the farmer's name. Ed Snedd. I don't know why Walter even bothered to prosecute him. He wasn't the first farmer in Parker County to fuck a sheep. Kids used to do it to learn how. No, not me. Walter didn't even win the fucking case. The ewe wouldn't testify. Ed Snedd walked. The first thing he did was he dumped a truckful of sheep dip on Walter's driveway.

The dream, she said.

I put that goddamn paperback in his coffin. In his hand. *Barrington, Q.C.,* that was the book's title. It was a series. *Barrington Takes Silk,* that was another one. I tried to get a periwig, but the costume shops in Kiowa and Cap City didn't have any, and there wasn't time to order one. I don't know why I wanted it there, I don't think I had his best interests at heart.

The dream, she said again.

I found him. Sunday lunch with Walter and Emily. I'd make it maybe once a month or so. Actually less. Three times in the year before he died. It's a hike from Cap City to Hamlet. Two hundred fifty miles due west across that goddamn table of a plain, the speedometer nailed to ninety, not even a shiver; then the same two-fifty back. Three and a half hours there, three and a half hours home, it's a chunk out of the day when you have to be in court the next morning. No, that's not the real reason. I didn't even spend that much time in court, most everything was pleaded out. We just didn't have that much to say to each other. What do you have coming up? he'd say. That should be interesting. Don't get many hostage situations in Parker County. Keep your eye on the sparrow. He was always saying some asshole thing like that. What fucking sparrow?

The dream, she said a third time.

Always underdone roast chicken. Pink goddamn chicken. Is there anything worse than underdone chicken? Fifty-two Sundays a year. He'd go to the coop, pick the chicken out, and whack off its head with the hatchet he kept in the barn, then he'd bleed it, my mother would pluck it, and then undercook it. It was pink. Rare. Rare goddamn chicken.

You said that.

So I was there that Sunday. What do you have coming up? Don't have much conspiracy to commit securities fraud in Parker County. Keep your eye on the sparrow. The chicken was a triumph, Emily. As always. Jamie saw a sign driving down here, Emily. PROTECT BEEF—RUN OVER A CHICKEN. That's one way to protect our economy. You follow through on that, though, you could call it a violation of private property, seek redress, might even have a case unless the driver of the vehicle could prove it was an accident. I think I'll go down to the barn, Emily, rinse the blood of our lunch off the hatchet. Tends to rust, you don't rinse it off. You stay here, Jamie, entertain your mother, she loves it, you come to visit.

The dream, she repeated.

You want to watch the game, my mother said. What game? I say. There's always a game on Sunday, she says, I thought you might want to watch. No, I don't want to watch the game, I think I should be getting back. Well, then, she says, and I look at her and she looks at me, and then I heard the shot. Correction. We heard the shot. You better go down to the barn, she says. Very quiet. Matter-of-fact. No excitement. Your father is so careless sometimes. He's getting old, Jamie. (He's not even sixty, he's fifty-five, fifty-six, and she says he's getting old.) I'll go down and take a look, I say. And I walk out the door and out to the barn, walk, not run, as if I thought a car on the road had backfired, as if I had never heard a gunshot before. When I was a kid, I used to shoot at a fence-post with that old Colt, my hands were so small I could hardly reach the trigger, and it had such kick it gave me a bone bruise in my palm. Some days when it rains I can still feel that bruise. I got to the barn and there he was, in the wheelchair, his head leaning over into the tub where he kept the scrub brushes, as if he didn't want to splatter the blood, and here's the thing, before he did it he ran water over the axe he used to kill the chicken we had for lunch, scrubbed it clean with a wire brush, and then hung the axe on the nail over the sink where he kept it. First things first. That was Walter.

Finish the dream.

What dream?

About your brother.

Emmett.

Yes.

His voice was a monotone.

Pushme, Jamie, pushmepushmepushmepushme, the pier jutting into the pond, blocking Walter's view. Pushing him, holding him down, calibrating the seconds, five, six, seven, eight, nine, ten, all the way to fifteen, maybe twenty, twenty-five, even more, I can't remember, Emmett's capacity for holding his breath stretched to the extreme, and beyond. Then he was free, but he wasn't gasping for air, no laughing, no again-againagain, just floating there facedown, and Walter, stretched on the rise, he'd fallen out of the wheelchair, he was grabbing tufts of grass, trying to pull himself down to the dock, it's not your fault, Jamie, it's not your fault, he kept on saying.

CHAPTER TWO

From Teresa Kean's journal:

M flossed his teeth with L's pubic hair.

Teresa's journal was full of odd, quirky items like this, entries that seemed on superficial first reading to reveal only some ill humor or private sexual gratification, but as I read deeper into the journal and as my translation became more fluent, these random jottings would usually end up making a point, illuminating something or someone, and the someone was often herself. It was here that doubt would make an occasional appearance and the chilly conviction usually on display would melt a bit. It was as if she needed to get something down before she lost it, something she heard or overheard, or suddenly remembered about *M* or *L,* if those were indeed their initials, something that pinned one or the other, like a butterfly onto cork. Or perhaps not *M* or *L* at all, but an attitude of her own toward them or what they represented. I had a similar experience once when I was in the Caribbean with Stanley (my only trip ever in search of the sun). In the house we rented on a white sand beach inhabited almost exclusively by naked young men whose bums were as tanned as their shoulders and faces (Stanley's nirvana), I found a moldy copy of Scott Fitzgerald's notebooks, left I supposed by some previous weekly tenant (along with twenty-three ribbed and lubricated Trojan-Enz condoms and two tubes of K-Y jelly), and I was more absorbed by the cryptic shorthand of "Erskine Gwynn," say, or "The war had become second-page news," or "He has a dark future, he hates everything," than I was by the latherings of Bain de Soleil or the silver reflectors beaming rays evenly onto the faces of the sunbathers on the beach outside our perfect six-thousand-dollar-a-week bungalow (four of Stanley's, two of mine, although I did the cooking). As I burrowed through Teresa's laptop, I sometimes had that same sense that I had reading Fitzgerald's notes that I needed an Enigma machine to decode exactly what she had on her mind.

In this state, people drive a hundred miles to buy a pack of cigarettes at two in the morning.

That was the beginning.
Or the beginning of the end.
At any rate, it was the only thing she put down about the trip where she saw the twister west of Quantum and east of Higginson. I suppose you could say, if you believed in such things as signs or premonitions, that the twister west of Quantum and east of Higginson was a warning, an augury, bad weather ahead.
Or as it happened in this case, behind.

Jim Hogg.

Jim Hogg County, she had said suddenly one night.
It had come up during one of those interminable discussions we would have at the end of the day when we were sick of preparing the case we would present on behalf of Duane Lajoie.
And would talk about anything that came into our minds.
The town of Randado, she said. Population fifteen. My father said it sounded like the perfect place for witness protection. Nothing but chaparral and mesquite. Ninety percent of the county is of Mexican descent.
How did he ever hear about it?
I saw an item in the *Times*. The National Briefing. Maybe a paragraph. No more. Wire service. Some local case. Sex, drugs, rock and roll. Follow the money right into Randado, Jim Hogg County. The local sheriff bugged the newsroom of the weekly newspaper. You know where he put

the bug? In the Mr. Coffee machine. He didn't figure the machine would melt the bug.

The rat would have to speak Spanish, I said. As always, I was being practical.

So send a Spanish-speaking rat, Teresa had said.

Max is devious.

No Enigma needed there. I hadn't realized how much of an impression I had made on her. No, that's not true. I know I had, as she had made a similar impression on me. What I hadn't realized was how she tried to sort it out behind the RECIPES password. Although what she was actually trying to sort out was not so much me and our relationship, as herself. Computer therapy, Stanley had called it.

Absolutely.

I thought I was vetting him [*she wrote*], but of course he was vetting me as well. He had decided to do the case even before I walked into his office in the Law Building (there was something so creepy and Central European about that place, it was like the headquarters of the secret police, no one ever quite met your eyes, the men in the elevators all had dirty suits and oily hair and ties that had food stains), pending his opinion of whether I was an idiot or not. Max has a way of dividing the world into idiots, or most people, and those he reluctantly identifies as not idiots, a number he claimed he could count on seven of his ten fingers. I apparently passed, although I think it was touch and go for a while. I took the liberty, he said after we felt each other out, neither of us giving away much, of checking for any outstanding warrants against Alice Faith Todt.

In other words it had never occurred to him that I wouldn't ask him to be my co-counsel. He was already on the case. Behind his head, I could see a huge elephant balloon floating by his window, like one from the Macy's Thanksgiving Day Parade, part of a two-day Midwestern Republican Conference a block away at the Rhino Carlton-Plaza where I was staying. It gave me a moment to gather my thoughts.

Carlyle, I said carefully.

The warrants identify her as Alice Faith Todt.

That was Max's way of telling me there were warrants.

How many? I said. Or recall that I said. So much has happened that I am no longer sure of anything I said that far back. Or even that it matters. But I do know this. One of the first things Daddy taught me when I went to work in his law office was that unless you know the answer already, you never ask "Why?" It is a defensive question, and a defense counsel always has to be on the offensive. "Why" will come out soon enough. Asking Max why he had checked to see if Carlyle had any outstanding warrants would probably have meant he would have struck me from his magnificent seven.

Three, he said. A bad check and an illicit credit card in Osceola County, a DUI in Loomis County. All three would have run through Juvenile Court. But she never showed up for any court appearance. Went to New York City and made her fortune. She could be arrested, if she plans to be here, as I suppose she will, and if she wants to get a coffee-table book out of it, with a sty in her eye and all. She'd probably just get probation, a little community service, but you never know. People might like to make an example of a little rich girl who thinks she's better than the law. J.J.'s run it through the computer, bet on it.

Allie Vasquez was the reason I could bet on it, of course. I didn't know then that it was Max who had hired her when he was running the Homicide Bureau in the A.G.'s office, or that she was a night school law student of his. J.J. was her boss now. And then some. It seemed the definition of split loyalties.

J.J. used to work for me, Max said. He knows how it's done. Max was not really vain, but he did like to point out that J.J. had once been his number two and, implicitly, that had it not been for Gerry Wormwold, J.J. still would be. He doesn't want to embarrass Alice Todt, he said, but she starts blowing Carlyle smoke and getting her face all over the tube from the courthouse steps, schmoozing with Alicia Barbara, say, he'll try to neutralize her, and the best way he can do that is, and it will pain him to have to do it (Max was milking the moment), probably on those same courthouse steps, probably with that same Alicia Barbara, J.J.'s tight with her, is to say that she forged a two-hundred-dollar check at Food Treasure on the account of someone called Waylon Madden. Bought two liter bottles of Diet Pepsi, two bags of Fritos, and an economy-size package of Butterfinger Bits. Total $11.27. She took the balance in cash. One hundred eighty-eight dollars and seventy-three cents.

It was as if he were reciting the figures to a jury.

There's an additional little problem with Waylon, Max said, and this is where J.J. will really bust her chops if he can.

Is the problem with Waylon Madden that he was already dead when she went to Food Giant?

Food Treasure, Max corrected. He seemed a little disappointed that I was up to speed on Waylon Madden.

Right. He drove his car into a train with some other guy.

Kile Purdy, I said. Kile was driving. It was his car, actually. A 1986 Crown Vic. Lowered. Chrome mufflers. He hit a Burlington Northern grain train in Albion. They were both drunk.

Max's expression did not change as I ticked off the details of the final moments of Waylon Madden and Kile Purdy. My answer to the Diet Pepsi, the Fritos, and the economy-size bag of Butterfinger Bits. On points, the sparring between us was even.

They spooned the two of them out of the Crown Vic, Max said after a moment. Alice Todt was so twisted out of shape she headed off to the Food Treasure with Waylon's check.

I watched the elephant balloon bobbing up and down outside Max's window, while on the street below a brass band was playing what I later learned was the SMU Rhino fight song over and over.

No big deal, Max said. She makes restitution to Food Treasure. Publicly. On her website. You pay for your mistakes, she says. It makes you a better person, she says. A stronger person, she says. I bet she tips a waiter two hundred bucks at dinner.

He didn't know Carlyle. She claimed she never carried cash. She always had an assistant around to pay the bills and take care of the tips, ten percent, not a penny more. Your business is Carlyle, she told the people who worked for her. The people who worked for her watched her cash outlays, or they didn't work for her long.

She had grown up poor, and she was never going to be poor again. I am sure she thought of me as an employee, and I suppose I was. Except I made sure that her check had cleared before I took up the business of Carlyle.

Food Treasure funds a Reading Lab program statewide, Max said. It's their good work. She gives the Reading Lab ten computers. In memory of Edgar Parlance. The credit card beef will just disappear, she's Carlyle, it was an honor to have her use my Visa card, dude, she just borrowed it, man. The DUI nobody gives a shit about, they can't even get a Mothers Against Drunk Driving campaign going in this state, the neutralizer is neutralized, and now we've just got Duane Lajoie to deal with.

And Edgar Parlance.

He's dead, Max said. He's not our concern.

That was a stupid goddamn thing to say.
As it turned out.

CHAPTER THREE

Now I had an associate [*Teresa wrote, a later journal entry*], but the question was who was the associate, Max or me. The last few years I had spent not in a courtroom but on public forums or testifying before congressional committees or matching wits on those ideological gong shows with people like Poppy McClure or Lorna Dun or Mark Berquist, the youngest member of the Senate and pride of South Carolina, already being promoted as a future Republican candidate for president, in 2012, say, or 2016. It wasn't the life or death you have before a judge and jury, acquittal or prison, it wasn't even smart, it was just bitchery on parade, thirty minutes less commercials. Take Lorna Dun, of course always called Lorna Doone. She was the anchor of a nightly half hour, seven to seven-thirty, called *Fixed Bayonets*, and the name tells it all. It had the highest rating of any news discussion show on cable, mainly because of her. She was blond, she was always called beautiful by men, never women, she wore vinyl miniskirts, had a voice that would cut metal, and would say anything, especially if it was hurtful, innocence or irrelevance no defense. At Harvard she had been president of the *Crimson*, and in her column had outed the football captain, a black tight end and Rhodes Scholar candidate from Baton Rouge named Gaylord Gaines, "Lordy" everywhere on campus except in Lorna Dun's column in the *Crimson*, where he was always called "Gay" Gaines. She also gave out the name and address of the gym where he worked out in the Roxbury ghetto, a place called Buff & Buns. The private life of a public person was not put in a blind trust, Lorna liked to say, and if a football captain preferred to work out at Buff & Buns, his fans in the Harvard community had a right to know. Right to know was a big item with people like Lorna, except when someone claimed the right to know about them. I never had much trouble with her (or with Poppy McClure, who occasionally filled in as host of *Fixed Bayonets*). I had a quick tongue and I was able to keep my private life more or less private, at least until Jack Broderick died in my bedroom.

What I am trying to say is that for all my alleged confidence I wondered if I had been away too long, if I had become nothing more than an aging media bunny who could only cut it on *Fixed Bayonets* and not on a capital murder case with a defendant even my co-counsel thought should go to the electric chair. I hated to think what my father would have said about my failure to check out Carlyle's outstandings. It was almost the first thing he had me do when I passed the New York State bar exam and came to work for Kean & Kean. What's he got that will stick to him, Daddy would say in that staccato machine-gun voice of his, the big stuff will take care of itself, but the little stuff you miss now will come back to haunt you, Teresa. He would never admit it, but I think he liked having me there, liked teaching me the ropes.

He could be surprisingly indirect. Sometimes we'd take the afternoon off and slip into the multiplex near the office on Twelfth Street, usually to see a gangster movie or a newspaper movie or a courtroom movie. With a box of popcorn in his hand, he'd talk out loud to the screen, pointing out errors of procedure. It was like a postgraduate course in criminal law. Now what's wrong with that scene? he would say. I thought it worked, I whispered, because I always whispered in a movie theater, even if it was empty. As a movie it works, but I'm talking real life, Teresa, he would say patiently, loud enough that I hunched down in my seat so no one would know he was talking to me. But he did. Look, De Niro throws the wise guy into the trunk of the car, slams it shut, then *bang, bang, bang*, he shoots the bad guy through the trunk door, what do you think is going to happen? At that point I didn't care, but I didn't say it, I was just trying to be invisible. What's going to happen, he said, is the car's going to blow up, because the wise guy is in the trunk, and the trunk sits right on top of the gas tank, a bullet hits the tank, no more wise guy, no more car, no more De Niro, no more movie. I had to admit it made sense. And after a while I began to like these afternoons at the Twelfth Street multiplex, and began to pick up things before he did. The point of the exercise was not to be a smartass about some Hollywood movie, but to learn how to think fast on your feet, to look for the opening that will help you out. Mr. Director, there are two bodies on the front seat of that car, they have each been shot in the back of the head, but the car is a two-door coupe; where does the hit man hide until he shoots them in the back of the head and how does he crawl out of the back seat past the victims whose brains are now splashed all over the windshield and messing up the seat leather, you better get yourself a four-door sedan and reshoot the scene.

Very good, Teresa, my father would say, and offer me some popcorn, but it's too expensive to reshoot the scene just because some hotshot from Yale Law School says so.

It was his way of expressing approval, I thought at the time. But now I can't help wondering if those afternoons at the movies were more than just a time-out, if instead they weren't his own unique way of introducing me to, and preparing me for, the kind of life my real father had led, secrets that Daddy was sure that I would one day unravel on my own. I can't believe it was unconscious. He lived in the present, and his empathy for introspection or the subconscious was almost nonexistent. At trial he loved to shred the pretensions of expert psychiatric witnesses. What he liked to do was lay in things, markings, he called them, markings that he could return to in order to show a trail of connections. All you have to do is tell the jury a story, Teresa, remember to keep it simple, a Mob hitter would know better than to shoot someone stuffed in the trunk of a car. And if this marking ultimately led me via the circuitous way the mind worked to dwell on his relation-ship with Jacob King, I suspect all he would have said was, It's a good story, honey; follow the trail, go with it.

CHAPTER FOUR

I suggested that we drive down to Regent before we interviewed Duane Lajoie at the Correctional Center. We should talk to some people in Loomis County, I said, and see if we can get a better handle on our client than we have now. Allie had told me he was threatening to gut Bryant Gover for dealing him out, not an immediate or likely eventuality since the Department of Corrections had placed Gover in the maximum-security wing at Durango Avenue, on the other side of town. Max, Teresa said (we had progressed by now from Mr. Cline and Ms. Kean to professional intimacy), perps are always threatening to gut snitches. True enough. In my night-school-professor mode I had this impulse to instruct her, although in point of fact she and her father had tried many more murder cases in New York than I had in South Midland, murder here not being the cottage industry it was there.

Edgar Parlance, she said as she rose to leave. That jail time he did in Colorado.

Twenty years ago in the Canon City state pen. Did the crime, served the time.

Isn't four years a heavy stretch for stealing a car?

In this part of the world, stealing a car is like rustling cattle used to be.

She persisted. No time off for time served?

No.

No good time?

He ought to be happy he wasn't hung.

A smart answer I would come to regret. She did not seem to fret. I checked all the prison databases, I said, turning to efficiency. He doesn't turn up again. Cross-indexed him with both Gover and Lajoie. No match. Anyplace.

Two other Parlances, Teresa said. A quick smile. So she had done her own computer search. I don't know why I would have thought she would not have. Other than my compulsive hostility to strangers. Which is essentially everyone. Fred and Cato, she said. Cato had a lethal injection in Arkansas in '91. Fred's a hundred and one years old, in a state hospital in Au Train, Michigan. Cato was Haitian, Fred's Caucasian.

It was the same information I had.

As long as we're going down there, let's close that circle, she said. Can you get a court order so we can examine the place where he lived?

I nodded. In the not too distant past, this is what I had babycakes do for me.

I walked her to the elevator, and then down to the lobby. It had been years since I had been subordinate in a courtroom, and I was uncertain as to how I would react to being overruled. As we chatted desultorily, the small talk like a smoke screen, I speculated about the nature of her relationship with her father. This is not to suggest anything deviant, but I sensed a dependency, a need to please his memory, and I half wondered if I had been tapped to be his proxy in South Midland. It was one of the many things I got wrong about Teresa.

The sidewalks were a dozen deep with spectators. A block away, by the front entrance to the Rhino Carlton-Plaza, the elephant balloon had docked alongside the equally large balloon of the USM rhinoceros, both now floating to the hotel's sixth floor. The banners hanging from every lightpost said, RHINO LAND WELCOMES MIDWESTERN REPUBLICANS. I could not recall the rhino balloon ever parading for a convention of state Democrats.

It was a turnout made for Poppy McClure.

She was sitting on the ragtop of a vintage Chrysler convertible at the head of the motorcade snaking its way toward the hotel. Beside her sat Clifton Snow, the aging movie-star president of the National Rifle Association, a huge Poppy Power campaign button pinned to his jacket. Poppy's gift for the exorbitant gesture never faltered. Of course she had snagged Clifton Snow to make the keynote address to the Midwestern Republicans. They would share the front pages and lead the local news, even if he upstaged her with his movie-star smile and the rugged good looks that would not have been misplaced on Mount Rushmore. Confetti streamed from the windows above and the sun glinted on the highlights of the silvery hairpiece cemented to his skull. A testament to Elmer's glue, I thought. He waved slowly to the crowds lining both sides of the street. He seemed to move in perpetual slow motion, the hand slowly rising, the craggy smile slowly enveloping his face. I tried to remember who said that movies were truth at twenty-four frames a second. His normal speed seemed to be sixteen frames a second.

Teresa looked for a moment, then turned and gave a little smile before striding into the throng. A few steps away, I saw her stop and rummage in her bag. A moment later she had a cigarette in her mouth. She lit it and inhaled deeply. I found it gratifying that she was a secret smoker. Then she was swallowed up by the crowd.

Stanley on the private line. "Well?"

"Well, what?"

"Are you going to do it?"

"I told you this morning I was."

"You said, 'Depending.' "

I didn't answer.

"Are you shrugging?"

Again no response.

"How much are you getting paid."

"None of your business."

"All right then. Did you pop out your bridge?"

"Yes."

"And?"

"She wondered if I was the product of a stagnant genetic pool."

"I like that." Stanley had an exaggerated way of talking in private that he knew I found intensely irritating. "I really like that."

I wish I hadn't told him.

"Listen. About tonight." He was lecturing at the university law school. "Erotic Psychopathology in the Criminal Mind" was the title he had attached to his talk. The criminal was Stanley's subject, and the way in which prisons were what he called cathedrals of crime. Prison aristocracies intrigued him, the world of men without women where the weak belonged to the strong and any member, any orifice, might offer sexual release. "Bum bandit" was the phase he used to describe the cellblock sexual imperialist, and he studied the bum bandits and the punks and all the subcategories in between with the eye of an anthropologist. "The dean suggested dinner afterward. Why not come along?" And dish about Teresa Kean was what I suspected he had in mind. "The university lawyer's joining us."

"Leo Cassady?"

"He said he knew you."

"He fired me, Stanley."

"Not fired, Max. Laid off. Downsized. Budgetary cuts."

"Fired, Stanley."

"Be boring, Max," Stanley said as he hung up.

It was the way so many of our conversations seemed to end.

I think a respite from Stanley was another reason I was so willing to involve myself with Teresa Kean and the Lajoie defense.

Chapter Five

In fact, Teresa had met Clifton Snow.

She had moderated a seminar on the Second Amendment at Georgetown Law School where he had been a participant one cold winter night two years earlier, maybe three, maybe more, she had lost track of time, another endless evening of spirited specious debate, Snow versus a representative from People for the American Way, also an actor whose name she had forgotten as well as the series he had starred in, then Q&A, biscotti, cheap chardonnay, false smiles, and we must get together sometime, no addresses or telephone numbers exchanged. The right to bear arms, burning the flag, *Roe* v. *Wade,* stem-cell research, and that hardy perennial, the Vietnam War, remembered most passionately by those who did not choose to fight in it—whatever the issue, Teresa Kean could be counted on to end the evening on time and not let the proceedings get out of hand, at least until the event in Baltimore after Jack Broderick died in her bedroom.

Teresa shouldered her way to the curb so she could cross to the hotel, but her way was blocked by an enormous young man waving a placard that said, I'LL GIVE UP MY GUN WHEN THEY PRY MY COLD DEAD FINGERS FROM IT. In spite of the cold he was only wearing a T-shirt and jeans. His breath was frosted and he was stomping a booted foot, shouting, "Clif-ee, Clif-ee, Clif-ee," trying to get Snow's attention. From the Chrysler, Clifton Snow acknowledged the sign by forming his left hand into a gun, pulling the trigger twice, then blowing away imaginary smoke. Beside him, Poppy McClure waved and clapped.

Teresa wondered if Poppy had recognized her. Wondered what the social amenities were when she was defending an alleged murderer Poppy's husband was trying to electrocute. She would let the amenities work themselves out.

The huge young man suddenly turned and brought his placard down as if it were a tollgate. Thick clumps of chest and back hair curled over the neck of his ripped and dirty white T-shirt, on which was printed the slogan GUNS, GUTS, AND GLORY ARE WHAT MADE AMERICA GREAT. A true believer. "Back on the sidewalk, lady."

She tried to be reasonable. What she wanted was a long soak in a hot bath, not a street fight with a steroid cretin. "I just want to get across to my hotel."

"There's no 'just,' lady, you wait like everyone else." Teresa had never seen anyone quite so big. A cohort of equally muscular companions, all wearing guts-and-glory T-shirts, now surrounded him. To their loud and ribald applause, he jabbed the placard at Teresa as if it were a lance. "You think you're from New York or someplace like that?" Another poke. "Back on the fucking sidewalk."

Teresa stumbled back, scraping the heel of one Ferragamo pump on the curb. The cohort jeered, a display of surplus testosterone that ratcheted her adrenaline up a notch. In a fury, she sprang forward, grabbed the head of the lance, and shoved it aside. "You pea-brained Gargantua," she hissed, "get out of my way." The brutish young man hesitated, the tollgate lance wavered. The thought occurred to Teresa that this might be the first time his authority had ever been questioned, his size the only credential he had ever needed to certify his lummox power. In the split second before he could respond, she swept past him and darted across the street, behind the Chrysler, behind Poppy and Clifton Snow, and into the hotel. She felt exhilarated. Gargantua. Where had that come from. Of course. Her father. When he was a boy, he had once told her, he ditched St. Cyril's one day and went into the city to see the Barnum & Bailey Circus at the old Madison Square Garden on Eighth Avenue. Specifically to see Gargantua, the great ape, who guzzled Coca-Cola by the case, then peed in his hands, and threw his urine through the bars of his cage at the audience who had gathered there just for that experience. A brain the size of a chestnut, Teresa. Mrs. Gargantua was the very fetching M'Toto, he said. Twice a day, afternoon and evening performances, they would pledge their troth, M'Toto's hairy face framed by a virginal white veil. Which was entirely appropriate. Because Gargantua, Teresa, did not seem to have much interest in his lady ape. Or any lady apes. King of the primates, perhaps, but queen of the May. More interested in Tarzan, Brendan Kean had said, than in his saucy little M.

She had never anticipated that Gargantua might be useful in Capital City, South Midland. Another debt owed to Brendan Kean.

It's like Washington here, Teresa thought with a chill as her eyes wandered over the jammed lobby of the Rhino Carlton-Plaza. Washington transported to Midlandia. Washington on one of its more unpleasant command-performance evenings. The Annual Dinner of the White House Correspondents Association at the Hilton, say. The din was like the noise of an open spillway. Midwestern Republicans clutched and greeted each other as if they had not been in hourly cell-phone communication or seen each other in Washington, Des Moines, or Manchester the previous week. There were huge posters of Dixon McCall everywhere. The president lecturing his colleagues at the G-8 meeting in Salt Lake City. Salt Lake was the real America, Dixon McCall had told them. *The Real America* was the Republican campaign theme, and the posters reflected it. Dixon McCall at Grand Coulee. Dedicating the World War II Memorial on the Mall. Escorting the pope to the Grand Canyon. Clearcutting timber in the Cascade Range. Hanging from an oil derrick at Alaska's Arctic National Wildlife Refuge. Branding cattle at his Oklahoma ranch. Speaking at Edgar Parlance's funeral. Everyplace Teresa looked she saw a familiar face. Faces she thought she had left behind. Faces that came with familiar stories that were the currency of Georgetown dinner parties she was no longer compelled to attend. The windbag pundits elaborately pretending they did not notice the attention they attracted from the county chairmen and national committeemen. Over there Mark Berquist bear-hugging Gerry Wormwold, laying down a possible marker for the future White House run the pundits, the county chairmen, and the national committeemen all were predicting he would make. In the anteroom off the lobby Lorna Dun with a camera crew from *Fixed Bayonets,* setting up an interview with Clifton Snow. Lorna Dun and Mark Berquist. Familiar faces with a familiar story too often told. Sex and politics. Politics without sex was a nonstory in dinnertime Georgetown. Lorna Dun and Mark Berquist had once been involved. Until Mark Berquist dumped Lorna Dun when he was appointed to complete the term of the ninety-three-year-old junior senator from South Carolina after he collapsed while chairing a hearing of the Foreign Relations Committee on Saudi Arabia. Dumped for the twenty-one-year-old daughter of the governor who had appointed him to fill out the term of the deceased former senator. He needed a wife who was a constituent, Mark Berquist told Lorna Dun. What Mark Berquist meant was that he did not want a wife who at that juncture of his political career was better known than he. What Mark Berquist also meant was that he might be able to find occasional quality time for Lorna Dun. What Lorna Dun did to Mark Berquist was to aim a garden hose through a dog door at his house in Cleveland Park, flooding his first-floor library and ruining his signed first edition of the speeches of John C. Calhoun. What Lorna Dun then did to Mark Berquist was call the governor of South Carolina and tell him that his daughter's intended had suggested that she and he continue the relationship that antedated his engagement to the governor's daughter. What the governor of South Carolina did was call Mark Berquist and tell him to get that woman out of his life.

Teresa knew all the stories.

Like Lorna Dun, she knew she had become one. Bared to the essentials, a dead man jumping her bones. Still on top of her when EMS came. Scout's honor. A reliable source on the Metro desk. A story chewed over along with the rack of lamb and the gratinéed potatoes. Washed down with the Sterling Vineyards 1997 cabernet sauvignon.

She paused by a booth that was selling campaign paraphernalia. Poppy McClure was the big-ticket item. Poppy Power buttons and Poppy Power straw boaters with a red, white, and blue band. A Poppy Power video with vintage Poppy sound bites. The EPA was the American gestapo. The wage-earning American male was an endangered species. Ayatollahs of unity. Stealth agents of the global national force.

There was once a story about Poppy. Out there in the ozone. It never made it all the way to the gratinéed potatoes. Poppy and . . .

Oh, yes.

She never believed it.

"What are you going to buy, Teresa?" Willie Erskine placed a Poppy Power boater on her head. "The Real America becomes you."

Teresa removed the boater and put it back on the counter. She had known Willie Erskine since he was a Republican staff AA with Mark Berquist on the Senate Intelligence Committee. Sharing an apartment on Dupont Circle with other true-believer AAs, including Lorna Dun. Foot soldiers preparing for the transition in Havana, mischief in the Middle East, and anything that would shift the tectonic plates in Pyongyang. Taking out whomever, whenever. What's up? What's going down? The word is. Yesterday's news. Today's bulletin. When Mark Berquist was appointed to the Senate, Willie Erskine had expected to be named to his staff, but Mark Berquist had informed him that politics was too important for friendship. It was then that Willie Erksine had attached himself to Poppy McClure. "Hello, Willie."

"Shame on you doing what you're doing here, Teresa. We always thought you were one of us."

Teresa smiled. Her Gioconda imitation.

"Did you ever expect to see Lorna and Mark in the same room together, greeting each other so benignly?"

"I never gave it much thought."

"His child bride is with issue again. Three times in four years. Barefoot and pregnant. An old South Carolina tradition. It leaves so many evenings free for our future president and leader of the free world."

He was milking the moment, like a bad actor in a touring company, treating her elaborate disinterest as if it were applause.

"One hears the senator might be flossing his teeth with Lorna's pubic hair again."

"You're a toxic waste site, Willie."

"How sweet of you to say so." He paused, flicking an imaginary piece of lint from his lapel. "I was so sorry to hear about Mr. . . . Broderick, was it?"

Teresa moved toward the elevator.

"Oh, there's someone you must meet, Teresa."

"Another time, Willie."

He put his hand on her shoulder. "Teresa Kean, J.J. McClure."

Size them up immediately, her father always said. First impressions are best. Make them prove you're wrong. You can always amend later. Big fish, small pond was her immediate reaction. "Mr. McClure, I was going to call you."

"I've been expecting your call, counselor."

"Perhaps tomorrow."

"I'm rather backed up tomorrow."

"I'm sure."

"Max Cline should help you over the jumps."

Then he knew about Max already. Word traveled fast. Word always did. And not just in zip code 20007. "If needed."

"You feel you're up to the job, then?"

So that was the way it was going to be. "We almost met once."

A slight hesitation. He was not expecting the unexpected. "We did?"

"In Washington. Your wife was on C-Span. With Brian Lamb. You were in the green room. I was scheduled to tape Brian's next show. I was late getting there. Or maybe it was the next day. Anyway we didn't meet. In the green room."

Not a flicker. "It's nice to meet you finally, Ms. Kean."

"And nice to meet you, Mr. McClure."

She awoke with a start. The digital clock on the bedside table said 9:37. Good God, she had slept all night. No. She was still dressed and sprawled diagonally across the bed. She must have fallen asleep. Her eyes focused on the Poppy Power button and the Poppy Power boater on the chaise opposite the bed. Jesus, I couldn't have bought them. Steady. Wake up. No. They were in her room when she came upstairs. Keepsakes to all the Midwestern Republicans from the Poppy McClure Reelection Campaign. Or was it Poppy McClure for Governor? She did not know and did not care. She wondered why Poppy needed Mr. McClure. Nothing more than a good-looking walker. She kicked off the Ferragamo pump that that had fallen from her foot, unbuttoned her blouse, arched her bottom, shimmied out of her skirt, and kicked it to the floor. In the corridor outside, Midwestern Republicans seemed to be partying loudly. The dinner must have ended. She knew what Clifton Snow had said in his keynote address. The same thing he had said at

Georgetown Law. The same thing he had said in meeting rooms and convention halls and hotel dining rooms across the country. The Speech. With local references. We have more in common with the valiant red men after whom the great city of Kiowa is named than we have with the cultural shock troops of today's liberal establishment. The Real America. Those wise old dead white guys who invented this county. Clif Snow can say "wise old dead white guys" because Clif Snow marched with Jimmy Baldwin and Dr. King. Freedom is our fortune and honor is our saving grace.

He could have sent a tape.

Outside her door a down-home country guitar was now playing "Bye Bye Love." Badly. Country music and Republicans. The anthem of the red states. More the curse of Lee Atwater in her opinion. She considered masturbating. When in doubt, masturbate, Marty Buick used to say at Smith. Click off, clear the mind. She wished the guitar player in the corridor would segue into "Let It Be Me," however badly he played it. The perfect background music for what she had in mind. *Never leave me lonely. Tell me you love me only.* Her hand slipped beneath the elastic band of her panty hose. No. That was self-indulgent. I'm forty-something years old. How many somethings is my business. And it's a mortal sin. That never stopped her when she was a little girl. Only now. At forty-something. God, I'll be going to mass next. And confession. Bless me, Father, for I have sinned, I had impure actions one hundred and forty-two times. Impure actions. I still know all the confessional euphemisms. They were like swimming or bicycle riding, something you never forget. The only one she could never bring herself to say was self-abuse. Where was the abuse? You tell me, Father. And you can also tell me, Father, how often you spank the monkey. A term she picked up from Budd Doheny. She supposed the reason he was on her mind was the fat girl in the pictures Max Cline had shown her. Merle Orvis. Doing herself with the banana and the dildo.

She had never done herself with foreign objects.

She did not care about the fat girl.

She did not care about the baby who had shit on the sheet.

The baby who was not the issue of Duane Lajoie.

Her client.

Soon to be on trial for the murder of Edgar Parlance.

When the facts are against you, argue the law.
When the law is against you, argue the facts.
When both are against you, attack the other side.
Easy for her father to say.
But where to begin?
She peeled off the rest of her clothes and opened the minibar. Absolut and nacho Doritos. Or Stolichnaya and Lay's barbecue chips. Bad dinner ideas. She considered calling room service, then changed her mind. It would take forever getting the tray through the drunk Republicans clogging every corridor. Maybe, however, she should order a Kiowa stripper medium rare, Rhino onion rings, a side of broccoli rabe, and a slice of pecan pie with a scoop of hazelnut just to see how much got past the ravenous revelers of the Real America. No. Not worth it. She caught her image in the mirror over the writing table. The mirror with a plaster-of-paris rhinoceros guarding the top of its gilt frame. A touch of cellulite on the back of her legs. A slight slippage visible in the buns. There must be a StairMaster in the hotel fitness center. A treadmill. But she hated public exercise. The kind of delta Carlyle thought was unfashionable. *Xan, don't you know pubes are gross, get them waxed, a Mohawk's so much cooler.* Yes, they were her own boobs, she had told Carlyle. Now in her hawkish gaze beginning to sag. Not hang. Sag. Be clear about that. At least it took to forty-something. She propped them in her hands and examined them for the stretch marks she supposed were just beyond the horizon in the pale of estrogen deficiency. Before long she'd wake up in the morning and have to chase them around her back.
It's a mood, she thought. It will pass.
PMS.
Except it was nearly two weeks until her next period.
Teresa sat on the bed and punched the TV remote. "Condom recall. Next on *Eyewitness News* after these commercial messages." Not tonight. Another channel. Lorna Dun on *Fixed Bayonets,* with the latest political potpourri. She tossed her blond mane and beamed at the camera. "My next guest will be Alicia Barbara, the genius crime reporter from *Courthouse Square* and feisty anchor for *The Courthouse Square Nightly Wrap-up,* and we will be talking to Alicia about the upcoming trial of the skel who brutally murdered Edgar Parlance, a crime that made Real America cry, and how it will affect Congresswoman Poppy McClure's political

prospects this fall. This savage, whose name I refuse to mention, will be prosecuted by Poppy's husband, James Joseph 'J.J.' McClure, the head of the Homicide Bureau in the South Midland Attorney General's office, who many call the best prosecutor in the Midwest. Poppy as you know is a regular guest on *Fixed Bayonets,* and she will be a frequent visitor to the courtroom where the trial will take place. What you may not know is that the savage will be defended by Teresa Kean, another frequent guest on this program, and former head of Justice for All, the victims' rights organization. I'll be asking Alicia why a victims' rights lawyer would defend such a savage, and I know Alicia well enough to predict that she will not try to fob me off with that innocent-until-proven-guilty non-sense that liberal apologists for criminal behavior are always spouting. Someone close to Teresa Kean recently passed away, someone very, very close, and maybe that grief can explain her aberrational behavior in taking this case. So. Alicia Barbara. Next."

Not next. Not ever.

M flossed his teeth with L's pubic hair.

I must remember that, Teresa thought.

She stretched out on the bed, a naked forty-something woman whose body was beginning to show the signs of aging's wear and tear, a naked forty-something woman in a city, in a state, where she had never been, a naked forty-something woman in a hotel room where the glasses and the towels and the ashtrays and the sheets and the lamp shades and the stationery in the desk and the notepads on the telephone table and even the bedspread she was lying on were monogrammed with tiny rhinoceroses. She felt as if she were going to be trampled by a herd of wild rhinos.

Maybe if I count them I can go to sleep, she thought.

What am I doing here?

Never leave me lonely.

Tell me you love me only.

TWO CONVERSATIONS

I.

"Tell me what she's like," J.J. said.

"Smart," Poppy said. "Tough. Like a lot of people in Washington."

"Smarter than you?"

"No."

"Tougher?"

"No."

"That's it?"

"I don't really know her, J.J. I'd see her. That's what you do in Washington. You see people. You don't know them. You really don't want to know them. Sometimes they're useful, most times they're not."

"So you keep them in the bullpen."

"That's one way of putting it. Her father was a Mob lawyer. He defended someone named Jacob King."

"A big someone. By all accounts."

"Big, little, it's the same thing."

"And before Jacob King he was a prosecutor who sent two guys to the chair. One more than I have. Mob guys. Pandro Cohen and Giusseppe Joie. Joey Joey, he was called. Sometimes Joey Twice. I'd have to say the criminal element back in those days had more picturesque names than Percy Darrow."

"Maybe that's why the Mafia hired him. So he wouldn't send so many of their people to the electric chair."

"A possibility."

"She worked with him."

"The reports I get are that she was pretty good."

"Then what else do you want to know?"

"I want to know why she left Washington, Poppy. I want to know why she took this loser case. She was a victims' rights bureaucrat. Now she's defending the most infamous murderer of the last ten years. There has to be some reason."

"Someone died in her bed. Someone she apparently had never met until that night. Someone she met at a White House dinner. He had a heart attack. He was sixty-something. Dead when EMS got there. People talked about it. Then they didn't. She wasn't that big a player. Something else came along. If it hadn't been for the White House, nobody would have cared."

"You are telling me that's why she left Washington? Because she was embarrassed?"

"You don't believe it."

"No."

2.

"Maximiliano."

"What do you mean?"

"It's my father's name. Maximiliano. Maximiliano Vasquez."

"Allie, keep your eye on the ball. The Max I'm interested in is Max Cline. Not your father Maximiliano."

"You don't think that's funny?"

"Think what's funny?"

"That my grandfather named my father Maximiliano."

"Okay. I'll bite. Why is it funny?"

"J.J. How many Mexicans name their sons after the Emperor Maximilian?"

"What has that got to do with Max?"

"He's got the same name as my father."

"Max is Maximiliano Cline?"

"No. Forget it. I just thought it was interesting. Max. Maximiliano. It'd never occurred to me before."

"Are you jerking me around, Allie?"

"I work for you, J.J."

"Then tell me why Max tied up with this woman. With this trial."

"Max doesn't confide in me. What he does, he does."

"You want to go back to the PD?"

"They wouldn't take me."

"Exactly."

"Meaning."

"Let me know what you know."

"I always do, J.J."

Chapter Six

MAX

I like to read the profiles of newly minted CEOs in *Forbes* or *Fortune* or *Business Week,* the only magazines you seem to find in the waiting rooms of dentists and doctors these days, leading me, admittedly a terminal hypochondriac, to the unfortunate, if highly speculative, conclusion that the M.D.'s and D.D.S.'s spend more time worrying about their investment portfolios and sheltering strategies than they do keeping up to speed on the latest innovations in anticoagulants or PSA counts or colonoscopy procedures or the advantages and disadvantages between generic and proprietary medications. Anyway. The cover photo is usually of a man in his late forties, with the start of a weight problem, a widow's peak or a comb-over beginning to go gray, wearing a blue suit and a frown if he wants to impart the cold distant numbers-cruncher look. Or shirtsleeves and riotously colored suspenders if he wishes to appear youthful and dynamic, the Turnbull & Asser gaiters suggesting the influence of a younger second trophy wife who probably gives good head, the first he has received since the birth of his third child by his first wife, who was more into motherhood and PTA than head, and in fact never really liked to do it. On the cover, the new CEO's hand rests on a globe, signifying his company's international synergy, or he is on the assembly line with the latest fiber-optic communications system, or in front of a picture window with a fleet of air-express cargo carriers in the background. The slash line is usually as peppy as the photograph, ending with an obligatory exclamation mark: UNICON'S BOB MACDONALD: "BACK OFF, UNCLE SAM!"

Inside the story relates how Bob MacDonald, the only son of an electrician and International Brotherhood of Electrical Workers shop steward named Sam MacDonald of Mattoon, Illinois, and Sam's homemaker wife, Harriet Winsted MacDonald, left Purdue with a degree in business and electrical engineering, and went to work in the Topeka plant of Harvey Engineering (later UniCon). Bob was already a family man, with his wife, Nancy, a high school sweetheart, at his side, along with daughter Rona, who was followed by Bob, Jr., and Sam, who has Down's syndrome, the tragedy of Bob's life (Bob's second wife, Lanna, is chairperson of the National Down's Syndrome Foundation). Bob advanced rapidly up the corporate ladder on the finance side, his fiery personality and ruthless cost-cutting catching the eye of UniCon's grand old man, Evans Harvey, who picked him out of the pack and groomed him to be his successor, supplanting Ev Harvey, Jr., who told his father he wanted to go off and do his own thing. Now here is the point. These twenty years only take three paragraphs in the profile, a fat three paragraphs, but still just three paragraphs. We have had two wives, Nancy, who seems to have evaporated into thin air, and Lanna, whose hair is tinted ash blond and who is deep into public-spiritedness, three children, Down's syndrome, cost-cutting, plant closings, union busting, and all of a sudden Bob MacDonald, the electrician's son out of Mattoon, Ill., and Purdue, is saying, as if he is some kind of corporate Dirty Harry, "Back off, Uncle Sam!"

What happened?

What exactly was it that caught the eye of Evans Harvey? Where did Lanna, last name LaVecchia, come from, and how quickly did she fit in or, to be more precise, take over? Why was Lanna the chairperson of the National Down's Syndrome Foundation and not Nancy, the mother of the Down's child? What did Sam MacDonald, the shop steward for the International Brotherhood, think of his son's union busting? In what way was Bob MacDonald ruthless? How was his personality fiery? Who did he roll over, push aside, whose ass did he kiss? What precisely was Ev Harvey, Jr.'s, own thing, and what exactly was the cost to UniCon of sending him off to do it?

These are the questions never asked and of course never answered in *Forbes* and *Fortune* and *Business Week*. The questions I have about these

CEOs, however, are not unlike the questions I have when I try to contemplate, try to parse, the relationship between Teresa Kean and J.J. McClure.

How did I miss it?

What was I not seeing?

And was I willfully not seeing it?

Of course Regent had a lot to do with it.

REGENT—A PLACE FIT FOR KINGS—POP. 3,679.

Regent gave it traction.

Loomis County is corn and sorghum country, along with some cattle that ranchers fatten up for the slaughterhouses in Kiowa. It's not exactly cowboy work these ranchers do—branding, riding fence, mending wire, like Paul Newman in *Hud*—it's more like stuffing geese for the foie gras, but you see them at the Bunkhouse, a karaoke bar in Regent, wearing their sunglasses and straw cowboy hats and boots and belts with big turquoise buckles, picking their guitars and singing "Mamas Don't Let Your Babies Grow Up to Be Cowboys," along with Willie Nelson and Waylon Jennings on the video. Every few minutes when Teresa and I were driving down from Cap City, the Top Forty on the car radio was interrupted by the latest crop reports and commodities prices. After the dust settled, Alicia Barbara, who rode the story all the way from *Courthouse Square* and *The Courthouse Square Nightly Wrap-up* to a three-year two-million-dollar contract on Fox 5, invoked Willa Cather, one Sapphist to another, as it were, the toxic tyranny and social straitjacket of the small prairie town, and all that moral-of-the-story crap. The fact is, I never much liked Willa Cather and her prairie wisdom. I had to read her when she was required tenth-grade reading in South Midland's high schools, and I never liked the archbishop, never believed Ántonia, never was interested in those obscure destinies. There was a Lady Bountiful, house-on-the-hill aspect to Cather that I couldn't stand, the woman of quality from Red Cloud, Nebraska, casting her cold eye on the lower orders of the Great Plains. You notice she cut out for New York first chance she got.

Forget Willa Cather.

Back off, Uncle Sam.

It happened.

CHAPTER SEVEN

Clyde Ray said he did not drink coffee.

Clyde Ray said he was opposed to stimulants.

He had arranged the seating so that he was facing the picture window in the Lovat Hotel restaurant and coffee shop. It was called Auntie Pasto's and promised "Italian Kwee Zeen." Clyde Ray's eyes never met Teresa's or mine, but slowly swept back and forth, covering the Regent town square and Loomis County Courthouse across the street as if he were checking for snipers in no-man's-land.

Clyde Ray said there were several things he wanted to make clear.

Clyde Ray said that the parts of the Bible with which he disagreed had been added by the Jews, and that Yahweh permitted polygamy, allowing him to marry, in addition to his legal wife, not only another woman, but that woman's three daughters, including the youngest, who was rising thirteen.

Teresa did not blink. The things that Clyde Ray wanted to make clear were not on her agenda.

She asked Clyde Ray how he happened to be on County Road 21 the night Edgar Parlance was murdered. Clyde Ray said he was on Yahweh's mission, and that Yahweh's laws took precedence over the perverted laws of Mammon. Teresa persisted. But you did see the car. It was not a car, Clyde Ray said. Excuse me, Teresa said, it wasn't a car? It was a pickup, I said quietly. A 1989 Ford 4x4 with a four-pin trailer-tow harness, Clyde Ray said as if by rote. He hesitated. His scan had picked up a fat woman in a lumber jacket exiting the basement door of the courthouse. She walked with the rolling gait of a sailor home from the sea, her girth making it difficult to put one leg directly in front of the other. Clyde Ray stopped talking until she climbed with effort into her van, making it on the second try, then backed out of her parking place, and drove off. There was a shotgun in the rifle rack over the steering wheel.

1989 Ford 4x4 with a four-pin trailer-tow harness, Clyde Ray repeated finally. Traveling at seventy-eight miles an hour, Clyde Ray said finally.

Not seventy-five miles an hour? Teresa said. Not eighty?

Seventy-eight miles an hour, Clyde Ray said. How can you be that precise? Teresa said. I am invested with the spirit of the Archangel Michael, Clyde Ray said. I see, Teresa said. And this Ford 4x4 with the four-pin trailer-tow harness had a bumper sticker? Teresa said. *Fornicate the telephone company,* Clyde Ray said. Teresa nodded, repeating as if to herself, Fornicate the telephone company. And this was at what time? she said after a moment. Two-forty-seven, Clyde Ray said. You looked at your watch? Teresa said. I am invested with the spirit of the Archangel Michael, Clyde Ray said. I'm sorry, Teresa said. I forgot. She stirred her coffee idly, watching the steam rise from the cup. Just one more question, Mr. Ray, she said after taking a sip. I'm sorry if I keep coming back to this, but I'd like to pin down exactly . . . exactly . . . what you were doing on County Road 21 at two-forty-seven a.m. last November the seventh?

I was on Yahweh's mission.

And what was the nature of mission you were conducting for Yahweh?

The questions of an unbeliever from the mongrel world do not need to be answered by a disciple of Yahweh, Clyde Ray said.

"Do they really practice polygamy?"

"Not in any formal way. The authorities from the mongrel world tend to frown on that sort of thing."

"What do you think he was doing out there at two-forty-seven in the morning?"

"Stealing something. Or looking for something to steal. Or bringing back something he had already stolen."

Teresa held her coffee cup in front of her face. "That seems unequivocal."

"When I was with the A.G., we were always looking for ways to prosecute that bunch. They have an encampment on the other side of the river. It's easier to get into Fort Knox than to get in there. Loony stuff. Yahweh sanctions bestiality, sodomy, torture. Only you never catch them at it. They're getting ready for Armageddon."

"That's not illegal."

"The stealing is. At one time we figured, all in, a hundred and twenty grand. Cattle. Hogs. Farm machinery. Construction equipment. Not easy to steal, not easy to hide. They were like night riders. They'd slip into Kansas, Missouri, the neighboring counties, justifying everything they stole as guerrilla warfare for the greater glory of Yahweh. Here's the beauty part. They'd fence it for ammunition, weapons, clothing, even food, stockpiling it for the ultimate conflict against the enemies of Yahweh. We never could get close to them. And no one ever jumped ship. They were too afraid of what might happen to them. Or their many wives. Or their even more many children. We'd hear stories about crucifixion."

"Stories," Teresa said.

"Seeing Duane's car is not a story."

"Fornicate the telephone company," Teresa said.

Marjorie Hudnut, the town librarian and historian, said that William Clarke Quantrill had once wintered in Regent. That would have been 1863, Marjorie Hudnut said, then that summer Mr. Quantrill and his raiders rode into Kansas, into Lawrence, Kansas, actually, and they rounded up one hundred forty men and boys, tied their hands behind their backs, and I am sorry to say, they killed them all. They had a reason, Eugene Hicks said. Well, yes, I suppose, Marjorie Hudnut said. She was a tall bony woman and she did not seem quite convinced that Mr. Quantrill and his raiders had cause to murder one hundred and forty men and boys in Lawrence, Kansas, in the summer of 1863.

And the reason was, Eugene Hicks said, and you know it, Marjorie, was there were these four young women making common cause with the Confederacy in a Union jail in Kansas City, and that jail collapsed and killed those four young women, crushed the life right out of them, and that was why Quantrill rode into Lawrence, Quantrill was Quantrill, always an eye for an eye.

Nothing wrong with that, Joe Salmon the barber said.

Quite possibly that's so, Eugene, Joe, Marjorie Hudnut said, twisting the yellow ribbon that was pinned to her dress, but I am not sure that Miss Kean came all the way down to Regent to hear about Mr. Quantrill. That is ancient history, Eugene. You too, Joe.

It was Eugene Hicks's pointer, Jesse, who had discovered the body of Edgar Parlance. Right out there in the middle of that field, Eugene Hicks said. There was a flock of geese, and I had taken down one, a traveling shot, left to right, like skeet, and I thought that was what Jesse was standing over, and then I saw Gar. Couldn't make him out, of course, didn't know it was Gar, fact is, I never knew Gar, it was Marjorie who knew him, and Joe here, and Claude, but there wasn't much left of his face, and his thigh where those boys skinned him, it was not a pretty sight, Jesse was guarding him like he was that goddamn goose, I really don't know why you bother defending that Lajoie boy, Miss Kean, he was no damn good, from what I hear.

No damn good at all, Claude Applewhite said. Claude Applewhite was pastor of Regent's Bethany Methodist Church, and Edgar Parlance had lived in the apartment above his garage, paying for his keep by raking the leaves and washing his car.

You knew Duane Lajoie? Teresa said.

I heard about him, Claude Applewhite said.

Gar played Santa Claus at the annual Christmas party at the library, Marjorie Hudnut said. Best Santa we ever had.

A colored Santa Claus, Joe Salmon, the barber, said. That's what kind of town Regent is, they have a colored Santa Claus, and it's no big damn deal, like it would be in some places.

Where you from, Miss Kean? Marjorie Hudnut said. They have colored Santa Clauses there?

Yes, Teresa said.

Fancy that, Eugene Hicks said.

He did the barbecue outside the courthouse on the Fourth of July, Claude Applewhite said. He had his own sauce recipe, guarded it with his life, so hot it made the top of my head sweat.

Absolutely, Marjorie Hudnut said.

I was wondering, Pastor Applewhite, Teresa said, if we—Mr. Cline and I—could take a look at Mr. Parlance's apartment.

What do you want to do that for? Claude Applewhite said.

Because we have a court order that says we can, I said.

Brutus won't let you in there, Eugene Hicks said.

The court order does not exempt Sheriff Mayes, I said.

You know Jocko Cannon is working with Brutus, Joe Salmon said.

Community service, Claude Applewhite said. He got a hundred hours after that deal in the Orange Bowl.

Teresa seemed not have heard about the Orange Bowl incident.

That Orange Bowl deal had a rank smell about it, Eugene Hicks said.

That referee was on the take, Joe Salmon said. What I hear is he had Florida State and the spread.

He shouldn't have done that to the Rhinos, Marjorie Hudnut said. It wasn't fair. The Rhinos had the game won.

Jocko says he was a sodomite, Claude Applewhite said.

Claude, there are ladies present, Joe Salmon said.

Beg your pardon, Miss Kean, Marjorie, Claude Applewhite said. But you've got to admit, Marjorie, there's a lot of books in that library of yours that talk about sodomites. Too many, you ask me.

I don't do a count, Claude, Marjorie Hudnut said.

A fag is what he said, Claude, Eugene Hicks corrected. Jewish fella.

I didn't know that part of it, Claude Applewhite said. That explains it, then.

Jocko'll get a good workout with Brutus, Joe Salmon said. Got this big damn rowing machine right there in the office.

Brutus put up a basket in the parking lot, Eugene Hicks said. Him and Brutus play one-on-one.

That's seven hundred pounds of horse playing basketball, Claude Applewhite said. They take up the whole damn parking lot, those two.

Scarcely enough room for that Mercedes automobile Jocko bought with his signing bonus, Eugene Hicks said. Prettiest car in Regent. He's got those people of his shining it up every minute.

Won't let anyone park next to it, Marjorie Hudnut said.

He takes three parking places, Eugene Hicks said. One on either side, plus the one he's in. He's afraid of getting a scratch on it.

You scratch that car, you'll hear from Jocko, Claude Applewhite said, you can bet the mortgage on that.

Brutus will teach him all the tricks, Joe Salmon said. What Brutus don't know about football ain't worth knowing. Damn shame about that knee of his.

The NFL lost a hell of a linebacker, Eugene Hicks said.

We got a hell of a sheriff, though, Joe Salmon said.

We seemed to be wandering away from the subject of Edgar Parlance.

Did Edgar Parlance ever have any visitors? I asked Claude Applewhite. In his place above your garage.

Gar had lots of friends, Marjorie Hudnut said. Didn't he, Joe?

This whole town, Joe Salmon said.

Claude Applewhite looked at me for a moment, suspicion slowly clouding his face. What kind of visitors? he said.

Just visitors, I said. People. When he wasn't being Santa Claus. Or making the best barbecue sauce in Loomis County.

Damn lawyers, Claude Applewhite said.

As you probably have already discerned, Teresa had, after a fashion, previously met Jocko Cannon. It was Jocko, of course, who had tried to block her way into the Rhino Carlton-Plaza after our first meeting in the Law Building. To Teresa it was an unexceptional street encounter she saw no reason to mention until she saw Jocko again in Brutus Mayes's office, glistening with sweat and wearing the torn and grimy white T-shirt that said GUNS, GUTS, AND GLORY ARE WHAT MADE AMERICA GREAT.

Jocko, not surprisingly, did not remember Teresa. Women did not generally show up on Jocko's radar screen. Unless they were underneath him. Pinned between his legs like a sacked quarterback.

The hundred hours of community service Jocko Cannon was doing under the supervision of Brutus Mayes seemed designed mainly to make Jocko physically ready for training camp with the Miami Dolphins, who had chosen him as the twenty-ninth take in the first round of the NFL draft. While doing his community service, Jocko was attended by an entourage including a barber, a wardrobe consultant, driver, agent, his own personal merchandiser from I-Bod, with whom he had signed a commercial contract, and a floating contingent of pals from SMU who picked up the laundry, got the girls, and roughed up anyone who invaded Jocko's space, the perimeters of Jocko's space constantly changing according to the volatility of Jocko's mood.

Jocko's posse. A surly bunch. Mostly large. All on the payroll. All who laughed at his jokes. No one laughed harder than Brutus Mayes.

I thought Jocko was atmosphere. My mistake. I did not anticipate that even Jocko would play a role in what I did not then know would become a narrative.

The narrative.

Jocko's Mercedes first. A silver S-600, reclining front bucket seats with built-in ventilation, Bose sound system, xenon headlights, Distronic cruise control, ZAS cylinder shutoff system, two TVs in the headrests, a DVD player, Sony PlayStation, fax machine, color copier, laptop computer, two hidden video cameras, one in the driver's sun visor, the other in the back seat reading light above the rear window, sticker price $115,200.00, fully loaded $241,945.00, tax and license not included, tax and license bringing the whole package up to two-five-oh.

Two-five-oh is ballpark, the I-Bod representative said as he buffed a fingerprint from the metallic paint job of the S-600. The I-Bod representative said his name was Duke. Duke did not offer a last name. Nor did any of the posse. There was Bobo, there was Pig, there was Sonny, there was Tater. The other names I can't remember. When they weren't doing for Jocko, they were working out, lifting weights, buffing their biceps. Talking about pussy.

Actually the incident at the Orange Bowl was a blessing in disguise, Duke from I-Bod said. Of course it knocks Jocko down to a low first-round draft choice instead of top five, it's all that image crap the NFL is into, the referee blew the call, everyone knows that, Cohen his name was, the last play of the game, a Hail Mary pass, for Christ's sake, you don't call roughing the passer, football is a collision sport, you can't blame Jocko, you can't fault his intensity either, he's a winner, intensity is his middle name, the Rhinos would've been national champions if it hadn't been for that Cohen's call. Jocko's going to be a credit to the I-Bod logo for years to come, you can bet on it, only the winner goes to dinner, this young man is going to be the first nose-tackle superstar in TV commercials, and isn't this vehicle a beauty, two-five-oh ballpark, a lot of automobile for a lot of young man.

Teresa recognized Jocko Cannon immediately. She had already noticed the poster Brutus Mayes had pinned to the bulletin board in his office: SEE DICK DRINK. SEE DICK DRIVE. SEE DICK DIE. DON'T BE A DICK.

It should say "dickhead," Brutus, Jocko Cannon said, sweating and heaving on the rowing machine, shaking his head so vigorously that his perspiration sprayed Teresa and me. Don't you think so? he said to Teresa.

The posse arranged around what available space there was in Brutus Mayes's small office giggled.

Only one other thing you do with this kind of motion, Jocko Cannon said as he continued rowing. In, out. In, out. In, out. The posse exchanged high fives.

Teresa concentrated on the photo blowups of Brutus Mayes as a Detroit Lion that covered the walls of the office.

Gatorade me, Jocko Cannon said. One of his retainers reached into a cooler, produced a bottle of Gatorade, and passed it to him.

The whole team wore Parlance doodads at the Orange Bowl, Jocko Cannon said between gulps, as he drained the bottle of Gatorade. We all wrote the letters *EP* in Magic Marker on the inside of our helmets.

Goddamn, what a swell thing to do, Jocko, Brutus Mayes said.

Jocko Cannon looked at me. That referee was a homosexual, you know what I mean, counselor?

Name of Cohen, Brutus Mayes said.

Relative of yours, was he? Jocko Cannon asked in my general direction.

More giggling from the posse.

We'd like to see where Mr. Parlance lived, Sheriff, Teresa said.

Why? Brutus Mayes said.

Teresa handed Brutus Mayes the court order allowing us to examine Edgar Parlance's rooms above Claude Applewhite's garage.

That Duane Lajoie broke up this jail when he heard Gover had ratted him out, Brutus Mayes said, not looking at the court order.

Should've taken care of him then, Brutus, Jocko Cannon said. He seemed to be evaluating Teresa's sexual potential. That would've saved the state a lot of trouble. But then I never would've met Miss What's-

Her-Name here, comes down to Regent to defend Duane Lajoie. Her and her friend. Mr. Cline.

He was standing astride the rowing machine, wiping his face with his sweat-soaked guns-and-glory T-shirt. My daddy tells me you used to work for Gerry Wormwold, Jocko said. Until he fired you.

The posse looked to see if Jocko Cannon would get a rise out of me. Not a chance. Teresa had nailed him. An ape with a pea-sized brain.

Gargantua. I have to say I loved the touch about Gargantua.

Goddamn court order, Brutus Mayes said. I had dealt with him when I was with the A.G. THE BIGGEST LAWMAN IN THE STATE was his campaign slogan. He hated court orders. His first instinct was always to balk, like the linebacker he once was. You had to push back. Explain it was not Lions *v.* Cowboys. He thought it was like making him say, Yeah, Marse.

Reta! Brutus Mayes shouted.

His secretary peeked into the office. Reta was wearing drop earrings shaped like handcuffs.

Get the key to Gar's place, Brutus Mayes said. He looked at Jocko. You go with them, Jocko, make sure they don't mess with anything.

They mess with anything, they mess with me, Brutus, Jocko Cannon said. And then to his posse: Uniform me.

Jocko Cannon took up most of the space in the tiny spare room above Claude Applewhite's garage where Edgar Parlance had lived prior to his murder. In his custom-tailored sheriff's uniform, five-gallon hat, and mirrored sunglasses, he looked like one of the guards in *Cool Hand Luke.* The room had a sink, a daybed, a portable heater, and a bedside table on which was a lamp with a three-way bulb, a pencil, and a notepad from Regent Pharmacy: YOU CALL, WE DELIVER. One of Edgar Parlance's odd jobs, according to the Kiowa *Times-Ledger,* was working as a delivery boy for the drugstore, "a chore that brought Gar into homes all over Regent, where he'd stop for a cup of coffee and exchange the time of day, one reason why his death was so keenly felt in this rural community." There was a small refrigerator and a wooden drying rack on which he apparently hung the clothes he washed in the sink. There was a mirror above the sink and a medicine cabinet containing a plastic water glass, two toothbrushes, a package of five Gillette MicroTrac disposable razors, a can of

Barbasol shaving cream, a bottle of Scope mouthwash, a tube of Colgate toothpaste, and a tube of Tuck's hemorrhoidal ointment. The toilet was at the foot of the stairs leading up to the spare room. There was a closet with no door except a sheet, and in the closet two pairs of jeans, four denim shirts, three pairs of heavy-duty yellow work shoes, a fleece-lined red-and-black-checked winter lumber jacket, and two baseball hats, one with a logo that said ZIV CHEMICALS, the other with a USM rhinoceros. A pair of earmuffs hung from a hook in the wall. In a green wooden military locker at the foot of the daybed there were several pairs of underwear, some socks (the socks and underwear freshly laundered and neatly folded), two pairs of worn work gloves, a Bible, a hand iron, and an overdue book of Ansel Adams photographs of Yosemite from the Regent public library.

I got the look of the room immediately. It had the anonymity of a prison cell maintained by a particularly fastidious inmate. There was no hint of personality anywhere. No sense of who Edgar Parlance was. Or what had led Duane Lajoie and Bryant Gover to skin him alive.

The only objects out of the ordinary were thirteen twisted votive candles on a serving platter placed on top of the refrigerator. It was as if they had been melted and then sculpted into strange otherworldly shapes by a demented artist whose medium was wax.

I had a hunch about the candles. They were included on the sheriff's inventory of the apartment, but not the exact number. Approximately ten, the inventory said. You could count on Brutus Mayes not to do things right.

Jocko picked up one of the candles and began playing catch with it. Throw it up with one hand, catch it with the other. He flipped it over his shoulder and backhanded it without turning his head. Teresa was reflected in his mirrored sunglasses. He snatched a second candle from the plate and began to juggle the two, and then without missing a throw, grabbed a third.

The juggling seemed to be Gargantua's mating call.

Teresa scrutinized the contents of the medicine cabinet. It was as if nothing interested her more than the Scope, the Barbasol, and the Tuck's hemorrhoid ointment. What did not interest her was Jocko Cannon.

Jocko was so close to her that his knee was grazing her hip. I was the Jew fag. I was not there. I took advantage of the opportunity.

I pinched a candle and put it my pocket.

Let's move on, Teresa, I said. There's nothing more we need to see here.

Merle Orvis had a teardrop tattooed under her right eye.

She had been in and out of juvenile detention since she was twelve.

Her last detention report said that she was five feet three inches tall and weighed one hundred fifty-nine pounds.

Merle Orvis and her son Boy lived in the Wuthering Heights Mobile Home Park, suggesting that someone had a sense of humor (not likely), an affinity for Emily Brontë (even less likely), or had simply appropriated the name as classy after seeing one of the many film versions of the book available on the cable movie channels. The park was across from the Regent town dump and next door to the VFW post (BINGO WEDNESDAY AND SATURDAY, PUBLIC WELCOME) and a topless bar called Bob's. Bob's had originally been called Boobs, Merle Orvis said, but the fucking town council, a bunch of limp dicks, forced it to change its name. The sign outside now said B OBS, without the apostrophe and with the first *o* painted over. Merle Orvis had danced at Boobs until the owner discovered she was only fourteen, and it was a penal-code offense for a minor to be engaged as a lap dancer. A pall of smoke hung over the dump from the small fires that burned trash day and night. Most of the mobile homes, including Merle Orvis's, had wind chimes, and when a breeze came up it blew the smoke and fetid fumes from the dump over the court and rustled the chimes so that the effect was like listening to a concerto for xylophones as you were choking to death.

Inside, Merle Orvis's trailer was a pigpen of dirty dishes, unemptied wastebaskets, open garbage bags, ashtrays filled to overflowing, and moldy French fries that seemed to be growing out of the sprung couches. Boy had no other name, although occasionally Merle Orvis called him Baby. After Baby was born, she said, she had made arrangements for him to be adopted by what she called a couple of muff divers from San Francisco, but then decided that lesbian parents would not give Boy the kind of upbringing she thought he deserved. Boy's birth had never been registered, and officially he did not exist. On Merle Orvis's rung of the societal ladder, birth control was seen as a dreary restriction—messy, expensive, unspontaneous—and because babies conferred a kind of status on teen mothers with nothing else going for them, abortion was regarded with disfavor. Women as well as men seemed to accept rape as an irrevocable clause in the sexual contract; Loomis County had not prosecuted a rape in seven years, or secured a rape conviction in the twelve it had been operating as an independent legal entity in the state court system. Boy wore no clothes and was not yet toilet-trained, although he was almost three. He piddled constantly, and was still being nursed. Titty, he would say to his mother, and Merle Orvis would hoist a flabby breast from under her T-shirt. Boy would line up the nipple and pop it into his mouth, picking his nose and viewing his surroundings as he slurped his mother's milk, sucking until he was full. Shitty, he would then say, and squat and crap. His legs and his ass were stained with dried excrement. The only other word Boy seemed to know was "Lester." Lester was Merle Orvis's current boyfriend. Lester Ray. Lester Ray, as it turned out, was the son of Clyde Ray, who had seen Duane Lajoie's 1989 Ford 4x4 with the four-pin trailer-tow harness making tracks down County Road 21 the night that Edgar Parlance was murdered. Like his father, Lester Ray never made eye contact. Nor did he volunteer a single word all the time Teresa and I were talking to Merle Orvis. I do not think Teresa in her wildest fantasies imagined that she would separately meet two members of the Ray family in a single day.

"You actually know Carlyle?" Merle Orvis said. "I mean, you met her and all?"

"We should get back to Duane," Teresa said. "It's Duane we need to find out about. Everything you can tell us. You never know what can be helpful."

"She told me she's coming out here to do a book."

"You talked to Carlyle?" I said.

"To her assistant. Consuela. Carlyle wants me to be an extra, Consuela said. You know, like one of the people Duane knew, she wants all Duane's friends and stuff. I told Consuela I could be her stand-in, all those famous people have stand-ins, I could be a very good stand-in, or I could do her nails, I always wanted to be a manicurist, maybe she could send me to manicurist college if it works out. I shadowed a manicurist once when I was at the Learning Center in Kiowa trying to get my GED, so I know all about nails and cuticles and that shit."

Teresa hesitated. I knew she did not wish to deviate from the subject of Duane Lajoie, but on the other hand Merle Orvis seemed to be speaking an idiom she did not understand. It was as if Teresa felt that she needed to get a working grasp of the local dialect before she could proceed. "What do you mean by 'shadowed'?"

"You shadow people in some job to see what the requirements are," Merle Orvis said. For her entire life people in authority had been asking Merle Orvis questions, and every response was tinged with an automatic truculence. "Like if I wanted to be a lawyer, I'd shadow you, you know what I mean? Don't they have shadowing where you're from?"

"I suppose they do," Teresa said.

"I suppose they do," Merle Orvis said, in a passable imitation of Teresa's tone. Then, staring at her: "I told Consuela I used to date Kile Purdy's brother Beau, Beau said Kile was so in love with Carlyle—she was Alice then, but just as pretty as she is now. The shit she and Kile did. You ever see *Taxicab Confessions* on TV, people who aren't real famous talk to taxi drivers about what they want to be in life, about fucking and stuff, I think I'd be a natural on *Taxicab Confessions,* I mean, the stuff I know about Duane, and shit."

"The night that Edgar Parlance was killed . . ."

"Who says they did it?"

"Bryant Gover," I said.

"They didn't mean it. It was like a plane crash or a car accident. It just got out of hand. Duane is such a nice person. Most of the time."

"What time exactly did Duane arrive here that night."

"That fucking sheriff asked me that same thing. He treated me all snotty like. He's so hateful. He ain't going to get my vote next election."

"One o'clock? Two o'clock?"

"Three. Four. I can't remember. You sound like that fucking sheriff."

Boy said, "Titty."

"Fuck you, Baby. You're not hungry. You just like fooling around with my boobs. Go see Lester. Lester, turn on the TV, watch it with Baby, do something fucking useful for a change around here. I'm talking to these people going to send me to manicure college."

"Let's say it was four a.m.," Teresa said.

"Closer to three," Merle Orvis said.

"And what did he say?"

Merle Orvis mouthed the words. "He wanted to fuck."

"Did you?" I said.

"No fucking way. I had the rag on."

"So what happened?"

Again Merle mouthed the words. "I gave him a blow job." And then in her normal resentful voice, "It took like fucking forever. It was like sucking spaghetti, you know what I mean?" She made a slurping noise as if she were drawing spaghetti strands into her mouth.

I wondered if Teresa would nod, but her expression did not change. She waited until Merle finished her slurp, then asked, "Is there anything he wanted you to say?"

"I told that to the sheriff."

"We are Duane's attorneys. We have different agendas. We need to hear it from your mouth, not from the sheriff's."

"What's an agenda?"

"It's what we need to defend Duane."

"He was brain-damaged at birth, you know that? That cord, the umbilical shit, it was wrapped around his neck, it really fucked him up, is that an agenda?"

"Possibly."

"He was a real fuck, Duane, you know that?"

"In what way?"

"He didn't like having Boy around."

"Why?"

"Because he's half colored. Duane was into that white-supremacy bullshit. He hated niggers."

Teresa took a deep breath. "So was there anything specific he wanted you to do?"

"He wanted some Clorox. He washed his fucking hands with Clorox and this fucking wire brush until they bled."

"Anything else."

"He wanted me to wash his shirt."

"Why?"

"I didn't fucking ask."

"Did you wash the shirt?"

"No."

"Why?"

"You ever get tired of asking those fucking questions? Why don't you get a job with that fucking sheriff?"

"Why?"

Merle Orvis ran her tongue over a canker sore on her lip. She seemed to be weighing the possibility of not speaking. But not replying might jeopardize an opportunity to become an extra in Carlyle's shoot. "He wanted me to say he'd been here all fucking night," she finally said. Hostility clashed with calculation. "I said I couldn't do that, I'd been over at Boobs, some people saw me. Shit, I didn't know why he wanted me to say that, but I knew he needed like some kind of alibi, like on TV, *NYPD Blue* and them. And I said fucking no, I'm not going to do it, and he fucking hit me. You don't love me, he said. Well, he got that fucking right."

Boy tapped Teresa on her knee. "Titty."

Teresa smiled and stood up. She reached down tentatively and patted Boy on the head. He began to cry.

"You've been very helpful," Teresa said.

"You going to see Duane?" Merle Orvis said.

Teresa nodded.

"Tell him I still love him."

Another nod.

"You know that Jamaal Jefferson? He was at the funeral. Put up the reward money." She shouted toward Lester Ray, who was slumped in a torn and sagging fake leather chair with its springs sticking out watching *Jeopardy!* on a small black-and-white TV set. "Lester, what is he? Six-ten, two-fifty?" Lester did not move. "I am fucking talking to you, Lester, you hear me?"

Lester Ray continued staring catatonically at Alex Trebek on *Jeopardy!*

"Fuck you, Lester." To Teresa: "Jamaal going to be at the trial?"

"I don't know," Teresa said.

"I read in *People* he prefers white girls," Merle Orvis said.

"Pee-pee," Boy said.

Teresa lit another cigarette. It was the last in the pack. She crumpled it slowly and searched in her bag for another. No luck. After three or four quick puffs, she threw the cigarette out the car window, and the crumpled pack after it. In the rearview mirror I could see the ash spark as it hit the highway. I did not tell her that it was a violation of the South Midland penal code to throw a cigarette out a car window. It could start a blaze in fire season that could take down six thousand acres overnight. "I generally only smoke on the street now," she had said when she asked if I minded her smoking in the car. "When I was a little girl, my mother said that only a certain kind of woman did it. What kind of woman? I would always ask. Just to see how far I could push her. Don't be bold, she'd tell me. 'Bold' was my mother's all-purpose word for any behavior she disapproved of. If she ever knew how bold I really was, I think she would've crawled up Golgotha on her hands and knees."

It was nearly midnight.

We had been on the go since dawn. I would not count the day as a success. We could not even get rooms for the trial at the Lovat Hotel across from the courthouse. The press had taken up all the available space, and the jury would also be billeted there. We finally got three rooms at a place called Motel DeLuxor on the outskirts of town, one room for each of us, and a third we would set up as an office. The owner had a droopy eyelid, which perhaps accounted for the unshaved patches of beard on his face. He seemed to think DeLuxor was a fancier name than DeLuxe. In every room he had placed a pamphlet that said, THE WAY OF SALVATION: "Before God Saves a Man, He convicts him of his sinnership. His blood can wash the foulest clean. Turn over to Him regulation of your life. Obey Him with all your might and He will conduct you to heaven."

Do you believe? he had asked.

Absolutely, Teresa said quickly. I think she was afraid I might say something smartass that would cost us the rooms.

We talk to the Lord every evening, the owner said, his eyelid flickering. We set up tables out by the food center.

The food center was the collection of vending machines. Chips, candy, cookies, soft drinks, and pre-packaged roast beef sandwiches, the meat a little green. Not even the ice was free. Fifty cents a bucket.

We'll definitely try to come, I said. I'm into the Lord.

A warning glance from Teresa.

Still. It was better than staying at the ranch Carlyle had rented. It's quite a spread, we were told. It looked a movie set. I thought it would be perfect for Carlyle, at least as Teresa had described her. Her whole life sounded like a location shoot. I'm sure she imagined herself going over the next day's legal strategy with us every night in the bunkhouse. Or was it around the campfire? With that photographer of hers snapping away in the background.

Even then I had a bad vibe.

Teresa hadn't spoken since the last cigarette. Nor had I seen another car for miles. It was as if we were on an abandoned highway. Then from out of the night the terrifying screech of an air horn and a tractor-trailer right on my tailpipe. It was like an early Spielberg movie I had once seen after sex with a stranger. *Duel,* I think it was called, paying more attention to it than to the prissy young civil litigator wearing a wedding ring and Jockey shorts. Chicago, as I remember. A conference on white-collar crime when I was with the A.G. Was it his room or mine? Mine, probably. If his, I would have been out of there. Watching the movie so avidly was an implicit invitation for him to leave. To get out. Go. There was a paper name tag pasted to the lapel of his suit jacket, which was hanging from the knob of the bathroom door. Hello, I'm Chuck Something. From Des Moines or Des Plaines. Maybe De Kalb.

As the trailer passed, air horn blasting, the airflow nearly knocked me off the road.

Teresa gave no indication that she noticed.

"You know, right after I got out of law school," she said suddenly, "I was studying for the bar, and my father defended someone named Rocco Campobosso. One of these people." She pushed her nose to one side of her face. "He was a collector for the Cuccinello crew. From one of the New York families. Which meant it was a full-ticket case. Large dollars. They ran a construction and carting company. A front, of course. Executive Red Ball. Exterior demo. Interior dismantling. That was Rocco Campobosso's line. Dismantling. People. Who couldn't or wouldn't make the vig." Her head rested against the window. She seemed to be in some other place. "He threw someone off the George Washington Bridge once. The Jersey side." Then briskly, "But that was a private thing. Daddy said he was doing a favor for someone. Hudson County couldn't make the case."

A private thing. A favor. I felt like an innocent.

"Usually he'd start off easy." She was back on Rocco whatever-his-name-was. "With a message. He'd send a hearse to your house. From a funeral home. A long black Cadillac. Usually from Pelluglio Funeral Services. Two guys in black suits and black fedoras would ring the door-bell. 'We're here to pick up the stiff,' they'd say. It usually did the trick and payment was forthcoming. But then there were those who didn't get the message. Or who maybe thought Pelluglio's made a mistake, got the wrong house." She stared so long out into the night that I thought she had lost whatever thread she was trying to knit into the narrative. Then: "He had a way of dealing with those people. You could almost call it unique." She paused. "He'd pour dry-cleaning fluid down their throats. They'd find the money. Oh, yes. They always found the money. It was not an experience you'd want to go through twice."

I jammed on the brakes.

A deer had bolted from the side of the road and stood frozen in the glare of the headlights. As the car skidded to a stop, the buck turned and bolted across the highway, disappearing into the blackness.

Again Teresa seemed not to have noticed.

While I wondered if anyone in the Cuccinello crew had ever seen a deer, let alone had any concept of the damage a twelve-point buck jacked in the headlights could do even to a sensible Volvo SUV like mine that happened to crash into it at seventy-five miles an hour. But then again I think I'd rather take my chances with the buck than with someone who might throw you off the George Washington Bridge. On the Hudson County side.

"However," Teresa said. She seemed to be talking less to me than to herself. "This one delinquent. He choked on the cleaning fluid and went into cardiac arrest. Suffered permanent brain damage. My father worked out a deal. Everyone knew everyone. The prosecutor had been a student of his at St. John's. He'd worked with the judge at the Queens D.A.'s. So. Aggravated assault. Rocco Campobosso would do a touch in Attica. That's what they called it. A touch. They treated it like summer camp. Three years. Five. I can't remember."

I concentrated on the road. In the distance I could see the lights of the two newest real estate developments south of Cap City. Rancho Rhino and Strong Valley. The second named after Dr. John Strong, who owned major parcels of the land on which Strong Valley was developed. Each parcel a gift from grateful Rhino boosters.

"You know what Rocco Campobosso's doing now since he got out of Attica?"

At last we seemed to be getting to the point. "No."

"He's a consultant. On wise-guy movies. TV. What color blue suit does a Mob guy buy?" She did a gangster imitation, deep and rich with phlegm. " 'Electric-blue mohair, don't you know nothing?' Does he have a razor cut or not have a razor cut? Do you say you capped somebody or you whacked him out? Do you wear the pinky ring on the little finger of the right hand or the little finger on the left hand? 'The left hand, of course, don't you know nothing? Because you use the right hand to hit somebody with, you wear the ring on the right-hand pinky, it might take out someone's eye, then some pain-in-the-ass A.D.A.'s going to load a charge of assault with a deadly weapon onto the indictment.' I think he actually makes all the stuff up, but you get the lowdown from Rocco Campobosso from the Cuccinello crew, it's got to be gospel, right? He's a made man, he's made his bones, everyone knows all the lingo."

Another long pause. I knew she was going someplace. I just did not know where. Finally: "I ran into him in the street in New York a year or so ago. On Park Avenue. There's a BMW dealership on Park, and as I was walking by, I heard this voice. 'Hey, Brendan Kean's daughter, it's Rocco.' And it was. It's not a voice you forget. It's a voice used to scaring people. 'I'll suck your fucking lungs out.' And his face. It was like nine miles of dirt road in Calabria. And he starts hugging me. 'Your father, God rest his soul, saved my life,' he said. I'm lost in his overcoat, it must be five thousand dollars' worth of vicuña, I can't move, I can't speak, all I can do is listen. 'The touch he worked out was just what I needed, I coulda done it standing on my head, but I thought I'll make use of my time, I'll rethink my life. In Attica. I'm driving a BMW now, just brought it in for servicing, on Park Avenue, you notice, not out in Ozone Park, I'm making more than I ever made collecting for Cooch, I got a summer place in Point Pleasant, I never ratted anybody out, life is good.' The dry-cleaning fluid was from another place, another time. Now he's got something to sell."

I thought I finally had made the connection. "Unlike Merle Orvis."

"She's like a paper boat. No rudder. Just floats through life any which way. That child. Boy. Baby. Maybe we should get child welfare involved."

"Getting Boy into foster care is not what you're getting paid five hundred thousand dollars for."

Teresa stared out the window. As I focused on the highway, it struck me that Rocco Campobosso or the more unsavory members of the Cuccinello family were probably more comprehensible to her at that moment than Duane Lajoie or any of his satellites.

But then again.

Her voice came out of some other part of the night. "Max, who actually knew Edgar Parlance?"

In other words, she had her own internal circuitry. She just got to places more indirectly than I was used to.

"If you believe what we heard today, Teresa," I said carefully, "he was the best friend of everyone in Regent. Couldn't have a birthday party or a barbecue without old Gar. Tie a yellow ribbon round the old oak tree."

The turnoff to Cap City loomed ahead.

"Tell me why you stole that candle from his room."

Chapter Eight

TERESA

Well, that went badly.

An insufficient answer, then ten miles of freighted silence past the malls and mini-malls and industrial parks that surrounded Capital City like a commercial moat. She wondered if there was such a thing as unfreighted silence, and how it differed from freighted silence. That was how the mind worked when two people were trapped in a car unwilling to speak to each other. One additional word and the nascent partnership of Kean & Cline would have vaporized. Could have vaporized. Might have vaporized. Perhaps. Possibly. So. Concentrate. Think good thoughts. Teresa counted the grain elevators rising in the night distance. A sudden unwanted image elbowed its way into her consciousness. The grain elevators reminded her of Jack Broderick's last hard-on. A prostaglandin E-1 event. That was an area of concentration she did not need. Her last sexual adventure. How long now? Stop counting, she warned herself. Celibacy was the operative ticket post-prostaglandin. She would give up sex as she used to give up peanut butter for Lent. Except she had never liked peanut butter. She had looked up prostaglandin E-1 in the *Physicians' Desk Reference* she kept in the small office adjacent to her bedroom. Next to the *Merck Manual.* Teresa Kean, she thought, prepared for any medical emergency. Except for a postmortem erection. Prostaglandin E-1. Warnings. Precautions. There were no indicators that the carnal interaction the prostaglandin E-1 was supposed to facilitate would lead to myocardial infarction. She implored a higher power. Please, get me off this subject. She looked over at Max. He was peering out at the highway as if it were an unmarked, unpaved road in a strange foreign land where he did not speak the language—Urdu, say, or Farsi—or understand the local alphabet. Driving required all of his attention. Teresa craved a cigarette. God, for ten years she had not smoked, and now she wanted a butt stop. Wal-Mart. Food Treasure. A carton of Salem Lights. Easy on the throat. How to occupy the mind rather than converse with Max.

"We'll talk," Max said suddenly.

The SUV had pulled up to the main entrance of the Rhino Carlton-Plaza. She had not even processed the trip through town. What she had noticed was that Max kept both hands on the steering wheel and did not make a move toward opening the door. She also noticed that the doorman who swung it open had a rhino emblem on his peaked hat. She wondered if when the case got before a judge she should wear a rhino emblem on her court clothes. She assumed everyone else would be wearing one.

"Tomorrow."

"Good night, Teresa."

"Good night, Max."

Teresa leaned back against the pillows. Plastic. Not feather. Housekeeping had said there were no feather pillows. If there were no feather pillows, she doubted that room service could rustle up a bowl of iced and thinly sliced cucumbers. Something to put on her eyes that would ease out the markings of age she so acutely felt. Forget avocado slices, her usual protection against the plague of time. Avocado was a rare delicacy in Cap City.

The telephone rang.

Twelve-ten. It had to be Max. Only he would call at this time of night. "Teri—"

"Who?"

"Teri Kean." Whoever was calling pronounced it *Keen,* not *Kane* as in *Citizen Kane.*

"Teresa Kean."

"Of course. Who'd you think I was calling. My girl never makes a mistake. A whiz with numbers. She can track anyone down. Doesn't matter where the location is, she'll find you. Right off the top of her head she can get Marlon. Tom. Julia. Beepers. Cell phones. She got Ridley once in Rabat. Rabat, for Christ's sake. That's in Algeria."

"Morocco."

"Morocco. Tunisia. Who cares. They're all the same. Sand-nigger countries, excuse my southern, you didn't hear that. The point is she tracked him down. Nine-hour time difference, he was setting up a five-camera shot, twenty-five hundred extras, beautiful downtown Rabat, he's losing the light, she gets his beeper number, he takes my call, everyone takes my call. Teri Kean. You take my call right. In wherever the fuck you are, Kansas City . . ."

"Capital City."

"You're better off in Rabat."

"Do you know what time it is?"

"Ten o'clock."

"It's after midnight."

"Not in L.A., it's not."

"Who is this?"

"Marty. Marty Magnin."

"Who?"

"A Martin Magnin Production. You heard of that, right?"

"No."

"Jesus. A kidder. Kansas City. The city of kidders."

"Mr. Magnin, I'm going to hang up now."

"Wait. You got the flowers, right?"

So he was the one responsible for the gangster-funeral mountain of white flowers that covered every flat table surface in the room. Tulips. Casablanca lilies. Freesia. White lilacs. A bouquet of white roses on her pillow rather than the nighttime chocolate. She had to put some vases on the floor so she could see the mirror to cream her face. The card simply said *Marty.* In her exhausted state after the endless day in Regent and the tense ride back with Max, she had assumed Marty Buick. But Marty would never have been so vulgar. A perfect *Phalaenopsis* was more Marty's style. Three hundred dollars for two sprays. Those flowers. They reminded her of death. Pellugio's on Sullivan Street. That's twice in one night Pellugio's came up. *Six Generations. A Hundred Years in the Com-*

munity. *Family Owned. Family Focused. Serving All Faiths.* As long as the deceased was Catholic and Italian. *Pre-Need Planning.* A sound feature, her father once said. Since most of its clients expected to get whacked. There was something reassuring about Pellugio's. Again something her father had said. They do it right. There was always someone at the rosary talking about what should have been done to Marlon Brando in *On the Waterfront.* They shoulda thrown that fucking snitch off the fucking roof of his fucking apartment is what they shoulda did. Naw, an ice pick in his eye is what they shoulda did. A hot poker up his ass like they did to one of them English kings, I saw it on A&E when I was inna can. They got cable inna can now? Ogdensburg. Minimum security. You can fucking order in almost. You tried this fucking cannoli? Every mourner at a Pellugio interment received a loaf of Pupella Pellugio's homemade lard bread, as well as a baseball cap that said PELLUGIO'S—PRE-NEED PLAN-NING. Angelo Pellugio, patriarch of the sixth generation, invariably called her father Mr. Brendan Kean. We meet again, Mr. Brendan Kean. Too often, Angelo, you know my daughter Teresa. I haven't had the plea-sure, Mr. Brendan Kean. Even though she had attended half a dozen wakes and rosaries at Pellugio's on Sullivan with her father. Lulu Con-stanza. Silvano de la Torre. Carmella Concetta, Dino Concetta's ninety-nine-year-old mother. It's a pleasure to meet you, Miss Kean. She favors you, Mr. Brendan Kean. Another thing Angelo Pellugio always said at the wake of one of her father's clients. Martin Magnin could have taken a lesson in manners from Angelo Pellugio.

Teresa saw no reason to acknowledge receipt of the flowers. Not with the memories they carried. Holy communion every fucking day, Dino Concetta had said of his ninety-nine-year-old mother. She wanted to make fucking a hundred. Dino Concetta was born without a right thumb. Which made him less than the optimum hitter Brendan Kean always said he wanted to be.

"No."

"You didn't get my flowers?"

"Mr. Magnin, I'm tired, I've had a long day, I want to go to bed."

"Wait a minute. We got to talk. We've got pals in common . . ."

"I think that is extremely unlikely."

"Jack."

Oh, God.

"Jack Broderick. He was a pal of yours, right?"

Is there anyone who did not know that Jack Broderick had died in her bed?

"He was my writer, Jack. One of them anyway. A pain in the ass, you want to know the truth. Like all writers. But I figure you know that already."

She did not know what to say. There had to be a reason Martin Magnin had called. And she knew she would not get to sleep if she hung up without finding out what it was.

He was still locked on Jack. "He did that thing about the kid movie star. The one that gave Shirley Temple a run for her money until she got all fucked up. Blue Tyler. I own that story. I mean, he did it on my tab, he never delivered, I figure I own the rights, I got to get my money out. I got my people busting his people's chops. If there's something there, it belongs to me. We go to court, we got a solid case, my people say. That kid, that Blue Tyler, there's a major motion picture there somewhere, and I want to make it, and no pain-in-the-ass writer's going to stiff me."

Teresa stifled a laugh. She tried to imagine the look on Martin Magnin's face if he knew that the woman he was talking to in room 1012 of the Rhino Carlton-Plaza Hotel, Capital City, South Midland, was Blue Tyler's daughter. Then a moment of panic. Had his people found something? Had Jack left something in his papers? Angelo Pellugio, Dino Concetta, Blue Tyler. Teresa felt depleted, as if she had been sentenced to solitary confinement in a prison of the past. LWOPP. "Mr. Magnin, why did you call?"

"Your rights, Teri."

"What rights?"

"We need you to sign a release."

"Why?"

"So we can use you in this picture."

So there had been something in Jack's files. Her voice seemed to rise an octave. "What picture."

"I got the wrong room? This is Teri Kean, right?"

Her voice was strangled. A step from hysteria. "My name is Teresa."

"Who said it wasn't? Teri Kean. The chick that's going to defend that nutcase who chilled what's-his-name, the schwartz, Eddie Parlance."

Teresa touched her forehead. It was damp with perspiration.

"Jessica's dying to play you."

"Jessica?"

"Lange. You're about what? Fifty? Fifty-five."

It's what I feel, certainly. Maybe even look like. A bowl of cucumber slices would be just the ticket right now. "No."

"Jessica's around there. Give or take. We put some clamps in, she can do thirty-five. No. That's a stretch. Forty. 'With Jessica Lange as Teri Kean.' That sounds good, right? You can get behind that?"

She could not think of anything to say.

"And I've got Jack sniffing around. He loves Jessica. From *Postman*."

Jack. Don't ask. Context clues, the nuns in seventh-grade English at St. Pius V would always say. *The Postman Always Rings Twice*. Jessica. Jack. Nicholson. "Really."

"He's never done a *fageleh,* Jack, and he might be a little long in the tooth, you got to be a hundred to get that Kennedy Center Honors thing, but he's a very good personal friend, and if the price was right, I think we could work something out with Sandy Bressler." She did not dare ask who Sandy Bressler was. Context clues again. Lawyer. Manager. Agent. "You think your partner would sign off on that. 'And Jack Nicholson as Max Cline.' "

It was too much to assimilate. "Mr. Magnin, I won't sign a release. I'm going to hang up now. Don't call back. Good night. And thank you for the flowers."

"I thought you didn't get the flowers."

"I made a mistake," Teresa said as she hung up. She took the bouquet of white roses from the pillow and held it beneath her nose, breathing in the aroma. *And Jack Nicholson as Max Cline.* Max would appreciate that. It could ease the strain. The considerable strain.

"Tell me why you stole that candle from his room?"

CAPITAL CITY—NEXT THREE EXITS.

Max maneuvered the SUV onto the turnoff.

"That candle is evidence," Teresa said.

He still did not answer.

"And yes, I did read the property report, and yes, I know that moron sheriff did not have the exact number down in the inventory. And it's a good bet

that cretin who was coming on to me copped one, too. Or maybe three. To improve his juggling skills. But I'm an officer of the court, Max. And so are you. If you were still with the A.G., and you knew I'd lifted a piece of evidence from the room where a homicide victim lived, you'd drag my ass up before the ethics committee of the state bar, right?"

"Right."

"Why then?"

"It's complicated."

"What isn't?"

Max shrugged.

Outside the car window she could see houses. Every one the same. Every one with a basketball net and backboard jutting out from its garage.

"I'd like to put this on hold, Teresa."

"There's a reason?"

"Conceivably."

"And that's all I'm going to get out of you?"

"Yes."

And it was.

CHAPTER NINE

MAX

The Magnin character called me that night, too. *Teri loves the Jessica idea, Max. Jack's never played one of you people.*

One of what people?

He's always looking for ways to stretch himself.

For his art.

Whatever. But first, you'll talk to Teri, right? Get her on board. We sign Jack, we sign Jess, then you bid a fond adieu to Cap City, you're off to the land of milk and honey. You like Malibu?

There's a trial I have to take care of.

If Teresa still wanted me.

Absolutely. We'll be in touch.

So.

Now to Stanley. Who always said that separate bathrooms were the secret of a happy marriage. Fat lot he would know about that. I wondered if Stanley considered our connection a marriage. Or even happy. He had usurped the large bathroom off the master bedroom. No reason why not. He was paying for most of the upkeep. Even as senior prosecutor with the A.G., I was not exactly rolling in clover. And less so now as defender of the odious and their right to be judged innocent until proven guilty. In any event, nothing I really believed, however much I prattled to my students, who believed it even less than I did.

My bathroom, half the size of Stanley's, was down the hall, off the small bedroom I had turned into a home office. Stanley had a tub, but I had the newer shower, three showerheads pounding water at me front, back, and side, with one of those handheld attachments I could use to wash the soap off my genitalia and out of my eyes. Stanley craved my shower, and was constantly talking about putting a new one in his bathroom. Which meant he would have to use mine during the construction. Not so fast. We had an implicit agreement. His bathroom and mine were like tabernacles. Stanley's word. Not to be violated by the other. A place of secrets. The place we kept things we preferred the other not see.

Like the candle I had left on my sink. I lay down. I could hear Stanley finishing up on the treadmill in the alcove where he kept his barbells and workout paraphernalia. He liked to be sweaty when he got into bed. He thought it was an aphrodisiac.

That damn mangled candle. Which Stanley was holding in his hand as he stood in the doorway. His abs were glazed with perspiration.

"What is this?"

"Stanley, you were in my bathroom."

"I saw it on the sink. I thought you left it there because you wanted me to see it."

"It's evidence."

"Someone was naughty, was someone?"

"I'm under a gag order."

"You are so professional, Max. Did Ms. Kean see the candle? Or is that under the gag order, too? And how could you be under a gag order? You haven't been to court yet."

"Put it back, Stanley."

"Does she know how it got twisted into this interesting shape?"

"Good night, Stanley."

"You are going to introduce me to Ms. Kean, aren't you? 'I'm Stanley, you're Teresa, Max has told me soooo much about you.' " He disappeared down the corridor. A moment later he was back, toweling himself vigorously. "She won't call me Stan, will she?"

Chapter Ten

Teresa picked up the phone on the sixth ring.

"Teresa."

"Max." Was he in or out? She was supposed to meet Duane Lajoie at the Correction Center today. Without Max she would have to re-schedule.

"Seven-nineteen. You watching TV?"

"I'm not awake yet."

"Channel Twenty-three. That'll wake you up."

She groped for the remote. She heard the sound first. ". . . The teenaged supermodel arrived last night from New York in a chartered jet . . ."

Alicia Barbara on-screen. In the background the chartered G-5. "Sources say that the cost of chartering a Grumman G-5 for a flight from New York to Capital City would be no less than forty thousand dollars . . ."

Carlyle wearing jeans, boots, a jean jacket and an oversized woolen cap with the peak turned backside front.

"She wasn't supposed to come until next week."

"Did she call?" Max said.

"No. Of course not. I don't want her here before I even see my client."

Alicia Barbara: ". . . was accompanied by a covey of assistants and prize-winning photographer Alejandro 'Alex' Quintero . . ."

Alex Quintero in a khaki camera jacket shooting Carlyle on the tarmac, his assistants reloading his battery of cameras and handing him a new one after every few shots.

Alicia Barbara: ". . . refused to speak to this reporter or say if or when she would see her half brother, Duane Lajoie . . ."

A still of Teresa. ". . . whose defense attorney is Teresa Kean, the well-known Washington victims' rights advocate and talk-show regular."

Jesus Christ.

". . . former colleagues at Justice for All, the advocacy firm headed by Ms. Kean, refused to comment when asked if it were true . . ."

". . . for a fee said to be one million dollars."

A shot of Carmen Furillo, her secretary, no, her former secretary, exiting the Justice for All offices with her hand over her face as if she were doing a perp walk. And behind her Lois Bercovici, her chief litigator, same mode, straight ahead, no stopping, no eye contact. In fact, Lois Bercovici had said plenty, but only to Teresa. Dishonest. Hypocritical. Contemptible. Judas. Four of the more measured words Lois Bercovici had used when Teresa had told her staff that she was leaving the firm and that she would defend Duane Lajoie.

"And now the supporting cast," Max said, into her ear.

". . . will be assisted by Capital City attorney Max Cline . . ." A still of Max, younger and with a beard. ". . . former chief prosecutor and director of the homicide unit in the South Midland Attorney General's office." Alicia Barbara staring at the camera, talking fast. ". . . resigned after a dispute . . ." Another still of an older unbearded Max. ". . . over what were said to be lifestyle issues . . ."

Teresa clicked off the remote. "That's enough. Any more surprises in it?"

"Just the usual Middle America crap," Max said. "A rural community asks why. Brutal murder. Beloved victim. National attention. The president of the United States. J.J. Poppy. Johnnie Cochran. Jamaal Jefferson. And a wonderful last shot for our side." Teresa waited. Max milked the silence. "Carlyle and her happy crew leaving the airport in three stretch limos. White. The kind kids use on prom night so they don't drive down the wrong side of the road drunk and kill themselves and the family of five in the oncoming Dodge Caravan. With two SUVs to carry their luggage."

She took a deep breath. "You want out?"

"I think we're stuck with each other, Teresa."

As Teresa stepped from the shower, she saw the red message light blinking on the telephone. She wondered who it was. Max was picking her up at ten-thirty to go to the Correction Center for their first interview with Duane Lajoie, so unless he was changing the pickup time, there was no one else she wanted to hear from. If it was Max, there was plenty of time to call him back. Deliberately, she wrapped herself in a towel, shook the water from her hair before wrapping it in another towel, then ran the back of her hand over the stubble on her legs. A quick leg shave with the disposable razor from the hotel gift pack, then a pass under her arms. She noted with satisfaction that she did not nick herself as she usually did.

A random thought: What is the physiological function, if any, of body hair? When did women first begin shaving their armpits as a fashion statement? Was Queen Victoria the first? Cleopatra? Marie Antoinette? Elizabeth I? Martha Washington? Sally Hemmings? Harriet Beecher Stowe? Emma Goldman?

She rubbed skin lotion into legs and face.

Why, she thought suddenly, am I taking such pains to pretty myself for Duane Lajoie? With all the care I'm giving this, I'll be putting in a diaphragm next. No, thank heaven, if there is one, she'd left that back in Washington. It was an inducement to casual carnality that she did not intend to pursue in South Midland.

Although she had brought her pills.

There were only a half-dozen left. She would have to reorder. From her pharmacist in Cleveland Park. She did not believe it would go unnoticed that Duane Lajoie's lawyer got a birth control prescription filled in Capital City. Or was that just paranoia? Maybe it was better to let the pills go, too. Another inducement she didn't need. The diaphragm always seemed ludicrous to her now, anyway. On a planned holiday trip to Israel the summer before her last year in law school, an impassive El Al security guard in the Frankfurt airport had removed an earlier pessary— she loved that word, it was so old-fashioned, so Mary McCarthy and *The Group*—from its case and carefully held it up to the light as if it were a repository for Semtex or whatever concealable explosive El Al security thought might blow up a plane that summer. He held it as if it were a Frisbee and for a moment she had thought he might scale it to another guard. Then he had put it back into the case, and motioned her through the metal detector. Where she had promptly set off the alarm and found herself staring at three automatic rifles. The detector, it turned out, was pitched so high that the underwire stays in her bra had triggered it. Two El Al security women watched her remove the bra in the ladies' room and returned it to her after she passed through the metal detector a second time without incident. In the departure lounge, she waited until the final call for her flight to Tel Aviv, and then as she was about to board, the last passenger, she turned instead and left the airport. She exchanged her ticket for a flight to Rome, and spent the next three weeks in a tiny Fiat wandering by herself, pensione to pensione, through Umbria and Tuscany. She never did put the bra back on, and in both Todi and Lucca the diaphragm had proved handy. Camillo and Frederic. Camillo was a Chicago policeman, recently divorced, with distant relatives in Montefusco he had decided he did not really wish to meet. He had tattoos on his arms and shoulders. One tattoo said *Fickel*. She wondered if he had spelled the word wrong, or if it was the name of someone once dear to him, but she did not ask. Frederic was a defense analyst at the Hudson Institute. He said his name was spelled like Lieutenant Henry in *A Farewell to Arms*. He said she reminded him of Catherine Barkley. One of the more repellent lines she had ever had foisted on her.

She still had not been to Israel.

She wondered if there was any method of birth control she had not tried.

Abstinence.

Although it makes the heart fonder. Or so they say.

Rhythm.

I got rhythm, I got music. What the just-menstruating girls at St. Pius V would giggle to each other in the school bathroom. She did not even know what rhythm was.

Still.

Duane.

She felt as if she had slept with him last night.

Not exactly with him. With his paper trail. The familiar product of discovery. Every reading bringing fresh discoveries. Rap sheets, probation reports, psychiatric evaluations, IQ tests, medical examinations, witness statements, character appraisals, and sentencing documents. The only history available to someone like Duane Lajoie.

Since birth an object of public and institutional scrutiny. There are two types of people, she used to think when she was in criminal practice. The scrutinizers and the scrutinized. The great divide in American life. She had always been on the right, or at least the safe, side of that divide, and wondered what it would be like instead to be in the crosshairs of authority. The examinee rather than the examiner. These were the thoughts that came with rereading the entire case file last night and into the early morning. How many times now had she done it? How many times had she questioned Max? How late was it when I finally fell asleep? she wondered. The sun was just coming up. But then the sun is always dramatically just coming up in these reflections. Lending the romance of dawn and its early light to their coloration.

Her father had always found the reading of these dark histories comforting and instructive. Throw everything up in the air, Teresa, and let it drift to the floor like the autumn leaves. Don't try to put it all back together, this with this, that with that. It defeats the purpose. Read it in the order you pick it up. It exercises the mind. Allows you to make connections. A little trick of the trade.

She would need more than a few tricks of the trade to mount a defense of Duane Lajoie. Even Brendan Kean, GRHS—God Rest His Soul, in the Pius V Sunday announcements—could not provide all the tricks she would need on this one.

Forget Pius V.

Think Duane.

Age 21. Height 5 feet 7 inches. Weight 136 pounds. Which would make him approximately five inches shorter and maybe fifty pounds lighter than Edgar Parlance.

Max, who actually knew Edgar Parlance?

Marginally retarded. Presumably from breech-birth oxygen deficit.

IQ 87, first test. IQ 84, a year later. IQ 91, most recently.

I've known judges with an IQ of 91. Or so I thought. Certainly politicians. Meaning mental incapacitation is a no-go defense.

Albion County, two counts residential arson. Convicted. Awaiting sentence.

No permanent address.

No permanent employment.

Had only met Bryant Gover two weeks before Edgar Parlance's murder.

Thirteen days. Maybe fourteen.

She could hear her father's voice: It's not how long they knew each other, Teresa. In the country of crime, two weeks is a lifetime. What's important is what they did together when they knew each other.

Okay.

They skinned Edgar Parlance alive. One of them did. Or both of them did. Bryant Gover got his story together first.

Could Bryant Gover be the soft spot?

It was a start.

A straw to clutch.

Max, who actually knew Edgar Parlance?

If there is an answer, neither of us has been able to find it.

She spread out the Gover files.

Father (unk). Mother: Maude (?) Gover (Grover? Tovar?). Education: Nathan Hale Juvenile Vocational & Detention Farm, Loomis County, SM; one yr HS (inc) Northeast HS, Lincoln, NE. Occupation: Food Treasure bag boy, Pratt, KS; day laborer, car wash attendant, etc., various venues. U.S. Army. Desertion, dishonorable discharge, three months confinement, Fort Sam Houston, TX. Involuntary manslaughter, Darwin, AK, convicted, one to three years, served thirteen months. Carnival roughneck, Galveston, TX, assault w/deadly weapon (knife), charges withdrawn. Beston, OK, accused domestic A&B, case dismissed. Questioned not charged homeless homicide, Loup City, NE. Assaulting a peace officer, thirty days, Paradise, NM. Drunk and disorderly, fifteen days county workhouse, Dedman, Wyoming, once called Dead Man until the town fathers changed the name to attract the Wind River & Western Railroad, which never came.

It was a life spent on the road, thumb out, and always the possibility of grand theft auto in the next car speeding down the empty endless strip of two-lane blacktop. *Where you going, son?* A dangerous question on the open road. Always leading to the same alibi. *The faggot made a pass at me.* D&D. B&E. Concealed weapon. Indecent exposure. Charges filed, cases dismissed. Fairholm, Colorado. Clifton, Utah. Jaco, North Midland. Theo Cummings, Idaho. Ewing, Missouri. Wilsonmeer, Montana. Mifflin, Kansas. Towns named after initial settlers long since vanished, along with their descendants. Bryant Gover was the sort of road rat who automatically attracted the highway patrol in whatever jurisdiction he happened to be moving through on his way to someplace else. A slowdown, a U-turn, red lights blinking, the officer slowly emerging from his cruiser, belly stretching the buttons of his beige polyester shirt with the sewn-in creases, the car door acting as a minishield in case the vagrant suddenly produced a weapon. May I see some identification, please, sir. It was a demand, not a question. A night or two in the local lockup while the sheriff skimmed the unsolved-crime file, and then he was on his way again, deposited by a deputy at the county line, no official apologies given and none expected. Leaving behind prints and front and side views for future reference.

Would he have ever met Edgar Parlance in his travels?

Possible. They were traveling men.

Where were the intersects?

None, Max had said.

None the SMBI had found.

None Teresa could find.

And yet.

Max, who actually knew Edgar Parlance?

The message light was still blinking insistently. Teresa dropped the towels and searched her body in the mirror for ripples and wens. She felt her breasts and remembered Marty Buick once telling her that if you found a lump in your tits, it was already too late, it might seem like a bing cherry pit to you, but to the oncologist it meant get your estate in order, sign the will, say goodbye to the near and dear, bury the necessary hatchets, take the chemo, go to the good wig-maker, real hair makes all the difference, keep a stiff upper lip, what you want them to say is, God, she was so unflinching at the end, so brave, so unafraid, what you don't want them to say is, You want the honest truth, she was such a pain in the ass, like nobody else had ever had it.

Better to punch the message button. "You have two unplayed messages," the computer voice said. "One, eight-oh-nine a.m."

"It's like the fucking Ponderosa down here," Carlyle's voice said. "I thought it was going to be some kind of dude ranch, but they got pigs and chickens and that shit. Not even any trail mix. No wonder Hoss Cartwright died. The smell got him. Listen, get me and Alex suites at that hotel up there, will you? And bed-and-breakfast places for . . ." Her voice trailed off as she talked to someone in the background. "Alex, how many people we got with us?" There seemed to be an argument. "That's too fucking many, Alex, that's all I'm saying. You're paying for yours, right?" Then back to Teresa. "Yo, Teresa? I want to see what's-his-name, Duane, you know, my bro . . ."

Teresa pressed the discard-message button and began brushing her hair. The computer-generated voice said, "Second message: eight-thirteen a.m."

"Teresa . . ." Martha Buick's voice, talking too fast. "It's Marty. You're not there. I guess you must be at the health club. Listen, I just heard from Carlyle. Has she called?" You know she's called, Marty, she called you as soon as she left the message for me. "She wants to see Duane, I mean meet Duane, since she's never actually met him . . ."

Teresa hung up.

She felt her breasts again. No tangible growths or bumps or cysts. Nothing to excavate her from the case upon which she was about to embark.

CHAPTER ELEVEN

VERBATIM AUDIOTAPE TRANSCRIPT

DATE: 5/8

VENUE: CAPITAL CITY CORRECTION CENTER,

CAPITAL CITY, SOUTH MIDLAND

PRESENT: Duane Lajoie, South Midland Dept. of Corrections No. 914609CCCC (hereinafter called DL); Teresa Kean, Atty-at-Law (hereinafter called TK), counsel for Prisoner No. 914609CCCC; and Max Cline, Atty-at-Law (hereinafter called MC), also counsel for Prisoner No. 914609CCCC. The record will reflect that Duane Lajoie was wearing the orange jumpsuit that is standard attire for inmates at the Correction Center and was in arm and leg restraints because of an incident with a Correction Officer as reported to prisoner's counsel by George Hennican, Warden.

TK: Mr. Lajoie . . . is it Laj-wah or La-joe-a?

DL: You're my lawyer, you can't even get my fucking name straight, what good are you, for fuck sake, women are pussy, they're not lawyers, it's La-zhoe-a, and you there, the other one, I heard about you, big-deal prosecutor, there's people he put in here, pussy, he gave them time because they wouldn't cop his dick, he's a Jew fag is what he is. . . .

MC: Good morning, Mr. Lajoie—

DL: Fuck you.

TK: Mr. Lajoie, may I call you Duane?

DL: I didn't even know I had a fucking sister, then she finds you, she's paying you a million, it says on the TV, shit, she gave that million to me, I wouldn't be in the shit I'm in now, fuck her, long gone, over the hill to grandmother's house, except I never had no grandmother, I never had nothing my whole life, I see my lawyers, they put me in leg irons like I'm guilty or something, what kind of impression does that give—

TK: Mr. Lajoie.

DL: I thought you were going to call me Duane. That's Doo-ane, not Dwane, Doo, that's what my friends call me, you can call me Doo-ane.

MC: About the leg irons. The warden said you stuck a correction officer—

DL: They ever find the fucking shank? No.

MC: Actually they did. It was the wire holding the straw together on a broom in a utility closet.

DL: It was only a fucking puncture then, man. And how do they know it was me—

TK: You've had previous incidents with this correction officer, Clarence Detroit—

DL: What kind of fucking name is Clarence anyway? You ever know anyone named Clarence wasn't a nigger? And Detroit? The capital city of Nig Nog from what I hear. Never been there, never going to go.

TK: These incidents—

DL: Every time he sees me, Clarence Dee-troit, he goes, "*Bzzzz,* that's what the electric chair sounds like, it's the last sound Percy Darrow heard, it's the last you're going to hear, *Bzzzz,* I'd pull that switch and hear the sweetest sound this side of heaven, *Bzzzz,* I'll have it with chitlins and greens. *Bzzzz.*" I'm going to tell that Dee-troit nigger something, I ain't going to no electric chair, fuck him and his *Bzzzz.*

MC: So that's why you shanked him.

TK: Let's move past Clarence Detroit. I don't think he's really part of our charter.

DL: What's a charter?

TK: In this instance, Edgar Parlance.

DL: I didn't know that motherfucker.

MC: You never met?

DL: I don't hang with niggers.

MC: Never met him?

DL: How many times I got to say no?

TK: Then it was Bryant Gover who knew him.

DL: I'll gut that—

MC: So we've heard.

TK: You and Bryant Gover were friends.

DL: He never was no friend.

TK: But you knew him.

DL: I only know him for a week. I just met him. He killed that nigger and now he's trying to blame me. I was just along for the ride,
he's a fucking animal, he said he'd kill me I didn't go along, he had
this .38 Detective Special, it makes a hole in you like a fucking cannon, he likes to off people, that's what he likes to do, then he
snitches me out, he doesn't want to hear no fucking *Bzzzz,* I got
friends up at Durango Avenue, they'll fucking take care of him.

MC: How'd you meet?

DL: How come you ask all the questions? You getting paid the million or is she? Who's in charge here?

TK: Duane, how did you and Bryant Gover meet? We have to estab-
lish a time line. Did you just run into each other? Were you just
hanging out?

DL: What do you mean "hanging out"? You mean "doing a little
weed"? That kind of pussy stuff people like you do? You know what
they do in here? The fat girlfriend comes in here on visitors' day
with little plastic bags of smack or shit in her panties or her
brassiere, or maybe she stashes it in her brat's shitty diapers, that's
the best place, no hack's going to go fishing through a whiny kid's
crappy Pamper, and she flushes the stuff down the crapper. And the
guys in the sewer plant, they know it's coming, and they swim
through the shit and piss like fucking scuba divers and fish out the
skag or the crack or the crystal meth, whatever it is. It smells a little
rank, but, fuck, it gets you up, it gets the job done. I'd like a piece
of that action, I'd be a fucking rich man in here, my so-called sister
wouldn't have to put up no million.

MC: Waste management in the cathedral of crime.

DL: What's that, some kind of faggot joke?

TK: Duane, we were talking about you and Bryant, how you met.

DL: He cold-cocked someone with a pool cue. I mean, that's what kind of violent person he is, a stranger, someone he didn't even know. It's like what he did to Wonder.

MC: Who's Wonder?

DL: It's fucking nobody. Some guy. Another guy.

TK: Let's concentrate on Gover and the pool cue. When you met. Who did he hit with a pool cue? Where?

DL: You know Feathers.

MC: The keno joint in Chippewa County.

DL: What're you, some kind of geography teacher, or something?

TK: You were at Feathers. And?

DL: This dude was flashing a picture of Merle.

TK: Merle Orvis?

DL: Has that cunt been talking to you?

MC: What kind of picture?

DL: I told her to keep her mouth shut.

TK: The photograph—

DL: She was giving him a blow job.

MC: Wonder?

DL: Forget Wonder, he's—

TK: Who, then?

DL: Who what?

TK: Who was she fellating?

DL: What's fellating . . .

MC: It's a lawyer's word for blow job.

DL: I got to remember that. Is that classier than sucking off?

MC: Judges think it is.

DL: Well, that's the only fucking thing she knows how to do, fel-lat-ing, and she's no good at that.

TK: Let's get back to the pool cue. At Feathers.

DL: So this guy, Ty or Ray or something like that, he's showing this picture of him and Merle around the bar, her fel-lat-ing him like, and I hit him with a beer bottle, and he comes at me, him and some other guy, he's got these like huge arms, like fire hydrants, I'm holding my own, I don't need nobody, and all of a sudden, they both go down, Bryant's broken the fucking pool cue on the back of their heads, he can't pass up hitting somebody, that's what kind of person he is, he doesn't even know Ty and the other guy, and we get out of there, we get in my pickup, and shit, we are gone, we go to Merle's, we do some stuff, she gives him a blow job.

CHAPTER TWELVE

The rest was more of the same.

It gives you an idea of what Teresa and I had to work with, and how even if he were innocent, which he wasn't, how difficult it would be to sell his story to a jury. We might be able to prove, although it was unlikely, that he did not cut or peel or shoot or stomp, but the fact was that he had been there, and the best spin we could put on it was to show that he was an unwilling participant, in fear of his life.

An old story that never worked.

His teeth were chipped and broken and looked as if they had never entertained a toothbrush. The space between his two front teeth was the same space that was the trademark of his half sister. All the time he was talking he was breathing his homemade buck fumes in our faces, Windex and raisins picked from prison rice pudding and fermented together. Another premium product in the inmate economy.

Bzzzz.

I had to admit it did have a nice sound.

Punctuation. A period at the end of the sentence.

We weren't surprised by his riffs and free association and stream of consciousness, if he indeed had ever been what is generally conceived of as conscious. So there is no point in printing out the whole transcript. A taste of it is like a swallow of buck. Nor would there have been any point in telling Duane that the mother who left him at St. Fintan of Cloneagh's Foundling Hospital in Halloween County had once been a keno waitress and part-time hooker at that same Feathers in Chippewa County, had married her first husband Bruiser Todt there when she was seventeen and already pregnant by someone other than the Bruiser. Pregnant with the half sister who was paying for his defense.

Coincidence as destiny.

Duane Lajoie, Bryant Gover, and Merle Orvis. For two weeks—or, to be exact, twelve days—they were the three musketeers of Loomis County, rolling over the back roads at such high rates of speed in Duane's old Ford 4x4 that the pickup received four speeding summonses, twice when Bryant Gover was driving, once when Merle Orvis was at the wheel, with Boy on her lap sucking a breast.

All for one and one for all until they began ratting each other out.

Each summons had mentioned the FUCK THE TELEPHONE COMPANY bumper sticker that Clyde Ray had seen on County Road 21 the night Edgar Parlance was murdered. Freeing Brutus Mayes from having to do much Dick Tracy sleuthing. There was only one pickup in Loomis County with that particular signature, and it was registered to Duane Lajoie, Wuthering Heights Mobile Home Park.

Merle Orvis's trailer.

Somehow Teresa and I were able to piece together a narrative from the gospel according to Duane. Which, as it turned out, was really not that much different from the gospel according to Bryant.

Except when, at the meaningful moments, the roles were reversed.

It was as if they were pitching the same movie with two different leading men.

Bryant had camped out in the back of Duane's pickup. They shoplifted groceries at the Food Treasure and skipped out of Domino's and KFC without paying and sang karaoke at the Bunkhouse and took turns fucking Merle Orvis. The bed of the pickup, according to the sheriff's impoundment papers, was a landfill of crushed six-packs and discarded fast-food containers and dirty laundry and cigarette butts and roaches and used condoms, each item like an artifact discovered on an archaeological dig. The underclass—a migrant civilization deliberately forgotten.

Another story in this saga.

So. Here is Duane's story. The short version.

Bryant was driving. On the road out by the falls. It was after midnight. There were no other cars. Duane was drunk. Two liters of malt liquor and a pint of apple brandy. He was pretending to be asleep against the passenger door. He was afraid of Bryant. Bryant was equally drunk and had already puked in the cab. His vomit was all over the steering wheel, the dashboard, the windshield, and Duane's trousers. Bryant said he would cut Duane if he didn't stop complaining. Bryant spotted a man walking by the side of the road. The man turns and puts out his thumb. He was colored. Bryant shakes Duane and says let's have some fun with the nigger. He guns the pickup and steers it straight at him. The man jumps away. Bryant turns and chases the hitchhiker into the field off the road. He was playing with him, man, Duane Lajoie said. Blocking the nigger off and knocking him down, I thought the fucking truck would get stuck in the mud, I tried to get him to stop, he wouldn't do it, he was having too much fun, now he wasn't even trying to hit him, you ever seen that bullfight movie, the fucking cow gets all tired and shit, he can't move, and then the bullfighter takes the knife and shit and sticks him, that's what Bryant was doing, he was playing with him, and finally the nigger just went down on his knees and then he rolls over and he's just lying there, man, he could hardly breathe, it was fucking awful, I felt really sorry for that nigger. And Bryant gets out of the truck, he takes a tire iron out of the toolbox and he goes over and he hits the nigger and what I'm doing is I'm trying to slide into the driver's seat so I can get the fuck out of there, but Bryant's got the keys and he comes after me, and he says he'll kill me if I don't help him, and then this nigger gets up, I never seen anything like it, he comes at me, like it was me who hit him, not Bryant, and Bryant hits him again, and puts him down, and then he gets some pliers out of the toolbox and he's got this box cutter and he gives me the tire iron and says if he moves hit him, you don't move, I'll skin you, and he starts slicing the nigger's pants and he slices a piece of skin and he takes the pliers and pulls this piece of skin off like it's a strip of bacon, you know what I mean, you buy a quarter pound of bacon, you peel the strips off, that's like what he was doing, then this nigger just gets up, I just want out of there, man, and Bryant says deck him, I drop the tire iron and Bryant picks it up and drops him, then comes after me, he is going to brain me for sure, and the nigger gets up again, I never seen anybody that tough, he's got pieces of skin flopping all over the place, and Bryant hits him again, and he goes down, and Bryant stomps him with his boots and shit, and then he starts to pull his tongue out with the pliers, and the nigger still tries to get up, and that's when Bryant shoots him with that .38 he always carried, it tore the back of his head off, he checks the nigger out to see if he's dead, then he takes this knife, it's a huge fucker, it's like one of those swords the soldiers wear in those movies before they had guns, when it was just bows and arrows and swords and shit, and he cuts something on the nigger's chest, he says to me kick some dirt over him, and I say no, and he says I'll put you down there with him, I'll cut your tongue out, and so I kick some dirt on him, we're about ten miles from the fucking road, nobody's going to see him, but I want to keep my tongue, and that Bryant's crazy, and when I'm doing that dirt he gets back in the truck, he's going to leave without me, he's going to leave me out in that field there to take the fall for offing that nigger, so I chase after him, I'm hanging on to the fucking tailgate and finally I pull myself on board, I'm lying in the back with all this shit, and he stops, Bryant, he gets out of the truck, I thought the fucker was going to shoot me, and he says we got to get rid of all this shit. So we finally get back on the road, it seems like hours, Bryant must've chased him halfway to Nebraska, I thought we'd get stuck before we ever hit the road, but then we do, and we head for the falls, and Bryant says we can get rid of the stuff there, they'll never find it, he wanted to keep the .38, he said that fucker had got him out of a lot of tight spots, and I say fine, you ought to keep it, they ever get to him and he's carrying that dude, they'll pin killing that nigger on him, and not on me, and that's how it happened, it was Bryant, it was Bryant's idea, it was Bryant that did it, then the fucker snitched me out.

It was implausibly plausible.

Or plausibly implausible.

Not that it mattered either way.

Divers found the .38-caliber DS-II Detective Special, the Tennessee Toothpick, the box cutter, the pliers, and the tire iron underneath Loomis Falls. There were no fingerprints on any of the weapons. Each appeared to have been wiped clean before being thrown into the falls, and the water apparently removed anything else incriminating that might have remained. In the attempt to retrieve the weapons, one of the divers drowned, and the Worm was trying to find some interpretation of the state penal code that would allow him to charge Duane Lajoie with the diver's wrongful death.

"You get everything you wanted?" Warden Hennican said at the guard station controlling Duane Lajoie's cellblock. He had that hard little smile of contained outrage that career bureaucrats in the Department of Corrections automatically seemed to cultivate. In a warehouse of criminals, moral superiority, however superfluous or spurious, was an additional weapon. "I'll tell you something, Mr. Cline . . ." He ignored Teresa, it was as if she was not there. ". . . you used to send people here, that was before you began defending the people who are sent here, but I like to believe you've still got a bit of the old you when you were a prosecutor, and so it's the old you I'm talking to, if I make myself clear—"

"Goodbye, Warden," Teresa interrupted. She picked up her attaché case.

". . . that man is a troublemaker . . ."

"People in prison tend to be," Teresa said. She moved to the door.

We walked silently through a series of security checkpoints. At each stop, a corrections officer examined Teresa's attaché case. It was as if she might have been slipped something between checks. Finally, for a moment before the gate was open, we were alone. "What did you think?" Teresa said quietly. "About our client?"

"I think he should've cut a deal before Gover got his. He wouldn't be looking at the *Bzzzz* if he had. What do you think?"

She waited a moment before she spoke. I knew what she was going to say. It was on my mind, too. "I think a lot about Edgar Parlance."

The gate to the prison exterior swung open.

You saw what happened.

Lorna Dun was there with her camera crew and Alicia Barbara with hers, each of them shouting questions at Teresa and me. Poppy McClure was not there, but Teresa saw Willie Erskine cheerleading a crowd of demonstrators who were waving placards scrawled with red-meat slogans, KILL THE BASTARD or A BULLET BEHIND HIS EAR. It was just another

mini-riot that the Cap City police did not expend too much energy trying to put down, viewing it in the same good humor with which they
viewed the downtown wreckage after the Rhinos beat the Cornhuskers
or the Vols. Teresa slowly pushed her way to my car, with me in my
rugby mode acting as her blocker, *I have no comment, please, no comment,
I'll have a statement on behalf of my client at the appropriate time, please,
no comment.* As we reached the car, she was hit in the side of the face and
crushed against the SUV by a KILL THE BASTARD sign, and as she righted
herself she found herself staring into a Nikon held by Alex Quintero,
who managed to squeeze off half a roll of film before she found safety in
the front seat. It was only then that we saw Carlyle. She grabbed Alex by
the arm and led him to a scrum between two groups of demonstrators.

"Who knew we were coming here today?" I said, pushing the SUV
through the throng draped over the hood, with some satisfaction making Alex Quintero jump out of the way, the satisfaction diminishing
when I realized it was the kind of shot he was looking for.

"Does it matter?" Teresa said.

CHAPTER THIRTEEN

About Alice Todt, aka Carlyle: Her sense of propriety was absent, and I intuited but did not act upon the danger I suspected she posed. She was after all financing the defense, such as it was. I always had difficulty calling her Carlyle, and in the aftermath find it impossible to do so.

She and Alex Quintero did produce and publish their coffee-table book, and hired an uncredited ghost to write the text. They called the finished product *Fit for Kings,* from those signs on every road leading into town: REGENT—A PLACE FIT FOR KINGS—POP. 3,679. For a long time I would not open the book. Not to read it, however, was like not opening a long-locked closet because of what one feared might be found behind the door, and so I finally picked it up as I was trying to assemble this record. The book was everything I expected it would be—mendacious, meretricious, and self-servingly dishonest or evasive about the events in which Alice was a catalyst, shot against the seamier backdrops of Loomis County, not the falls or the epic, undulating prairie. Theirs was a mean, marginal Regent of trailer parks and pit-bull breeders, of karaoke bars and the Burlington Northern switching yard, of a cemetery overgrown with weeds and a dump where old tires burned around the clock. It was a place that seemed entirely populated by people wearing jeans that rode lower than the anal crack and soiled T-shirts that did not cover the belly button; by men and women with 56-inch waists, the product of bad weather, too little exercise, too much television, and too much sugar-saturated junk food; by women with black eyes and men with missing teeth and swastika tattoos.

In the book, I found things I had chosen to forget, observations I had opted not to confront, not least about the forbidden subject of class. I remember the predatory bookers for the daytime tabloid talk shows, cruising Loomis County in stretch limos looking for anyone who had known Bryant Gover or Duane Lajoie, or better yet had fucked or sucked one or both. The talent pimps offered these gullible souls, dressed like streetwalkers, craving this last best chance for a way out of Regent, a ride to Kiowa and first-class plane fare to Chicago or New York, a night in a big city, bright lights hotel, a prix-fixe steak-house dinner, drinks not included, and an economy ticket home. Those who signed up did not understand that to the bookers they were only human debris allowing their producers to fill another mud-wrestling half hour purporting to show the underprivileged at play. When the red light on the camera dimmed, they would return to the anonymity of the vegetable counter at the Food Treasure, or the perils of single motherhood, or the weekly visit from the domestic-abuse counselor, with a memento matchbook from the Howard Johnson Motor Inn to show for their visit to the high life, a swizzle stick from Sullivan's on Broadway, and an eight-by-ten glossy signed by Montel or Jerry Springer.

Fat blustery Merle Orvis with her teardrop tattoo was on the jacket of *Fit for Kings,* smoking a cigarette and nursing Boy, his tiny little pecker nearly erect as he stood tippy-toed on a wood stump and hung like a monkey to his mother's pendulous breast. It was celebrity of a sort, or at least Merle Orvis chose to think so. She called Alice Todt Carlyle, or Carl, sometimes Carly, and said that Carly was her best friend and asked Carly to be Boy's godmother, although she did not know exactly what a godmother's duties were, except to give presents, you know, like on birthdays. Carly said she would check with her attorneys and her financial advisors, and if there were no contractual obstacles, she would consider the request; Alex are you getting this? Alex Quintero captured it all, roll after roll. The book was a slippery New York item, a Christmas present artifact for decorated living rooms, the artist dropping in on Midlandia, and it made me fiercely protective, outsider though I was myself, of the place I called home.

For my own peace of mind, I would like to think I would have felt the same way even had the casualties not been so prohibitive.

BOOK TWO

SURVIVORS

PART ONE

ANGKOR WAT

20:54.16. *She opened her purse and scooped out three coins. The camera zoomed close and paused on the bag. He made out the* F *clasp.* F *for Fendi, he supposed.*

She dug in the purse. No more coins except the three she had in her hand. She removed the cigarettes and snapped the bag shut.

Hold on the cigarettes, please.

Come in tight, please.

Gauloises. French and unfiltered.

Why not.

She slipped the cigarettes into a blazer pocket and then pumped the three quarters into a twenty-five-cent slot. The third quarter brought a return of six more.

She gathered the coins and quickly dropped three into one slot and three more into the adjoining machine. This time no return from either slot.

A delicate Asian cocktail waitress materialized at her side, holding a bamboo drinks tray. The woman in the dark blazer and the white blouse and the dark pleated trousers shook her head no. No complimentary soft drink, no beverage at all. The Asian waitress was wearing a white bustier and a long skirt that clung to her legs.

The waitress looks like Princess Tuptim, I said to the chief of security.

Who's Princess Tuptim? the chief of security said.

From The King and I.

That's the general idea, the chief of security said.

Of course. The dealers and croupiers were dressed in pantaloons and silk shirts, their hair shorn to the skull, like King Mongkut. Actually more like Yul Brynner. When Rex Harrison played King Mongkut, he had a full head of hair. Midgets in exotic dress scurried around the casino floor. The keno runners were all Asian, sloe-eyed, the brochure said, the waiters and the bellmen dressed in the orange robes of Buddhist monks. The sound system played "Shall We Dance?" and "Getting to Know You."

It was definitely erotic.

Like a very expensive whorehouse.

Or a male brothel.

Everything is authentic, the promotional video in each room said. Down to the smallest detail. Verified by a panel of world-renowned Asian scholars. Silk spun from privately owned silkworm ranches.

Except that Angkor Wat is in Cambodia, and Mongkut ruled Siam. There was no reason to explain this to the chief of security. One does not argue with a world-renowned panel of Asian scholars.

It's a long way from Jim Hogg County, I said to the chief of security.

Say again? the chief of security said.

Just thinking out loud, I said.

She was at the front door now. She seemed to appear and disappear like Zelig. A male dwarf in silks from the privately owned silkworm ranches offered her a scented towel.

We're going to lose her for a moment, the chief of security said. Until she gets to the pedestrian bridge.

She seemed to be laughing.

I'd like to send her home, the chief of security said.

Chapter One

Raw interviews conducted by print and electronic journalists with Alice Faith Todt, aka Carlyle, after the events herein described played out to their logical, illogical, and in some instances unexpected conclusions. They were edited, elided, and rearranged into a seamless monologue. The questions of the various interlocutors have been excised in the interest of narrative clarity. Every word, however, is hers, picked up from audio or video recording devices obtained or made available to the narrator.

For fuck's sake, Alicia, everyone blames me for what happened, like it was my fault, and it wasn't. No, no, no fucking way was it my fault, I was not responsible. You want to start blaming, start with my agent, my former agent, I'm going to own her fucking business by the time I get through with her, I'll even take her plane, it's her husband's plane, a G-4, you mark my words, I'll get that, too. The way she foisted that lawyer off on me, when all I was trying to do was keep my brother Duane out of the hot seat, I never even knew they ever called it that. The hot seat. It's cute in a way. I bet you could make a lot of money out of it, you know, a toy like a whoopee pillow, instead it gives you a little shock instead of blowing a fart. At least that's what Alex said. Alex's got a good head for business. It was his idea for me to go after Three V, he'll want a piece of it, of course, Alex wants a piece of everything, it's from growing up in Washington Heights, he thinks he's the only person in America that grew up poor. I've seen that Washington Heights of his on the way to

Teterboro. I don't fly commercial anymore, it's too much of a hassle, people want my autograph and ask me questions about Jacquot and Yo! Carlyle, I don't have time for all that shit. I always ask the driver to slow down, the windows in the limo are smoked, but you can see out and it's not so bad, Washington Heights, try a mobile home in Cap City, me on the couch, and my mom grinding away in the sleeping area, it was from my mom I learned you're supposed to go "Oooo" and "Ahhhh," like it's some kind of big deal. Everyone thinks I was getting off with Alex, but you know, we never did it. Except for that time at the Gritti, we were there for a Jacquot shoot, I hate Venice, all that water, it makes me seasick, it was only twice anyway, I think a model of my stature should stay away from photographers, they're just people who work for you. Except for Irving what's-his-name, shoots the flowers and fruit and shit. Anyway, he's been married twice, Alex, first to someone from the hood on West 153rd, the second time to that Jap model, maybe she's Chinese or something like that. His first wife's married to a dentist in Riverdale now, and the second wife, the slope, she's in rehab, Hazelden this time, she's tried them all, Silver Hill, where Billy Joel went, Promises in Malibu, Charlie Sheen's home away from home, Alex always picks up the tab for her, he should tell her to take a hike back to Tokyo, but he never will.

So what I mean is, I got my own troubles, without taking the blame for those four people dying. I mean, who shows up in Regent but my mother. She's got a little red dot in the middle of her forehead, like they wear in India and shit, she'd told me she wasn't coming to the trial, it was too painful, they were going to try and say her baby Duane did those awful things, and I know my baby Duane didn't do them, and she puts her two hands together like she's praying, and she says, Call me Shehnaz. In a pig's ass I'll call her Shehnaz. Alex says I should call her Dot for that little red dot. It was the Roshi, she said, who'd sent her to Regent. Roshi Gurjanwaia, or however the fuck you pronounce it. She said she was so happy at Amritsar University, remaking her life according to the Roshi's five principles, and I say, What principles are they? And she says the Roshi's five precepts for living are to abstain from killing, stealing, lying, and intoxicants. And I say to her, That's four, what's the fifth? And she says to abstain from all sexual activity, and I said to her, You got to be fucking kidding, and she says to me, bowing and pressing her hands together and closing her eyes, like she's praying and shit, I am here on a mission from the Roshi, and the Roshi asks if you would make a small pledge to Amritsar University, and I said, What kind of pledge, and she said, A small fraction, and I said a small fraction of what, and she says, Life has been good to you. Then I get it, and I said, It hasn't been all that good, and no matter how good it is, I'm not dumb enough to get hustled by some Roshi with his mitts out, thinking I'm going to shake the money tree in his direction. You are an ungrateful child, she said, and I said, You better believe it, and while you're at it, you can take you and your red dot back to Amritsar and abstain from balling.

Anyway, so I get in to see Duane after my mom leaves. I'm feeling kind of bad we had this fight and stuff, so I say I'll go see Duane, I'll leave out the Shehnaz part. My fucking lawyer doesn't want me to go, and I say to her, Listen, you're here on my tab, don't you forget it. I know all about prisons, I was at Riker's Island, you know, doing that Prada shoot that all the assholes got so pissed off about, prison's not so bad, they had some good-looking dudes at the Prada shoot, you know black guys and Spanish guys, Alex could speak Spanish to them, *Quien sabe* and stuff like that. There was this guy at Riker's, Alex knew his brother, him and the brother had gone to school, he'd been shot or something, by the cops or something, or another dealer, they thought Alex was great, these guys. Anyway, Duane comes in, and I say, Hi, Duane, but shit, I thought he'd look like those guys at the Riker's shoot, but he's like he crawled out from under a rock, he's got this breath, I nearly fainted. I had some Binaca, and I tried to give him the Binaca, and this guard takes it away from me. You can't pass contraband to the prisoner, he says, and I say it's not contraband, it's fucking Binaca, and he says, He'll drink it. I felt so sorry for him, and he tells me his story, it's the other dude that did it, what's-his-name, Gover, well, you know what happened, everyone knows it, how the fuck was I supposed to know. No one else did either.

That first day in court, everyone was ganging up on me, right from the start. I'm waving at Duane, you know, during jury selection, and I say, Hi, Duane, and he's giving me an over-the-shoulder wave, he's got these chains and shit around his ankles and he can't turn around, and Alex has this little camera, it's about the size of a goober, and he's snapping away, great pictures, you've seen them, when this fat guy in a uniform, he's some kind of bailiff or shit, whatever the fuck a bailiff is, he says I can't wave at the prisoner. And I say that's my brother, and he says, real smart, Well, that's your tough luck, isn't it. Sweetie? Fuck him, I bet he doesn't make a hundred thousand dollars a year even. Then that midget judge, she wouldn't let me use my beeper in the courtroom, it rings with the first few beats of the Jacquot commercial, you know da, da, da-da-da, it's really cute, Alex's Jacquot video won the Eddie Award, and when I accepted it with him, the strap on my dress broke, the Jean-Paul Gaultier print, and I showed a little tit on the tube, but it was only cable, so it didn't matter that much. Anyway, the beeper goes off that first day, I want to keep in touch, keep my dates straight, I got Milan coming up, and I want to do Giorgio and Donatella, but they overlap you know, Giorgio wants my hair one way, Donatella wants it another, we have to work that out, and this judge, she's got a mustache, she goes nuts, she asks whose beeper it is, and I'm not going to tell her, no way. So she closes the courtroom, she won't let anyone out, and there's this stink of sweat and shit, everyone in the courtroom could use a shot of Jacquot Skin Pearls, you ask me, and she has this spade sheriff and his fucking deputies pat everyone down, like it's some kind of big criminal deal your beeper going off.

So that's how I met Jocko. He's one of the deputies working the courtroom, and he comes up to me, he's about the size of the *Intrepid,* you know that aircraft carrier on the West Side Highway, I did a shoot there once, some pansy French photographer, not Alex, I got him fired, this frog, he thought out of focus was arty, and I said to him, Get lost, go back to France, where you from Nancy, that's a town in France, I bet you didn't know that. Anyway, Jocko brings me outside in the corridor, and he says to me, Put your arms over your head and let me pat you down, a real Mr. Smooth act, and I say, No fucking way are you going to touch me. And he says, Well, give me the beeper then, and I say, How do you know it was my beeper, and he says, Come on, everybody in the court-room knows, the people around you were pointing at you, just go up and tell the judge you thought it was turned off, fuck her over a little bit, Your Honor this, Your Honor that, my brother's on trial for his life, I am so upset, she'll give you a warning, she'll take the beeper, make it the property of the court, don't worry, I'll get it back for you, she'll never even know it's gone. So to make a long story short, Brutus, that big black sheriff, he makes Jocko my bodyguard, it's part of the community service he was doing, like there was so many people around when I was shooting, and Jocko, he was like a one-man crowd control, no one's going to fucking mess with him, and those pals of his, Tater and Bobo and the rest, and I get to ride around in his air-conditioned Benz, he had this red light he puts on the roof, he even had a siren in it, he comes to a light or a stop sign, forget it, the siren is blaring, the red light is going round and round, he is the law. Jocko. His name sounds exactly like my cosmetics line, Jocko, Jacquot, it's so cute, I thought it was, like, fate. Some fucking fate.

Chapter Two

MAX

I talked earlier about the rich seam of chance that governs events.

The coinage of coincidence.

Or is it a skein? Or does it matter what you call it?

So much happened that first day in the Loomis County Courthouse, so much that seemed at the time no more than the commonplace maneuverings of the judicial system. Whatever else one calls coincidence, call it implacable.

Begin with Harvey Niland. Gray, ectoplasmic, failed Harvey Niland.

Harvey Niland was originally meant to be J.J.'s number two. He was safe, he would not open his mouth, he knew the case law, he would take care of the errands and the menial assignments without obvious complaint, and most importantly he would not pull focus away from J.J. But then, mirabile dictu, the Committee on Judicial Appointments, after a decade of waffling and passing him over, graded Harvey as "very qualified" for the bench ("very qualified" means that anything above traffic court is a stretch for the nominee), and the judgeship that Harvey so devoutly desired was at last his. I would guess that the committee took his age into consideration—Harvey was within three years of mandatory retirement—and could view his accession as a kind of tombstone promotion to a position where he could do no real harm.

This is where it began to get complicated. J.J. wanted to pick a younger assistant prosecutor from the Homicide Bureau to be his backup, but Gerry Wormwold insisted he use Patsy Feiffer; she had worked with

Maurice Dodd on the case before he died, she was familiar with the details, and she had been present when Maurice debriefed Bryant Gover. All sound arguments. The only case J.J. could make was that Patsy was both bone-stupid and legally inert. It was a case, however, he declined to make. He knew the Worm could not be budged, and he knew why. It was Poppy. Poppy McClure had let it be known that whenever the press of business in Washington allowed her to do so, she would attend the trial. Poppy's capacity for agitation could not be underestimated. She had not yet declared if she would challenge the A.G. in the Republican gubernatorial primary, but she knew her presence in Regent would make him jumpy. Hence the Worm's intransigence about Patsy Feiffer. He wanted someone in Regent who would report to him on every detail of what happened in and out of the courtroom, and Patsy was too much a creature of ambition, however limited her talents, not to provide this service.

Duane Lajoie arrived from Cap City shortly after sunup, a ninety-minute trip in a high-security unmarked police van, wearing leg irons and handcuffs and guarded by two marshals. I had seen him for a moment in the holding cell adjacent to the courtroom, and ignored his imprecations about my Jew faggotry while Brutus Mayes oversaw the exchange of the orange jumpsuit Duane wore at the Correction Center for a white shirt, khaki pants, and sandals without socks. Every evening during the trial, he would change back into his jumpsuit and his leg irons and be returned to Capital City. Bryant Gover, when he was called to testify, would travel in a second van from Durango Avenue. They would occupy cells on different floors of the courthouse, and when Gover took the stand, Duane Lajoie would be shackled in his chair and guarded by two deputy sheriffs so that he could not try to wreak physical vengeance on the witness. These security arrangements had been negotiated by Maurice Dodd and Duane's previous attorney and there was nothing Teresa or I could do to change them.

The press was everywhere; satellite trucks had taken every available parking space around the courthouse. There were rumors that Jamaal Jefferson was on his way, and a bailiff told me he had heard that Jack Nicholson was in town to get the feel of the courtroom. Lorna Dun and Alicia Barbara were making do with Eugene Hicks and Marjorie Hudnut, in her Sunday best, until Jamaal and Jack and Carlyle and Poppy showed up. On the courthouse lawn, special correspondents once more recounted the hideous scene off County Road 21, milking every shocking detail with all the attendant pieties on how the murder of Edgar Parlance had forced a reconsideration of the unresolved role played by race in the heartland. I had taken samplings on the black-and-white TV set in the tiny office Teresa and I had been assigned in the courthouse basement. In the absence of real news, everything was fodder: the crop-management and weed-control pamphlets in the wire racks on the ground floor of the courthouse, the plaque honoring Loomis County's war dead—sixty from World War II, five each from Korea and Vietnam, the promotional brochure published by the Regent Economic Board that said, "The crime rate is low, the standard of living high." Arched eyebrow and sign-off: From the Loomis County Courthouse in Regent, this is Brent Baker, Acme 1, all news, all day, every day.

"Hello, Max," J.J. McClure said when I walked into the courtroom and placed a legal pad and three pencils at my place at the defense table. Some lawyers are neat, others are always scurrying through documents and transcripts, looking busy. I was one of the neat ones. I thought the busy bees tended to distract the jury when they should be concentrating on the witness being examined. J.J. smiled, the kind of smile that did not affect the laugh lines, but he did not offer his hand. "Long time."

"I've been around."

"So I've heard."

I looked at the *Courthouse Square* cameras set up at either end of the jury box. Technicians with earphones linking them to a mobile unit outside were trying to synchronize their movements. "Is Poppy going to be here?"

"You know Poppy. Last in, first out." The edge in his voice was almost but not quite imperceptible.

As if via a conjuror's trick, Patsy Feiffer suddenly materialized at J.J.'s side, bustling with efficiency, her dusty rose courtroom suit perfectly complemented by a cream-colored blouse. Ostentatiously not acknowledging my presence, she began to ask J.J. a question about the demographic analysis of the jury pool.

"You used to pick the first twelve that came out of the box, J.J.," I said. "Having a confidence problem?"

J.J. hesitated for a moment, then said, "You know my number two, Patsy Feiffer, Patsy worked with your friend Maurice."

Patsy Feiffer stared at me as if I were unclean, which I suppose by her lights I was. I had been fired by the A.G. and I was a homosexual. It was the second time that morning that what some would call my sexual irregularity had been questioned, this time implicitly.

"I've seen you around the courthouse in Cap City. Always on the run. I'm told you're J.J.'s eyes and ears." After a moment I added, "Or someone's."

Her expression did not change. "J.J., Judge Tracy's here, she's going to want to meet counsel in chambers before court opens."

J.J. nodded, and when he seemed disinclined to respond further, Patsy Feiffer disappeared as if the conjuror had waved his wand a second time.

"That wasn't necessary, Max," J.J. said.

"It was fun though, wasn't it?"

"Patsy forgets everything except a grudge."

"Forewarned."

"Where's your boss?"

He was trying to see if he could rankle me, but Teresa *was* my boss, and I had signed on knowing she would be. "Taking care of some business."

In fact, I did not know where she was. We had checked in to the Motel DeLuxor the day before, and I could see the look of distaste as she surveyed the gloomy rooms that would be our headquarters for the duration of the trial. I found the Motel DeLuxor invigorating, or to be more accurate, I found the prospect of what I hoped might be a vacation from Stanley invigorating. The grudging largesse of Alice Todt had allowed us to take over more rooms than we had originally planned. We had computers with passwords ("Northampton" was hers, "Lemberg" was mine, for the Galician railhead where the Kleinbaums began to evolve into Klein and then Cline), and e-mail and a fax and a printer and a shredder, all those things that in my pre-Teresa life as a defense attorney I found at Kinko's. We had a secretary to answer the telephones we had installed independent of the motel switchboard (the calls to my office in Cap City were referred to the DeLuxor), an answering machine, a legal typist on call, and a retired deputy sheriff from Albion County to serve both as

part-time driver and nighttime security. It was not that our files were at
risk, but with the interest in the case high, Teresa thought it best to have
a line of defense against the curious, or the malicious. That morning, she
had woken me at six and said she was going jogging, and would meet me
at the courthouse. I think she only wanted to be alone, to get her thoughts
in order, like an officer in the trenches before he led his troops over the
top in a hopeless and unwinnable battle.

"Tracy hates tardy lawyers."

"I do remember that, J.J."

Ellen Tracy. Another knot in the skein.

She had not become a lawyer until she was forty, and she ran a tight
no-nonsense courtroom. Alice Todt was right. She did have a mustache.
She was tiny and she wore huge white square glasses that drew attention
to the shadow of hair clearly visible on her upper lip. She had been
brought up poor in a hamlet called Dead Center, because it was in fact
the dead center of the state of South Midland. When she was sixteen, she
married a hitchhiker passing through Dead Center, and forty-three years
later, they were still together, the former hitchhiker now a mid-level construction manager in the state Department of Roads. They had a son
and a daughter, both now over forty, and when the children married,
Ellen Tracy, who had never graduated from high school, took a GED
and applied to SMU Law School, where she finished in the top ten percent of her class. For seven years, she was a prosecutor in Kiowa County,
then spent the three years before her appointment to the bench in the
Kiowa public defender's office. She had seen everything, was not swayed
by sentiment, and with her abundance of hard-earned common sense
easily climbed the judicial ladder to senior-judge status. She ruled, she
moved to the next order of business, always decisively, never ratcheted by
doubt. Any decision was better than indecision. She did not tolerate
delay, showboating, or imprecision in examination; a contempt citation
was something she would promise once, and order without hesitation a
second time. When she was assigned the Parlance trials, she immediately
ruled that the difficulty in finding an impartial jury in a jurisdiction as
small as Loomis County, where everyone seemed to know or be related
to everyone else, mandated that the jurors and their alternates be selected
from the larger pool available in Kiowa County. A panel of potential

jurors would be bused to Regent, and those finally chosen would not be sequestered until the start of deliberations, although, Judge Tracy suggested, people used to the bright lights of Kiowa might consider having the freedom of Regent a form of sequestration.

For Ellen Tracy, that passed as humor.

"You're late, counsel," Ellen Tracy said when Teresa knocked on her door and entered the judge's chambers. Teresa was carrying her briefcase and a large orange-and-white shopping bag with cord handles. A not auspicious start.

"I apologize, Your Honor. There was a demonstration outside the . . ."

Ellen Tracy interrupted. "Then you should have made allowances for it, Miss Kean. This is not New York, it's not Washington, where I think you are used to practicing. Here you run on my schedule, and my schedule is meeting in chambers if necessary at eight-thirty, court opens at nine, it ends at four." She ran the words on together, one long sentence without pausing for punctuation. Stop. Breathe. And then the example she expected the attorneys to follow, always somewhat self-serving. "I got here at six-thirty." Having driven herself down from Kiowa, listening to a Great Book on tape. I don't think Tracy had actually read a book in forty years, but she was famous throughout the legal community for having listened to most of the prominent works of modern literature on the high-end audio system in her Land Rover as she dashed around to the various state circuit courts, and she was not above sneaking in a quote or two without attribution if she thought it appropriate to a situation at hand. Happy families are all alike, she might say without a trace of irony, or Isn't it pretty to think so, and only the better-read members of the state bar would know that the obiter dictum was a literary reference. Treating your adversary with respect is giving him an advantage to which he is not entitled, she once said to a callow young attorney who was appearing against me, and it was meant as a rebuke as much to me as it was to him. I knew she had not thought that up herself, and I finally found the remark in a book of quotations. It would have been madness to suggest to her that I was not aware of her affinity for Samuel Johnson; that I found it was victory enough.

Teresa was still in her sights, a target of opportunity. She pointed to the shopping bag at Teresa's feet. "Are you planning a shopping expedition at the end of the court day, Miss Kean? Are you going to take her to the mall, Mr. Cline?"

"I'm not sure there is a mall in Regent, Your Honor."

"Don't get smart with me, Mr. Cline."

"I beg the judge's pardon."

A smirk creased Patsy Feiffer's lips. Tracy was on her in a flash, fresh prey. "You, what's your name?"

"Patsy Feiffer, Your Honor." Her voice was tremulous. "Appearing with . . ."

Judge Tracy cut her off. "I know who you're appearing with. Your given name is actually Patsy?" Incredulity was just another arrow in Tracy's quiver. "Your parents had the effrontery to christen you Patsy? Patsy must have stuck in the minister's throat."

"My given name is Patience, Your Honor."

Judge Tracy considered the name. "Patience." Her head rocked back and forth. "Well, Miss Feiffer, you smirk in my courtroom and I will lose whatever patience I have allotted to give you, and that is not much."

J.J. tented his fingers and stared at Judge Tracy expressionlessly. Even had he been so inclined, which I doubt, he would not have come to Patsy Feiffer's defense. This was a rite of fire, he had seen it before, as had I, it was something to survive. Like a lioness marking her territory, Tracy was staking out the perimeters of her authority, and woe unto anyone who violated her space.

"Now, Miss Kean, back to your shopping trip."

Teresa was rustling around inside the bag. She pulled a straw boater from it, and two large white campaign buttons. The Poppy Power boater, the Poppy Power buttons. J.J.'s eyes flickered, and he inhaled and exhaled quickly.

"If it pleases, Your Honor . . ."

"It pleases."

"Congresswoman McClure, Your Honor, was passing these . . ." Teresa seemed to search for the right word, but I suspect she had it at her fingertips. ". . . artifacts . . ." She let the word hang there. ". . . artifacts out on the steps of the courthouse. When the bus from Capital City with the jury panel arrived, her staff gave these hats and pins to them as they got off the bus. And it appears that a Mr. Erskine, who works for Congresswoman McClure, I think as chief of staff, although I think Mr. McClure here is more able than I to define his proper job designation . . ."

I have to admit that I had doubted Teresa's ability to persevere in the adversary culture of the courts, but she was good, she was very good, she had rocked both J.J. and Judge Tracy back on their heels, and she made it seem as if it was one of the most distasteful things she had ever been forced to do.

"Mr. McClure . . ."

"Mr. Erskine is the congresswoman's chief of staff, Judge." He made it sound as if Poppy were the congressional representative of his district, a distant figure whose hand he had shaken once or twice at campaign events he had been forced to attend.

"And Mr. Erskine did what?"

"The marshals who escorted my client from the Correction Center this morning told me that Mr. Erskine had tried to give them these artifacts." Teresa waved her hand vaguely toward the boater and the buttons on Judge Tracy's desk. "But they of course are officers of the court, and they refused." No one spoke. "I would hate to think that the jury panel has been contaminated," Teresa said hesitantly after a moment.

Tracy did not hesitate. "I don't need some New York lawyer to tell me how to do my job, counsel."

"I apologize, Your Honor."

"You have exhausted your quota of apologies this morning, is that understood?"

"It is, Judge."

Tracy ran her tongue over the furze of mustache. "All right. I'll have the bailiffs go into the jury room and remove anyone who is wearing either this . . . this hat or one of these pins." With a ballpoint pen, she moved first the boater and then the pin to the edge of her desk. "I hope we have enough left to sit a jury. In the meantime, I'm imposing a gag order on these proceedings that is absolute and unequivocal. No speeches outside the courtroom. No appearances on television. No interviews or comments. Any objection?"

The four of us shook our heads.

"Any deviation from this gag order is grounds for contempt, and I will remand to custody that person or those persons who violate it. Understood?"

The four of us nodded.

"Now Mr. McClure."

"Judge."

"You are in sort of a special category here."

J.J. tested the ice. "In what way, Your Honor?"

"Your reputation for charm precedes you, Mr. McClure. I hate charm. Do we understand each other?"

The ice was too thin. "Yes, Your Honor."

"I'm going to bar Congresswoman McClure from the courtroom. Any objection?"

J.J. tapped his thumbs together. "If Your Honor so orders."

"I do."

I knew another shoe was going to drop.

"I suppose I can't include Congresswoman McClure in this gag order, but . . ." She had our attention. ". . . if she intrudes on these proceedings by word or deed . . ." She nodded crisply in the direction of the boater. ". . . while in the jurisdiction of this court, I can hold you in contempt, Mr. McClure."

J.J. shot forward in his chair. "I'm not sure you can do that, Judge."

"Try me, counsel. You can appeal this decision, of course, but I have a good record with the appellate division in this state. If you so desire, I'll bring the court reporter in and we can put this in the record."

J.J. pinched his lower lip between his thumb and forefinger and held it for a moment before speaking. "That won't be necessary, Your Honor."

Tracy looked at each of us in turn. "Okay. Let's go to court."

We rose and headed for the door.

"Miss Kean."

Teresa turned. "Your Honor . . ."

"Welcome to South Midland." Tracy was putting on her robe. Even in high heels she was scarcely five feet tall. "And the court wishes to thank you for bringing this matter to its attention."

So that was it. I don't know what J.J. said to Poppy, but there was clearly no reason for her to stick around if her presence would compromise the case against Duane Lajoie, not to mention complicating her ambition for higher office, whatever that office might be. She released a pro forma statement about greasing the wheels of justice, a Willie Erskine special, then went back to Cap City and from there to Washington and what the statement called the nation's first order of business, holding the line against the poison of collectivism. Her banishment was a contentious topic on *The Courthouse Square Nightly Wrap-up* ("Viewers are encouraged to e-mail their remarks and comments to alicia@cswrap.com"), where the response encouraged Alicia Barbara to mention Poppy at the top of the show three nights running. Tracy threw Alice Todt out of the courtroom, and after two days of jury selection, she swore in twelve jurors—five women and seven men; two of the women and one male juror were black—and four alternates, all four women, two of them black. She told them she liked things to move along quickly and that the proceedings should not last longer than two weeks. It was a Thursday morning and unexpectedly she delayed opening statements until the following Monday, giving everyone a free four-day weekend. The jurors returned to their homes with instructions to be back in Regent by Sunday evening, and the press decamped to Chicago, Washington, New York, and points in between. The recess she ordered allowed Judge Tracy to drive halfway across the state to Dead Center so that she could preside over the fiftieth anniversary of its incorporation as a municipality in Central County.

Ellen Tracy never understood how the mundane decisions she made that day affected the way things turned out.

By the time Ellen Tracy filed a formal complaint with the state bar association recommending that disbarment proceedings be initiated against Teresa Kean, LLC, and James Joseph McClure, formerly chief deputy attorney general in the Office of the Attorney General of South Midland, the play was long finished.

Chapter Three

PARTIAL TRANSCRIPT   PAGES 1–188

IN THE DISTRICT COURT OF LOOMIS COUNTY,
SOUTH MIDLAND

THE STATE OF SOUTH MIDLAND

(CASE NOS. 2391, 2392, 2393, 2685),

PLAINTIFF, *vs.* DUANE LAJOIE, DEFENDANT.

Proceedings heard before Hon. ELLEN TRACY, Judge, at
Regent, Loomis County, South Midland on March 14.

THE COURT: Mr. McClure, you may begin.

MR. MCCLURE: Thank you, Your Honor. Ladies and gentlemen of
the jury, my name is James J. McClure. I am the chief deputy in the
homicide division of the Attorney General's office up there in Cap
City, which as you know is so ably run by the A.G., that's our shorthand for attorney general, Mr. Jerrold Wormwold. I'm going to be
prosecuting this matter, along with my co-prosecutor, Patience
Feiffer, you see her over there at the prosecution's table with all
those files and law books stacked in front of her. Where to begin? I
think the best place to begin is for you to take a good look at the
defendant, Mr. Duane Lajoie, whose current address is the Capital
City Correction Center. Look at him. Look at him closely. Look at
the way he avoids your eyes—

MS. KEAN: Objection.

THE COURT: Sustained. Move on, counsel.

MR. MCCLURE: This story begins not with the defendant, but with the good man he is accused of so wantonly murdering and disfiguring. His name was Edgar Parlance, and he was a man like so many of us, trying to make do. He was a black man, an African American, an American, and to the defendant that was enough to maim and dismember and kill him. You are going to hear things, good people of the jury, that will make you sick to your stomachs, hear those things in the most brutal and specific detail, and you will see photographs of this good man, Edgar Parlance, that will make you turn away in horror. It is no wonder that Duane Lajoie would not look at you earlier, he knows what you are going to see, he was responsible for what you are going to see, and see him now, brazen, looking at you finally with that terrible smile, he seems to think that the crimes with which he is charged are funny, and not, as they are, an affront to man and the God we worship.

It was Thanksgiving season. The season for giving thanks. Edgar Parlance was walking that early morning out near Loomis Falls, as he often did. Edgar Parlance was a walker. There was scarcely a foot of ground in Regent that he had not explored. When the weather was kind, Edgar Parlance liked to sleep out by the falls under the stars. . . .

THE COURT: Miss Kean.

MS. KEAN: Thank you, Your Honor. Good morning, ladies and gentlemen. My name is Teresa Kean and I am counsel for the defendant in this action, Mr. Duane Lajoie. Appearing with me as co-counsel is Max Cline. Now. You have heard the state, in the person of Mr. McClure, lay out the case it will try, and let me repeat the word "try," try to convince you it has against my client. You notice I say "the case." I say "the case" because the state has no idea what the facts are in this matter as they pertain to Duane Lajoie. Facts. Who. What. Where. When. In the absence of facts, the state relies on emotion. The state would like your power to reason, your ability to reason, to give way to emotion. And there is reason for emotion. The victim in this case was a good man. The crime against him was so horrible that it is almost impossible to assimilate. You would like to cast it from your minds and think good thoughts. My concern, ladies and gentlemen, is that the emotional issues, the goodness of Mr. Parlance and the ugliness of the deed done to him, will overshadow the facts as we will come to know them, the facts that do not implicate the defendant, Mr. Lajoie.

I direct your attention, ladies and gentlemen, to the spectator seats. I expect this courtroom has never been so packed. As you look at the spectator seats, you will see many familiar faces. Not people from Regent. Not people from Loomis County. Or Kiowa or Osceola counties. Not even many people from South Midland itself. No. The familiar faces are those who have talked to you, in many instances shouted at you, from your television screen. These familiar faces have told you what happened that awful night in November. The fact that they don't know what happened is irrelevant. They have told you who is responsible. Again, they do not know. They have told you what the verdict will almost certainly be, given the facts of the case, the facts that neither they nor the prosecution know. These familiar faces who have invaded your homes have arrived at conclusions before a word of testimony is heard. Let us not pretend you are not aware of the tumult surrounding these proceedings. Have you jurors and you alternates all been on Mars since the events of last November that snuffed out the life of Edgar Parlance? Have you been on Jupiter? Uranus? I didn't think so. So I daresay you are familiar with the phrase "plea bargain"—

MR. MCCLURE: Objection.

THE COURT: Overruled.

MS. KEAN: —with the phrase "cut a deal"—

MR. MCCLURE: Objection.

THE COURT: Let's see where counsel is going with this, Mr. McClure.

MS. KEAN: The prosecution cut a deal with Bryant Gover because it could not make a case against Duane Lajoie, and Bryant Gover was afraid he would go to the electric chair if he did not cut a deal with—

MR. MCCLURE: I request a sidebar, Your Honor.

THE COURT: I don't like sidebars.

MR. MCCLURE: Then I request a meeting in chambers.

THE COURT: No.

MR. MCCLURE: I would ask that the jury be excused.

THE COURT: No. But Mr. McClure, I'm going to sustain your

objection. Miss Kean, you've taken this far enough. You can continue this line when the witness, Mr. Gover, is sworn. Agreed?

MR. MCCLURE: Yes.

MS. KEAN: Agreed.

By that Monday morning of opening statements, Teresa and J.J. had already been together for four days.

CHAPTER FOUR

The dream, she said.

You want to watch the game? my mother said. What game? I say. There's always a game on Sunday, she says, I thought you might want to watch. No, I don't want to watch the game, I think I should be getting back. Well, then, she says, and I look at her and she looks at me, and then I heard the shot. Correction. We heard the shot. You better go down to the barn, she says. Very quiet. Matter-of-fact. No excitement. Your father is so careless sometimes. He's getting old, Jamie. (He's not even sixty, he's fifty-five, fifty-six, and she says he's getting old.) I'll go down and take a look, I say. And I walk out the door and out to the barn, walk, not run, as if I thought a car on the road had backfired, as if I had never heard a gunshot before. When I was a kid, I used to shoot at a fence post with that old Colt, my hands were so small I could hardly reach the trigger, and it had such kick it gave me a bone bruise in my palm. Some days when it rains I can still feel that bruise. I got to the barn and there he was, in the wheelchair, his head leaning over into the tub where he kept the scrub brushes, as if he didn't want to splatter the blood, and here's the thing, before he did it he ran water over the axe he used to kill the chicken we had for lunch, scrubbed it clean with a wire brush, and then hung the axe on the nail over the sink where he kept it. First things first. That was Walter.

Finish the dream.

What dream?

About your brother.

Emmett.

Yes.

His voice was a monotone.

Pushme, Jamie, pushmepushmepushmepushme, the pier jutting into the pond, blocking Walter's view. Pushing him, holding him down, calibrating the seconds, five, six, seven, eight, nine, ten, all the way to fifteen, maybe twenty, twenty-five, even more, I can't remember, Emmett's capacity for holding his breath stretched to the extreme, and beyond. Then he was free, but he wasn't gasping for air, no laughing, no againagainagain, just floating there facedown, and Walter, stretched on the rise, he'd fallen out of the wheelchair, he was grabbing tufts of grass, trying to pull himself down to the dock, it's not your fault, Jamie, it's not your fault, he kept on saying.

"It wasn't. He's right. It wasn't your fault."

"I held him under, Teresa. I knew what I was doing. I knew his legs had stopped kicking. He was trying to push my hand away. I had his life in my hands. It was mine to save or take away. I was like Caesar at the Colosseum. Thumb up, thumb down, the losing gladiator lives or the losing gladiator dies. Thumb down. Walter knew what I was doing."

"Jamie, you were seven years old."

"Almost eight, and I was drowning my brother. No. I drowned my brother. Deliberately. With malice aforethought. I wasn't jealous of him. He wasn't my parents' favorite. There was none of that psychoanalytic crap. The fact is, most of the time Walter and Emily didn't even know we were around, Emmett and me. I don't think they knew the other was around, either. I can't remember their ever having a conversation with each other. 'You should get the tires rotated on the Plymouth, Emily.' 'I'll get Fred to do it, Walter.' That was the extent of it. Fred was the handyman. Fred Riggs. He drank. My mother liked him. I don't mean they shared drinks or anything like that. God knows, not the other thing. He'd show up. Then he'd disappear. He didn't have a phone. Fred just seemed to know when my mother needed him for some chores. The tires on the Plymouth needed rotating; there was Fred the next day, knocking on the kitchen door. 'I think I ought to take a look at the tires on the Plymouth, Mrs. McClure.' That's how he pronounced it, 'Miz.' He wasn't tugging a forelock. And he was never presumptuous, either. I suppose in a way he was like Edgar Parlance. Except he was white."

"We said we wouldn't talk about Edgar Parlance."

"Right." J.J. seemed lost in thought. "When she died," he said after a moment, "Fred was the only other person at the grave. Except for the minister. He'd lost a leg, Fred. Diabetes, he said. He was living in a VA hospital someplace in Kansas." J.J. hesitated, as if trying to decide if he should continue. "You know, Walter's family had been in Parker County for a hundred years or more."

"And Fred Riggs with one leg was the only person at the funeral."

"Yes."

"How did he get up from Kansas."

"I didn't ask."

"What did she die of."

"There was no reason not to."

He was drifting away.

"Jamie," Teresa said, "tell me more about Emmett."

"What's there to tell? He was only three. Emmett and I, we were like extras in the movies, bring on the kids, don't be too cute, don't look at the camera. And it wasn't like I was trying to get Walter's attention. You never knew Walter. He was the biggest pain in the ass in any room he ever wheeled himself into. I was seven, eight years old and I knew it. I think he knew it, too. And that was why he killed himself. Not because I held Emmett under. That was a factor, though. He wanted me there, too."

Teresa was insistent. "It was an accident."

J.J. drew the back of his fingers slowly over the her body. "A gun in your mouth is not an accident."

"You're angry."

"I've never told anyone about the way Emmett died. I don't share my life. So it must mean something that I told you." Outside it had begun to rain. After a moment, he said, "Tell me about the man in Washington. The one who died at your house. Poppy says he's the reason you're here."

"I thought Poppy came under the ground rules."

It was as if he had not heard her. "Poppy said you'd never met him before. She said if there hadn't been a White House connection nobody would've cared."

"Poppy's full of information."

"Now you're angry. That makes us even."

She heard thunder, then saw a flash of lightning. "This is madness, what we're doing."

From the darkness, he said, "Yes. It is."

All this Teresa told me later. Not all at once. Over days, weeks. Here and there. Giving it up reluctantly. In stops and starts. Sometimes with flashes of hostility. The attraction was something they picked up in each other. Immediately. An encoded signal giving the latitude and the longitude where their lives could intersect.

She remembered J.J. staring at her intently. "We can go back to Regent," he had said. "Nobody the wiser. Just one more folly in two lives pockmarked by folly."

"It's seventy-five miles."

"In this state, people drive a hundred miles to buy a pack of cigarettes at two in the morning. In case you ever wonder why traffic accidents are the third leading cause of death here. After cancer and heart disease. Gunshot wounds are right up there, too."

"No. I don't want to go back to Regent."

"I didn't think you did." He touched a finger to her lips. "Do you remember the first time we met? In the lobby of the Rhino Carlton-Plaza? And you told me we'd almost run into each other years ago in the green room at C-Span in Washington."

She kissed his finger.

"The site of an earlier folly. As I knew you knew. That's why you mentioned it. It was your way of saying don't mess with me. And I knew then we were so much alike. Walking on the edge. No seat belt. No safety helmet." He hesitated. "I think, Teresa, if we had met that time in Washington, both our lives would be so different."

Teresa drew the feathery patchwork quilt around her. "I want to tell you something."

"You don't have to. It's not truth or dare."

Through the half-open window she could hear the wail of a train whistle. "Poppy is not exactly right about the reason I'm here." He listened. "I had never met Jack before that evening. Broderick. That was his name. Jack Broderick. He knew my mother."

"Before she had Alzheimer's?"

"No. My real mother. The one I never knew. The one I never met. That's why he came back to my house that night. One of the reasons."

J.J. waited.

"He seemed to know he was going to die sometime soon. And he wanted to tell me about my parents. It was as if telling me would allow him to die in peace. This was like his last confession. A perfect act of contrition for an imperfect life." A cloud slipped in front of the moon, darkening the room. "My father . . ." She faltered and broke off, before beginning again. "My father was a gangster. A murderer, in fact."

My father never knew he was my father. He was shotgunned to death before he knew my mother was pregnant. He was building a hotel in Las Vegas called King's Playland (his name was Jacob King), and there were shortfalls and overruns. . . .

"Stop, Teresa, don't go on."

"No. I want you to know all of it."

My mother was a movie star. A child movie star who was trying to cross over and become a grown-up movie star. Her name was Blue Tyler, and there was a time during her adolescent years when her name on a marquee was a guarantee of gold. My father was killed, and my mother's career failed for one reason or another, my father's occupation and his rather dramatic and bloody public demise being two good reasons that fell under the moral-turpitude clause in a motion-picture contract. She worked for a while in Europe, and then she disappeared for nearly forty years until Jack found her quite by accident in Detroit, an itinerant bag lady, one whose truest love had been a killer unimpressed by her fame and wealth and whose daughter she had borne and given up for adoption after he was murdered.

"Teresa. Teresa. Teresa."

Chapter Five

Allie had figured it out by lunchtime Saturday.

Friday afternoon she had telephoned J.J. at home to report that Bryant Gover was on a hunger strike at Durango Avenue as a protest over some infraction of prison rules that cost him cigarette privileges. Exaltación, the latest Sonoran domestic brought up from the hacienda at Bacadé-huachi, told her that Señor McClure was not expected in Cap City for the weekend and that Señora McClure had already left for Washington in Señora McClure's own *avión*. Exaltación seemed delighted to talk to someone who spoke Spanish. *¿De Sonora?* she asked. *De Hermosillo,* Allie replied. Exaltación said she had laundry for Señor McClure, his shirts on wooden hangers as he liked them, and his underwear ironed, not just folded, and she wondered if Señora Vasquez could see that they were delivered to him in the city where he was performing as an *abogado*.

Let him pick up his own shirts, Allie said, I don't make deliveries.

The Lovat Hotel in Regent said that Mr. McClure was not answering.

The next morning I ran into Allie in the elevator in the Osceola County Courthouse.

"I thought you'd be in Regent," she said. "Working on your opening statement. Getting ready for Monday." No conversation with her would be complete without a final dart. "Looking up the case law for your appeal when the guilty verdict comes in."

There was no way not to explain why I was in Cap City. "Stanley had an accident."

A skateboarding accident. Stanley had taken up skateboarding in the all-out way he did everything. He had a skateboarding instructor. He wore a blue plastic state-of-the-art helmet, with lightning bolts on it, and matching tights like the riders in the Tour de France. He wore aerodynamically designed board shoes and elbow guards and knee pads and leather gloves and plastic wristbands and yellow-tinted wraparound glasses. He jumped curbs and did three-sixties in the air. He said he wanted to compete in the X Games. Then in a time run Thursday he had come down wrong doing a victory three-sixty at the finish line and had dislocated his wrist. A Mayday message was dispatched to me in Regent, and my holiday from Stanley was cut short.

"I told Teresa I'd be back this afternoon. I've been trying to get hold of her. She doesn't seem to be picking up. I haven't been able to get through to her since I came back here Thursday."

A look crossed Allie's face. I had seen it there before. Blank. Eyes narrowing and unblinking. I often thought that suspiciousness beat in her like a second pulse. She attached fact to suggestion, suggestion to hint, hint to insinuation as if she were assembling a jigsaw puzzle, blindfolded, by feel. The elevator door opened. Neither of us moved to get out. The door closed.

"J.J.'s not picking up either."

Think of a dream. Think of telling that dream to a friend, a psychiatrist, a lover, a significant other, even a stranger sitting next to you in the passenger cabin on a flight to somewhere. A dream is just shards of memory, images, flashes imperfectly remembered, and when you try to explain them, you add connective tissue to give the dream shape, to make it understandable. The house in the dream is not exactly the house where you grew up, but it could be, it's a little larger, as houses in dreams tend to be, unless they're smaller, claustrophobic, and the closet where you found the thing that scared you, whatever it was, maybe it was just the dark, is not the closet where the winter coats and the mud gear were kept, but it could have been. And what scared you might not have been just the dark, or the door behind the coats that you forgot was there, the little half door that led under the eaves, and it was under the eaves behind the little half door behind the winter coats and the mud gear and the wet galoshes, the little half door with the loose pull knob and the simple rusty hook latch that didn't catch, it was under the eaves that you saw, or thought you saw, what it was that scared you in the first place, and then you woke up.

Think of this as connective tissue.

Galoshes and mud gear, a loose doorknob and a rusty hook latch.

Teresa's memories.

Sporadic, like summer lightning.

Thursday.

The day Judge Tracy swore in the jury and then declared a four-day recess until the following Monday, opening arguments at 9 a.m.

Early that afternoon I got Stanley's call summoning me back to Cap City. Doctors at University Hospital had put a cast on his wrist, and he was feeling beleaguered.

I asked Teresa if she wanted to come up to Cap City with me. You can spend the weekend in the relative comfort of the Rhino, I said. Everything you need is available in my office, and what's not you can log in on the computer.

Will you introduce me to Stanley? Teresa said.

Not a chance, I said.

Then I'll be fine here, Teresa said.

You can't stand it here. You called it limbo's waiting room.

I'll work on the statement. Read the record again. Visit the scene of the crime again, bring myself up to speed.

Don't overtrain.

You know who you sound like? Wright Ingersoll at Yale. He taught criminal law. Forget he never tried a criminal case. He wrote a textbook about cross-examination. *The Art of Cross-Examination,* I think it was called. My father loved to read it out loud and laugh. The artist follows that line of questioning, he'd say, then his client better book a room at Sing Sing. Anyway. I think the Rhino's probably less enticing than the DeLuxor. And I won't have the diversions of Capital City to distract me.

She smiled.

A heartbreaking smile as I remember.

But then of course I now know, as does most of the sentient tabloid world, that she found a more dangerous diversion in Regent than she ever would have in Cap City.

If you need company, you can always catch up with Carlyle's shoot, I said. She and Merle Orvis are real tight, I hear.

Peas in a pod, she said. I got a message from Marty Buick. Carlyle wonders if she can sue Judge Tracy for removing her from the courtroom.

Maybe we should have done this pro bono, I said. She smiled, and I told her I would check in periodically and see her back in Regent on Saturday.

My mistake.

I could not have guessed that Stanley's orthopedic adventures were helping to shape the narrative.

She had been perusing the menu at Auntie Pasto's when J.J. passed by the table.

"Do you usually have dinner at four-thirty, counselor? Or is this a late lunch?"

Teresa put the menu down. Except for a waitress shaping her inch-long false fingernails, the restaurant was empty. "I didn't expect to see you still here, Mr. McClure."

"Taking care of odds and ends. I'll be leaving in a while. I'm hoping that if I wait long enough, Exaltación won't feel she has to make me dinner. She has many household skills, but cooking isn't one of them. She'd much prefer watching *Jeopardy!* and trying to learn English. It's amazingly effective, you know. Who is Thomas Jefferson? 'Señora McClure, Tomás Jefferson, did he have a *negrita*?' 'Liberal slander,' Poppy said. I don't think it penetrated. What is Yankee Stadium? 'Señora McClure, why is Luis Gehrig in his *beisbol* suit the happiest man in the world if he is crying?' Poppy let me handle that one."

He rested his hands on the chair opposite.

"I'm sorry, Mr. McClure. Sit down."

J.J. looked at the menu. "They spell ravioli R-A-V-O-L-A."

"I noticed that. I thought it might be a specialty of the house, but ravioli is what it is."

"I hope you won't think this is improper . . ."

"Not until I've heard it."

". . . there's a place called Catfish Cove in Albion. Fresh catfish right out of the Albion River. Sizzled in hot oil. Dunk, two, three, four, and out. It's about as close to a delicacy as you are going to find in South Midland."

"I'm sure it is, but I don't think it's a good idea, Mr. McClure."

"Not one word about the proceedings we are both involved with."

Teresa watched the waitress stick her emery board into her beehive hairdo and move slowly toward the table. Her name tag identified her as Raymonda. "Snagged my nail," she said to neither of them in particular. "Ravola's the special, we got two orders left, it's filled with cream cheese, it's our big favorite usually."

I don't think it was the ravola that did it. Or the emery board sticking out of Raymonda's beehive. Those are just picturesque details, freezing the moment. But no one really does anything because of the piquant, as much as writers would have you believe it's what pushes people over the line. Teresa was simply attracted to risk in the way a moth is attracted to light. I don't try to scan the tea leaves for reasons. People do what they do.

"I think I'll have the catfish," Teresa said, getting up from the table.

J.J. didn't mention to Teresa that Albion was seventy-five miles away. I don't think it occurred to him. For J.J., it was a drive around the block.

They never did have catfish.

It turned out Catfish Cove had burned to the ground a few weeks before. The sizzling oil had caught fire, and by the time the Tri-County volunteer fire company arrived, there was nothing left but cinders and smoke.

They had dinner at the Best Western at the I-60 turnoff.

Three-star accommodations, the South Midland TourBook said. Offering amenities and a degree of sophistication.

They split the dinner bill. Down the middle. Twenty-four fifty-seven each.

We can stay, he said.

She nodded.

It was as simple as that. They were not heedless of possible consequences. It was not a suicidal impulse. Caution was for other people. They were just running a yellow light, as each of them always had. Without slowing down.

A yellow light, each thought, was not a red light.

My father was a gangster. My mother was a movie star.
Pushme, Jamie, pushmepushmepushme. . . .

Chapter Six

Over the next three days, they drove nearly two thousand miles. I looked at the speedometer, she told me later, holding steady, not quivering, ninety-five, a hundred. Over a hundred. That's when I stopped looking. I wondered what would happen if he lost control. She had imagined the headlines. PROSECUTOR AND DEFENSE ATTORNEY KILLED IN CAR CRASH. QUESTIONS ARISE.

They headed west.

Always talking.

About the years before Catfish Cove. A summing up of two lives, of compromises made, of secrets kept and promises unkept. Some episodes were edited, some in ciphers easily and silently broken. The usefulness of Allie Vasquez. "Useful" was a precise and appropriate way to describe Allie. Nothing further needed to be added. Useful to J.J., useful to Teresa and me.

Allie will know before we get back to Regent, J.J. said as they passed into Parker County. It's what she does. It's why I put up with her. And if she knows, Max knows.

Teresa had tried not to think of Allie Vasquez. Allie was part of J.J.'s former life, the way Budd Doheny had been part of hers. And Camillo, the Chicago policeman in Todi. And the husband she had gone to Nantucket with.

Somebody else, J.J. said.

Who? Teresa said.

Just somebody. Somebody always knows. Somebody out there. A Lotto shot. The winning ticket bought in a Wal-Mart in Ottumwa. It happens. You can't worry about it.

She remembered that he accepted the inevitability of it with a stoicism she found both comforting and a little frightening.

You deal with it, he had said after six or seven miles.

In the distance Teresa could see a water tower with the word HAMLET lettered on it. The town where J.J. grew up. The town where he had found his father dead in the barn.

The town she supposed was the true north of his life.

When I was a kid, J.J. said, someone climbed that water tower one night, and painted LINDA KRONHOLM PUTS OUT on it.

Did she?

Yes.

She wondered whatever had happened to Linda Kronholm. As if he were reading her mind, J.J. said, She's a county supervisor now.

On the edge of Hamlet, they stopped by a chain-link fence circling a high school football field. The yard markers had faded and the metal goalposts needed paint. There were sagging wooden grandstands on either side of the field. A scoreboard identified the site as MCCLURE FIELD, HOME OF THE PARKER COUNTY PACKERS—*Spring Practice* April 15.

Up on the hill where the school is, that's where we lived, J.J. said. The pond's been drained. There's a swimming pool in the gym. They wanted to name it the Walter McClure Memorial Pool, and I said no.

Still west.

Past cattle and a few herds of buffalo.

The Midlandia Motor Hotel and Campground in Lower Meridian. Budget accommodations, according to the South Midland TourBook. Slightly older-style décor. Coin laundry. Communal grilling. PLEASE DO NOT FEED THE BUFFALO.

J.J. had mentioned Charley Buckles. And Gordon Sunday. Gas Station Gordy. The most famous murderer in South Midland history until her client. Duane Lajoie. Our client. They were following Gordy Sunday's route, J.J. said. J.J. knew the name of the Rawlings sporting goods salesman Gordon Sunday had killed while he was asleep in his car at the gas station in Boudreaux.

And the names of the husband and wife shot dead at the Sunoco station they ran in Fort Shaw.

A strange hegira, I wanted to tell Teresa, but did not. A pilgrimage along the Gordon Sunday Trail.

They traveled light, buying toothpaste and toothbrushes and mouthwash and razors and combs and shampoo and bottled water and six-packs of Midlandia Lager at service-station convenience stores.

I suppose condoms.

A couple of wool shirts at a general store in a town called Viking when it turned cold on Saturday. The jean jacket with the fake fleece collar she was wearing when she walked into the DeLuxor early Sunday afternoon.

She checked for messages on her cell phone, usually calling from the ladies' room when they stopped for gas. There were urgent messages from Martha Buick. Carlyle says she wants someone else to handle her money, Martha Buick said. Another message: Who the hell is Ralph Cannon, Sr.? A third: Why don't you answer?

Call me, was the message I left three times on Teresa's machine. She had never given me her cell-phone number.

J.J. was calling in too, from gas station pay phones. He had turned off his beeper and his cell. I don't want to hear the phone ring, he had said. I don't want to hear the beeper beep. Two sounds from the real world they would have to return to. At the general store in Viking, he said Poppy had left a message that she was appearing on *Fixed Bayonets* discussing judicial tyranny with Lorna Dun, and no, she would not mention Judge Tracy. Allie had also called. Friday afternoon and that morning. And Patsy Feiffer. Twice. Patsy said there had been stock footage of him on *The Courthouse Square Nightly Wrap-up*. Kean, too. That's how she referred to you, J.J. said. As "Kean." It seemed to amuse him. Is there anything you want me to do, Patsy asked in her second call. No, J.J. had said to Teresa, answering her unasked question. She's not smart enough. She doesn't do connections.

Cando lay ahead. Teresa remembered that she had pronounced it "can dough" when she saw the highway cutoff sign. It's "can do," J.J. had corrected. We keep things simple out here. It was the territorial motto before we became a state. Can Do. Then North Midland put it on its state flag. Which meant it couldn't be our state motto. People from here call North Midland the No Can Do state.

I remembered thinking he loved this place, Teresa told me a long time later.

Give J.J. that.

West of Cando, J.J. said, When you were in Washington. The sentence trailed off. Teresa waited for him to continue. In a far field, she could see a bull trying to mount a cow. When he began again, his tone was casual. In Washington, he repeated. Another pause, and then: Did you ever hear anything about Poppy?

All the time, Teresa had said.

About Poppy and Lorna Dun.

No, Teresa said quickly. And then: Not really.

They drove on, eyes fixed on the road that stretched in front of them, a taut black hawser disappearing into the horizon.

Saturday afternoon, they saw a twister in the far distance, black and then milky when the sun caught it, moving like a huge reticulated vertical snake.

We can head for Higginson, J.J. said. He searched the horizon, but did not slow down. Or we can go back to Quantum.

He had one of those expensive extras on the dashboard that told you where you were, where you were going, and where you had been, along with the mileage. Thirty-eight miles to Higginson, he said, forty-one back to Quantum.

Can't we just stop? Teresa said.

Not unless we find a root cellar out there in the fields, J.J. said. His voice was calm. He was still doing ninety. And if we find one, it'll be locked, and it will take too long to break in with the jack and the tire iron. And I don't carry a rifle in my go-to-court car. There's a handgun in the glove compartment, but it's just a little pissy-ant thing, and anyway, I don't see any root cellars around. So Higginson or Quantum?

Teresa remembered being frightened. Of the twister and the little pissy-ant handgun she had not known was in the glove compartment. It had not occurred to her that J.J. was so familiar with guns. As was I. Even Jewish boys got hunting licenses in South Midland before their voices changed.

Either one's a pretty safe bet, J.J. said. She remembered that he seemed unconcerned, remembered his saying Higginson had been flattened in '77, Quantum in '93, and twisters never hit the same place twice. Higginson's closer now, he said. Thirty-three miles, a Sunday picnic ride.

The tall grass bent under the high wind, then snapped back. It reminded her of an ocean swell. She remembered he wasn't wearing a seat belt. She remembered his saying that seat belts were Eastern.

The tornado finally set down without incident just across the Wyoming line.

That night in the Step Right Inn, at the junction between Higginson and Higgins, Teresa asked if was true that tornadoes never hit the same place twice.

I don't know, J.J. said. It seemed logical. Like lightning. You were worried. I didn't want you worried.

It was as close a declaration of love as J.J. was capable of making.

They were up before dawn Sunday morning. Complimentary instant coffee at the Motel 6 food center, with sugar substitute and creamer that did not dissolve, a bag of nachos and a can of apple juice.

They drove east toward the sun, which was trying to break through the gray cloud cover of late winter. Their other life lay dead ahead, Duane Lajoie and the harsh fact of felony murder. They had not spoken in miles, each lost in thought. *Two roads diverged in a yellow wood, And sorry I could not travel both.* She remembered the lines somewhere between Fort Shaw and Buffalo Creek, remembered an aging failed former Broadway star doing a one-man show of Robert Frost's poetry when she was at Smith. He had bad makeup and a bad white hairpiece and a suit that was several sizes too big, all supposed to make him look like Frost, and the croaking voice he affected to imitate Frost was inaudible. She did not think Frost would have thought Buffalo Creek the road not taken.

She remembered she had gone to the reading with Chipper, later to be husband number one. Chipper had said he loved poetry, he really did. Chipper said he wished he had taken a poetry course at Amherst. Who are your favorites? Chipper had said. Chipper said he was not familiar with Robert Lowell. Chipper said the Bob Frost surrogate was really one hell of an actor. A little light on his feet, maybe, but hell, he's an actor.

It occurred to Teresa that for four days she had been assaulted by her past.

Teresa, J.J. said softly. His voice was like a caress. He was wearing sunglasses and the last of the clean white T-shirts he had bought at a mini-mart in Parker County two days before. It seemed like years. Years of sharing.

Yes.

Nothing, J.J. said. Just Teresa. Teresa Kean.

And miles to go before we sleep.

PART TWO

CHAPTER ONE

MONDAY

"We're late," Ellen Tracy said at nine minutes past nine. "In my court, nine o'clock means nine o'clock, everyone in their places and ready to go. No paper shuffling, no 'May it please the court.'" Her weekend reign as the grand marshal of the anniversary celebration in Dead Center had not made her courtroom demeanor any less intimidating. I tried not to think of her reaction if she discovered how opposing counsel had spent their recess. "Mr. McClure, you may begin."

"Thank you, Your Honor." J.J. looked as if he had spent the weekend getting a haircut and a manicure. He was wearing a severe dark blue suit, white shirt, and a blue tie with tiny replicas of the scales of justice worked into the fabric. Only his soft black running shoes suggested the casual, and they were polished to a high sheen. I hated to use the word *sangfroid,* especially under the circumstances, but it described J.J. perfectly. "Ladies and gentlemen of the jury, my name is James J. McClure. I am the chief deputy in the homicide division of the Attorney General's office up there in Cap City, which as you know is so ably run by the A.G., that's our shorthand for attorney general, Mr. Jerrold Wormwold. I'm going to be prosecuting this matter. . . ."

"Max, don't say a word," Teresa had said when she walked into our tiny offices at the DeLuxor early Sunday afternoon. She was in the jeans and the jean jacket she had bought somewhere on the roadside hundreds of miles to the west. She looked like the wild thing that I had half suspected was at Teresa's core, but had never seen, buried as it was under layers, years, of public propriety. The dress she had been wearing when she ran into J.J. at Auntie Pasto's four days before was stuffed at the bottom of a plastic shopping bag under a half-dozen bottles of water, like the detritus of a former incarnation. "Don't say reckless. Don't say irresponsible. Don't say willful. Especially don't say willful. I hate willful. The goddamn nuns used to say it. And don't ask if we talked about what we're here for. We didn't. Is there anything else you want to know?"

"Hello to you, too, Teresa."

She opened a bottle of water and drained it in one long swig. Then she arced the bottle into a wastebasket, removed her jean jacket, sat at her computer, and typed in her password. She was wearing a V-neck T-shirt, a man's size, too big, with a spot of something like ketchup just under the vee. Her arms were folded, and her right hand nervously scratched her left breast as she waited for the document to come up. I do not think women are erotic, but looking at Teresa at that moment I was willing to reconsider the prejudice. She pointed to the monitor and I looked over her shoulder at the notes she had made for her opening statement before she had succumbed to her wanderlust. I did not tell her I was so sure she would not return in time that I had written my own opening statement.

Hers was better.

"We counterpunch, Max," she said. "Hope for an opening. It's the only way we're going to keep Duane Lajoie out of the electric chair."

One thing I knew about J.J. McClure.

He didn't give many openings. Whatever had happened outside the courtroom would not affect what happened inside. He would still try to beat Teresa Kean's brains out.

This is something else I knew.

Teresa would not give him an inch either.

Judge Tracy demanded speed, and the first witnesses were called before lunch Monday, immediately after Teresa finished her opening statement.

A woman juror asked for a restroom break, and the judge said she would have to wait until the lunch recess at twelve-thirty. In other words, she would run the proceedings her way, bladder discipline was the order for all involved. The witnesses were the lesser investigators and forensic specialists who laid the foundation and applied the mortar, establishing that violations of pertinent clauses in the state penal code had been perpetrated by a person or persons then unknown. J.J.'s questions were direct, uncomplicated, and pro forma. When did the Loomis County Sheriff's Department receive the first call of a possible incident? Was the call logged? Was there an audio recording? Where was the body of the victim discovered, what was the state of the victim's person, what was the approximate time of the victim's death, when was the identity of the victim confirmed?

I watched Teresa and J.J. closely. It was as if they were strangers who shared only the contagious dislike of each other that prevails in the adversarial system. The basic facts from the witness box were not in dispute, only the odd detail, a mistake about time or the caliber of a weapon or the depth and exact nature of a wound, and she and J.J. felt each other out, gauging how the other would react, jabbing like prize-fighters, seeing if blood could be drawn. As theater, it was not bad, but at that moment there were only two members of the audience who understood the play. I was one, and Allie Vasquez the other; Allie, as J.J.'s chief investigator, was sitting at the prosecution table next to Patsy Feiffer, who acted as if she were not there. The principal actors were playing their parts to the hilt, like the road company hams who would occasionally visit Kiowa or Cap City in bus-and-truck revivals of Broadway musicals, recalling enchanted evenings and hills alive with the sound of music. Teresa was dramatically exasperated when she would object that answers supplied by the witnesses J.J. had called, lacked either specificity or foundation, and J.J. was genially contemptuous in his responses.

"Perhaps counsel is a little trial-rusty," he said after one objection, "since it's been half dozen years since the last time she defended a criminal—"

"Objection."

"Excuse me, Your Honor, alleged criminal."

Ellen Tracy whacked her gavel. "Counsel, Mr. McClure. You're acting like lawyers on TV. You're not auditioning. Don't waste the time of this court with your prefabricated bickering." Another whack of the gavel. "You may continue, Mr. McClure."

So Tracy got the performance aspect, too. Good instincts.

Duane Lajoie sat next to me at the defense table. He never looked at a witness, never shook his head, never sighed heavily. He just drew penises and vaginas on a scratch pad, showing them to me and then to Teresa, and a sketch of Ellen Tracy with a Hitler mustache not unlike her real one. It had not occurred to me that he might be so observant.

The morning's only moment of levity came just before lunch when J.J. allowed Patsy Feiffer to examine Brutus Mayes. He was as trim as a 350-pound man could be, his arms bursting like tree trunks out of his short-sleeved dark brown uniform shirt, his Sam Browne belt and shoulder strap highly polished, his equally polished holster empty, since only marshals were allowed to wear guns in court.

Patsy Feiffer's first question was long and rambling.

Teresa was on her feet.

"Sit down, counsel," Ellen Tracy said before she could speak. "I'll handle this. Miss Feiffer, that's not a question, it's a speech."

"I'll repeat the question, Your Honor." She did. Hesitantly.

"Miss Feiffer," Judge Tracy said. "That's not a question. It's four questions. You only get to ask one at a time."

She tried again.

"Miss Feiffer, where is the foundation to that question?" And so it continued. What appeared to be a sweat stain started down the crease of Patsy Feiffer's jacket. Brutus Mayes tried to help her out, and was cut short. "Sheriff, this is not the National Football League. In this courtroom, I call the plays."

At last it was over. "Mr. Cline," Judge Tracy said.

I was down to handle the cross. Patsy Feiffer had made that unnecessary. "We have no questions of the witness at this time, Your Honor. We reserve the right to recall."

"Granted," Ellen Tracy said. "We're running late. I'm going to take it out of the lunch break. Forty-five minutes not an hour, everybody back here and ready to go at one-forty-four, understood?"

Romantic dramatist that I had become since the weekend, a totally unaccustomed role for the hardheaded realist I thought I was, I wondered if Teresa and J.J. would acknowledge each other as they exited the courtroom. They did not. J.J. brushed by, talking to Patsy, while Teresa waited until Duane Lajoie was led away to the holding cell, then engaged me about the witness list, and who would cross-examine whom, decisions we had in fact already made. We both knew that the only witness of any consequence was Bryant Gover, who was scheduled for Thursday morning. Until then there was nothing we could do except try to score debating points against the secondary witnesses. We could ask Clyde Ray what he had actually been doing on County Road 21 when he spotted Duane Lajoie's pickup at two-forty-seven in the morning, and we could ask Merle Orvis the exact nature of her sexual relationship with Bryant Gover, but we would just be marking time.

It was only Allie Vasquez who had anything to say to us after the morning session, and as always with Allie, there was a mocking insolence just beneath the surface. "Professor Cline," she said. It was how the more problematic of my students at Osceola Community College referred to me, as if they thought the undeserved honorific might flatter me into inflating their grades, thus making it easier for them to inflict themselves on the state bar. That kind of flattery was foreign to Allie. Imperfectly veiled mockery was her chosen method of address. "Putting your classroom lessons into practice, I see."

"Ms. Vasquez," I said. I would play along. "I don't think you've met—"

Allie interrupted. "I'm Altagracia Vasquez," she said to Teresa. I had never heard Allie use her full first name before, and only knew it myself because it was on the student list sent me by the college registrar.

"Teresa Kean," Teresa said. Each waited for the other to speak again.

"I have to go," Allie said finally.

"I imagine we'll see each other," Teresa said. "In court."

"I imagine."

In that brief exchange they had managed to size each other up, each recognizing a wary adversary not without a danger quotient. I knew that Allie did not care about J.J., or about Teresa as a rival for his affection, in Allie's case an attraction that had only been physical, but J.J., and to a lesser extent me, offered her and her daughter passports out of what she regarded as the negligible circumstances to which she felt them sentenced. This was a passport application that she would not allow to be compromised, and this was, I realize now, why she was able to function as a double agent with such unerring equanimity. One of us, either J.J. or me, might ultimately be more useful than the other.

Outside the courthouse, Teresa and I picked our way through the gaggle of reporters and cameramen hurling questions and snapping our pictures. We kept moving, not even bothering to say "no comment." I saw another group gathered around J.J., who deflected questions with an expressive gesture or a quip, always pretending to put a gag in his mouth when any reporter veered toward the morning session and the effectiveness of the presentation. Patsy Feiffer stood at his side, her face frozen into a rictus smile, like a royal princess at the trooping of the colors. I knew J.J. too well to think he had bothered to take her to task for the shortcomings of her examination of Brutus Mayes. He knew she was Gerry Wormwold's person, and I expect he was reasonably certain that Ellen Tracy, who ate ill-prepared young attorneys alive, would feast on her. Poppy was another subject of general interest. Yes, he had been in touch with Poppy. What had they talked about? Tax reform, J.J. replied. There was general laughter. What else? The cherry blossoms are in bloom, J.J. said.

At the edge of the fray, Alex Quintero recorded the scene, his assistants reloading his cameras, the star photographer photographing the proletarian photographers at their labors. Alice Todt and Jocko Cannon hovered behind him. Alice Todt's makeup people had applied the sty she wanted on her left eye (after the right eye had been rejected, the right side of her face being what she thought the better side), and she was wearing an oversize lumberman's shirt, not tucked in, but hanging loose over black jeans torn at the knees. Jocko Cannon's arm was draped over Alice's shoulder, suggesting a broader definition of his community-service bodyguard activities than had been contemplated. He was wearing a Miami Dolphins ocean-green home-uniform jersey, number 99 (the number negotiated by his agents in the contract he had signed), with just the name JOCKO on the back, not his last name (another contractual stipulation). Jocko was the name with commercial possibilities, not Cannon. Merle Orvis crouched nearby as if on a catapult, ignored except when an order was shouted, watching everything, a runner always available to fetch and carry. The only person who seemed to be missing was Boy. I wondered into whose custody he had been delivered, and whether his sitter had to offer a breast to keep him quiet. To Alex Quintero and Alice Todt, Boy was a prop, and until he was needed, he was to be consigned to the property master, along with the Rollerblades and the lowered Impala and the 1969 Harley.

Merle Orvis opened a bottle of water, passed it to Jocko, who swallowed half and passed the rest to Alice.

"How's Duane holding up?" Alice Todt asked.

"He's been helpful," I said. I had torn the sexually explicit drawings from his scratch pad and stuffed them in my pocket.

"Is he fucking smart enough to be helpful?"

Teresa stared at Alice for a moment, as if trying to deconstruct the question. Since the weekend, her concentration on the dangers inherent in her own situation, while still trying to present a viable defense in court, had led her to misread, at least momentarily, the degree of Alice Todt's self-absorption. To Alice, Duane Lajoie was only the most valuable of her props. The five hundred thousand dollars she was paying for his defense she saw now as an investment in the broader future she could have when she could no longer sustain being a teen nymphet, a possibility she had never previously considered. When the jury returned its verdict, she would be ready for her close-up.

"You like the sty?" Alice Todt said.

Teresa seemed trapped. "It looks real."

"I fired Marty this morning," Alice Todt said. She had an effortless ability to change gears. "I mean, my lawyer in New York did. Jocko's dad is going to handle my money from now on. He's so smart. He says I need to diversify more. Lessen my liability. Get higher yields. Have my money working for me. Go offshore. He wants to leverage some shit, whatever the fuck leverage is, but he's so rich it has to be okay, cut down the tax burden. He says maybe I should buy a plane, the fucking deductions I could get, you know lease it out to people when I'm not using it. Jocko says he wants to learn how to fly—"

"I'm sure you and Marty can work it out," Teresa said.

"She wants to fly out here," Alice Todt said. "I mean, she's your friend, and all. I don't know why the fuck I should talk to her."

"We're due back in court in twenty-five minutes," I told Teresa. "We should get something to eat."

"Try the catering truck," Alice Todt said. "I hired Auntie Pasto's."

Teresa leaned back against the headrest as we drove to the DeLuxor. Her eyes were closed. "I want this trial to be over, Max," she said after a moment. "I've always loved the courtroom. I love the competition. I even love a pain in the ass like Tracy. I love getting around the petty tyranny. I love trusting my instincts. It's like playing chess with some-one's life. Some pawn who otherwise isn't worth an instant"—she snapped her fingers—"of your time. I even love knowing I'm going to lose, because I'll go down knowing I did my best. I love the whole thing. And here it is the first morning, and I want it finished."

She was trusting those instincts. She was not an alarmist. She only knew there was a storm ahead. She did not know where it was coming from, but she knew it was coming, she smelled it the way sailors smell foul weather two days off, and she knew that hatches would be battened down, people would drown, that survival itself was at risk.

When we walked into our office at the motel, Mrs. Idella Primrose, the local woman we had engaged as our secretary, said there had been a collect call forwarded from my Cap City number from a man who iden-tified himself only as Tugboat. Mrs. Primrose had a worn pinched face, and she did not meet our eyes. I asked if Tugboat had said anything else. Things I wouldn't even tell my late husband, Mrs. Primrose said. Tug-boat had left a callback number, but said he could not be reached and would try to call again at dinnertime.

"You know anyone named Tugboat?" Teresa asked.

"No," I said. "But you can bet I'm going to accept the charges if he calls again. Chances are a solid citizen named Tugboat has a sheet, done some time, and knows something he thinks I might want to know, if the proper arrangements can be made. The area code he called from is in Sunflower County. I think I know what that means."

I picked up the telephone and dialed the number Tugboat had left. "You have reached the Sunflower Facility of the South Midland Depart-ment of Corrections," the voice on the automated answering machine said. "For general information, press one—"

"The Sunflower supermax," I said to Teresa. "It's only been opened four months. Top of the line. State of the art. Privately operated under a concession from the DOC. Making it a profit center. It's the envy of the upper Midwest. Twenty-four-hundred beds, five hundred screws with automatic weapons and open fields of fire. No windows in the cells, just slits that let in a little light. Plus death-wire electrified fences, one touch turns you into toast. It's going to warehouse all the hard cases in four states. Kansas, Nebraska, North Midland, they'll all pay Sunflower to take their worst guys off their hands."

Teresa picked at the greens Mrs. Primrose had ordered from a nearby mini-mart.

"If he calls back, he'll call at five. That's when they have dinner. He probably won't go to dinner—"

Teresa seemed to perk up. "Because the pay phones in every prison I've ever seen are out in the open and he won't want anyone to hear what he has to say."

"Right."

"There's probably a tap on the line," Teresa said.

"Count on it," I said.

"And people called Tugboat tend to know things like that."

"In my experience, yes."

"Can we find out more about him?"

I took a deep breath. There was one way to find out quickly, but I knew Teresa would not like it. "I'll ask Allie Vasquez. She's got sources all over the system. Give her twenty minutes, she'll know how many teeth he has left in his head."

Teresa considered the proposal. "Max, I'm not sure that's a good idea," she said finally. "She works for"—she searched for the right words—"for the other side."

"Teresa," I said. "We don't have a case. We need all the help we can get. You don't get it free."

She did not reply. It wasn't a yes, but it wasn't a no either.

The option of checking with Duane Lajoie was one we did not consider.

In the afternoon session, there was a detailed analysis of the blood evidence by medical technicians from the state Bureau of Investigation. Some of the jurors were having difficulty staying awake. One started to take notes and was immediately told by Judge Tracy that she did not permit jurors to take notes, and ordered a bailiff to confiscate the notebook. It was the function of jurors to listen to the evidence and weigh it carefully, she said, and if during their deliberations they needed parts of the record to be read back to them, she would so order. A juror writing, she continued, was a juror not paying attention. She was like a pedantic kindergarten teacher, I thought. I watched the courtroom clock ticking toward the end of the day and wondered what Tugboat would have to offer. I was not wearing a watch and had told Teresa not to wear hers in the courtroom. It was just another of Ellen Tracy's idiosyncrasies: The sight of an attorney peeking at a watch guaranteed that she would ask the offender if he or she had another engagement.

Judge Tracy called it a day at four-twenty.

Again J.J. and Teresa ignored each other.

I stopped Allie as she left the courtroom and quietly asked if she could get a heads-up on a con named Tugboat at Sunflower. No other information available.

"Do I get to ask why?" she said.

"No."

"I can't do it, Max."

"Okay. No harm in asking."

"None."

We told Idella Primrose to take the rest of the afternoon off.

At five-oh-five, the phone rang.

"Max, I'm going to tell you this just once," Allie Vasquez said. She was on her car phone. In the background I could hear Springsteen. "His name is Albert Curwent, aka Leo Lutz, aka Tyrone Powers—like the actor, but add an *s*—aka Wally Korn—Korn with a *k*—aka Tugboat, aka Fat Albert. Nobody calls him Fat Albert to his face. He's sensitive about his weight. He likes to hear the sound of bones breaking. The pelvis is his specialty. A stone criminal. He's been inside somewhere seventeen of the last twenty-one years. You name the joint, he's passed through. Sunflower's just the latest stop. He's looking at five LWOPPs to be served consecutively. He contracted to torch a house in KC and there were five people in it. The guy's girlfriend, the girlfriend's mother, and three kids. The starship *Enterprise* will be back before he gets out."

Suddenly Allie turned up the volume on her tape deck, and as the E Street Band boomed behind the Boss, she clicked off the mobile phone without a further word. Typical Allie. No frills. Waitin' on a Sunny Day.

"What's that going to cost?" Teresa said.

"Something," I said. With Allie, it was never tit for tat. If it became necessary, she would make Albert Curwent available to J.J. If not, there would be something else. Allie's upward mobility was predicated on the flexibility of her allegiances. Calling me was just another deposit to the capital she hoarded away in her survivalist savings account.

Ten minutes later, I told the operator I would accept the charges from Mr. Tugboat. Teresa was listening on the extension. Tugboat got to the point immediately.

"You know Princess, right?"

"Sure," I said. "I know Princess up in, you know, and I know the other one, the fat one." The idea was to keep the conversation going, even though I did not know what he was talking about. Professional criminals suspect that every stranger and most friends are wearing a wire, that every room is bugged, and all telephones are tapped. Names and places are rarely mentioned, and never with any specificity. This guy and that guy, your guy and his guy, their guy and the other one. Where? There. You're kidding me. No, there. What's-his-name goes there, right? That's the place. No shit, I don't know that. Now you fucking do. Well, I thought he went to the other place. No, this place. Down in . . . Yeah. So that's where. Right. Right.

Entire arias of miscellaneous felonies and mayhem between every silence.

"Your guy," Tugboat said.

"The fat one?"

"No, the one on the TV."

"Oh, that one."

"He worked for Wonderman."

"I don't know Wonderman."

"The whatchamacallit. The tongue-tied guy, you know what I mean?"

"Oh, that guy."

"Wonderman."

"I didn't know that."

"In Oklahoma."

"That makes sense."

"That Wonder, he was something."

"I heard that." I was beginning to see an outline of where this might be heading. Duane Lajoie had done time in Oklahoma. Thirteen months in McAlester for stealing an eighteen-wheeler and turning it over on a van full of German tourists from Düsseldorf. "So Princess worked in Oklahoma."

"Let's just say your guy worked for that guy."

"Okay. In Oklahoma."

"Getting his shit pushed."

"Wonderman?"

"No, man. Wonder wasn't getting his shit pushed. Wonder was pushing shit. Big-time."

Tugboat said that dinner was nearly over. He said he worried about his back. He suggested a face-to-face. He thought tomorrow would be an excellent time for a face-to-face. Or else he'd have to make other arrangements.

Tugboat said he was not comfortable at Sunflower.

"Max," Teresa said. She was flipping through a transcript. "The first time we met Duane. He said something. I'm trying to find it." She ran her finger down a page, then the next, then the one after, and the ten after that. "Here. Got it." She read it as if she were a court reporter reading playback testimony to a jury.

> TK: Duane, we were talking about you and Bryant, how you met.
> DL: He cold-cocked someone with a pool cue. I mean, that's what kind of violent person he is, a stranger, someone he didn't even know. It's like what he did to Wonder.
> MC: Who's Wonder?
> DL: It's fucking nobody. Some guy. Another guy.

"He got pissed off," I said. I remember we had not pursued it. It seemed just another violent encounter in the kind of existence where periods of nonviolence were at best interludes.

"There's something else," Teresa said. "Something that's been floating around in my head. Something I haven't been able to put my finger on.

Something Jack said the night we were together. The night he died. Something about Edgar Parlance. And making a movie about him." She pulled it up from the fog of memory. "He said there was no one to root for. He said you can't root for a dead man. He said . . ." She paused. "He said, 'What's his backstory?' " We looked at each other for a moment.

"I think we're about to find that out, Teresa."

CHAPTER TWO

TUESDAY

I left for Sunflower before dawn. If my absence came up, Teresa would say that I was doing defense business at her request.

She saw me off, bundled in her jogging sweats, stamping her sneakered feet against the dark morning chill. She seemed to be holding something back, then told me as I was getting into the car that J.J. had called from Cap City just after midnight. It's Jamie, he said when she picked up the telephone. She would not tell me what else they had talked about. Things, she said. Just things. I had never thought of J.J. as Jamie before. The childhood name gave him a vulnerability I had not thought he possessed.

I wondered if he knew about Tugboat.

I wondered if she had told him about Tugboat.

I wondered if they were already keeping secrets from each other.

"I am a double-up, triple-up snitch," Tugboat said. We were talking through the glass partition in the visitors' room. I had signed in as counsel to Albert Curwent. There was a camera scanning the visitors' room, sending its images back to a guard station. The camera was attached to a TV monitor on which I could see the back of my head and Albert Curwent's face. At that moment, he and I were the only two people in the visitors' room. Like all seasoned cons, Albert Curwent shielded his mouth with his hand so that his lips could not be read. "Some guys, they

296

done so much stuff their brains are like scrambled eggs, they can't remember who they ratted out. Not me. I remember every one. When I did it. Where I did it. What happened to the guy I ratted. You know why I move around so much? I keep moving, I keep alive. Staying alive is important to me. Then I get sent here two weeks ago. Already I see three guys in the yard I ratted, and I hear another one's due in next week from Eastham ad seg. This is not a safe environment for me. The day I get off the bus, I'm not even processed yet, some guys are doing a snitch in a day-room. Twenty-eight stab wounds. You got to admire the professional-ism. A shank spatters blood, so they bring along a change of clothes. That shows planning. So now I watch out for guys carrying laundry. I been thinking Alaska. What do you think of Alaska?"

"It's cold."

"Of course it's fucking cold. But I never ratted out an Eskimo I know of. That's what makes it appealing to me. I see pictures of Spring Creek. It's got a fucking totem pole outside. Like you see in the *National Geographic*. How tough can a joint be that's got a totem pole by the front gate?"

"Hawaii's warmer."

"Are you crazy? You ever seen the size of those fucking Samoans they got out there, man?" Tugboat was huge. I wondered if he could turn around in his cell without brushing the wall. "They all got like eighteen letters in their names. Tuifatasopo, and names like that. The only thing I got going for me in a place like this is I'm fat. I know the moves. Fat Albert can take care of himself. For a while anyway. So I don't want to go no place where I'm like a midget, and that's what I am next to those Samoans, forget Hawaii, forget aloha."

"Alaska," I said. "It might be doable." I was not sure how, but there was no reason to tell him that. He would know it anyway. He was a pro-fessional snitch, and he had learned to play his cards very close to the vest. Facing five LWOPPs, he knew that prison was the only home he would ever have. Snitching was just a way to improve his standard of liv-ing. As Albert Curwent's lawyer, I could speak to the Department of Corrections about his snitch jacket. The correctional center at Spring Creek with the totem pole at the front gate was probably a reach, but at least it would be on the record that Albert Curwent's attorney had said his client, with reason, felt himself at risk. If Albert Curwent came to an untimely end at the hand of another inmate or inmates, the possibility of civil litigation would be implicit, if far-fetched.

"I thought it might be." Albert Curwent was ready to put his cards on the table. "You used to put people like Princess away."

I said I did.

"And now you defend her."

There it was. "You knew her at McAlester."

"She worked for us."

" 'Us' is you and Wonder?"

"Me and Wonderman."

"Wonder have a first name?"

"Earnest. Like in 'He's an earnest individual.' Not the other way."

"Earnest Wonder."

"We called him Wonderman."

"So you said. He have another name?"

"Christ, man, everyone's got another name."

"You've been Leo Lutz."

"Hey, you're not bad."

"Wally Korn, Korn with a *k*."

"That goes way back. Haven't used that one since Saginaw. Or maybe it was PNM in Santa Fe." He paused. "Chick Bailey."

"I don't know that one."

"Of course you don't know that one. I just made it up. I'm very good at names. I'm known for it. Guys are getting out, they already got a score set up, I sell them a name. Give me two butts and I come up with Jack Beale. Harry Schott. Easy names. Randy Ford. Easy to get ID. Lost my license, some bastard lifted my wallet on the number nineteen bus, you know, going to Overland and Main. What's your name? Lew Smith. Lewis J. Smith? Or Lewis M. Smith? No. Lew. Just Lew. My old man was half Chinese, he didn't like middle initials, that's a thing with Chinese people. They got this thing about middle initials. Lew. It's a big Chink name. There's seventeen people behind you in line, they're getting pissed off, it's time for lunch, you walk out of the DMV with a temporary that says you're Lew Smith, 1291 Overland. The thing with most of these dumb bastards, they're not smart enough to make it up as they go along. It's like fucking Ping-Pong. They see me, I tell them what to do, they write it down with their pencil, they try to memorize it, these guys can't remember the last time they took a leak, and they say to me, Is it the number eighteen bus or the number nineteen, as if it fucking matters. They already got a score set up, they're going to knock over a jewelry store, and they don't know how to get a fucking driver's license."

It occurred to me that if the pseudonymous Lew Smith ever did knock over that jewelry store, Albert Curwent would have someone else to rat out. No wonder he felt as if his situation demanded constant movement. "So what was another name Wonderman used?"

As if I did not already know.

"Hey, man, the guy Princess did."

Earnest Wonder. Edgar Parlance.

Max, who actually knew Edgar Parlance?

Tie a yellow ribbon round the old oak tree.

Best Santa we ever had.

Gar.

"So you and Wonder were in business together."

Albert Curwent stared at me through the glass. I wondered as I had all the way to Sunflower why he had called me instead of J.J. Prosecutors can offer snitches more in the way of promised favors than can defense attorneys. But that was a question I would hold off asking until our business together was finished.

"I was his associate," Albert Curwent said carefully. "Associate" was not a con word. It was as if he were already testifying under oath, stressing his importance while claiming to be only a junior partner. "Wonderman was a natural-born business leader. I get to McAlester, he hasn't been there all that long, he's already running the yard and gen pop. Him and me, we hit it off. I have a low tolerance for shit and so does the Wonder. I'm like his bodyguard. That's how smart he was. He believes in harmony between the races, he says, but he don't want no black guy covering his back. We are all bros. He cuts me in. We'd get these little matchboxes full of weed, sell them for fifteen dollars each. He'd give me two, keep five, the rest goes to the screws. The joint is what you call a cash-on-demand economy, you can get anything you want, even early release, but you got to pay for it."

"He was running the punks too."

"Him and the hacks. Wonder always said the warden took his cut, and the chaplain. It was just like a big-time whorehouse, like in one of them places in Nevada, Mustang Ranch, like. The hacks free up this old trailer and bring in some videos, buttfucking and shit, and it was like Saturday night at the movies, people were lining up outside, and the girls were there, Wonderman's got them all dressed up pretty, they're wearing blusher and mascara and bandannas and bikini underwear, parading around like they do at Mustang, and there's a screw with a counter by the door, so Wonderman doesn't short him, he's too smart to do that, this is a good deal and he doesn't want to lose it. I get to name all the girls. Nancy Sue and Ava Gardner and Caroline Cooz. And this one big black girl, she used to play arena football or some shit, she must be six-six, six-seven, queer as a pink hairnet, and I call her Queen Kong, and she is the star of the string. Queen Kong could do thirty johns a day, no sweat, she loved it, around the world in ten minutes. She didn't need no candle like the other girls, that bitch was always ready."

Tell me why you stole that candle from his room.

I had suspected its provenance.

It was not the sort of thing easily discussed with a relative stranger.

What was it Stanley had said? When he spotted the candle I had lifted from Edgar Parlance's room over Claude Applewhite's garage? *Someone was naughty, was someone?*

I took the twisted candle from my bag and put it on the counter on my side of the glass partition. "Like this?"

"Is that his?"

"It was in the place where he resided."

Albert Curwent nodded thoughtfully. "He kept some in his cell." After a moment, he said, "You knew what it was, right?"

"Right," I said. "Tell me about Princess."

"Wonder thought she'd be an addition. A real moneymaker. Small, you know. Red hair. Niggers would love her."

"What did Duane think of that idea?"

"Let's call her Princess, okay?"

"Right. My mistake. What did Princess think of that idea?"

"Not much."

I could not imagine that being turned out by Earnest Wonder would have much appeal. "Was she a punk?"

"No more than anyone."

An answer with layers of meaning.

"And Wonder says to me, 'Tug,' he always calls me Tug, he says, 'Tug, I want you to do something grievous to that girl.' "

The absolute monarchism of the prison yard. King Wonder the First. "What exactly constitutes 'grievous'?" I said.

Tugboat laughed, a frightening, unpleasant sound. "Wonder ran the sports book. Softball games, basketball games, boxing matches. That shit. The hacks are taking their piece, they let him keep a bat, they look the other way. I was like what you call the batboy. It was one of those aluminum jobs they use now. Wonder used it for protection."

"Or to do something grievous?"

"It's very good for doing something grievous."

I could imagine the extent of the grievousness. "In the . . ." I wondered if I could say anal sodomy with a foreign object: to wit, an aluminum softball bat. Not likely in this venue. Just avoid it. "It must have been very convincing."

Albert Curwent seemed to enjoy my squeamishness. "Very. We took turns, Wonderman and me. Made her chew on a towel so she wouldn't make no noise. She changed her mind." An aluminum softball bat up your ass might have that desired result, I thought. "She was cute. I named her Princess. She was a good earner. Regular johns. Wonder liked to watch her. She wasn't a natural like Kong. But Wonder made her keep the candle in so she was always ready."

So Duane Lajoie had a motive.

Princess was cute. Princess was a good earner.

"Albert, one thing," I said as I prepared to leave Sunflower. "Why'd you come to me and not to Mr. McClure? That's the usual drill."

"I did. Friday. He wasn't around. I got this bitch who worked for him. She blew me off. She said the case was airtight. She said I was just trying to ease my situation. The dumb cooz. What's she think a snitch does? You were my shot."

I wondered if Patsy Feiffer had ever been called a cooz. J.J. would have heard Albert Curwent out. But then J.J. wasn't around.

Earnest Wonder had pleaded guilty to selling narcotics in Ada, Oklahoma. Charges of assault with intent to kill were dismissed when the victim of the assault declined to testify against him. The sheriff's department in Pontotoc County, Oklahoma, faxed to my office in Capital City the arrest report on Wonder, Earnest, Case Number 3345. The state's attorney faxed a copy of the plea-bargain agreement signed by Wonder, Earnest, Case Number 3345. Wonder, Earnest, Case Number 3345, was represented by Jane Leo, now deceased, of the Pontotoc County Public Defender's Office. Wonder, Earnest, Case Number 3345, was sentenced to two years at Oklahoma State Penitentiary in McAlester, Oklahoma. The Oklahoma DOC faxed photographs to my Cap City office of Wonder, Earnest, Prisoner Number 83992-1, full face, left profile, right profile. The sentence of Wonder, Earnest, Prisoner Number 83992-1, was commuted to early release after fifteen months and seven days.

Duane Lajoie, Prisoner Number 84411-1, arrived at OSP McAlester three months before Earnest Wonder's early release.

CHAPTER THREE

WEDNESDAY

Bottom line. Teresa and I now perhaps had the extenuating evidence needed to keep Duane Lajoie out of the electric chair in the penalty phase of the trial after he was convicted. That Duane Lajoie would be convicted was as near a certainty as the gods allowed. I wondered if the *P* carved into Edgar Parlance's chest with the Tennessee Toothpick was meant to signify *Princess.* Certainly not *Parlance.* The man Duane Lajoie and Bryant Gover had run into on County Road 21 was known to Duane Lajoie only as Earnest Wonder. Edgar Parlance was someone else. The kind of black man better white people could identify with. Good-hearted. Independent. Not weighted down by the faults of the society that so many black folks (a construction of the better white people) blamed for their straitened circumstances.

Earnest Wonder. The backstory no one had thought to consider.

Wonderman. The flip side of Gar.

Wonderman could short-circuit the buzz. Blow the fuse.

Teresa looked tired. Well, she had said when I told her about my hours at Sunflower, you had a more interesting day than I did.

Clyde Ray had testified and was no more forthcoming about how he had happened to be on County Road 21 after midnight on the night of the murder than he had been when Teresa and I had talked to him at Auntie Pasto's. Judge Tracy had chastised Teresa for pursuing the matter, and said that whatever Mr. Ray's reasons for being out that night, those reasons were not the business of the court.

Merle Orvis had also testified. Merle Orvis had tried to have Boy sit on her lap while she was on the stand, but Judge Tracy had ordered him removed. Boy had begun to scream *pee-pee!* and *titty!* when a female deputy sheriff carried him out of the courtroom and placed him in the custody of Children's Aid. Judge Tracy then called for a fifteen-minute recess; in the corridor outside the courtroom, Marjorie Hudnut, the librarian, and Claude Applewhite, the Methodist minister, seemed embarrassed by the episode. Both said these people did not represent the finer elements of Regent. It was as if they wanted to say, and were loath to say it, that the glare of the spotlight, the spotlight focused on Regent, Loomis County, South Midland, had lost its transient appeal; the thrill of recognition had paled. The accused and to some extent the victim had contaminated the upbeat ordinariness the community had prized, even raised into a virtue. Being interviewed on the way into court and on the way out was like being caught in a bear trap; there was no escape.

Alicia Barbara had asked Marjorie Hudnut and Claude Applewhite to define "these people" and "finer elements."

Marjorie Hudnut said these people weren't from here.

They were just passing through, Pastor Applewhite said.

Not gone soon enough, Marjorie Hudnut said. We don't mean Gar, she added.

We definitely don't mean Gar, Pastor Applewhite said. Gar was like an old shoe, wasn't he, Marjorie?

Just a vagabond, Marjorie Hudnut said.

Neat as a pin, Pastor Applewhite said.

Teresa said that J.J. had called that night from Cap City.

What did he say? I said.

He said it would be over soon.

Teresa, I have to ask you something.

Max, no. Not a word. I wouldn't do that. I have a professional obligation to Duane Lajoie. That takes precedence.

It was the kind of speech I gave to my law students. I usually said it with all the gravity of Oliver Wendell Holmes or Felix Frankfurter.

Duane Lajoie said, "I told you my story."

"Tell it to me again," Teresa said.

"Bryant was driving," Duane Lajoie said.

"He said you were driving," Teresa said.

"He's fucking lying."

"He said Edgar Parlance was walking by the side of the road and you passed him, then you jammed on the brakes, backed up and nearly ran him over."

"You're going to believe me or believe him. You're my fucking lawyer. I want Alice in here. I want you fired. I want a new lawyer. Alice told me all about you."

Exactly what Alice Todt had told Duane about Teresa did not seem at that moment a profitable area of discussion. Time was the enemy. Bryant Gover would begin his testimony the next day, with J.J. leading him through it, point by point, as if it had been scripted, which indeed it had. Judge Tracy had already arrived from Kiowa, and she would call the morning session to order in less than two hours. In the middle of the three holding cells adjacent to the courtroom, Duane was still dressed in the CCCC orange jumpsuit he had been wearing when he was transported that morning from Cap City to Regent. His court clothes were folded on the table where Teresa and I were sitting, hands folded, files in front of us, like hearing officers at a parole hearing. Duane Lajoie stared venomously at us through the bars of the center cell. If he could have grabbed Teresa, I think he would have. Without expression, she listened to his stream of profanities.

It was time for me to jump in.

"Tell me about McAlester," I said suddenly.

He stopped in mid-tirade, as if struck dumb. He seemed to be analyzing what I had said, and with the con cunning that is like a reflex in professional criminals, he was looking for a way to lie his way past it. "I don't know no McAlester." And then: "Yeah, wait a minute, I know fucking Kenny McAllister. He had this girlfriend Mitzy, she was a whore in Mobile, Galveston maybe, she had a tattoo of her cunt on her boob, the left one, I think, no, the right one, I remember now. Kenny wanted to join the army, he wanted to be a paratrooper, the crazy bastard, fuck that, what this country ever do for him." The words were tumbling out of his mouth, one on top of the other, the fabrications mounting up like corpses on a particularly bloody battlefield, vagina tattoos and place-names adding what he thought was authority to his demented barker's spiel. "Anyway, he goes to this air show in Ponca City, I was there, Casey was there, Casey was his new bitch, Casey worked both sides of the mountain, you ask me, and Kenny, he's wearing this hat like a fucking football player, you know, with the buckle under his chin, and he puts on his parachute, and he goes up in this fucking plane, Mitzy was clap-ping and pissing away, no, it was Casey, the new one, the dyke, and Kenny goes up in this fucking little airplane, and he jumps the fuck out, and his parachute don't open, it's what they call a Roman candle, I don't know why they call it a Roman candle, I never seen a Roman candle, except once at a Fourth of July fireworks in Dothan. Kenny hits the fucking ground, splat, he hits it so hard, it's like a bomb, it must've shook every house in Ponca City."

He stopped only because he had run out of breath. "Kenny McAllis-ter. Shit, I haven't thought of Kenny in a long time. Whatever happened to Casey, I wonder."

"No, not Kenny," I said.

His face turned sullen. "I don't know no other McAllisters."

"McAlester. It's a place in Oklahoma. You spent some time there. Thirteen months and twelve days. To be exact."

Duane Lajoie said he did not understand what the time he had spent at OSP had to do with anything anyway. He was like a deflated balloon. He knew where I was going, he knew Teresa knew, he had exhausted his bluster, there was nothing he could do, and there was no way he could attack us physically.

"Albert Curwent," I said. "He was there when you were there."

Duane sat on the steel bunk. His foot tapped the floor of his cell in a staccato fashion.

"He went by the name of Tugboat. He's about the size of one."

"I never seen no tugboats."

"Akimbo Thorne. Another big guy. Huge guy. Black guy. Akimbo's name in the yard was Queen Kong. The Kong was a big favorite there."

Duane curled up on the steel bunk and turned away from us.

"Wonderman." I opened my briefcase. The candle was there. The candle I had been sure was going to affect this trial since the day I first saw it in Edgar Parlance's cell-like room over the garage. Don't show it yet. Play it out. "I have some pictures of him here. Earnest Wonder. Prisoner number 83992-1. You want to see them? They're just mug shots, but it should jog your memory. He pretty much ran things at OSP, didn't he?"

Duane did not move.

"You might say Wonderman scouted talent," I said. "And then he had Tugboat cut the deal."

Teresa put her hand on my arm. "Tugboat told Mr. Cline here that you were a good earner," she said quietly. "When Mr. Cline saw him. Yesterday."

"Actually, Teresa," I said, interrupting her, "what Tugboat said was that Princess was one of Wonderman's best earners."

Duane Lajoie said he would kill Teresa and he would kill me if we exposed Edgar Parlance as Wonderman and himself as Princess. Duane Lajoie said he had the resources to have us killed if he was not able to do it himself.

Teresa very patiently tried to explain to Duane Lajoie that life without the possibility of parole was not in the cards without the Earnest Wonder evidence. Very patiently tried to explain that without that evidence Duane Lajoie would go to the electric chair.

Duane Lajoie said he would rather go to the electric chair than have it introduced in court that he was a prison whore. That he wore thong underwear and a bra and eye shadow and lipstick. That he was forced to insert a candle into his rectum to keep it pliable for the tricks he would service.

Duane Lajoie was enough of a jailhouse lawyer to know that this evidence could not be introduced without his permission. Enough of a jailhouse lawyer to know that attorneys were obligated to abide by the wishes of their client.

We could only hope to persuade him to change his mind.

As it turned out, we never got the opportunity.

PART THREE

PART THREE

CHAPTER ONE

The narrow two-lane river road between Albion and Capital City is lightly traveled except on weekends, when the teenage drag racers appear after midnight with their girlfriends and hangers-on and by the beams of their headlights try to survive speed runs without crippling or killing themselves. I-63 gets most of the heavy traffic that runs from North Midland through South Midland and into Kansas, three lanes in either direction, straight as a plumb line, for trucks and passenger vehicles, no posted speed limits. I-63 has view lookouts and weighing stations and truck stops offering the best coffee in three states and full-service gas stations with eight pumps and diesel fuel and Best Western and Howard Johnson, off-the-road home living.

The river road then, following the configurations of the Albion River, some gentle, some not so gentle. Rain slants down. The sky is unpolished pewter. No thunder, no lightning, just sheets of rain, like panes of storefront window glass, exploding onto the river road and onto the hood and roof of the black van with the smoked windows that is moving smartly north at a high rate of speed, probably eighty, or faster, maybe a hundred. There is a road sign that says DANGEROUS WHEN WET that the driver no doubt ignores as most drivers in South Midland ignore highway admonitions. The driver makes no allowances for the rain. Water shoots from under the wheels as if from a high-velocity spray. North of Sherlock, the driver appears to lose control of the van. It slipstreams from the northbound lane to the southbound, and back again. Ahead is the Albion Bridge between Sherlock and Roscoe. CAPITAL CITY 19 MILES. The driver seemed to apply the brakes, according to the Highway Patrol's accident report. The accident report said it appeared that the van had fishtailed onto the bridge. It appeared to crash into the railing of the southbound lane, then appeared to turn completely around and crash through the railing of the northbound lane. The hood of the black van appeared to hit the water first, because it was largely crushed. The river was in full raging flow and apparently flipped the van over onto its roof and swept it downstream. It was two hours before a highway lineman on emergency duty discovered the breach in the Albion River Bridge between Sherlock and Roscoe, and two hours after that before the wheels of the upended black van were seen being pushed steadily down-river by the Albion's floodwaters. By late afternoon the rains finally abated. The black van was righted, and deputies from the Loomis County Sheriff's Department removed the bodies.

Chapter Two

Do you remember that four-day recess before the trial started? Alicia Barbara said a long time later. She had stopped off in Cap City for an hour-long special she was doing for *Fox 5 News*—"The Peace Lobby: What Are Its Secret Ties to the Military-Industrial Complex," or something like that, and she had called and asked me to lunch. She wanted to talk, she said. Chew the fat. Old times. Talk about the Angkor Wat.

I've never been to Angkor Wat, I said.

Have it your way, she said, I'll buy you lunch anyway, *Fox 5*'s not chintzy about expenses the way *Courthouse Square* was, *Courthouse Square* wouldn't okay a tip of over ten percent, and even that was a fight. Why do you have espresso when regular coffee is cheaper, that snooty cable crap, is that how you sneak drinks onto your bill?

It was just a matter of knowing where to look, Alicia Barbara said the following Friday when we met at the Rhino Carlton-Plaza restaurant. She had an expensive haircut, an Armani jacket, and good makeup, but she was gaining weight around the face and the chin, not bloat, but impacted. She plowed into her Chicken Caesar Salad like a field hand, pushing every bite down with a piece of bread. My love life was a mess that weekend, and so I worked, didn't go home. You ever had a weekend like that, you didn't want to see your . . . She let the sentence trail off.

There was no reason to reply.

I drove all around Loomis County, she said finally, I went out to where Parlance's body was discovered, I read everything I could find on the Net. Open and shut. Your client was going to the chair. Check the fuse box, you don't want a short when they turn on the fire. Still. There was something that bothered me. Waiter, can I have some more bread?

The waiter brought another basket of bread. There was a rhinoceros embroidered on his white jacket. Alicia Barbara tore off a piece and sopped up the dressing and the few remaining croutons. Where was I? she said.

Asking for more bread, I said.

It was her. Teresa Kean. Why was she doing this? She was a big deal. All the right schools, law review at Yale, Harvard, whatever. You must've asked her. Why was she defending this mutant? You, I understand. You wanted to get back in the game. It wasn't the money. She had enough. I checked. I went to all the places. The house in Washington was free and clear, her father had left her something, those Mob guys he defended, and the white-collar Wall Street crooks, they all paid top dollar, usually in cash, the IRS was all over him, but he reported every nickel, the Feds couldn't lay a hand on him, and then there was this trust fund, she was the beneficiary, I did a D&B, I did a Bishop. . . .

She was showing her mastery of the process. To people like Alicia Barbara, the process was more important than the conclusion. Her words washed over me like a wave.

. . . Brendan Kean . . .

. . . you open up one hole, you get to another.

. . . Jacob King. You know about him?

. . . Blue Tyler. You know about her?

. . . imagine what 24/7 would have made of those two if it had been around then.

. . . and all roads lead to this Broderick guy, the guy who was humping her when he died . . . he knew the whole story, he fit all the pieces together, what do you think they talked about that night he was . . .

. . . you put two and two together. You hope it adds up to four. Maybe four and a half. Five even. Close enough.

. . . and so by the end of the weekend, I was fairly certain she was the daughter of Jacob King, the guy who gave us Las Vegas, and Blue Tyler, the wanker's Shirley Temple . . .

. . . I could make an educated guess . . . that's all it's about, really . . . it was the biggest story I ever had. An Alicia Barbara exclusive. I don't

share this with anyone. I'm already counting the zeroes in my new contract. I just had to get her alone and ask her . . .

. . . all I had to figure out was a way to get past that gag order.

. . . do I want to spend thirty days in the can for freedom of the
press . . .

. . . that was the tricky part.

. . . I sit on it until I could spring it . . .

. . . I thought I knew everything about her . . .

"You were wrong," I said.

Somebody always knows, J.J. had said that Friday afternoon when he
and Teresa took the turnoff into Hamlet, past the water tower where
someone had painted that Linda Kronholm put out.

J.J. had called that one right. He had conjugated the possibilities.
The narcotic of twenty-four-hour television. Shows repeated at midnight and 3 a.m. for the insomniacs and the lonely and the night people.
Handheld video cameras. Security checkpoints. The availability of websites. Shock jocks. Talk radio. Share your thoughts with. E-mail your
remarks to. Randy from Higginson. Yo! Carlyle.

Somebody out there, J.J. had said. A Lotto shot. The winning ticket
bought in a Wal-Mart in Ottumwa.

You can't worry about it.

It happens.

It wasn't the Wal-Mart in Ottumwa.

It was Randy from Higginson.

Randy from Higginson was the night manager at the Step Right Inn.
The graveyard shift. Eleven p.m. to 7 a.m. Randy from Higginson toned
his abs with Carlyle's exercise tapes as a way of staying awake. Randy
from Higginson had twenty-seven Carlyle postcards. He had a Carlyle
do-rag. He e-mailed Yo! Carlyle every night after midnight. Yo! Carlyle.
What's going down? That judge had some nerve. Hang in. You got a pal
in Higginson. Yo! Carlyle. You and Jocko. He's my favorite Rhino. Your
pal in Higginson. The first thing Randy did when he reported for work
each evening at the Step Right Inn was check the number of cars in the

parking lot. If there were more cars than there were rooms occupied then Randy knew that someone was piling extra people into a room without paying extra for them. He would get them in the morning. Five in a room was the limit, but that included two kids. At 1 a.m. he turned on the NO VACANCY sign. A house rule. Step Rite Inn management took the position that anyone who tried to check in to a motel after 1 a.m. was probably up to no good. Better safe than sorry. No room at the Inn. Then he would rerun the surveillance tape from the camera over the desk so he could put faces to the names of the people who had checked in before he came on duty. A habit of his in case a room was busted up or sheets were stolen. Yo! Carlyle. People will steal anything. Randy from Higginson. T.M. Kean had signed in at four-thirty that afternoon. The gentleman who accompanied her was J. McClure. J. McClure paid for the room with a hundred-dollar bill. Thirty-three dollars and eighty-four cents change. Yo! Carlyle. I didn't recognize them until they were checking out the next morning. I mean, they'd been all over the TV last week. I mean, that's cool. My bud Tommy said he could copy the tape. Your pal, Randy.

CHAPTER THREE

From the unedited interviews of Alice Faith Todt, aka Carlyle.

Well, for fuck sake, of course I put it on my Web page. Usually I don't see those loony e-mails from Nobody in Nowhere, I got people who handle that shit, but someone sees the one from this dude at the Step Right Inn—can you fucking believe that?—and one way or the other it gets to me and Alex sees it, and he says it looks like Duane's lawyer and the D.A. were balling their way across the whole state. Higginsville or Higginsport or whatever the fuck it's called is like five hundred miles from Regent, maybe even a thousand, why didn't they hire a chopper, a small plane, or something, I get carsick if I drive thirty miles, and what were they doing except cooking up some deal for Duane while they were bouncing up and down on some motel bed, those fucking beds are like trampolines, I remember from when I was a kid, you know with me and Waylon and me and Kile. I bet Duane's deal was going to be some kind of parole or shit in thirty years and stuff, that's not bad, I don't want to see him that much anyways, thirty years is about right. Alex hires a chopper, it goes out to Higginsport and picks up Rudy, or Randy, and Randy's got the dupes of the surveillance tapes when they're checking in, you can't see them all that clear, but they look all shifty-eyed and shit. Alex says those tapes are gold, everyone's going to want them, they got to pay to use them, one-time use only. He's always thinking business, Alex. You got to maximize, he says. Always maximize. Whatever maximize

317

means, it's going to put money in Alex's pocket, bet your ass on that. Anyway, this old lesbian, Alicia, she must be forty or something, hears about it, and we negotiate, and you know that cunt never told me what she had about Teresa's mom, typical, you can't trust them. You know, I know a lot of gay chicks from the shows, you're changing backstage, and you see them casing your box, don't get me going on that. Anyway. Alicia goes on the air in her nightly wrap-up with the tape and Blue Tyler and that gangster and shit, and it's like a zoo the next morning at the courthouse, they even got camera teams from the *Today* show and *Good Morning America*. It's pissing rain, Alex got some terrific shots of me with my hair all mussed to shit and my clothes plastered against me like with glue, and it's just that fucking rain, and Duane is there and that other fucker, Bryant, he was supposed to start testifying that morning, and nobody knew what was going to happen, and I talk to *GMA* and that perky one on *Today*. . . .

CHAPTER FOUR

Willfully indiscreet, Ellen Tracy said that morning. She stalked her office in the courthouse, her face contorted with rage. Willfully arrogant. Willfully this. Willfully that. I remembered what Teresa had said Sunday afternoon—was it only four days earlier?—when she returned to the DeLuxor. *Don't say willful, Max.* She hated willful. I stared straight ahead. Patsy Feiffer seemed afraid to blink. J.J. and Teresa sat side by side in the chairs placed in front of Judge Tracy's desk. The judge was walking behind them, as if straining at a leash, talking to the backs of their heads. Judge Tracy. Spencer Tracy. Spencer Tracy and Katharine Hepburn had once been in a movie in which he had been the prosecutor of a woman accused of murder and she was the defendant's attorney. *Adam's Rib.* They were married. They called each other Pinky. He was a Republican, she was a Democrat. Or vice versa. Presumably they had not taken a vow of celibacy during the course of the trial. Move away from there. *Adam's Rib* was not a productive line of rebuttal.

In violation of every known ethical precept. Tracy had caught her breath and was starting over again.

I have examined my options, she said. We could continue the trial we began last Monday, but in my opinion this case has been irretrievably compromised by the willfully unprofessional behavior of counsel for the defense and counsel for the people.

It was as if Tracy were already marshaling the case she would present at a disciplinary hearing.

She would declare a mistrial and dismiss the jury. The indiscretion of counsel had become a matter of public debate and would taint any further proceedings. The defendant would be returned to the Capital City Correction Center, and the witness, Mr. Gover, to the state penitentiary in Cap City. Counsel was advised that the court's gag order was still in effect. After reading the record and the precedents, the court would recommend an investigation by the disciplinary committee of the state bar.

Teresa and J.J. left the room without looking at each other. Patsy Feiffer's cell phone suddenly began to ring. She stopped as if she had been shot, then fled through the door, slamming it in my face.

I was going to ask you to remain behind anyway, Max, Ellen Tracy said. It was the first time she had ever called me by my first name. She sat down heavily in her desk chair and stared at me for a moment. Could you have stopped that? she said finally.

Am I speaking to a potential witness against me at a disciplinary hearing?

Ellen Tracy's face froze. No, she said.

Then I couldn't have stopped it. I didn't know until Saturday. And then I took a leap. You were the only one who could have stopped it, Judge. That four-day recess. When you went home to Dead Center. If we'd started last Thursday . . .

Are you blaming me?

No, Your Honor. I'm just saying that indiscretion cannot occur without opportunity. That recess was opportunity.

You can leave now, Mr. Cline.

The vehicle that was meant to deliver Bryant Gover back to Durango Avenue had developed a crack in the engine block and could not be driven. Because of the rain, it would be impractical to bring another secure police transport down to Regent until the next day. The state marshals assigned to Bryant Gover declined the offer from Brutus Mayes of a Loomis County sheriff's van to replace the van with the cracked engine block. The marshals assigned to Duane Lajoie said they could deliver both men to their respective destinations in Capital City, and after many discussions over who would be in charge of the vehicle, it was

decided that one of Gover's marshals and one of Duane Lajoie's marshals
would escort the two convicts. The two other marshals would have no
problem catching rides back to the capital. Both prisoners would be in
leg restraints; their hands were cuffed and duct tape was wrapped around
the mouth of each to stop the stream of invective that each shouted at
the other in the parking garage under the courthouse. Piece of cake, the
marshal driving the van said as he prepared for the trip. Two pansy boys,
no problem, the second marshal said. They would take the river road.
No traffic, good time, the driver said. Duane Lajoie was in the back seat
with his guard, Bryant Gover in the front with the driver.

No one is quite sure what happened just short of the Albion Bridge
nineteen miles south of Cap City. What is known is this. There was a
shank in the car along with the four bodies. The shank was a nail file that
had been melted into a toothbrush; the toothbrush was the handle, the
nail file the business end. Whether the shank belonged to Gover or to
Lajoie was unknown. I would assume it was Duane; when his body was
pulled from the car he seemed to have slipped from his iron restraints.
He was slight; perhaps the rush of the river as he was drowning might
have aided his escape from the irons. Perhaps he thought he could escape
from the car. Perhaps he thought this was his last opportunity to kill
Bryant Gover, sticking him through the mesh screen separating front
seat from back. Perhaps the driver saw him in the rearview mirror and
took evasive action.

Perhaps the driver was the target.

Or perhaps the shank was Bryant Gover's last best chance for escape.
Or settling a score with Duane Lajoie.

Something he used because he liked to hurt people.

Did it matter?

The car went into the river, and floated downstream until it was
stopped by an uprooted tree.

Bryant Gover was still wearing the duct tape over his mouth.

What had been a sensational mistrial was now a sensational mistrial
that had resulted in the death of four people, two of whom were members of a South Midland law enforcement agency.

Film at six. Supermodel Carlyle—*Larry King Live!* "Solved at Last:
The Mystery of Blue Tyler!" Killer's lawyer in seclusion. Poppy McClure:

no comment. Wormwold: now clearly in the lead for Repub nomination for gov. Film at nine. CNN: "Blood on the Prairie—a Report!" Rush: What kind of lawyer defends scum like this?

Film at eleven.

The fact is, we will never know what really happened the night Duane Lajoie and Bryant Gover ran into Edgar Parlance on County Road 21. We can make certain surmises. We can surmise that Duane Lajoie was driving the Ford 4x4 pickup. We can surmise that Edgar Parlance was walking by the side of the road. We can surmise that the headlight beams on the 4x4 picked up someone Duane Lajoie recognized as Earnest Wonder. We can surmise that he backed up to make sure the man walking by the side of the road was the man he had known at OSP as Wonderman. Earnest Wonder. We can surmise that when Edgar Parlance saw himself caught like a deer in the headlights, he began to run. We can surmise that when he was run down he might not even have remembered Duane Lajoie.

Who he knew as Princess.

We can surmise that Duane Lajoie was not an innocent bystander in the death of Edgar Parlance. We can surmise that Bryant Gover was equally culpable.

We can ask if it is worth caring about.

PART FOUR

CHAPTER ONE

Teresa did not contest the proceedings against her conducted by the disciplinary committee of the South Midland Bar Association. Nor did she appear at the hearing. She also chose not to be represented by counsel. The committee, however, insisted that an attorney representing her interests be present, and so she designated me. Your only instructions, she wrote, are to make sure that my name is spelled right and in verbal testimony that it be pronounced correctly. The proceedings were brief, and the unanimous written verdict of the committee was that Teresa Kean, LLC, be herewith and forever barred from the practice of law in South Midland. Her disbarment only applied to South Midland, meaning that there were forty-nine other states where she could practice law if she so desired, although when she applied for a license in a state where she was not already licensed she would have to make known the action taken against her by the state of South Midland.

James Joseph McClure was reprimanded by the disciplinary committee and his license suspended for four months. He had already resigned as chief deputy prosecutor in the office of the Attorney General of South Midland. In a written statement, he said that the committee had acted properly and with dispatch and he would like to thank the committee for taking into consideration his years of service to the state of South Midland.

Oh, fuck him, Allie Vasquez had said.

Poppy McClure said she would give up her seat in Congress when the

current session ended and would not run for governor. Neither she nor
J.J. would comment on the future of their marriage. Poppy moved per-
manently to Washington, and is still in demand, preaching the conserva-
tive sermon on talk radio, where, she says, she is not frustrated by the
moral cripples and mental defectives in the Democratic Party who run
both houses of Congress and seek to stifle the wishes of true Americans
who worship flag and country. Stanley tells me that in the gay under-
ground, stories occasionally flourish about Poppy and Lorna Dun. He
hears the stories in the clubs he visits from time to time.

Gerry Wormwold won the Republican nomination for governor. In
the general election, however, to his great surprise and the surprise of all
the Sunday prognosticators, he was trounced by the incumbent, Guy
Kennedy, whose moribund candidacy was revived by the slogan VOTE
FOR A WORM, GET A WORM.

Merle Orvis tied up briefly with Randy from Higginson.

Edgar Parlance's reputation remains more or less intact, but iconic
black men are no longer much in demand as a story line, nor is the evil
that men do to each other. Martin Magnin had put the Edgar Parlance
story on hold, back burner (Jack didn't want to play you anyway, he told
me over the telephone), and he was throttling up the Blue Tyler story,
did I know how to get in touch with Teri Kean, I'm working up a whole
new approach. I suppose that Albert Curwent is still out there, hopeful
that he can sell his tale to someone, but it is devalued currency. Every
now and again, I look at the mug shots of Wonder, Earnest, Prisoner
Number 83992-1, Oklahoma State Penitentiary, McAlester, OK.

I am told that a gun cannot appear in the first act without its going off in
the third. I don't know who said that or even if it is true in real life. I have
been around guns my whole life and never felt the need to shoot anyone.
Stanley sometimes, but never to the point of lifting the weapon for heft
and seeing if there was a bullet in the chamber.

And yet.

Case in point: The Manurhin 7.65 with which Alice Faith Todt aka
Carlyle accidentally shot herself in the arm at a Donna Karan AIDS
benefit in Miami Beach. Jocko Cannon of course made a move on Alice
in the back seat of his Mercedes-Benz S-600. Tater was driving. Jocko

pinned Alice to the back seat and grabbed at her underwear with one hand, taking his dick out with the other. Alice did not fight him. He outweighed her by two hundred pounds. She groped in her bag and located the Manurhin 7.65. The first shot caught Jocko in the stomach, the second smashed the front windshield. No charges were brought against Alice, because Brutus Mayes forgot to remove the film from the two hidden video cameras in the S-600, one in the driver's sun visor, the other in the back seat reading light above the rear window, both of which recorded the assault. By the time he attempted to confiscate the film, it was already in the hands of the lawyer from Chicago that Alice had retained, and who himself drove that same model Mercedes. Jocko recovered. He now wears a colostomy bag. He never reported to the Miami Dolphins.

The film library of Furlong Budd Doheny did turn up on Famous Flesh and Boobs & Pubes. Or some of it did. There was no footage of Teresa, nor was the man identified by name. The only woman I recognized, in a remarkably clear still photograph, was Martha Buick. She was naked, kneeling on a bed, talking to a man I took to be Budd Doheny. She was laughing, he was smiling. They were prepared for whatever they were going to do. What struck me was the room where this coupling would take place. There was a riding helmet on the bedside table, the kind worn in dressage, trimmed in black velvet. There was a lithograph over the bed, an *Ocean Park* by Richard Diebenkorn. There were photographs in silver frames and a silver baby cup filled with sharpened pencils. The pillow slips were patterned, perhaps Porthault, and the bedspread looked as if it might come from Pierre Deux. In other words, it was an upscale venue, not the seedy Motel 6 room of most pornographic photographs. Someone had taken this picture. Someone engaged as a photographer, one with professional skills, and who perhaps was also meant to be a participant in the revels clearly about to begin. I wondered if Teresa knew that her best friend and her second husband were or had been so engaged.

Does it matter? Teresa had said to me the day we walked into a mini-riot outside the Cap City Correction Center.

I think now she meant does anything matter.

It was, needless to say, Alice Todt who found the photograph, in her daily perusals of Famous Flesh and Notable Nookie.

She used it as a bargaining chip against Martha Buick.

Allie Vasquez passed the bar and is an immigration lawyer in San Diego, where I suppose she will never run out of clients. She is also married, to a widower, a retired navy rear admiral with grown children who don't like her. Allie's daughter Rhea is thirteen. She runs the hurdles for her school track team and is an aspiring ballet dancer. Her ballet teacher wants her to give up the hurdles and her track coach wants her to give up the ballet.

Fuck them, Allie said. It's her choice, I'll let her make it.

Allie and I talk every now and again. Just checking in, she will say.

How's the admiral? I will say.

Happiest gringo you ever saw.

I find it difficult to imagine Allie at the officers' club in Coronado. The wives in teased hair must hold their husbands in hammerlocks when she is around.

You play bridge with the wives?

I learned how. Anson taught me. Anson was her husband. Rear Admiral Anson Cunningham, USN. I was very good.

That's past tense, Allie.

I wanted to play for money. They didn't. It's against club rules, they said. So play for matches, I said. It's still gambling they said. All very pissy. So Anson and I go to Del Mar instead.

Mrs. Cunningham, I said.

How's Stanley?

Stanley and I stagger along. We're used to each other. I think we've even come to like each other. At least more often than we dislike each other. Stanley has this lecture he gives. The title is "Offal," and it, and Stanley, have become big hits on the Midwestern lecture circuit, helped along by the fact that Stanley is an M.D. as well as a professor of medicine at the SMU Medical School. It is Stanley's theory that people in long-term relationships have three subjects they talk about more than anything else. The first (or the second) is sex. The second (or the first) is money. And the third is shit. Shit is the public unmentionable. Did you go? When did you go? Can you go? Why can't you go? What does it look like? Stanley claims that the world is divided up into two kinds of people—those who look at their body waste in the toilet bowl, and those who don't. Most people claim they don't, which is a lie, because most people do. By this point in his lecture, Stanley has his audience rolling in the aisles. Color. Consistency. Shape. Odor. Farting. Laxatives. Softeners. Enemas. Constipation. Diarrhea. Strain. Couples will never admit how much they talk about this, Stanley will say. Then he names famous people, historical personages, royals, and current favorites. Do you think the president or the queen or the diva or the movie star does not talk about this? Get real. The lecture began to catch on. At one point Stanley was invited to be on a nightly talk show in New York. He was greeted at the airport by one of the show's bookers who said he was delighted to meet Dr. Poindexter, or as the show's host had called him in that morning's storyboard meeting, Dr. Dump. Stanley took the next plane back to Cap City. He did say that he thought the booker was cute.

J.J. returned to Parker County when his suspension was up and he was free to practice law again. After an appropriate interval he and Poppy quietly divorced, an action filed in Hermosillo, the capital city of Sonora, where Poppy's maternal family still had extensive interests; the suit did not even make the South Midland papers until months after it was concluded. I ran into him once in the checkout line at a Rite Aid drugstore in Cap City. I turned around and he was standing behind me. There were three other cash registers taking customers, so I can only assume that when he saw me he deliberately pushed his shopping cart into my line. He was buying the usual toiletries, plus, I could not help but notice, a box of Tampax. Hello, Max, he said. J.J., I said. We went and had coffee at a diner down the street. I did not mention Poppy nor did he ask about Teresa, I think because we both knew the other would volunteer nothing. I also refrained from asking what he was doing in Cap City. Surprisingly, the conversation was easy. J.J. was always good value, and the missteps of the Worm's campaign for governor were a subject made for him. He told me that Patsy Feiffer was so devastated by the

Worm's defeat that she had gone back to Connecticut, where her father pulled some strings and got her an appointment to the state parole board.

No early releases in Connecticut, J.J. said with a smile.

What about you, J.J.? I said.

I'm just a country boy, Max, J.J. said, counting out his half of the check. Can't wait to get home and do country things.

What country things he might be doing he did not say.

Then Allie sent me a photograph of him from a newspaper in eastern Montana. How she had come upon it I have no idea. I think perhaps she just liked to keep up with her past, and she searched the Internet like a code breaker. The photo was of J.J. at a cattle sale in Miles City. He was wearing a shearling coat and a cowboy hat and reading glasses that made him squint. He had gained weight. His face was jowly and he had a mustache. He went by the name of Jim McClure. Jim McClure was a cattle lawyer and head of the cattlemen's committee of a rangeland anti-environmentalist group. His wife Linda had recently died of cancer. Linda McClure had been a county supervisor in Parker County, South Midland, when she had married Jim McClure and moved with him to a small spread on the Powder River.

Linda Kronholm puts out.

Jim McClure.

Teresa would keep in touch by postcard. There was one of the Temple Mount in Jerusalem. *Finally got to Israel. A suicide bomber blew up a coffee shop across the street from my hotel the night I arrived. I slept through it. I hope that's not a metaphor. xoxox T.* The postmark was not from Jerusalem but from Trieste, with an Italian stamp, which suggests that she held it for a while before she mailed it. Another showed the changing of the leaves in Vermont. *This is so beautiful. To think I never saw it. xoxox T.* In fact she must have seen the leaves in autumn every fall when she and Martha Buick were at Smith. This card was postmarked Lake Louise. Occasionally there were notes scribbled on hotel stationery, from the Bristol in Paris, say, or the Kahala Mandarin in Honolulu. *Have you ever seen the Musée de Camondo?* the note on the Bristol paper said. *It made me cry. xoxo T.* The postmark was from Delhi. And in the Kahala

Mandarin envelope: *I saw the Pacific Fleet Band doing Mozart's Symphony 29 in A at the Foster Botanical Garden. They all arrived at the ending at the same time. xoxo T.* Postmarked Mantoloking, N.J.

We talked only once.

The telephone rang and the voice at the other end said, "Hi."

"Are you all right?"

"Of course I'm all right. I missed the sound of your voice."

"I'm hard to reach from Delhi. Where are you, now?"

"Teaching English to little Mexican kids."

"You don't speak Spanish."

"The object is to teach them English, not teach me Spanish. Anyway. I pick up languages fast."

"Where are you, Teresa?" I made the inductive leap. "Randado, Texas. Jim Hogg County. Over by the Rio Grande. Your father said it was the perfect place for witness protection. Who'd want to go there? I remember that. We talked about it."

"You don't forget much, do you?"

"True?"

"It's good talking to you, Max."

"Wait a minute. Teresa. I can fly there. Where do I go? DFW?"

"Laredo."

"I can get a plane tomorrow."

"Don't come, Max. That's a favor. I just wanted to hear your voice. And remember how smart you were. Are."

"Teresa."

"I'll keep in touch."

When she hung up, I got the area code for Jim Hogg County, Texas: 361. I dialed information. There was one Kean. T.M. Kean in Randado. It was the last time I heard from her. A month later I called the number in Randado.

It had been disconnected.

"Max," Allie Vasquez said on the telephone from San Diego. "Teresa Kean. What do you hear from her lately."

It was best to wait Allie out. Press her and you would get a lot of mouth. I wondered how the admiral coped with Allie's mouth. Maybe she spared him because it was worth it to her being Mrs. Cunningham. Allie already knew it had been two years and counting since I had last heard from Teresa. No postcards, no hotel notepaper. "Not much."

"That hotel in Vegas that her father built. The hood. Playland, right?"

"King's Playland," I said.

"Got him whacked."

"It did."

"It got torn down, right."

"Imploded."

"On the History Channel. *Great Demos.* I saw it."

I tried to contemplate Allie watching the History Channel. Hand in hand with Admiral Cunningham. *Great Naval Battles. The Age of the Dreadnoughts. The War Under the Sea. History's Mysteries. Great Demos.*

"You know what's there now?" Allie said. "The Angkor Wat. Built on the ground where King's Playland once stood."

I knew where this was going.

I had read the item.

An AP story about an unidentified and unclaimed Jane Doe in Las Vegas.

I had not put it together.

ANGKOR WAT

No one has come looking, the lead Clark County detective said. You're the first. Her fingerprints don't match any in law enforcement files. There is no missing persons report that matches her description. She could have come from anywhere. We don't know who she was, where she came from, and what, you know, made her do it. She left a SportSac bag on the roof, one of those big jobs, over the shoulder, like. There was nothing in it. No wallet, no ID, no driver's license, no money, no note, no cosmetics. Just a small bottle of saline solution, you know the stuff you use when you wear contact lenses, but she wasn't wearing contacts. And some kind of votive candle, you know, you go to mass and light a candle, that kind of candle, all twisted out of shape. Now it's possible someone inside the parking structure rifled the bag when there was all that commotion downstairs on the ground. You saw the surveillance tape. There was an abandoned Toyota Camry on the top-floor parking roof, but it had been there for two weeks and was traced to a gambler who had tapped out and left it there. She wasn't a street person, she had nice clothes. Her body has gone unclaimed for forty-three days. The holding period in the Clark County morgue is forty-five days. If she goes unclaimed, she will be sent to a local funeral parlor and be buried in potter's field. The county will pick up the tab. Her stone will read 08-12517.

We call her Jane Doe Jumper, the younger detective said.

We do not call the victim that, the lead detective said.

I meant around here, the younger detective said.

The lead detective stared him down.

With all due respect, the younger detective stammered.

She was sober, the medical examiner said. Unlike most impulsive suicides. There was nothing in her stomach, and no alcohol or controlled substances in her system. She doesn't fit the demographic profile. Your typical suicide victim is a male Caucasian, sixty-five years of age or over. No indication of prior injuries, nothing to suggest a struggle, nothing to indicate any sexual activity in any time frame the post-mortem could discover. This wasn't out the third floor, this was off the roof of a twelve-story structure, this was a woman who knew what she was doing, wanted to do it. It took a lot of courage.

I buried Teresa in Mantoloking, N.J., alongside Brendan Thomas Kean and Moira Twomey Kean. Stanley came with me to Mantoloking. I always wanted to meet Teresa Kean, he said, bundling himself against the cold. She always wanted to meet you, too, Stanley, I said.

Allie Vasquez was the only other person I told. For a long time, she didn't speak, and then she said, I'm sorry, Max.

I thought of calling J.J. up in Powder River country, but there was no reason to.

He was Jim McClure.

I think Teresa was the victim of her own blood.

She was her mother's daughter.

She was her father's daughter.

In the end Blue Tyler and Jacob King drew her in, drew her under.

Push me pull me.

Would she have gone to the Angkor Wat had the father she never knew not been murdered there?

Going to the Angkor Wat had a perfect symmetry to it.

Would she have defended Alice Faith Todt's psychotic half brother had the mother she never knew not come to mind every time she looked at Carlyle?

Carlyle in the perfection of her self-absorption. Who had no sense that acts have consequences. Who treated the acceptance of responsibility as if it were a disease. Who thought life a game in which she was always the winner. Who was ignorant of and uncaring about the devastation she had left in her wake.

All that was a long time ago.
I think of Teresa every day.

MONSTER
Living Off the Big Screen

In Hollywood, screenwriters are a curse to be borne, and beating up on them is an industry blood sport. But in this ferociously funny and accurate account of life on the Hollywood food chain, it's a screenwriter who gets the last murderous laugh. That may be because the writer is John Gregory Dunne, who has written screenplays, along with novels and nonfiction, for thirty years. In 1988 Dunne and his wife, Joan Didion, were asked to write a screenplay about the dark and complicated life of the late TV anchorwoman Jessica Savitch. Eight years and twenty-seven drafts later, this script was made into the fairy tale *Up Close & Personal*, starring Robert Redford and Michelle Pfeiffer. Detailing the meetings, rewrites, fights, firings, and distractions attendant to the making of a single picture, *Monster* illuminates the process with sagacity and raucous wit.

Film/Biography/0-375-75024-X

THE STUDIO

In 1967, John Gregory Dunne got unlimited access to the inner workings of Twentieth Century Fox. For one year Dunne went everywhere there was to go and talked to everyone worth talking to. He tracked every step of the creation of pictures like *Dr. Dolittle*, *Planet of the Apes*, and *The Boston Strangler*. The result is a work of reportage that, thirty years later, may still be our most minutely observed and therefore most uproariously funny portrait of the motion picture business. Whether he is recounting a showdown between Fox's studio head and two suavely shark-like agents, watching a producer's girlfriend steal a silver plate from a restaurant, or shielding his eyes against the glare of a Hollywood premiere where the guests include a chimp in a white tie and tails, Dunne captures his subject in all its showmanship, savvy, vulgarity, and hype.

Film/0-375-70008-0

VINTAGE BOOKS
Available at your local bookstore, or call toll-free to order:
1-800-793-2665 (credit cards only)